What people are saying about
Echoes from Deane Mountain...

"*Echoes from Deane Mountain* is a refreshing page turner. Beverly Knowles has a passion for her family heritage, the Deanes of Temple. Ancestral life stories are seen through Jennie's visions of her long-ago family spirits. For Jennie, Amadeus, and the cast of characters, there are happy endings."

—Tammy Mills, quilter, avid reader, and advance copy reader

"The two main characters, Jennie and Amadeus, kept Mrs. Knowles awake some nights in conversations with her. She listened to them and has crafted an engaging story as their lives unfold and their future becomes clear. An intriguing novel, set in Maine, with twists and surprises that will keep the reader turning the pages of this compelling book."

—Gail Hagelstein, media specialist and horsewoman

"Beverly Knowles's debut novel, *Echoes from Deane Mountain,* is a fascinating story. Near a mountain at the end of a road in rural western Maine is the tiny town of Temple. Here live the Deane ancestral spirits with a history filled with love, adventure, tragedy, hope, and most of all faith. Their story will both captivate and intrigue you."

—Jackie Pribble, teacher, avid reader, and advance copy reader

ECHOES FROM DEANE MOUNTAIN

A novel by

Beverly D. Knowles

Designed and produced by:
Maine Authors Publishing
12 High Street, Thomaston, Maine
www.maineauthorspublishing.com

To the descendants of the Deane, Parkhurst, and Stolt families of Temple, Voter Hill, and West Farmington, Maine.

AUTHOR'S NOTE

Echoes from Deane Mountain is a work of historical fiction. Amadeus and Jennie, the children, and others of present time are characters created by the author's imagination. Henry and Charlotte Deane, also fictional, bear no resemblance to the author's parents, other than sharing family trips to the cemeteries. The family seeking freedom was also fictional in order to record Cyrus and Mary Deane's involvement with the Underground Railroad.

Beloved grandmothers and a great aunt of the author's ancestry portrayed Jennie's angels.

Through Jennie's visions with the family spirits, the author shares her own ancestry in western Maine, which is drawn from family stories, the author's memories, the collection of Deane ancestry, and research.

The places and the ancestors are nonfiction. It is the author's intent to record and honor her family history, never to be forgotten.

To Jen –

Family history + memories are found within these pages.

– Aunt Bev

In 1854, Zibiah Deane (1793–1864) wrote this poem describing the Deane homestead and the family's life there as a letter to a family member in the Midwest. Zibiah was the daughter of the original settlers on the homestead in Temple, Cyrus and Mary Deane. The poem was found in the Deane family ancestry collection.

A Letter by Zibiah Deane (1854)

Let me describe our quiet peaceful home
'Tis no magnificent or costly dome
But a convenient cottage snug and warm
Which well protects us from the wintery storm.
Just large enough for what our wants require
And why should we a better house desire?
Stands on the sunny side of a large swell
And at the west a lovely pleasant well
Which yields for us a plentiful supply
Of soft pure water, and will not be dry
We trust for it was sunk when spring was low
When some perennial fountains ceased to flow
With a chain pump the water we procure
Which works with ease and keeps it very pure
'Tis platformed even with our dwelling floor
Within the wood house ten feet from our door
Nearby our dwelling north and east a rill
Proceeding from a spring far up the hill
Runs through a pleasant grove of forest trees
Which would, dear sister, I thy fancy please
Oak, ask *(ash)*, and maple, birth *(birch)* and cherry tree
Beech, basswood, poplar, at one glance we see
Osier and will also find a place
And elms are found within little space
And at the south a small neat garden lies
To furnish us with plentiful supplies
Of various kinds of sauce for table use
Some shrubs and flowers also does produce
Our fields and orchard yield an ample store
Of fruit and bread for our supply and more
Our pastures feed the grazing flock and herd
Which milk and butter flesh and wool afford
Our horse, strong, active, faithful, good and kind

A great assistance on the farm we find
As well as in a carriage to convey
Our persons and our loads on the highway.

Our swine and poultry each a proper share
Contribute towards our comfortable fare
And our industrious active watchful cat
Preserves our treasures from the mouse and rat
Two fire frames and a stove contribute toward
The comfort which a good warm fire affords
And in the small north room we build a fire
In a brick fireplace when our wants require
And our dear aged father's presence here
Contributes much his children's hearts to cheer
At night we see his wants all well supplied
And in the night if sickness should betide
We may attend on him at any hour
And do for him all that is in our power
His pain and suffering to alleviate
Which privilege we count a blessing great

A monitor with our sweet harmonious chime
Hourly proclaims to us the lapse of time
And holds a mirror to reflect the change
Which time has wrought on us in his long range
Kind admonition to prepare to go
From all these transitory schemes below
And find a home which time cannot invade
And treasures, which can neither fail nor fade
This monitor which daily care demands
To keep in motion her kind tongue and hands
Stands 'twixt two windows on the southern side
From which we sometimes see the white sails glide
O'er the smooth silvery lake which lies below
Around whose margin verdurous forests grow
And in whose placid waters fish abound
Among which salmon trout are often found
And when old winter's bridge is hard and strong

Stout heavy reams from various points do throng
Across the even surface to convey
The scholar's frequently short visits pay to us
But make no long-protracted stay
And when the scholars are from school set free
We hear their noisy mirth and childish glee
That full exchange of voice to childhood dear
Soul of their sports is duly cherished here
In the same schoolhouse people meet to pray
And to receive instructions in the way
That leads to life the way of holiness
To such I think we well may wish success
And in our new location here we find
The neighbors fair and peaceable and kind
Our little meetings now become quite small
Consisting of but six or seven in all
Are at our dwelling now allowed to meet
Where we I hope sit at the Savior's feet
As Mary did to hear His gracious voice
May that good part she chose be made our choice
Say have we not as many blessings here
As we should have if we should move out there
And who can doubt the way to heaven remains
As near from Maine's bleak hills as from the plains
Of rich Iowa's fair and fertile lands
What more can our necessities demand?
May peace and health be yours
And length of days
And may we all advance in wisdom's ways
And when our pilgrimage on earth is past
All be prepared to meet in Heaven at last.

PROLOGUE

Ten-year-old Jennie Abigail Deane followed her mother and grandmother across the lawn among old weather-stained stones in the village cemetery in tiny Temple, Maine. She carried a trowel, a miniature rake, and a small watering can. Mom juggled pots with red geraniums, and Grandmother Sarah hefted pink and white ones. Dad was up ahead, always up ahead, wandering around memorials near the pines, remembering Temple families he had once known. Even Jennie could see he was feeling the gentle breeze, the sun's warmth, the peace of the cemetery. He was a person, like anyone else!

Charlotte, Jennie's mother, bent to her knees, and Grandmother Sarah followed more slowly. They pulled the weeds that had grown in front of the gravestone: dandelions, purslane, and goldenrod. Not just any flowers were allowed to grow here! Jennie fell to her knees beside the women, dropping her gardening tools, and silently read the name on the stone. "Mom, was Mary Daddy's aunt?"

"Yes, Jennie, you know who she was."

"I only know that she grew up on the homestead and cared for Dad when he was a kid. But I don't know her story. Daddy doesn't tell me."

"He tells you what he knows, sweetie."

"But I want to know more. I want to know my great-aunt. Did she like children? Did she love Daddy?"

"Here, sweetie, take the trowel and dig three small holes, please."

Jennie picked up the trowel and dug a hole, a second, and a third, while the women planted the geraniums. Jennie's hands were getting so dirty!

"There's a faucet over by that tree. Fill the watering can, please," said Mother.

Jennie wiped her hands on her skirt, grabbed the can, ran over to the tree, and turned on the faucet. The cold water splashed her legs, skirt, and sneakers, as she let it pour into her cupped hands. Looking around, then leaning forward, she raised her hands to her mouth, tasting the cool liquid, as it dripped down her arms onto her blouse. Holding the can under the running water, she looked up at the fluffy clouds floating by, unaware of the can overflowing, a puddle forming under her feet.

As she turned to run back, her father, Henry, spoke firmly. "Jennie, walk quietly. This is a cemetery. Don't step on the graves. You're spilling the water!"

Jennie pulled up short, stood straight and tall, walked slowly, stiffly without bending her knees, holding the full watering can at arm's length in both hands, eyes forward, watching her step, and repeating her father's words: "Don't run. Graveyards are quiet places. Don't step on the graves. *Don't* spill the water."

Mom and Grandma had moved to the next gravestone honoring Charles and Anna Stolt. Mom dug three more holes, and Grandma Sarah planted the flowers. Dad still wandered in the back rows, not watching her, not seeing her. Jennie slowly set the can on the ground and turned three perfect cartwheels in a row, not touching a single grave. She retrieved the can and walked slowly, proud of her accomplishment.

At the gravestone of Great-Aunt Mary, Jennie watered the flowers, droplets on blossoms, the ground soaking up the water. Kneeling, she studied the engravings and traced a stem following the circle around to the center. Sensing the twirling, swirling, she instantly pulled back her hand. "Mom! Grandma! Come! Look!"

Mother said, "What is it, Jennie?"

"Look at the spiral!"

Grandma said, "Many things are shaped like spirals: flowers patterns, seashells, and cinnamon rolls."

"Was Aunt Mary like me?"

"Like you, Jennie, honeybee. It's only a fiddlehead." Mother opened her arms. "Come, sweetie, let me hug you."

Jennie bent to her knees in the grass between Mom and Grandma at the headstone of Charles and Anna. Mom and daughter shared a warm hug, and Mom kissed her on the cheek. Then Jennie watered the flowers.

Grandma leaned close, whispering, "My dear, perhaps you have found Mary's secret. Don't ask your father about the fiddlehead."

Mom rose to her feet. Rubbing her lower back, she sighed, eyed Grandma, and then said to Jennie, "Sweetie, tuck your skirt under your knees."

Wiggling around, adjusting her skirt, Jennie caught her reflection in the stone.

"Mom, tell me about Charles and Anna."

Charlotte stood near her daughter, letting the breeze cool her face as she listened to the birds chirping. "Honeybee, they were your great-grandparents and lived down the road at the four corners. You've seen the house, barn, and pasture." She smiled. "I'll tell you a story about an orange."

"A life story?"

Mother nodded. "When Charles immigrated from Sweden, the ship docked in England. He had never seen or tasted an orange. He bought one from a fruit vendor and bit into that tart, sour taste, not the sweet, citrus flavor of an orange. It was a lemon!"

Jennie's mouth fell open and, fingers touching her lips, she laughed with Mom.

Grandma rose to her feet, securely holding onto the stone. Feeling tired and achy, she rubbed together her arthritic hands. "Charles's accent was difficult to understand."

"You knew them, Grandma?"

Charlotte picked up the tools. "Mother, please, you know her curiosity gets her into trouble. Besides, Henry loved his grandparents." Walking over to Agnes's stone, Charlotte proceeded to dig more holes.

Grandma joined her and sighed. "I know. We have to walk on eggshells around your husband." Together, they planted the geraniums.

Jennie twirled over to the grave with the faint imprint of flowers. Great-Aunt Agnes, a young woman and wife, had died an early death. Kneeling beside Mother, Jennie traced the etchings and read aloud the epitaph: GONE BUT NOT FORGOTTEN.

Removing her daughter's hand from the epitaph, Mother said, "No, sweetie, they're not forgotten."

Grandma said, "Look at the dates, Jen. Aunt Agnes died when she was eighteen."

"Eighteen! What happened to her? She was only eight years older than me."

But Grandma had gone mum, seemed to drift into her thoughts.

"Mom, why did she die?"

Hearing the snapping of twigs and seeing Dad's shadow approaching, the three women stiffened. Jennie knew to stop talking, as Mom placed her hand on her daughter's cheek and hugged her close. Dad passed by the women, unconcerned, taking lazy strides over to the Deane row, clearly remembering the family of his boyhood.

Grandma leaned close to Jennie and whispered, "Don't ask your father about Agnes."

"Mother, stop encouraging her!" said Charlotte.

"I'm not encouraged!" Jennie protested.

Grandma thought that was funny. Mom did not.

Jennie brushed off her hands and skirt and met her father at Mary's grave. Cautiously slipping her hand in Dad's rough, work-worn one, she said, "We're going over to Grandma Jennie's grave now. Will you come?"

Enclosing his fingers around hers, he smiled and said. "Yes, of course, sweetie."

"And sometime could you tell me stories about Great-Aunt Mary?"

"You and your stories! I know very little about Aunt Mary. We may still have her recipe for ginger cookies. Ask your mother."

"Oh, thank you, Daddy. I will ask her."

With the weeds pulled and geraniums planted and watered at Agnes's grave and Grandfather Stephen and Florence Deane's grave, the two women rested a moment, pleased with their work. Grandmother Sarah slipped her hand into Charlotte's, and her only daughter tightened her grip, the strain between them now an inner strength. Remembering loved ones, they meandered over to Grandmother Jennie's grave.

Following behind, Dad said, "The flowers are pretty. Thank you for helping."

Jennie smiled, held tighter to his hand, and walked along with her father. Then, she said sadly, "You know, Daddy, I'll miss my best friend, Amadeus. I wish we could stay in Dixfield. Why do we have to move away?"

"My job. Living in Aroostook County means I'll be home more often."

"I won't like it there, and I'll never see my best friend."

"Amadeus has been a good friend to you, and you'll make new friends."

The family gathered in front of the gravestone of Jennie A. Stolt, young Jennie's grandmother, her father Henry's mother, who had been laid to rest long ago.

Jennie quietly fell to her knees in front of the monument with the engraved leaves. Grandma stood beside her and Mom and Dad farther back. In this solemn moment, sunlight shone on the aging granite stone, cool to the touch. Eyes closed, Jennie traced her finger slowly, lightly, across the etchings, seeing leaves, reading words and dates. Tracing cursive letters, she read the epitaph: BELOVED ON EARTH, WE LOVE THEE STILL.

Suddenly, Jennie spiraled, ascended high above treetops, whirled around, and descended in graceful twirls at the four corners on the Cummings Hill Road. The house, barn, and pasture all seemed familiar.

The rustling of crinoline, the voices of girls. In the front yard, Grandmother Jennie, a young woman, laughed with her sisters, brown-haired Esther and Agnes, the little blond. Grandfather Stephen Deane, a young man, walked down the road toward the house and the girls. Grandma Jennie smiled and ran to him. Stephen caught her in his open arms and hugged her close. Her younger sisters hid their eyes and giggled shyly.

Spiraling a second time, unafraid, she ascended and then descended in the familiar Varnum Pond neighborhood. Inside an old schoolhouse, low benches sat in an arc around the fireplace. Black paint on a wall served as the blackboard. A teacher's desk sat on a raised floor. Grown-ups were there, not children. Two ladies, mother and daughter, Great-Grandmother Anna Stolt and Grandmother Jennie Deane, sang in melodious alto voices an unfamiliar hymn in an unfamiliar language.

The spiraling sent her back, descending to Temple Village Cemetery. Jennie opened her eyes. She had landed on her knees in front of Grandma Jennie's grave and her finger still touched the epitaph. Mom, Dad, and Grandma stood where they had been—Grandma Sarah, near the headstone and Jennie, and Mom and Dad farther away—absorbed in their own thoughts.

Jennie couldn't contain herself. "I saw her!" she cried. "I saw Grandmother Jennie! I saw her sisters! I saw Grandfather Stephen! I heard voices and music! And I saw Anna!"

Father caught her arm, held it roughly, pulling her closer to him. Stiffly, Jennie stood straight, her head hanging down, eyes squeezed shut, as he barked, "Stop! You must stop this now! You can't see dead people! They're with God! Respect the dead!"

"Daddy, I did see them! I know what I saw. Please believe me. It's the truth."

"Enough of your imagination! It's too wild." He let go, she crumpled, and he stalked away. On the ground, trembling and holding her arm, Jennie sobbed.

Mother caught Grandmother's eye, an unspoken message passing between them, and hurried after Henry. Grandmother Sarah helped Jennie to her feet. "Come, my dear."

Still sobbing, Jennie said, "He doesn't believe me. He doesn't understand me."

Holding Jennie's hand, Grandma walked with her past the headstones to the other side of the cemetery toward an ancient, gnarled oak, far from her father's voice, now raised at her mother. "Now, sweetheart, calm down. Stop crying, and we'll talk."

Jennie calmed her sobs, inhaling the soothing scent of lavender, of Grandma. She said, "Daddy scares me."

"I know, but he's scared too. Your father, blind as he is, does not see your gift."

"But you see it."

"I do indeed. I have the same gift. Sweetie, you must not share this gift. Those who do not see do not believe. You will see and know the stories of your ancestors, but you must keep these revelations to yourself."

"Grandma, I could tell Dad the things he doesn't know, and maybe he wouldn't be so angry and scared."

"No, my girl, you must not. Telling him you saw his mother—a mother he has never known—hurts him. He has no memory of her. Accept only the stories he shares with you. Ask for no more."

"Amadeus liked my stories."

Grandma laid her hand over her heart and said, "Amadeus is a sweet boy."

Jennie sniffled, "I'll miss him."

"Yes, my dear, you will." Grandma sighed and said, "And so will I miss him." She held Jennie's eyes in hers. "Now, please obey my words. Our gifts must be held in secret, undisclosed to others. Share with me, if you wish. I am here to hold your hand."

Grandmother Sarah and Jennie strolled back toward the family graves. Mother and Father were already there, picking up the garden tools, watering can, and empty pots. Jennie ran to them and overheard Father's words: "Graveyards and pretending to see the dead won't help Jennie differentiate between the present and past, between reality and imagination. We must never return to Temple."

Racing back to Grandma, Jennie cried out, her hands shaking, "Dad's not coming back, never, ever!"

Grandma caught her in a hug. "What did you hear, my girl?"

"Because of me! I'll never see Temple again! I'll never know their stories!"

Holding Jennie's face in her hands, Grandma said, "Look at me." She paused. "You will come back. You may be grown, but you will return. And the stories will still be here. Now, calm down, dry your eyes." Jennie wiped her tears with her hand, and they strolled over to Mother and Father, waiting in the Deane row.

Standing in front of father, biting her lip, Jennie said, "I'm sorry, Dad."

"I shouldn't have yelled at you, my girl. I love you. It's just that…." Dad sighed. "Well, I don't have a memory of my mother or some of the others." He raised his voice and snapped, "I tell you the things I know, the things I've been told. Yet you persist." He breathed deeply. "But know that I love you."

"Oh, Daddy, I love you too." Dad hugged both his wife and daughter. Grandma Sarah watched, unconvinced. Looking up at Daddy, Jennie said, "Can we go to the homestead now, please? Your heart always finds peace there."

"I should say no, but I can't say no to your beautiful eyes. No more pretending to see dead people and no more making up stories about them."

"I promise. I won't talk about dead people, but Daddy, did Grandma Jennie have eyes like mine?"

"Yes, we've told you the story before. Grandfather Stephen asked us to give you my mother's name, for you have her brown dancing eyes. Now, it's time to go."

Walking backward slowly, along the dirt road toward the car, Jennie preserved in memory all she had seen: gravestones in the Deane row, geraniums and a fiddlehead, the gnarled oak, visions of Grandmother Jennie. She hummed sadly the song she'd heard in the vision—a long-ago tune, familiar to Dad but unknown to Jennie. Dad walked beside her and, feeling a sudden chill, surveyed the sky, the trees, and the cemetery.

Father drove back to the Intervale, the floodplain around Temple Stream. Deeply saddened, silent, chin trembling, and holding Grandma Sarah's hand, Jennie saw familiar sights from the back seat—Hodgkins General Store and the bend in the stream where they'd once seen a beaver. Still so alive in her imagination, sisters on the front lawn.

Everyone was quiet, somewhere else in their own thoughts.

Dad turned onto the Varnum Pond Road and then onto the logging road. The Ford bounced merrily through potholes along the overgrown road, barely wide enough, two plank bridges, tree branches scraping the car. Dad decided which rocks to go around and which to bump over. He turned onto the old beaten path at the Deane Homestead and parked beneath maple, oak, and pine.

Jennie jumped out and ran as fast as she could across the meadow, breathing deeply the mixed scents of wildflowers. She bent over, inhaled lilacs, then ran farther into the orchard, inhaling the scent of apple blossoms. Jennie fell to her knees, hidden by the trees, dug a small hole, buried a small object, and cried for her Amadeus, her beloved Temple, its stories and visions.

Dad stepped out of the car, "Jennie!"

"Let her go!" Mother stood behind him. "Just as your heart finds peace here, so does hers. Give her time!"

Grandma listened quietly, a witness to Mother's words.

Dad stood silent, taking in the ruins of his childhood home: the lilacs gone wild; the apple trees grown over; the wall still crumbling; the cellar hole; and Deane, Varnum, and Derby Mountains, Middle Hill, too, in the distance. He breathed deeply the fresh air, walked into the clearing, missing Jennie, and stood among orange day lilies, dandelions, and buttercups growing at the edge of the cellar hole. This was where the cabin once stood, old when Dad was young, now eaten by the earth. The trees and tall grasses swayed. The wind blew his jacket open, as he said his own goodbye.

Charlotte had followed. He reached for her hand, and they walked through the overgrown meadow, past the old crumbling stone wall, where he took a moment to remember the boy who'd walked on that wall. These things, the things of nature, held close the stories of the generations of the Deane family who had lived and loved here.

"We should find her," said Dad.

"No, leave her be," said Mom.

"Jennie could get lost."

"She's already lost. It's a mistake to not bring her back to Temple again."

At the edge of the orchard, Jennie waited and watched, knowing her father's heart was sad too. Once Mom and Dad were out of sight, she ran to Grandma at the old crumbling stone wall. Together they picked a wildflower bouquet.

Balancing herself, Jennie walked across the tumbled rocks. She stood, head up, a circus performer on the tightrope, and stepped carefully to the other end of the stone wall where the beaten path had once been a carriageway with wagons, horses, the milkman's cart. With perfect posture and grace, she bowed and curt-sied to an appreciative audience seen and heard only in her imagination. Jennie jumped to the ground. Grasping Grandma's hand, she said, "Come on! Let's go to the old cemetery."

"You and your graveyards!"

"The dead lived history," said Jennie. "We learn about life from their stories."

"If only everyone would open their eyes and hearts to see."

They walked slowly down the path, shaded by a canopy of tree branches, that led to the Deane–Huse Cemetery. Climbing the cracked granite steps, they entered through the open iron gate. In tall grass it was difficult to read names on the weather-beaten, sunken stones. "Come, Jennie," said Grandma. "Let's look over there on the far side."

Hand-in-hand, they walked slowly, carefully, until Jennie noticed the name "William Deane," her great-great-grandfather. She fell to her knees, wiping dirt and debris from the stone. Tracing the letters, dates, and the epitaph, she suddenly spiraled and whirled. Instantly stopping, she found herself in the same spot in time past.

A man, dressed as a Quaker, raked away the leaves from the graves. A couple stepped cautiously up the granite steps. She carried a basket. He held her arm.

Their skin was dark and their clothing torn and soiled. The Quaker looked directly at them, nodded, and turned his head toward the woods. The couple hurriedly passed by him, by the big rock, vanishing in a maple grove. The man continued to rake.

A dark-skinned boy in tattered clothing popped up from the other side of William's gravestone. Jennie stared into his wide-open eyes. Her complexion turned ashen, her lips and chin trembled, and she held her breath. He stared back, not seeing; then he turned and ran into the woods with the man and woman.

Grandmother Sarah tugged at her hand. Jennie spiraled back to the same spot. Father was coming. She stood, straightening her skirt. Phew! He hadn't seen.

"There you are, ladies," Father called happily.

Mom followed, her eyebrows drawn together, posture stooped, arms folded. He wouldn't listen to her. He was angry, unreasonable, denying Jennie's stories and visions, denying the peace both of their hearts found here. She had told him that his decision, an unforgivable wrong, would drive a wedge between father and daughter.

PART ONE

ONE

Awake before sunrise, Jennie crawled out of bed. As her bare feet met the cold floor, she folded her arms, shivered, and rubbed goosebumps with cold hands. Oh, the chill in this cold unforgiving house! She donned her old blue cardigan, threadbare from years of wear, buttons missing, but comfortable, like being wrapped in the arms of a dear old friend. On the porch, she bent over the dwindling wood pile, picked up and carried a few last sticks into the kitchen. Stacking them in the old pot-bellied woodstove, she lit a fire, the only source of heat.

Jennie prepared a cup of herbal tea, steeped exactly five minutes, adding honey. Sitting in the wooden rocker, she leaned forward with hunched shoulders and warmed herself by the crackling fire. Heat from the stoneware mug penetrated her hands as she sipped the steamy tea.

Through the window over the sink, the morning sunlight flittered on the bright yellow kitchen wall. Jennie replayed yesterday in her mind, the last day of the school year, saying goodbye to her students, and to Eleanor, a friend, a Treasure. Eleanor had offered her friendship on her seventeenth birthday, the day she moved into this house. Today, Eleanor was flying home, west to her family. Forty-year-old Jennie was alone.

Setting the mug on the marble slab that lay on top of a wooden stand, a family heirloom, she slid her hand across the smooth, cool surface, white with grayish markings. Memories of Temple, Maine, and stories of her ancestry invaded her mind. She would gather the family history, photographs, and memorabilia to remember that time of childhood.

Crossing the living room, her bedroom for many years, furnished with a bed, a small dresser, and a rack for hanging clothes, Jennie stood in front of the rickety stairs and rested her hand on the polished but unstable railing. Upstairs was a place she rarely went anymore, as the ghosts of the past lived there.

Breathing deeply and with dread, Jennie stepped up the creaking stairs. Halfway, she stopped, held her breath, listened intently for the voices, scanned the walls for the shadows. Then she silently climbed to the top. One thing she liked up there was the wide pine floorboards, but the closet loomed ahead. Floor to ceiling, dark wood, heavy sliding doors.

Jennie slid one open, as slowly and quietly as she could so as not to disturb the ghost. Spying two green boxes marked *From My Daughter* and *From My Students* and one more belonging to Rebecca, she piled them on the floor.

Caressing an old book, a faded pink cover with gold lettering, *Pollyanna,* she opened to the fly leaf and read, *Florence Deane,* written in an old-fashioned longhand.

On the highest shelf, the ancestry boxes and a paper shopping bag had been collecting dust for years. As she reached for a blue box and the bag, dust drifted down all around her. She coughed, sneezed, blinked, and reached again for two plain cardboard boxes and a shoe box. After one last look at the shelves, she slid the doors closed and wandered into Rebecca's bedroom.

In her mind's eye, Jennie saw her lovely ten-year-old daughter with shiny brown eyes, light brown hair styled in a French braid, and an inquisitive mind. Rebecca concentrated on old maps spread on the floor, on the bed, and tacked to the wall. Smiling, she said, "You know, Mom, someday, I'll see the world." Jennie's memory fading, she remembered that young girl, now a woman, still wearing a French braid, a history teacher, excited by the discovery of artifacts and the stories they revealed. Her only child, living on her own, still close by, but not in this miserable house where no warm hearts lived anymore.

Unintentionally, Jennie fixed her eyes on the dark wooden door of the locked bedroom, a skeleton key above the molding. The faint scent of alcohol still lingered in her memory. Inside the room, a small table—an altar with two wedding rings, a whiskey bottle, and a photograph of a teenage boy—was a reminder of that time of fear twenty-one years ago. She'd been nineteen.

It was time to leave. But where would she go?

Jennie carried boxes and the bag downstairs, leaning her shoulder against the horsehair-and-lathe wall covered with stained flowered wallpaper, the same as had been pasted to the living room walls several generations ago. Three trips, and she was done. She'd never walk up those stairs again.

The kitchen table was her workplace. She pushed aside her Bible, a few bills, empty schoolbags, her purse, a journal, and a pen. The glass vase she set on the counter.

The shoe box weighed nothing at all. Jennie slowly untied the white ribbon and lifted the lid. Removing old letters, she noticed a plain white sealed envelope, addressed, simply: Jennie. Dad's handwriting. What's this about? No need to hurry reading it. Jennie dropped the letters back into the box, concealing the white envelope.

Next, she saw a black-and-white photograph of two children, the boy taller than the girl. Teary-eyed, she recognized them: Amadeus, her best friend, and Jennie herself. Grandma Sarah's script on the reverse: *A sweet boy who knows how to keep a secret and how to protect my lovely girl, my Jennie.*

Another favorite black-and-white photograph: Grandma Sarah, the frail, old woman hugging five-year-old Jennie, the two of them sharing a secret on a summer day's family picnic. She remembered the day of Grandma's funeral in her thirteenth year. What was that song, Grandma's favorite hymn? Humming, she'd forgotten the tune.

Jennie opened a small box: a single small pearl set in a gold band, a gift to Grandma Sarah from Grandpa Harold, who always referred to her as the pearl in his life. Could she ever be a pearl in someone's life?

Replacing the contents in the box, she set the lid on it and re-tied the ribbon.

"What's this?" Grandma's handwriting on a cardboard box! *For Jennie.* How had she ever missed it?

Unfolding the flaps, dropping crumpled newspapers onto the floor, and holding a well-wrapped object in her hands, Jennie carefully removed soft white flannel. Grandma Sarah's silver teapot! Oh, the scent of peppermint tea in Grandma's kitchen. A family heirloom, such a precious gift. Suddenly, Grandma's voice filled her mind: *Come home. It is time.*

Grandma! She'd missed her so! She longed to go home!

From the second cardboard box, Jennie pulled out three-ring binders filled with ancestral charts of the Deane and Parkhurst families. Flipping through the pages of the Deane family, she saw names and places, and she remembered Temple, the Varnum Pond neighborhood, the little girl spiraling and seeing their stories.

Spilling the contents of the shopping bag on the table—documents and her grandfather's recollections of Varnum Pond—she caught sight of an old newspaper, the *Franklin Journal* from July 1912. Someone had drawn circles around paragraphs. Reading, she remembered the old Deane–Huse school: the raised floor, fireplace, and low benches without backs. Two women, Grandmother Jennie and Great-Grandmother Anna, sang a Swedish hymn. That's why she didn't know the words! They were singing in Swedish.

Hugging the newspaper to her breast, lips quivering, tears welling, Jennie marched onto the porch and plunked herself down on the top step between pots of geraniums. Dad, he knew, didn't he? Why had he taken away what she loved—her visions, stories, her beloved Temple, even Amadeus. Didn't he see, didn't he know, that she was lost without them? Unfolding the newspaper, she raised her arms and held it toward the sky, as though she were thrusting the evidence in his face. How could he, how could he say those words, *I love you*? For he did not love her. He could not accept who she was.

Trembling, she was unaware of a soft voice, of Rebecca's gentle touch. "Mom, are you okay? What's happened?" Her daughter sat next to her.

Jennie squeezed Rebecca's hand and sighed, "Even from the grave, your grandfather pours salt into my wounds."

"Oh, that. Mom, he's dead. Forget about him."

Jennie wiped her eyes. Rebecca didn't want to hear her complaints. "Well, so, tomorrow you're off! How exciting, your first archaeological dig!"

"It's not exactly my first, but I am excited about Malaga Island."

"Well, my dear, I have my own dig."

Frowning, Rebecca said, "What are you talking about?"

"I'm going on a quest of self-discovery. I'll be digging up the past, finding my ancestors and their stories again!"

"Where? How long will you be gone?"

"Temple, my beloved Temple, and then I guess I'll follow my heart." Squeezing Rebecca's hand a bit tighter and breathing deeply, she said, "Here's the thing. I'm resigning my teaching position and walking—no, running—away from this house."

"Mom, wait! What?"

"I just told you, a quest."

"But, this is home! I grew up here! My room, my things are here. You are here."

"Honeybee, this is home to you. You were born and raised here. To me, it's a cold, lonely house which ceased to be a home when you left. My home was my child."

"What about my things?"

"In the kitchen, packed in a box. Take them with you today, if you want them."

"Mom, suddenly, you're walking away from a career you love, and from me."

"Never from you. Just a letter or a phone call away. Sweetie, I need to find my life, a purpose, a place to belong. Here, I live with ghosts."

"How long have you been planning this?"

"Today. I cleaned out the upstairs closet." Jennie paused. No response. Still, no response. "Come inside, honeybee. You love all things history. Dig through the ancestry. It's all there in Temple and on Voter Hill."

At the kitchen table Rebecca was soon absorbed in family history: documents and handwritten notes. Noticing the silver teapot, she said, "Where did you find this?"

Jennie shared the history of the teapot, her love for Grandma Sarah, the pearl ring, and the photographs.

Holding one, Rebecca read the words in an unfamiliar script. "Who are the kids? The cryptic message, a secret? What's it mean?"

"Oh, yes, my best friend, Amadeus, and me. Perhaps you will learn its meaning at a later time. How about a sleepover and pizza tonight? My treat."

Rebecca opened the blue box, filled with photographs. "Sure, at my home."

"I was hoping for your apartment, but, okay, one last night here."

Jennie ordered pizza and salad, grabbed her purse, and left, smiling. Her daughter was hooked, and she'd be in Temple this summer.

That evening, the sunset, a fireball of reddish yellow rays spread the last light of day over the fields and beyond the tree line. Potato plants grew in straight rows, soon to be adorned by purple-and-white blossoms. Jennie and Rebecca, arm in arm, strolled down the field road. "Sweetie," said Jennie. "I built a life once. I can do it again."

"You're really going, aren't you, Mom?"

"It's time. The ghosts, the suffering, the pain is overshadowing the pleasant memories, all the pleasantries of life. And I fear they're winning the battle."

Turning toward home, they ambled up the rutted dirt road. A tear slid down Rebecca's cheek. "All the Treasures have left, even Eleanor."

Jennie held Rebecca's hand. "Honeybee, you are alone by choice. Remember the old maps? They're in the box. Dig them out. See where they take you." Pulling Rebecca into a warm hug, she said, "Would you like to have Eleanor's vase?"

"Oh, Mom, thank you. I love Eleanor. She's like a grandmother to me."

They stepped onto the porch and through the kitchen door.

Later, settled in bed, curled next to her mother, Rebecca closed her eyes. Jennie lay there staring at the ceiling, unable to sleep. Did she make the right decision? Coiled springs creaking, Rebecca fluffed her pillow, pounded it with her fist, fluffed it again, and settled down. Her daughter was never still, even in her sleep.

"Mom, perhaps you shouldn't pack your clothes. Go shopping and get a new look. I mean, since you're going into the world."

Jennie smiled. "Good night, honeybee."

"Good night, Mom. Oh, Mom, tell me what happened between you and Grandpa."

"Not tonight, sweetie, it's a long story. Another time."

"Once, when I was six, I talked to him."

"You did. What did he say to you?"

"He was at the grocery store with Grandma Charlotte. I ran down the aisle to him, and I said, 'Why don't you want to be my grandpa?' He said, 'Ask your mother.' So I'm asking. Grandma smiled, turned me toward frozen foods and I ran back to you."

"Good night, my sweetie."

"Good night, Mom."

Late in the night, while Rebecca slept undisturbed, Jennie awakened to weeping and moaning. Footsteps creaked on the stairs and moonlit shadows appeared on the wall. A chair scraped across the kitchen linoleum. *Smash*! Jennie jumped out of bed, rushed to the kitchen, and flipped on the light switch. On the floor lay the glass vase, a million tiny pieces. The silver teapot teetered on the edge of the counter. It tipped. In midair Jennie caught it, held it securely, and wrapped it in flannel, packing it in the cardboard box. She knelt by the broken vase, eyes watering, picked up the one and only shard large enough to hold between fingers. "Damn you, ghost!" A gift from her Treasure. For twenty-three years she had carefully cared for it and now had given it to Rebecca. Sweeping up the pieces, she emptied the dustpan into the trash.

Jennie picked up the ancestry binders and papers and filed them back in the other cardboard box and the shopping bag. She replaced the lid on the blue box. Stacking them by the door, she set the green boxes, the shoebox, and the book on top. At sunrise she would pack these things and the slab of marble in the Jeep, adding one clay pot of geraniums, a trowel, and a rake. Now she wrapped herself in the quilt and rocked in the creaking chair by the woodstove.

In midmorning, Jennie walked Rebecca to her Mustang, ready for her summer dig. "I'm so sorry about the broken vase, honeybee."

"It's okay. Not like it's an antique or an artifact. I still don't understand how you knocked it over." Rebecca held her mother's hand. "I'm more concerned about you."

Jennie shrugged. "No need."

"Mom, you didn't think this through. You cleaned a closet and you're making a life-changing decision. What about your career? And us? Your safety, a woman alone?"

"And so are you, traveling alone. Let's keep in touch—postcards."

"Perhaps we could go together during Harvest Break."

"I've taken care of myself since my seventeenth birthday. You have my address."

Rebecca opened the driver's side door. Several manila envelopes from universities lay scattered on the passenger seat. "Well, Mom, I'd like to visit you."

"I'll be there, waiting. I love you, honeybee."

They shared a warm hug and a few tears. "Be safe. I love you," said Rebecca.

Jennie stood in the driveway, waving, as Rebecca turned onto the field road and left onto McBurnie Road, heading toward Presque Isle. "Safe journey, my child."

Jennie drove to the cemetery on the hill where her parents were buried. Carrying the clay pot, bottled water, and gardening tools over to the gravestone, she knelt, planted, and watered three geraniums: pink, white, and red. "Mom, I'll not be visiting again. I'm going home, seeking my heart's peace. I'll plant the flowers, like we once did. I'll visit Grandma Sarah. I don't know where my journey will lead me. I love you, Mom."

A soft kiss on her cheek. Jennie felt wrapped in her mother's scent, lilac, and in her gentle touch. Mother's voice, a whisper, filled Jennie's heart: *I love you, my honeybee. Embrace your quest and you will find what you seek. Safe journey, my child.* Another soft kiss and Mother was gone.

Back at the Jeep, she stood by the door. One last look. She had not spoken to Dad, but was sure he knew. Seeing the old maple tree in the far corner, she remembered standing there at the grave sheltered by that tree. Farewell.

Leaving the cemetery, she drove to the bank and withdrew a large sum, leaving enough to pay the bills still lying on the table. Next, she stopped at the home of the farm family who owned the land and the farmhouse, thanking them for a place to live.

At the unforgiving house, Jennie placed telephone calls, canceling electrical and phone services. Sitting in one of the mismatched chairs at the kitchen table, she paid the bills and wrote the letter. In the fall, she would not be there to teach her children, the little sweeties who gave her joy. As heart-wrenching as that was, Jennie would be true to the quest—a journey into the past, seeking new life, a purpose, a place to belong, and an escape from the ghosts of her own past. And what of Rebecca? Would she accept her mother's decision and follow her own dreams?

Inspiring words gripped her mind: Mother's—*Embrace your quest and you will find what you seek*—and Grandma's—*Come home. It is time.*

Unwilling to spend another moment in this place, haunted by the ghost, the voices, and the shadows, Jennie opened the dresser drawer and pulled out a small box, her mother's pearl necklace, a gift from her father. Did he ever tell her? Did he know? Did Mom know she was the pearl in his life?

Throwing some essentials in one school bag, she boxed the rest of her clothes. Into a second bag, she tossed recipes including ginger cookies, teas, honey, the ceramic teapot, her camera, sketchbook, pencils, and important papers.

She carried the box and bags to the Jeep. Then, swinging her purse over her shoulder, she picked up the skeleton key, her Bible, and the mail. Stepping onto the porch, she laid the house key under a flower pot. Depositing the other things in the Jeep, she carried the mail to the box and raised the red flag.

One last look at the old house: white shingles with peeling paint, a front porch with a few sticks of wood scattered on the green-painted floor, a swing, and geraniums and herbs in clay pots. A shadow in sunlight clouded the window of the upstairs locked bedroom and the house wept.

As she turned onto the dirt road and left on McBurnie Road, the fields, homes, and neighbors became a memory. In Presque Isle, she parked in front of the thrift store and deposited the box of clothing at the front door. On Route 1, she drove past the university and the dealership, heading for Houlton, I-95, south to Bangor.

Two

L ate afternoon the next day, Jennie turned onto I-95 south, leaving Bangor. Traffic slowed to a stop as blue lights flashed up ahead. She tuned the radio to classical music. New clothes, hair style, soft, pretty manicured hands. How attractive and self-confident she felt!

Jennie combed her fingers through her hair, soft and thick, light brown with golden highlights and long layers. It would certainly shine in the summer sun. In the rearview mirror, she admired waxed eyebrows and pulled her hair back, touching gold posts. What had the hairdresser said: *Whoever he is, his eyes will be on you.* Jennie smiled again at the comment. She had been alone now for more than twenty years. No handsome lover in her life to tell her she was beautiful.

Earlier that day, in need of a summer wardrobe, Jennie had entered an anchor store at the mall. With help from the store associate, a young stylish woman, and multiple trips to the dressing room, she had created a wardrobe of comfortable, favorite clothes in natural fibers, different cuts, lengths, styles, and colors. Cotton shirts, matching cardigans, skirts, and jeans all fit her shape. Spying a dark blue dress, she had held it up in front of the mirror. The associate had commented, "That shade is your color." So Jennie had purchased it, adding gold jewelry. In other departments, she had purchased more items and hurried toward the exit. A display of cloth quilted bags caught her attention. She'd bought two for packing her wardrobe. Shopping bags spoke of new purchases, and Jennie preferred not to look like she had dressed off the rack. She'd replaced her old purse with the soft gray leather shoulder bag that lay on the passenger seat. Credit card receipts were tucked inside. Two old photographs in new frames sat next to the gray bag.

At the laundromat, Jennie had cut out the tags and labels with the tiny pair of scissors she carried in her purse. Labels were itchy, scratchy, and, like some fabrics, made her fidgety, even as a child. Once her clothes were washed and dried, Jennie packed them. The quilted bags lay next to her ancestry.

Carried away by intermittent high cheery notes in the symphony, she imagined little girls dancing and twirling in fields among spring flowers.

Traffic began to move slowly, but after the downtown exit, it sped up, and the orchestra played on. Jennie, the child, lay in a pile of brightly colored leaves as more floated downward in the wind. Seasons changed, and snowflakes fell gracefully. Open hands reached up. The child caught tiny flakes, watching them melt into water droplets. Lower deeper notes spoke of storms.

Taking exit 157 at Newport, Jennie stopped at a fast food restaurant. Inside she ordered a soda and a salad and sat alone eating an early dinner. Turning back onto Route 100, she stopped at the gas station and convenience store, filled the tank, and purchased a candy bar and bottled water. Then she left, weaving around and through a stoplight until she was headed west on Route 2, traveling through small towns. In Skowhegan, she passed by a wooded park, drove around narrow streets, and crossed the bridge over the mighty Kennebec River, a monument to a mill town of bygone days. As night fell, Jennie arrived in Farmington.

Checking into the Capital Motel, cheap rates, high upon a hill with a view of her childhood peak, she carried a few essentials inside. As she turned on the light, mice scurried out of sight. She didn't sleep well that night: scurrying noises in the dark; voices and shadows calling her back; the air, hot, humid, no fan, no air conditioning. Jennie sat in the one chair by the window, and, as the sun rose, her heart felt nearer home. Voter Hill, Mt. Blue, Day Mountain, all so familiar.

On Saturday morning, Jennie stood at the foot of Voter Hill. Her memories of Grandma Sarah and her mother, Charlotte, had drawn her to this place. Forgetting about the steep incline, she parked her Jeep near the old boarded-up radio station and began to walk up the hill.

Hayfields on both sides. Daisies, buttercups, and brown-eyed Susans grew wild. Solid stone walls bordered the fields. Halfway up on the left, a tree-lined avenue led to the old farm that once belonged to her grandparents, Harold and

Sarah Parkhurst. Temperatures rising, the sun heating the earth, Jennie stepped into the field and rested on a stone wall. Remembering that old farm and the family who once lived there, she felt a kind of ascension, then a spiraling, and she landed with a bump back against the wall.

Horses pulling a wagon trotted slowly down that avenue toward the road, toward her. From old photographs, she recognized Grandpa Harold, seated next to his daughter, Charlotte, chatting happily. Mother! In the back were wooden boxes of fresh, big, bright red strawberries. Jennie could smell the sweetness and taste the sugary fruit, as she imagined the juices trickling down her chin. Grandpa turned the horses onto the narrow roadway and skillfully held them at a slow pace, descending the steep hill. Jennie knew from her mother's stories that they were going into town to sell the berries.

Once they were out of sight, Jennie looked back up the avenue. Settled in her rocker, Sarah picked up her sewing. Peggy, their dog, lay at her feet. "Grandma!"

Again, she ascended, spiraled, and descended, still seated on the wall. She was back! She hadn't spiraled for so long!

Jennie climbed up the hill, a steeper grade, toward the dairy farm of times past, toward the place at the summit where she could touch the sky, a place closer to God. Distant mountains and treetops below—a magnificent view.

It had been a slow and tiring climb as the sun grew brighter and hotter. Feeling dehydrated, Jennie walked slowly across the road from the farmhouse to a log home with a well in the yard. A man was throwing wood off a truck. At the well, she lowered the bucket, seeking cool thirst-quenching water.

"Can I help you? That well has been dry for a couple of years."

Startled, Jennie searched for the brusque voice, and saw a woman approaching. "Oh, dear. I'm sorry. I'm just…."

"Your face is so red! I thought you might be in trouble here. Come inside, I've got a cool refreshing drink, and we'll get out of the sun for a while."

"Thank you for your kindness. I don't feel very well."

"Where's your car?"

"At the bottom of the hill," said Jennie.

"You walked all the way up here! Good heavens!"

"For the view."

"Well, it is gorgeous! I'm Alice Murphy."

"I'm Jennie Deane. My grandparents met at the farm across the road."

"My mother, Sylvia, grew up here, up on the backside."

"What a coincidence! My mother, Charlotte, grew up on the Parkhurst farm."

"Oh, my! So, we meet again!"

"You're *that* Alice? Walking stone walls, sticking fingers in sap buckets, reading in the hay loft?"

"I am, my friend." The two women hugged.

In the backyard of Alice's house, a large pile of firewood caught Jennie's attention—another reminder of the old days. "Getting your wood in?"

"Yes, getting my wood in. But I pay a fellow now. Lovely man, though I can't figure out why he chose this hot day to throw wood. Amadeus."

Suddenly stopping in her tracks, Jennie said, "Amadeus Stuart?"

Alice smiled. "I thought you might know him."

"Oh, my goodness!" Turning quickly to rush to Amadeus, Jennie almost fainted. Alice held her steady and escorted her into the kitchen. Resting in one of the two rockers sat in front of the woodstove, a rock wall behind it, Jennie sipped cool, refreshing well water. Alice made her a sandwich and sliced a few strawberries. On the opposite wall, small clay pots hung in a black metal frame. Sunlight nourished the herbs.

Passing the plate to Jennie, Alice said, "I hope you like chicken."

"Looks delicious. Thank you."

Alice took a seat in the other rocker. "What brought you here?"

"Reconnecting with my ancestry," said Jennie.

"How long are you staying?"

"As long as my heart is here."

Eight-year-old Annie rushed inside, slamming the screen door. "Mom, it's hot outside. Can I have a drink?" Stopping instantly, she said, "Oh, hi, I'm sorry for interrupting."

"Meet my daughter, Annie."

"Hi, my name's Jennie. What were you doing outside?"

"Waiting for Amadeus."

"Is he your friend, Annie?"

"Daddy's best friend."

Giving Annie a glass of cold water, Alice said, "Sit here, drink slowly. Then cool down with a good book."

While getting reacquainted, they heard the roar of Amadeus's truck, as he sped down the hill.

Feeling refreshed and full of the thought of him, Jennie thanked Alice for her kindness. "Could you tell me where I could find Amadeus?"

"One doesn't find Amadeus. He finds you. He'll be around. How fun, meeting an old friend. Where could he find you?"

"The Capital Motel."

"What a perfectly dreadful place. You simply can't stay there."

Jennie shuddered. "It's okay, once you get used to the mice."

Alice extended an invitation to share her home. Reaching for Jennie's hand, she said, "I'd love the company. Come and go, as you please. Annie would love our stories."

Time with friends, here in this lovely home on the hill with all its memories. So tempting to accept, but she would be imposing.

"Shall we get your things?"

Jennie nodded and smiled, "Sure, I'd love to spend time here with you."

They drove to the motel, where Jennie collected her things, said goodbye to the mice, and paid the bill. Returning, they stopped at the old radio station where Jennie had parked her Jeep. She drove up the hill.

Upstairs in Alice's home, Jennie entered the guest room with light blue painted walls and maple furniture, including a comfortable bed with a soft, blue comforter and a quilt at the foot. A rocker sat in front of a huge window with long white curtains pulled open. Just down the hill, the old Parkhurst farm. "What a lovely room!" said Jennie.

Jumping on the bed, Annie said, "My room is across the hall. We have a bathroom, just for us. Mommy and Daddy have their own."

"Where is your daddy?"

"Away working. He builds log houses." Annie fell to her knees. "I have a brother, too, but he's not here. Mom, is Daddy coming home today?"

"Tomorrow, he'll be here for Sunday dinner."

"Well, Annie, I think we will become great friends."

A few trips up and down the stairs, toting the ancestry, green boxes, school bags, quilted bags and one old book, and Jennie was moved into this lovely room. As she sat on the bed—no squeaky coil springs—Jennie touched the smooth surfaces of the maple nightstand and the pottery lamp. A round table with matching straight chairs sat in the center: a place to study ancestry, write letters—there were more than a few to write—and, perhaps, read and play games with Annie.

"Jennie, would you like to join us at church tomorrow?" Alice smiled, "Someone of interest usually attends."

"I'd love to join you."

Left alone in her room to rest and get settled, Jennie thought about penning a postcard to Rebecca, but the bed was so comfortable. Snuggling under the log cabin quilt, she soon slept.

✳

At Grace Church in Temple's Intervale, Alice, Annie, and Jennie sat in the third row from the back. Two friends of Annie's, Maggie and Gracie, joined them. Maxine and Madeleine, elderly sisters, grandmother and great-aunt to Annie's friends, occupied the pew just in front. Maxine's complexion appeared grayish, not rosy like Madeleine's.

Passing by the third pew, Sharon Bailey and Sadie Jackson welcomed Jennie. Two noisy boys ran ahead, a smaller boy following, and settled in a front pew. Pastor Andrew and Jill Griffin introduced themselves. Pastor had a wizened expression, white thinning hair, and crow's feet around his eyes. Jill had neatly styled gray hair and soft, wrinkled hands. Alice had told Jennie that they were missionaries and ten years ago had accepted the call to this rural town.

An older woman tapped Jennie on the shoulder. "Welcome, you must be visiting. I'm Emilie Stuart."

"Nice to meet you. Wait! I know you. I'm Jennie Deane."

"Yes, yes, Dixfield. We were neighbors. You played with my little brother."

"Oh, my goodness, you gave me piano lessons."

"That's right, I did," laughed Emilie. "What brings you to Temple?"

"Exploring my roots. Hoping to meet with the archivist."

"I'm the archivist. How about tomorrow, one o'clock, at the red schoolhouse?"

"Sure. That would be fine." Jennie kept her voice even, not wanting to betray emotion. "What's Amadeus doing now?"

"Oh, a little of this, a little of that. Keeps to himself." Hugging Jennie, Emily said, "Gotta go. See you tomorrow. I'm the organist."

The service proceeded with prayers, congregational singing, and Pastor's sermon from Matthew 13:1-9—The Parable of the Sower.

Four-year-old Maggie climbed off the pew to sit next to Jennie, plopping her hand in her new friend's. Jennie smiled into Maggie's sweet face: shiny blue slanted eyes, long, light blond hair, small chin, light complexion, a flat nasal bridge—Down syndrome. Maggie giggled her sweet laugh and Jennie smiled, gently holding the little girl's hand.

A trio—Jill on cello, Emilie on piano, and Pastor on violin—played an old familiar hymn. The service ended with prayer, and the parishioners filed out of the sanctuary. Alice and Jennie left together, followed by Annie, Gracie, and Maggie. Sleepover!

"Jennie, why do you look so glum?"

"It seems the someone of interest didn't show."

"Be patient. He'll find you."

They strolled back to Alice's caravan with the three girls. Twin boys followed Sadie Jackson. The smaller boy, who had a pronounced limp and a sloping shoulder, walked slowly, hand-in-hand with Sharon Bailey. Pastor Andrew, his arm linked with Maxine's, escorted the two elderly sisters to his SUV.

That night a tired Jennie crawled into a comfortable bed in a charming bedroom, window open, warm breezes blowing, and excited little girls across the hall. Rising out of bed and knocking on the open door, Jennie said, "May I join you? Tell you a story?"

"Sit here with us! We love stories!" said the girls, piling fluffy pillows.

Inside Annie's cozy, pastel-green room, Jennie crawled onto the big bed covered with a pink comforter and leaned against the soft heap, while three girls surrounded her.

Jennie told this story: Once upon a time, a little girl named Honeybee loved to dig holes. Inside her purple plastic pail, she carried small toys, spoons, cups, crayons, a shovel, and a rake into the potato field. She dug small holes and buried small things. Then she carried the pail, shovel, and rake back to the house and left them on the porch. At the kitchen table with paper and crayons, she drew a map of holes, potato plants, and mounds of dirt. Later, when her mother wanted to bake cookies, she said, "Honeybee, please, dig up the measuring cups and spoons." Honeybee put on her green sunglasses and a straw hat so big that it fell over her eyes, and she carried her map. Finding the holes, she dug up the things, put them in her pail and filled the holes again. Carrying everything to the porch and giving her mother the cups and spoons, Honeybee said, "Look, Mommy, old things! Mommy, when I get big, I'll dig in the dirt, find more treasures!"

"Did she?" said Annie.

"Does she find treasure?" said Gracie.

"She does. That little girl is my daughter, Rebecca. She's grown, a teacher, and still likes to dig holes. Now I see sleepy faces, and our Maggie has already fallen asleep."

Jennie tucked the girls into Annie's big bed. "Good night, my sweeties."

"Jennie, can we meet Rebecca?" said Gracie.

"Isaac digs holes, too," said Annie.

"I think you'll meet her one day. Happy dreams."

In her bedroom, Jennie closed the door and settled under the comforter. Falling asleep, she dreamed of blessings—little girls, Alice, and her lovely Rebecca.

THREE

The next afternoon Jennie arrived fifteen minutes late—yikes—at the old Day Mountain Schoolhouse, now the Temple Historical Society. It had twelve-pane windows, a school bell high in the belfry, peeling red-and-white paint, and a roof in need of repair. She parked on the roadside, hurried across the lawn, up two stone steps, and opened the door without knocking—did you knock to enter a museum?

"Jennie, it's wonderful to see you!" Emilie got to her feet, and the old acquaintances hugged, the nearly fifteen years between them meaningless now. "Are you all settled? How was the sleepover? You know, Maggie and Gracie really wanted to meet you."

"Sharing memories with an old friend and loving time with sweet little girls."

The old woodstove was cool now—Jennie's father had warmed himself in front of it. The woodbox was empty. Old historic maps lined the walls. The blackboard was made of local slate, the teacher's desk of local cherry, and the students' desks likely birch. Scattered around the room were donations of memorable collections in open cardboard boxes. Despite the big windows, it seemed dark, as only a small lamp sat on the table.

Jennie said, "The memories, the history of times gone by these walls must hold."

"One of Maine's oldest, I guess you know," said Emilie. "The historical society is restoring it to the period of the 1880s. It was the Temple School from 1811 to 1958."

"You know, my grandfather Stephen Deane attended the Deane–Huse School at Camp Dresser. He probably completed grade six, or perhaps eighth."

"The Varnum Pond neighborhood school. 1804 to 1900."

Bookcases containing binders of ancestral and community history lined one wall. Framed photographs and artifacts were displayed on the top shelves. File cabinets stood in front of another wall. A copier sat on top of one. Papers, files, and three-ring binders covered the long table where Emilie and Jennie sat, browsing through documents—births, deaths, marriages, land acquisitions—that were on file at the historical society. The afternoon flew by, and it was already three o'clock.

"Jennie, would you like a cup of tea? I have fresh mint, grown in our garden."

"Thank you. Mint, a lovely aroma. Do you raise only herbs?"

"Herbs for tea, mostly. It's just a small box garden." Before stepping outside, Emilie handed Jennie a folder. "I copied a few articles for you."

Jennie thumbed through the articles. Cyrus and Mary, the original settlers on the homestead, 1827. Her notes said they arrived in 1826. They belonged to the Society of Friends and held Quaker meetings in their home. The Underground Railroad! Cyrus Deane and his family were operators! Her vision at age ten, the dark-skinned boy hiding behind the gravestone. Who was the Quaker raking?

Another article—*Franklin Journal* 1912. The Deane–Huse School. She had the original newspaper, circles drawn around paragraphs, proof of her visions denied by her father. Spiraling, she had seen that school. Jennie hid it under other papers.

Emilie set the tray on the table, poured the tea, and offered Jennie a cup and the jar of honey. "You look like you found something disturbing."

"Oh, well, I just didn't know about the railroad."

"Had you ever seen a Deane Apple Tree? There are still a few growing here."

"Dad told me about Cyrus's chance seedlings, and I've been in the old orchard."

Emilie leaned back in her chair, sipping her tea. "How long are you staying?"

"I haven't really gotten that far, but I *am* enjoying myself. And I can't wait to explore." Jennie paused, sipped her tea. "Emilie, could you tell me how to find my family's homestead? I'm not sure I remember the way. It's been too many years."

"Let's step over to the wall map, and I'll show you." They set their teacups on the table next to the research.

A truck pulled up outside. Shit, an interruption. Emilie seemed not to even notice. After a moment, a tall man entered. Jennie followed Emilie's lead, ignoring him. He stood near a window, folded his arms, leaned back on the wall, and waited. The late afternoon sun shone on him.

Emilie traced the map with an elegant, long finger. "The line between Wilton and Temple crosses here. Varnum Pond is located on the Wilton side. Here on the Temple side is the old Deane Homestead. And here...."

Jennie couldn't ignore the stranger. He seemed to fill the space with his beaming grin and his clear, bright blue eyes. His face was tanned, his red beard trimmed short, and his reddish hair shoulder length. She smiled in response to the tip of his cap.

Emilie hadn't missed a beat. "As I was saying, here in this location is the Deane–Huse Cemetery. Walk down a steep narrow path to a clearing. This area of Temple and Wilton was the Varnum Pond neighborhood."

"Now, Camp Dresser, where? Oh, dear, a small tear." Emilie reached for the scotch tape on top of the file cabinet, then she closely examined the map. "It should be near the homestead. If only I hadn't forgotten my magnifying glass!"

The interloper stepped right over. Standing too close behind Jennie, he stretched his arm around her and said, "What's your interest in the Dressers?"

Scent of male sweat! As it filled her senses, her breathing grew shallow. She watched his finger, roughened by hard work, trace the town line to the Deane Homestead and then to Camp Dresser. Jennie needed air. "One of the Deanes taught at the school there."

Emilie flattened the small tear and placed the tape over it. "Yes, Temple School District Number Four. That article from the *Franklin Journal* was about the reunion meeting."

Jennie couldn't help herself; she stared. She knew this man. And he knew her. He grinned. Amadeus! In front of the old Temple map, he caught her up in a bear hug.

Emilie stepped back, giving them this moment.

Her hand and cheek pressed against his soft plaid flannel shirt, Jennie felt the strength of his chest and arms, the odor of sweat still pervading her senses. Just as quickly, he held her at arm's length and noticed her watery eyes. "You still cry at every little thing." His voice, his words spoken softly, comfortingly. Giving her time for tears, no words, only the warmth, the gentleness of his arms holding her, he remembered how often the little girl needed time for tears.

Jennie stood back. "How did you know I was here?"

"Well, no big mystery. You were in church yesterday with Alice Murphy."

"Oh, Jennie, I telephoned him. We've been praying you'd find your way to us. Our prayers were answered when you walked up Voter Hill into Alice's yard."

"Wait, what? Why?"

Touching her hand, Amadeus said, "You've been in our hearts for a long time."

Emilie handed Jennie the package of tissues. Dabbing at her eyes. Jennie said, "Alice, both of you, friends I didn't know I had."

Amadeus thought a moment, shook off some doubt, and said, "I have a couple of things I need to do. But I can be back shortly. Would you have dinner with me?"

Waiting patiently for her answer, he turned to Emilie. "Any work to be done?"

"There's plenty to do, but nothing right now."

He turned back to Jennie. "Would you have dinner with me?"

"Yes, that would be nice."

He smiled. "Then I'll see you at six at Alice's."

"Okay, I'll be ready."

Tipping his cap to both ladies, he left and hurried to his truck. Starting the engine, he shifted gears, tires sliding on gravel, and the truck roared down the Temple Road.

"What did I just agree to?"

Emilie held her hand. "A simple dinner date with an old friend."

"It's not a date, just a visit with my old friend. And as for you, the next time we meet, I'll share my information."

"Can we give thanks?" asked the archivist.

"Of course."

They stood by the front window, looking upward to the clear blue sky and prayed silently until Emilie said aloud, "Thank you, Lord, for bringing Jennie home. You know, Lord, those two belong together."

Amen

Jennie fought the impulse to argue.

"Jennie! Jennie! Amadeus is here!" said Annie and Gracie, stomping excitedly up the stairs. Bursting through the bedroom door, they instantly halted. "Oh, pretty!"

Jennie stood in front of the mirror for a last-minute check: jean skirt, light blue cardigan, matching blouse, bracelet, necklace, sandals. Her hair was long, thick, and straight. She did feel pretty.

"Thank you, girls. Where's Maggie?"

Bouncing on tiptoes, Gracie said, "Downstairs with Amadeus."

Clasping Jennie's hand, Annie said, "Come see. He looks nice."

Jennie grabbed her gray leather bag and, on second thought, tossed it back on the bed. She descended the stairs with a skip in her step and a smile on her face, two giggling girls following close behind. In the kitchen, Maggie climbed down from Amadeus's lap, took Jennie's hand, and looking up, said, "Pret-ty, Pret-ty."

Hugging her little friend, Jennie looked into shiny blue eyes and squeezed her chubby cheek. "Pretty, the first word I've heard you say, honeybee."

Sitting at the table with Tom and Alice, Amadeus gazed at Jennie and Maggie. "Isn't Jennie pretty, Amadeus?" said Annie.

"She is pretty, isn't she?" said Gracie.

He blushed, still gazing. "She certainly is pretty." To Jennie, he said, "Ready?"

"Yes," she said. He was handsome in a blue dress shirt that was definitely his color, khaki slacks, hair washed, brushed, neatly tied back in a leather throng, beard trimmed.

Amadeus held the door for Jennie, and behind them three little girls tumbled onto the front porch. Tom and Alice clung to them. Amadeus and Jennie walked down the path toward his truck in the driveway.

"Mom, look," said Annie, "they're holding hands!"

"Good for them," said Alice.

Jennie turned toward the girls, and Amadeus caught her eye. He gave her hand a squeeze, and she felt a flutter in her stomach. "Good night, my sweet girls."

There, in the driveway, directly in front of her, Jennie beheld The Beast—scratched brown paint, slight evidence of rust, and bald tires. When Amadeus opened the door, foam cushioning protruded through cracked leather upholstery. She could let him drive the Jeep, but on second thought, that was a bad idea. The Jeep had bucket seats. He held her arm, and she climbed into the passenger seat.

Amadeus drove down Voter Hill, the engine a dull roar. A car whizzed by them, heading up the hill. "Emilie's driving faster than usual. She must be going to Alice's."

"I expect we are the talk of the kitchen table," she said.

He laughed. "Do you remember our flower garden?"

"Your mother gave us seeds to plant. I called it my butterfly garden."

In their garden, morning glories bloomed. Butterflies fluttered from blossom to blossom. Sunflowers reached for the sunny sky. Every morning, he had seen her out there waiting and watching for green sprouts to break through, for the sprouts to become stems, and for the flowers to grow, to bloom, displaying a mix of bright colors.

"What do you remember?" she said.

He chuckled, "Getting muddy, planting, weeding, watering, and soaking you."

"I got you back." She laughed.

"Yeah, you did." He laughed as well.

He turned onto Route 2 West and speeded up. The engine roared.

✳

Entering the Wilson Lake Inn, he held her hand. It felt so natural twining her fingers with his. Seated by the hostess at a table for two with corner windows, the view breathtaking, Amadeus ordered a bottle of their best house wine.

"Did you request this table?" she asked.

"Yeah, a table with a view, anyway," he said.

The lake was placid and glassy. The evening sun mirrored itself in blue. They gazed at the view and sneaked peeks at each other from behind the menus, until the young waitress served the wine and took their orders.

He poured and they sipped. Thirty years had passed, and tonight the woodsman and the teacher were becoming reacquainted.

"Your hair shines in the light. It's lovely," he said.

"When did you settle in Temple? I left you in Dixfield," she said.

"Eighth grade. Liked it, so I stayed. What brought you back?'

"School's out. Lost something here and came to find it."

"Care to elaborate."

"Not now." She sipped her wine.

The waitress served their dinner—lobster, cold, fresh, piled into warm, baked rolls, and no mayo. Pleasing to the palate.

"So, are you more than just the wood guy to the Murphys?"

"Yeah." He chuckled. "Tom and I have been best friends since junior high. Joined and retired from the National Guard together. It was his idea to join up."

She laughed, "And yours to retire?"

"Mutual agreement," he laughed. "What about you?"

"Raising Rebecca and teaching."

"Tell me about Rebecca."

"She's grown but still tied to me. It's most always been the two of us."

"You look sad suddenly."

She sipped her wine and sighed. "It's time for my little bird to fly." A breath. "Do you have children?"

"No, I don't."

"You look pretty sad yourself."

"Ha," he said. "No time for that!"

She slid her plate over to him. "Have some fries, not greasy, not too salty, hot."

He slid his over to her. "Have some onion rings, not greasy, but hot, spicy sauce."

"They look delicious, but I simply can't eat anymore."

The waitress took their plates and offered dessert choices. He asked for the tab, adding the cost of two wine glasses. Grasping the wine bottle, he took her hand, and she carried the glasses. They strolled across the lawn to the sand beach. At the edge of the lake, he helped her into the rowboat, pushed it off, and stepped in.

Summer breezes whispered. Shades of yellow and orange streaked under the calm still water, cut only by the silent oars. As the sun set behind the mountains, he serenaded her with songs of nature, while rowing into paradise. Enjoying his baritone, she removed her sandals, pulled her skirt above her knees, and dangled her feet over the side, letting the cool water splash over them.

"Sing with me," he said.

"I haven't sung for a long time," she said.

"You once sang like an angel."

"That was before."

"Before what?"

"A story for another day. I don't want to disrupt untroubled waters."

He rowed and sang in his deep-toned voice. Tears forming in her eyes, her heart sensed tranquility in the water, woods, mountains, in his baritone.

He laid the oars down, gently turned her face, gazed into her eyes and asked softly, "What has hold of your heart?"

She swung her feet inside the boat. He held out his hands, and she clasped them. His warm hands, calloused from hard work, fit perfectly with hers. He helped her to the middle seat, next to him.

"I've lost my heart. I came to find it."

Amadeus wrapped his arm around her, holding her close. Jennie wrapped hers around him, resting her head on his shoulder. "I buried it at the homestead thirty years ago. I was ten."

"This weekend we'll go there."

"I'd like you to go with me."

The wind grew stronger as ripples, gentle waves lapped at the sides of the rowboat.

Holding tightly to each other, they sensed the mild rocking. Leaning down, he lifted her chin, kissed her softly, entangling his fingers in her hair. She touched his face. His kisses were inviting, his touch, warm and tender. Moonlight shone on the lake, on them. With one arm around her, holding her close, she held out the glasses, and he poured the wine. In silence, they sipped, listening to the night sounds: water lapping, a loon calling, frogs croaking, crickets humming. They would have stayed there, far into the night, holding, caressing, kissing, but the bottle was empty and the mosquitoes were thick.

Jennie felt comfortable, sitting close to Amadeus and holding hands on the ride back to Voter Hill. She sensed that he felt the same.

"Do you have plans tomorrow?" he said.

She smiled, "That depends. What do you have in mind?"

"Want to help me deliver firewood and spend the day exploring our past?"

"Sure, it's a date. Oh, I'm sorry, not a date…just time between friends, right?"

"Yeah, right," he said.

Amadeus pulled into the Murphys' driveway and turned off the engine. He wrapped his arm around her and she laid her head on his shoulder. "Thank you for a nice evening," he said.

She tilted her head, caught his eyes in hers. "I enjoyed it too."

He leaned down and they kissed softly. "Let me walk you to the door," he said.

On the porch under the light, she said, "A lovely evening."

"I'll see you in the morning." He turned to leave.

She grabbed his hand. He saw into her eyes. One last kiss and she stepped into a quiet house. Creeping barefoot up the stairs, Jennie peeked into Annie's room. Three sleeping girls were snuggled together under the comforter. "Good night, my sweet ones. Happy dreams."

In her room, the lamp by the bed, dimly glowed; the open window, curtain blowing; and on the table, pages of an open book fluttered. Gazing at the twinkling stars and down the hillside, she let the breeze blow her hair. Jennie was back on the hill, and her Amadeus was here. She'd always known they were more than friends. "Grandma Sarah," she said, "help me find belonging, a life, and a purpose here."

The scent of lavender filled the room. Startled by a sudden noise, Jennie turned toward the table. The shoebox lay open and the framed photograph of the boy and the girl stood on the table. The aroma was gone.

Alice tapped lightly on the door, entered, and wrapped her arm around Jennie like an old friend, like a mother.

Leaning into the hug, Jennie said, "With him, it felt like those thirty years were erased. Thank you, Alice, for extending friendship to a wanderer."

"Not wandering now, but seeking." Alice closed the bedroom door on her way out. Jennie crawled under the comforter and soon fell asleep with thoughts of Amadeus.

FOUR

Curtains fluttered in the breeze. Little girls with inquisitive minds sat cross-legged, chins in hands, and three sets of eyes stared. Hands covered mouths, muffling giggles. One set of little hands patted Jennie's face. She stirred, yawned, stretched, and stuffed pillows behind her. Leaning back on the maple headboard, she said, "What's going on?"

"We waited up for you," said Annie.

"Were you with him all…that…time?" said Gracie.

"Did he kiss you?" "Do you love him?" "Are you marrying him?"

Annie said, "Jennie, you just met him yesterday!"

"Now, wait! I need you girls to slow down."

Maggie wiggled around for a close-up view of Jennie's face, giggled, and poked her in the nose. "Morning, pretty girl, my sweetie," said Jennie, hugging Maggie.

A gust of wind ballooned the curtains. *Crash!* Jennie flew out of bed. The photograph of the boy and the girl lay on the floor with a broken frame and shattered glass. "Oh, no," whispered Jennie, picking up the pieces and staring at the window. The curtains now hung straight, still, not even a flutter. The broken vase, the teetering teapot, the weeping window, and now the broken frame.

Annie asked, "Who are the children?"

Gracie patted Jennie's shoulder. "The children. Who are they?"

"Huh? Oh, oh, the children. Amadeus and me."

"You knew him when you were a kid!" declared Annie. Blue eyes stared into brown eyes and mouths were O-shaped.

Holding Maggie's hand, Jennie said, "Be careful where you walk." Setting the picture on the nightstand, she sighed and crawled under the comforter. The lake, the rowboat. Was he thinking about their evening, too?

The Beast roared up the hill. "Amadeus! Amadeus!" said the girls, running by Alice with folded clothes in her arms, and squeezing through the door. "Wear these. They're old, but clean," Alice said, laughing.

Ten minutes later, Jennie ran downstairs, "Sorry, I'm late."

"Slow down. Take your time. We have all day," said Amadeus.

Alice set a breakfast plate and a cup of tea on the table for Jennie. Tom and Amadeus talked, coffee mugs in their hands. Three girls gathered close to Jennie, staring as she ate. "Are you going out again?" said Gracie.

"Yes, sweeties, I am, with him," said Jennie.

"You know, girls," said Amadeus. "Jennie has a surprise for you tomorrow."

"A surprise!" said Annie.

"For us!" said Gracie.

"What is it?" said Annie.

"Be good listeners today," said Amadeus.

Thanking Alice, Jennie rinsed her plate in the sink. Amadeus waited by the door.

Amadeus gripped the steering wheel with joyous abandon, laughing and singing, bouncing and roaring west on Route 2, his old F-350 work truck clanking and groaning past Agway, the Dutch Treat, and Dexter Shoe, the landscape changing from town to countryside. Trees in various shades of green lined both sides of the road. Wildflowers grew along the edges. Distant mountains seemed to meet the clouds. The road, hilly, up and down, around curves. Traffic, stop-and-go, road construction.

"So, what is this big surprise you promised the girls?" said Jennie, laughing.

"I don't know," he sang, a deep operatic bass. "It's your surprise. I'll not be around for a few days, camping with the Boy Scouts, Cub Scouts, too, so there should be crying in the night."

She tried on a contralto, "Oh my word. You're a Scoutmaster, too?"

So much for opera: "Ha! No, I just go once a year. Show them life in the woods."

"So you promised a surprise, and now you're abandoning me."

"The girls are always excited when you're around. Anything will please them."

"They're excited when you're around, too," she said, cheeks dimpling.

In East Dixfield, he turned off Route 2, sped down a dirt road, his truck loaded with firewood, and turned into a hidden drive. Mountains sheltered the valley and the small white farmhouse with a green-painted porch floor. Clay pots with colorful flowers sat on the steps—a reminder of the farmhouse where Jennie, until about five days ago, had lived. Following her gaze, he said, "No one's home. So, we won't be stopping to visit." She shook it off and climbed into the truck bed. They tossed wood and stacked it on the porch. Back in the truck, he drove down the road and onto Route 2 West.

"Did you forget to leave an invoice in the door?" she said.

"The Browns live on a pension from the mill. They'll pay when and what they can. But, no matter, pay or no, we'll be back midwinter with another load."

She noted his words, *we'll be back*, but said, "How kind of you. For years, wood was delivered to my house. I never knew where it came from."

The Androscoggin River flowed east. Sticks and broken branches floated in the current. On Route 2 in Dixfield, he parked near the hardware store and coffee shop.

"Is there a nursery nearby?" she said.

"We could check the hardware store."

"Before I left, I promised Mom I'd plant the flowers."

"I suppose you saw her," he said quizzically.

She laughed. "I heard her voice and felt her touch."

Holding hands, they wandered around the center of town remembering it as it once was: the skating rink nearby; the doctor's office in his home; the Stanley Hotel, now gone, where Grandma Sarah and Grandpa Harold had lived during his last years. At the hardware store, they bought the last two potted geraniums, red and white, and at the coffee shop, Amadeus got two donuts, cream-filled, sprinkled with powdered sugar.

At the cemetery, they ambled over to the chain link fence. Carrying gardening tools, plant food, and geraniums, they stopped in front of the granite headstone, shaded by the branches of an oak tree. Engraved in the center was the name Parkhurst. Flowers with stems and leaves had been etched into the stone. A Masonic emblem adorned it. Acorns were scattered in the grass. Jennie knelt by two flat stone markers in the ground, one with an etching of a cross honoring Grandma Sarah and the other with a flag and a marker honoring Grandpa Harold, a World War I veteran.

"You visit with Grandma," he said and carried the watering can to the spigot.

Tracing the letters and numbers, Jennie whispered, "Grandma Sarah, I've missed you all these years. I found the photograph with the note. I've come back, like you said." Inhaling the soothing scent of lavender, she closed her eyes and breathed deeply the aroma of Grandma.

"I have missed you, my girl," said Grandma—her voice was silvery. "I heard your words through the window. You're on the right path."

"I came home to find my heart's peace."

"Keep seeking. Do not falter, even when you think you can't go on." Grandma paused, seeing Amadeus approach. "A kind, loving man. He has a story too. Love him through the telling, as he will love you through yours."

"What does he have to tell?"

"Listen to him with your heart and trust in his love."

The lavender scent grew faint. Jennie said, "Are you leaving?"

"I'll be close by always, and there are others watching over you."

"I love you, Grandma."

"And I love you, my girl. Remember, this journey is not yours to walk alone." The aroma of Grandma vanished in a gentle wind.

Amadeus bent down, dried a tear from Jennie's cheek, and laid his hand lightly on her shoulder, waiting silently.

At the headstone, they knelt down and pulled weeds—dandelions, purslane, and primrose. He dug two small holes. She planted the flowers, covered the roots, and raked the dirt smooth. He poured a slow stream of nutrient-rich water, droplets raining down over the blossoms and puddling in the grass.

Jennie set an acorn on the headstone, as Amadeus bent down by the flat marker—time with Grandma. In the same moment that he listened to the silvery voice, she inhaled again the scent of lavender.

They gathered up the empty pots, tools, and plant food and strolled back to the truck, storing these things in the bed. He held the door. She slid to the middle. He started the engine, shifted into gear, shifted back, turned off the engine, and, with both hands clutching the wheel, stared straight ahead.

"Did you recognize Grandma's voice or her scent?" she said.

"Why would you ask me that?"

"I know the clues. So, what did you, two talk about?"

Holding her hand, he whispered, "I have a memory to share with you."

"Could it be?"

He grinned, started the engine, drove back onto the street, turned down a narrow lane and parked near Jennie's old house: faded shingles, torn screen in the crooked door, broken steps, a shed that leaned. Time had not been kind to this house.

Amadeus helped Jennie out of the truck and carefully swung a backpack over his shoulders. Carrying his violin in one hand, he held hers in the other, as they rushed through meadow grass, daisies, buttercups, and dandelions to their maple tree. He gave her a boost, and she grabbed onto the lowest branch, hung there, swung her legs, pressed her feet against the solid trunk. Then she pulled herself up, swung one leg over, pulled some more, and perched herself on the branch.

Passing the violin case up to her, he climbed much more quickly and seated himself next to her. Unzipping the backpack, he handed her two long-stem glasses, poured the wine, and hung the backpack on a limb. They clinked, sipped, and kissed softly, right there in the maple tree, where the boy and the girl had once played. A few more sips, kisses too, glasses empty, she held them and he shouldered Alastair [from the Scottish: *protector, defender, helper*]

"You're still playing that old violin?" she asked.

"You know the story," he said

"I sat up here and listened to you practice."

"Sometimes I sat here and played for you."

"Like you did on the day I left."

Alastair's notes resonated in her mind, her whole being, drifting into the air carried along by the melodies. In memory, she saw best friends: planting the butterfly garden, reading in the meadow, jumping into heaps of autumn leaves, laughter ringing out. Then, that summer day, she in the back of the station wagon, and he standing in the lane, waving, crying, hearts breaking, best friends parting. The music silenced. Drying her tears, he held her close.

"I sat right here many times, remembering, missing you," he said.

"I found an oak nearby, climbed it often, sat there, always with you," she said.

"Jennie, let me walk beside you on your journey."

"Together, like we once were, always together."

Shouldering the violin, he played a few more songs. They shared a few more memories and ate the donuts. She wiped sugar off his beard; he tidied the corners of her mouth. Tying a knotted rope to a higher branch, she descended first, he followed, and arms around each other, they slowly walked to the truck.

"Where to now?" he said.

"My first home was in Carthage. I have no memories of it, just stories."

"Do you know the way?"

"Not really, but I'll recognize the house from old black-and-white photos."

The engine a dull roar, Amadeus headed for Carthage. Dense woods, few houses, yards with uncut grass lined the paved road. Jennie watched for nature's landmarks that she could recall from stories: a small orchard, a field of lupine, an eagle's aerie high in a tree. At the outskirts of this rural woodsy town, she said, "Take a left."

"Familiar sites?" he asked.

"Just a guess," she replied.

He took the left, crossed a plank bridge, and followed the narrow, paved road up a gradual incline. Woods and only a few homes on both sides. They stopped by a field, too small for planting. Bushes and trees had overtaken it. A moose stood at the road's edge.

Her father, Henry, had raised beans in that field, sold them to canneries, and let neighbors glean. During the days, he worked the land, cared for their few animals, and cut wood. At the paper mill in Rumford, he worked the night shift—a long commute from Carthage. Her mother, Charlotte, felt the loneliness, only one neighbor, no phone, no car; she missed life in town.

"The house is at the top of the hill," she said.

"Still waiting for the moose to cross," he said patiently.

Finally, the moose, ambling along in front of The Beast, vanished into the thickets. Shifting gears, Amadeus drove slowly and pulled to the side. Jumping out, she hurried up the hilly, unpaved driveway, and he, taking long strides, called out, "Wait!"

But Jennie jogged.

The two-story house loomed in front of her. Mother's words: *cold, drafty, nights fearful, little time for family life.* Her sister's words: *nooks and crannies to explore.*

He caught up to her and saw her eyes circling, staring faraway, unaware of him. Her posture was stiff and straight. She was ascending, spiraling, descending.

Jennie found herself standing on the front lawn in midsummer—or not quite standing, but hovering over it. Nearby, her eleven-year-old sister softly stroked the lamb's wool. A book lay in the grass. On the blanket, one-year-old Jennie played with a few hand-sewn toys. The screen door creaked. Mother! Charlotte stood on the porch, waving to her daughter. The older sister carried the younger to Mother, ran to the woodpile, the lamb following, and, arms full, slowly trudged back and forth. A few trips and the lamb still followed. Mother was displeased to see the lamb in the kitchen!

Charlotte filled the woodbox in the blue enamel cook stove. Heavy pots filled with potatoes, green beans, and carrots simmered on the stovetop. Chicken fried in the cast-iron pan, feathers still on the floor. From the warming oven, she removed a pan of homemade rolls and set it on the table. A bowl of wild strawberries, fresh-picked, the pleasant aroma permeating Jennie's senses. Mother wiped her brow, sweat running down her face. A hot kitchen, a hot day.

Spiraling again, ascending, Jennie landed in the widow's walk. High above the treetops, she viewed endless miles of downward slope, green fields, tall, dense woods. At the edge of the trees she glimpsed movement. Nine deer ambled downhill single file, halting as if alarmed, then moving forward with caution.

Spiraling downward, warm, gentle arms enfolded her, and whispered words spoke to her, but she resisted his voice, his touch. On the porch, the older sister held two-year-old Jennie's hand, as they walked down the steps.

"Where are you?" he said.

"Safe in your arms."

They stood there, she leaning back on him, and he wrapping his arms tighter, holding her close. "You were always there," she said.

Kissing her, he said, "Always will be. Have you always been able to…well…see?"

"Only since I returned. No visions for the last thirty years. Dad took it all away when I was ten. That same summer he took you from me."

"Were the visions and wanderings the reason you moved?"

"Hmmm. He never admitted it, but now that you mention it…."

Holding hands, they walked slowly to the truck. From behind the seat, he pulled out the woven picnic basket and an oversized quilt, and carefully swung the backpack over his shoulder. "Hungry? No one's home."

Spreading the quilt on the front lawn in view of that downward slope, he poured the wine. She opened the chips and offered him a turkey sandwich. Blazing yellows, mixed with red and a little orange, descended behind distant mountains. Here, at her first home, she had a memory and a vision.

"Can you imagine never being allowed to be yourself, to be who you are?"

Lying back on the quilt, he traced her spine and said, "I know who you are. I know your heart. Always have."

Kissing him softly, she laid her head on his shoulder. "And I know yours. I spoke of my father."

Holding her close to him, they lay there until the sun had made its full descent. In moonlight, they strolled back to The Beast. She sat in the middle seat, as he drove down the road, and nearing the beanfield, he suddenly slammed on the brakes. Bald tires swerved on the dirt shoulder, brakes squealed, front tires ditched. An old farm truck pulled onto the road. Passing by, in the opposite direction, a man tipped his cap to Amadeus.

"Why did you stop?" she said.

Overwrought, he said, "Didn't you see that old truck? It appeared from nowhere."

"I saw nothing."

"Oh, Jennie, I'm freaking. And speaking of your father, the driver was him."

"Don't freak. Is it our gift? Have you seen before?"

"Today, Grandma Sarah, and not for the first time. Now, your father," he said, his voice edgy, his muscles taut. "It's eerie, seeing the spirits of the dead!"

"Well, it's wonderful to see Grandma, but, truthfully, I ignore *him*, and you should too. Enough salt poured into my wounds by that man!" Then, frowning, she said, "When did you see Grandma?"

"You're so calm about these visiting spirits!" he said.

"You may have seen into my vision. We're sitting so close." Then, laughing, she patted his thigh and said, "Wait! I didn't see him. You did!"

Amadeus shifted gears, pulled back on the road, held her hand, and headed home.

✳

In the Murphys' driveway, she woke to gentle fingers tracing her face and quiet words spoken in a husky whisper: "Are you okay with me leaving?" Soft, lazy kisses spoke of love.

"Go, have fun traipsing through the woods with the boys," she whispered. "Don't forget, I have a surprise for the girls."

Amadeus held her close, smoothing her hair. She rested her head on his shoulder, feeling his soft breath on her face and neck. Grasshoppers and katydids chirped. A dog barked. Stars twinkled in the sky. Turning her face, he kissed her, and she returned his kiss, deeper, more intimate, their arms enfolding one another. His warm hands drew her closer, gently slid around her hip to the small of her back, pressing her even closer to him. She felt the heat, her body tingling, weakening, knotting inside. Slipping her hand inside his flannel shirt, touching his skin, she slid it slowly down his chest. His hand under her shirt slid slowly up her spine. She needed air. Too fast. Slow down. Stop. Laying her head on his chest, her breaths slowed.

His chest expanding, contracting, his breathing slowing, he said, "I love you."

"Yeah, really," she said, breathless, her voice weak.

"For real, Jennie."

"I love you for real, too, but privacy is important."

"So, you're not returning north? To your classroom?"

"I resigned," she said. "Remember, my quest."

"My cabin is hidden in the woods, very private. Only Rosie lives with me."

"Rosie?" She had not yet heard of Rosie.

He chuckled. "My three-year-old chocolate lab. She'd love you."

"Oh, well, I like dogs."

He walked with her to the door. One last kiss. "See you Friday afternoon."

"I'll be here, waiting."

From the porch, she watched the taillights disappear down the hill. Oh, how she loved him!

And, of course, he loved her.

FIVE

Through the window over the sink, Jennie peered into the starry sky, filling a glass with cold well water. She took a sip and leaned on the island. A plate of cookies sat on the black granite countertop, and as she bit into one, she savored the sweetness of brown sugar mixed with the buttery taste of shortbread. Tracing the rim of the glass, she let her mind and her heart linger over their words, their shared memories.

Setting the glass in the sink and taking another cookie, she crept quietly up the stairs, so as not to disturb the sleeping family. Turning on the lamp by the bedside, Jennie set the cookie next to the photograph, touched the boyish face of Amadeus, picked up her pajamas, and stepped into the bathroom.

Ready for bed, Jennie stood by Annie's door, hesitated, then entered. All three girls snuggled together. As Jennie brushed Gracie's light brown hair out of her face, those deep brown eyes popped open. "Happy dreams, sweetie."

"You'll play with us tomorrow?" Gracie whispered, her eyes closing.

"Yes, honey, all day. Now sleep." Kissing Gracie on the cheek, she leaned across and kissed Maggie and Annie. "Sweet dreams, little ones." Her mother's soft-spoken voice had once said those words—*sweet dreams, my honeybee*.

Back in her room, she crawled into bed, held the photograph with the broken glass—Amadeus and herself—and whispered, *I love you*. She felt a little foolish, so sentimental, tried for a more formal attitude: "I pray our love is everlasting and true."

Setting the photograph back on the nightstand, she munched the cookie and turned out the light. Night breezes blew through the window, ballooning the curtains. Wrapped in an old log cabin quilt—red center squares, hearth and home—she visualized Amadeus's face. Immersed in the strains of Alastair and the creaking rocking chair, she inhaled the fragrant scent of lavender and slept, still and silent, a deep rest.

In the darkest hours, Jennie snapped awake, tossed, and turned. His face was still there, guarding, protecting. "Amadeus! Amadeus!" The ghost had invaded her dream! A gentle hand softly caressed her face, pushing back her hair. The music played on. Her beloved, yes, *her beloved*, stood at the foot of the bed, while the hand still massaged her face. Sarah's chair rocked and the aroma of lavender permeated the bedroom.

Next thing she knew, it was Wednesday morning, and sunlight streamed through the window and across the wood floor. Amadeus was not at her bedside. The lavender scent was gone, and the rocker sat motionless.

"You're awake," said Alice, holding Jennie's hand. "You didn't sleep well."

"Silly dreams of a schoolgirl."

"More like nightmares." Alice wriggled in next to Jennie, leaning against a mountain of pillows. "Talk to me, girlfriend."

Leaning her head on Alice's shoulder, Jennie said, "I dreamed. I dreamed that Amadeus and Grandma Sarah were here with me."

"Stacking wood and memories. A great date."

"Packed full of the past. Wonderful, really wonderful, just being together."

Alice laid her head on Jennie's and said, "It was like that with Tom and me. Just being together *fulfilled* us."

"You miss him, don't you?"

"I miss the togetherness of the early years, when his business was just an idea."

"Well, my friend, invade his space. He'd welcome you."

Three little girls burst into the room, jumped on the bed, crawled on top of the women, hugging and giggling.

"Oh, no," whispered Jennie. "Alice, the surprise."

"Got it covered. Need you to do one thing, though."

All attention on Gracie! She stood, straight and tall, at the foot of the bed, bounced a little, and spread her arms wide. "Watch me! I can fly!" Annie moved aside and held onto Maggie. Gracie let her herself fall forward, face down, onto the bed. Jennie caught her just before they bumped heads.

Midmorning, Maggie carried her baby doll and a brown-and-white stuffed puppy, and the girls each had a bag of fun things. Sitting with Jennie in the backseats of Alice's red Dodge Caravan, they sang silly songs and laughed at silly jokes. Alice, in the driver's seat, and Emilie, in the passenger seat, sat comfortably on cushioned, bucket seats, singing along and laughing too. A fun day!

Annie and Gracie dumped their bags, spilling a heap of dolls, mommies and children dressed in play clothes, ball gowns, jeans, T-shirts, and high heels. The pile lay on Jennie's lap. "Will you play dollies with us?" asked Gracie.

Jennie divided the dolls among the girls and herself and asked, "What's the story?"

"A picnic. They're going on a picnic," said Annie.

"They need to pack lunch," said Gracie.

"What are they packing in the cooler?" said Jennie.

"Cookies," said Maggie.

While Emilie and Alice conversed in the front, Jennie and the girls took the dolls on a backseat picnic with a lot of conversation about cookies.

Fixed on golden specks glittering in Emilie's salt and pepper hair, Jennie was carried into a vision. The girls' loud happy voices silenced, and the van slowed and stopped. The Temple Historical Society. Emilie, there alone, dialing the telephone, waiting, waiting, as if multiple rings.

"Hello," said a male voice, as if it were Jennie holding the receiver.

"They're together," Emilie said clearly.

The golden specks vanished, replaced by the van, gaining speed, and by the girls' voices, their hands patting her. "Jennie, Jennie, play with us," said Gracie.

"Jennie, the dollies," said Annie.

"What are the dollies doing now?"

Whose deep voice was that on the other end of Emilie's call? And whose business might it be that she and Amadeus were, well, more than friends?

Alice slowed down, turned right, and parked inside the entrance to the community playground by the lake. Their dolls piled on the seats, the girls teetered and wiggled, waiting for the women to remove the cooler and a beach bag. Piling out behind Jennie, Annie grabbed Jennie's hand, pulling her. "Come play with us!"

Jennie, her hand in Maggie's, hurried behind the girls into sprays of cool water. Letting go of her little friend's hand, Jennie stood still in the wet mist, hoses and sprinklers, pooling water. Laughing, she saw happy faces and heard joyous sweet sounds of girls running, jumping, and splashing.

"Jennie, come over to the swings!" said Annie.

"Just follow us!" said Gracie.

Running across mowed grass, past the benches shaded by maple trees, Jennie, with Maggie in tow, followed the girls. Alice and Emilie walked behind them.

"Push me, please, Jennie!" said Gracie, and Annie chimed in, "Me, too!"

She pushed them high, up toward the sky and said, "Now pump, girls."

Smiling brightly, blue eyes shining, Maggie held tightly to the ropes as Alice pushed her on the swing. Emilie was also pushing the girls, and Jennie swung, too, pumping until she drew nearer to the sky—pure joy.

"Stop us! We want to get off!" said Gracie.

"We want to go sliding!" said Annie.

With a little help, the swings slowed to a stop. The children ran over to the slides, and the women followed. Jennie joined them in sliding.

Later, at the picnic table, they opened the cooler. Drinking cool water and eating snacks of crackers, cheese, and fruit, they felt refreshed and ready for more play. Annie asked, "Mom, can we walk up that path over there?"

"Certainly. Let's go," said Alice.

Hiking uphill and around the trail into the woods, they stopped at the clearing. The women sat on pine benches in the shade of white birch. Running into the meadow, lavished with colorful blooms, the girls picked a lovely bouquet of wild daisies, dandelions, and buttercups. Hurrying back, they happily presented their gift to Jennie.

"Thank you so much. I love wildflowers, and I love you!" She had not received a bouquet as lovely as this one since her own little girl had picked flowers for her.

Gracie and Annie skipped ahead up the trail. Emilie held Maggie's hand and followed them back to the picnic table. Alice and Jennie walked more slowly with the beautiful bouquet. "Sweet, loving girls. Such a fun day." Linking her arm with Alice's, Jennie said, "Is it customary for sleepovers to last three or four nights?"

"Customary is one, but Maxine is not well. She's battling cancer," said Alice. "Madeleine, in her eighties, cares for her sister and the girls."

"Such a sad, difficult time. How can I help?" said Jennie.

"You already are. The girls love you. And I'm sure they're into the cooler, wanting lunch."

Picking up the pace, Jennie said, "Tell me about Sharon and her little boy with the uneven legs."

"She works at the supermarket and has a boyfriend. No one I know," said Alice. "Tim's a kind, likable boy, one of Annie's friends. He has some problems, but I'm sure you, as a teacher, can figure them out better than I."

At the table, hungry girls had already found the fluffernutters and devoured the small bags of chips and the cucumber slices. Emilie poured lemonade. Alice passed tuna sandwiches to the ladies.

Annie asked, "Mom, can we have dessert?"

"Yes," said Alice. From the cooler she removed a container of cupcakes, chocolate with white icing, and colorful candies. From the beach bag, she removed two wrapped presents and three cards with drawings by Jennie. Giving the gifts and cards to her friends, Annie said, "Happy Birthday! It's from all of us."

With happy faces, rosy cheeks, and bright shiny eyes, the girls tore away the paper: there were dolly dishes for Maggie and a Spirograph for Gracie.

"Thank you," said Gracie, now seven. "I like drawing."

Annie nodded, "I know you do, you play with mine."

Smiling sweetly, Maggie, now five, said, "Oh, my dollies?"

Squeezing Maggie's cheeks, Alice said, "For your dollies, sweetheart."

The girls admired their cards: a flying girl in midair, clouds above her, on light blue for Gracie; and for Annie, a girl rocking and reading on pastel pink. Running to Jennie, Maggie pointed to her yellow card and said, "Dolly. Maggie's dolly."

Hugging her and smiling, Jennie said, "Maggie rocks her dolly."

"Mom, why did I get a card? It's not my birthday," said Annie.

Jennie said, "It's a belated card. I missed your birthday."

"Oh, thank you. I love it."

The ladies and Annie sang to the girls. Then they all enjoyed the sweet taste of sugary cupcakes.

After washing chocolatey faces, corners of mouths, and fingers, Jennie raced with the girls back to the water sprays. Emilie and Alice cleaned up the area, carried things to the caravan, and strolled over to the sprays with towels in hand.

Alice said, "Your drawings have so much detail, even the children's expressions."

"It's just something I do. Like Gracie, I enjoy drawing." Turning to Emilie, she added, "I have time tomorrow, if you'd like to talk ancestry?"

Emilie said, "I'd love to see your collection. My place. I'll make lunch."

In the air-conditioned caravan, heading home, the girls sat quietly, bodies cooling, eyelids drooping, dollies forgotten. Maggie laid her head on Jennie's lap. Smoothing her hair and squeezing Gracie's hand, Jennie's thoughts turned to sisters and a loving grandmother. The wildflower bouquet lay on the seat.

Six

On Wednesday morning, the Boy Scouts, Cub Scouts, two hapless Scoutmasters, and several fathers, all to varying degrees outdoorsmen, gathered around at the base of the North Trail up Potato Hill, a mountain to a child. Their supplies lay in a heap.

Jack Warner, US Marine Corps, recently retired, Vietnam veteran and Scoutmaster of Troop 79, ordered the boys to share the load and work together: everyone needed to carry supplies! Eight-year-old Cub Scouts, holding onto their backpacks, grabbed one weighty pack. Mike and Calvin Jackson, twins, and Tim Bailey, all best friends, spirited boys, plodded onto the trail dragging the pack, and sat on it, ready and waiting.

Amadeus ambled over with Rosie alongside. "Hey, guys, you sure about carrying that? It's a steep climb."

The boys grinned up at him and said, "Yup."

"Okay, let me know if you need help."

"It ain't too hard for us. We can do it," said Mike.

Tim sat quietly, petting Rosie, and Amadeus said, "Hey, you like dogs?"

All three boys nodded, grinning.

"Well, this is Rosie, and she likes kids."

All the supplies were divided up, to be carried on shoulders or in arms: older boys and adults hefted heavier packs and the camp stove, and small boys carried lighter, smaller items. Each boy also carried his own backpack.

Usually, Amadeus was in the lead, but not today. Eagle Scouts led the way up the hill; Boy Scouts followed along with Jack Warner; Cubbies came behind them with the amiable fourth grade teacher, Bob Adams, their Cub Scout leader; fathers were scattered among the group; and, last, Amadeus and Rosie kept an eye on three small boys — Mike, Calvin, and Tim — whose dads were not present.

The North Trail passed through dense hardwood forest: old trees, new growth, fallen trees, and stumps. Elevation 1526 feet at the summit.

Halfway up, the narrow, steep trail became a challenge for the Cub Scouts. They tried to keep up with the older scouts but fell behind. With encouragement from Bob Adams and a few fathers singing, the Cubbies tramped along slowly, but not Mike, Calvin, or Tim. They just sat there on that massive pack, tired, parched, and teary-eyed. The pack was too heavy, the trail too steep, and the sun too hot.

Amadeus knelt down, pulled four canteens out of his backpack, offered one to each boy, and said, "Well, I'm thirsty. How about you guys?"

The boys looked at each other, at Amadeus, and at the canteens.

Drinking from his own, Amadeus said, "Cold, refreshing. Go ahead, have some."

Calvin said, "Well, you're drinking, so I guess we can too."

"Guys, sit right here. I've got something to show you."

Thirsty boys sat on the pack, gulping cool water and watching Amadeus disappear into the evergreens. Rosie sat next to Tim, allowing the boys to pet her. Not gone too far or too long, Amadeus reappeared. Kneeling down and handing twigs to the boys, he said, "Now this twig is from a pine tree, this one from a hemlock, and the third from a balsam fir. Look at the needles. What do you see?"

"They're all green," said Mike.

"That one. Needles are shorter," said Calvin.

"It's from a hemlock tree. Now look at the balsam fir. See how both have short needles. But hemlock needles are darker green. And pine needles are long and straight."

"This one is sticky," said Calvin.

"This one ain't sticky," said Mike.

"Mine's sticky," said Tim.

"The pine feels sticky. It's called pitch. The hemlock has no pitch on the twig. The balsam fir has blisters with Canada balsam, a liquid, inside. Now, boys, smell the twigs and tell me about the scent."

"These two smell the same," said Tim.

"The balsam fir and pine smell piney. Christmas wreaths are made with balsam tips. Now put the twigs in your backpacks." He paused, waited, and then gave them three cones. "One is pine, one hemlock, and one balsam fir. What's different about them?"

"This one is short and round, and those two cones—" said Calvin.

"Those two are long, like a stick," Mike broke in.

"You three are good observers. The long ones are a pine cone and a balsam. The short, oblong one is a hemlock cone."

"Look, there's purple on my hands!" said Tim.

"That long cone is balsam fir. The cones fall apart in August or September, after they ripen. Only the straight stalk is left. Put the cones in your backpacks too." Amadeus waited for the boys to pack nature's gifts before reminding them to pack the canteens. "Ready to carry on?"

"Ready!" all three nodded.

"Backpacks over both your shoulders keep you balanced. Perhaps you two could take turns carrying that side of the heavy pack. I'll take this side. Tim, hold onto Rosie's collar. She'll be proud to hike with you. Stay in front of us. Take your time, and we'll get to the top." The boys nodded again.

They trudged up the hill, way behind the others. *No wonder Tim's having difficulty; his left leg's shorter than the right, and his shoulder is bent over. His back must ache from carrying that backpack. He's a determined little guy.*

At the summit and hidden by the forest, Amadeus set the heavy pack down. "They're just through those trees. Stay on the path and you boys carry the pack into camp. Tim, you and Rosie lead the way." Beaming up at him, they finished the hike, just ahead of Amadeus.

Bob Adams gave the boys high-fives. He served them a lunch of sandwiches, chips, and cookies, and the hungry, thirsty boys gulped water from their canteens.

Later, hiking through the woods with the Cub Scouts, Amadeus showed them the different species of trees. Mike, Tim, and Calvin identified the pine, hemlock, and balsam fir by their needles and cones and all the boys learned to identify deciduous trees by the shapes of leaves. Creeping silently behind Amadeus, the boys followed deer tracks to a clearing, and hidden behind bushes, watched them graze, until, as if alarmed, the deer bolted into the forest.

While the Cubbies were involved with pack activities, Amadeus hiked with the Boy Scouts and talked about clear-cutting, selective cutting, and reforestation. He told the boys about the reasons to protect trees: the production of oxygen, protection of the land from erosion, and provision of shelter for forest animals and birds.

The scent of sizzling burgers and hot dogs called the Boy Scouts back to the campsite. Gathering around the cooks, they lined up behind the Cubbies with mess kits in hand. Tin plates full, baked beans and chips added, and tin cups of sugary, fruity drinks, the scouts devoured their outdoor feast around the campfire. The sky darkening, the moon rising, scouts and leaders and fathers sat on logs, while Bob Adams on guitar and Amadeus on violin jammed. Everyone joined in singing camp songs, roasting marshmallows, and eating s'mores. Too soon, the Cubbies grew fidgety, restless, slapping themselves—Bugs! Mosquitoes! No-see-ums!

"Boys, settle down! Bugs live in the woods!" Jack Warner said, his voice overpowering the jam session.

Amadeus reached into his pocket for a bag of herbs, rosemary mixed with sage, and threw some into the fire. It produced a pleasant aroma, but one unpleasant to insects. Tossing another bag to the boys, he said, "Crush a few citrosum leaves. Rub them on your skin. Share with everyone. You only need a small amount."

Jack rolled his eyes and insisted, "These boys need toughing up."

"It's nature's relief from bug bites," said Amadeus, calmly. "A naturalist knows about the woods." Rejoining the guitarist, he lost himself in music.

Late that night, the boys in their tents, Amadeus wandered around the campsite. Satisfied that all was quiet, even in the tent of Mike, Calvin, and Tim, he settled into his own tent, rubbing crushed leaves on himself. Lying there, resting, he thought about Jennie and her childhood nightmares. Did she still have nightmares? Dozing off, he was awakened by voices outside his tent.

"Mr. Amadeus," called Mike. "Help! We can't find Calvin!" called Tim.

Unzipping the tent flap, Amadeus looked down into the Cubbies' eyes and said, "Where did Calvin go?"

"We don't know," said Tim, shaking his head.

"That's why we can't find him," said Mike, shrugging his shoulders.

"Go back to the tent, boys. I'm sure he's fine. I'll have a look." With Rosie by his side, he soon found Calvin standing under a tree, lost, teary-eyed, and fearful of night sounds: owls hooting, sticks crunching, branches swaying, and creatures moving about.

"Well, what are you doing out here?" Amadeus said.

"I had to go to the bathroom real bad." Calvin whispered.

"You just got yourself turned around. Come with me. Where's your flashlight?"

"In the tent. I forgot it. Do you have to tell everybody I got lost?"

"Our secret. We'll tell Tim and Mike you were on an adventure. Because that's true, and a Cub Scout never lies."

Calvin grinned up at Amadeus and, holding his head high, trekked back to camp with his friend.

When all three boys were corralled in their tent and told to stay put, Amadeus settled himself again. Restless, he was unable to sleep. Images of Jennie, thoughts about his own past, and Grandma Sarah's words — *The time is coming* — occupied his mind.

Before dawn, Amadeus had fallen asleep with Jennie in his heart. He saw her, tossing and turning, waking, pushing back the quilt, and rising out of bed. Moonlight surrounded her. She covered her face with a cool cloth. Her skin, sweaty, breaths calming. Picking up two picture frames, glass broken in one, she sat in the rocker, crying. She missed him. She was afraid. She needed him. He reached out, smoothed her hair, and knew she sensed his presence.

Too soon he awakened to the sounds of boys rustling around the campsite and the scents of bacon sizzling and eggs frying. From outside his tent, Cubbies called out, "Mr. Amadeus!" "Rise and shine, Mr. Stuart!" "Breakfast!"

Yawning and stretching, he sighed. "Coming, boys. You go eat. I'll be right there." Later, he and Rosie would find a place to hide, take a nap, perhaps see Jennie again. "Come, Rosie." Seating himself on a log, lost in his thoughts, he was startled by a slap on his shoulder.

Jack Warner, a steaming cup of coffee in hand, plunked himself down and said, "You look like you got hit by a truck."

Cringing, the image of a broken body flashed in his mind, and Amadeus glared.

"Hey, sorry. Poor choice of words," said Jack.

"Yeah, poor choice."

"You've had something on your mind since yesterday. Could it be that woman you've been seeing? Gotta keep 'em in their place." Jack slapped him again and left.

Lowering his head, Amadeus rubbed his forehead and sighed.

Mike said, "Mr. Amadeus, we brought you breakfast!" All three stood in front of him, his platoon, grins on their faces, their offerings in hand: a plate of eggs, bacon, pancakes, a cup of hot chocolate overflowing with marshmallows, several pats of butter, and a bottle of imitation maple syrup.

"Mr. Adams fixed us a real good breakfast," said Tim.

"Yeah, and those two dads helped him. It's real good!" said Calvin.

"Thanks, I really appreciate this. I'm hungry. Enough to share with Rosie too."

"Wait!" said Mike and Calvin running back to Mr. Adams. Tim sat next to Amadeus, petting Rosie. In a flash, the two returned with a plate for Rosie.

"Thanks, you guys are great kids," laughed Amadeus.

The boys sat on the log with their friend as he partook of the delicious food.

While the scouts spent the morning working on merit badges with the Scoutmasters and the Eagle Scouts, Amadeus and Rosie hiked a short distance away. It was peaceful in the shade under an oak with Rosie curled next to him.

In a deep sleep, images of Jennie flashed in his mind's eye: the child, collapsed in front of a gravestone; the young woman, holding a little girl's hand, standing in front of another; the young mother and her little girl huddled in front of a woodstove.

Bright white light encircled the oak, glimmering on Amadeus and Rosie. The scent of lavender pervaded their senses. Alerted, whining, Rosie sniffed and barked. Amadeus blinked and blinked again. "Grandma Sarah."

"So, you've been having some dreams."

Stroking Rosie to calm her, he said, "Yeah, you could say that."

"Tonight, she will need you. For the time has come," said Grandma.

Eyes popping open, he sat up straight. Tonight. Time. The bright light, the scent of lavender evaporated in the breeze. Running his hands through his hair, he shook his head and trekked back to the campsite with Rosie by his side. *The time has come.*

Late afternoon, Amadeus, Rosie, and a small group of scouts blazed a trail through the woods, west about half a mile to the bald summit to see the view from the ledge—Mt. Blue and Day, Deane, and Varnum Mountains, valleys, and forested land.

Tossing aside branches, stepping on twigs, hiking around clumps of trees and stumps and climbing over fallen logs, the scouts, with compasses in hand, trekked west. Philip Warner and another boy followed, marking the trail. Mike, Calvin, and Tim walked behind them at a slower pace, and Amadeus, last, kept an eye on the group.

For Tim, walking over uneven ground and unable to see obstacles clearly—rocks and holes hidden in tall grass—the hike was difficult, and he was tiring quickly. Mike, Calvin, and Tim climbed onto a fallen log, Tim more painstakingly. Spotting movement in the trees, Tim said, "Look over there!" Squirrels scurried up oaks, and rabbits hopped away to hide, as Rosie, her tail wagging, was on the chase.

Noticing Tim, Phillip, his chest puffed out, arms swinging, strutted over, and from behind gave Tim a push. Lying prone in the tall grass, he heard Phillip's words: "Stupid kid. Can't even walk like the rest of us."

Immediately, Amadeus knelt next to Tim. "Are you hurt?"

Tim shook his head, trying but failing to hold back tears. Amadeus helped him to his feet, sat him on the log, Mike and Calvin beside him, and checked for broken bones, cuts, and bruises. Then he called to Rosie. "You sit right here. Hold onto Rosie. I'll be back."

Scouts backed away from Phillip as Amadeus caught up with him. Towering over Phillip, he glared at the boy, his voice low and angry. "Son, in the woods, careless behavior causes injuries. You could have done great harm. There's no place for bullying here. What's more, I'll bet the boys your size don't take any crap from you. Now, head back to camp."

Eagle Scouts flanked Phillip, others followed, and the three friends walked slowly with Amadeus, Tim holding onto Rosie.

At the campsite, Amadeus was packing his gear as Bob Adams approached him. "I heard about it. Leaving?"

Three Cubbies hurried to their tent, as Amadeus replied, "Yeah, I've had enough of the Warners this trip."

Jack advanced on him, "Hey, stay away from my son! I'll deal with him!"

Amadeus stared angrily at Jack, his voice still low and angry. "You tell me how a Boy Scout gets away with bullying little kids! I won't tolerate it! And you know that!" Shouldering his pack, he saw two Cubbies racing toward him and a third trudging along. All carried backpacks. "Where are you three going?"

Calvin said, "Where you go, we go, and Tim goes too."

Amadeus and Bob exchanged goodbyes and shook hands.

With Tim, his hand on Rosie, close behind Amadeus, and Mike and Calvin following, they descended Potato Hill—a slow walk down into the woods, into darkness, resting frequently. Flashlights showed their way, as old dense trees blocked the moonlight.

The hours passed and the moon rose higher. Amadeus dropped Mike and Calvin home, safe with their mother, Sadie. On the way back down Orchard Hill Road, he said, "Tim, tell me where you live."

"It's too dark. I don't know how to get there from here."

"Tell me the name of the road or what's around your house?"

"Well, there's woods, a pine tree, and graves near it."

Amadeus wiped his brow. Many cemeteries here. Acres and acres of woods and pines everywhere. "Do you know your neighbors?"

"Yup." Tim nodded. "Pastor Andy and Mrs. Andy. Umm…Maggie and Gracie."

Back on Route 43, he sped through the Intervale to Cummings Hill Road. Tim spotted a house, lit only by the moon. "Right there. That's my house."

With his truck parked in the drive, headlights on, Amadeus walked Tim onto a porch with a loose railing and floorboards. Turning the knob and pushing hard on the door, Tim cried, "It's locked!" No one turned on the porch light, welcoming Tim home, but he wasn't expected until the next day.

Amadeus walked cautiously around the house. There were no lights inside, no car, no truck. In the backyard, he bent down, and investigated a mountain of empty beer cans and whiskey bottles. Hurrying back into the front yard, he said, "Tim, are you sure this is your house?"

"Yup, it's mine. They go out, and I stay by myself. But the door's locked."

"Is there someone with whom I can leave you?" *The time has come.*

"Yup, sometimes I stay with Mike and Calvin."

Back to Orchard Hill. He didn't have time. "Anyone closer to your house?"

"Yup, Pastor Andy. We play checkers. I eat there, and they let me stay all night."

Amadeus drove to the parsonage, not far, just back to the Intervale.

Tim said, "I seen you before. You brung wood to Pastor Andy's house."

"Yeah, he's my friend too."

As they pulled into the drive, Pastor Andrew met them and helped Tim out of the truck. "Go inside. Mrs. Andy baked cookies."

Tim hurried into the house. Amadeus shifted into reverse and said, "New family in town?"

"Been here a few months. Tim's safe here."

Back on Route 43, The Beast roared its way to Voter Hill and to Jennie.

SEVEN

Voices! Shadows! Jennie tossed and turned, perspiring, pulled by the ghost into the past. Struck by the back of his hand, her head spun, and she fell to the floor. Drawing up her knees, arching her back, arms pulling her head forward protectively, she rolled into a ball.

"Bitch!" He kicked her again and again. "You get that bottle!"

"Stop! You're hurting me! Let me go!" A deep breath. Her baby. Another breath. Crying, afraid! Another breath. "Let me go!"

Hitting and kicking ceased: the bedroom—an eerie calm—only breathing, hers shallow, his deep. Powerful hands clamped onto her, hauled her upright, punched her in the abdomen, doubled her over, shoved her out the door. "You get me that bottle! Bitch!" The door slammed.

Jennie collapsed on the faded-blue, painted floor in front of the upstairs dark wood closet. She lay there, clenching her ribs—excruciating pain! Breathing brought sharper pain. Sobbing, she held her hands over her face. Oh, the pain! She needed to get up. Her little girl was not safe there. Pulling herself to her knees, she fell back onto the floor. In a weakened, trembling voice, she answered her daughter's cries. "Mommy's coming." Another shallow breath or two. "Mommy's coming."

Curled on her side, knees drawn up, Jennie lay on the bedroom floor in Alice's house, sobbing, arms folded around her ribs. She couldn't find the way out of her nightmare. Small, gentle hands touched her face. "Mommy! Mommy!" Her little girl's voice, her cries. "Mommy! Mommy!"

Bent to her knees, Alice stroked Jennie's cheek and smoothed her hair. Alice's tears — droplets mixing with hers, mixing with Rebecca's.

Warm, familiar, large hands massaged her back. The scent of Amadeus mixed with the aroma of lavender — her angel, Grandma Sarah. Another angel? She had seen her somewhere in the past — Grandma Jennie.

Helping Alice to her feet, Tom whispered, "Come with me."

Wait! Alice don't leave me! Come back! The door closed quietly. Gone.

Amadeus cradled Jennie in his arms and carried her to the bed. Lying beside her, the mattress sinking with his heavy weight, he held her close, safe in his arms. "Jennie, wake up. Wake up, Jennie." His voice, soft and low. "Come home to me, my Jennie." Now, humming in his calming baritone.

The scent of him! Her Amadeus! So gentle. Awakening, she looked into his loving eyes. "You found me. Like always, you found me."

Drying her tears, he kissed her softly and whispered, "Sleep now. I'll stay beside you. Hold you close." Laying her head over his heart, she listened to its steady rhythm and wept. Held by him, she was safe. Together, they relaxed into a peaceful rest.

As darkness yielded to morning light, shining on the hill, sunlight pirouetted on the blue wall and wood floor. The ghost, the angels, and the lavender scent were gone. Jennie softly traced Amadeus's face. Kind, loving, clear blue eyes, nose a little crook — once broken — red beard in need of a trim, lips sensuous.

Caressing Jennie's hand, he kissed her palm tenderly. Tracing her face with one roughened finger — beautiful brown eyes, puffy and damp, straight nose, and soft, sensuous lips — he said, "Honey, please tell me who abused you?"

Wrapped in warmth, the gentleness of him, she searched his eyes. "You were here during my dream."

"I was and I saw. So, please, tell me."

Hiding her face in his shoulder, she cried out, "The ghost!"

"We need time together. Would you stay with me for a few days at the homestead, at my cabin?"

Setting her eyes on his, she said, "Alone, with you?"

"Yes, alone, except for Rosie," he said, giving her a slight smile.

Jennie lay quietly in his arms. Curtains swayed in the breeze. Sunlight reflected off glass, like a prism, glittering around two photographs. "I'll stay with you."

A hint of a smile on her face, she said, "I'm sure I'll like Rosie."

Shower taken, dressed, and refreshed, Jennie packed a few essentials in one of the old school bags, and in the other a sketchpad, charcoal pencils, and camera, hanging them both on the straight chair at the table. She set her other things in the corner with the ancestry and made the bed, leaving no wrinkles. Folding the quilt, she laid it neatly at the foot.

As he sat at the table yawning, Amadeus noticed a white sealed envelope lying there, addressed simply, Jennie. Familiar handwriting.

She placed two picture frames, one with broken glass, in a school bag but did not see the white envelope tucked inside.

Descending the stairs and entering the kitchen to the aroma of eggs, bacon, and toast mixed with coffee, Jennie stepped over to the sink and, teary-eyed, wrapped her arm around Alice. "I need to leave for a few days, sort out the nightmares, find my way. I'll be with Amadeus. Please understand."

In the warmth of sunlight and friendship, the two women hugged. "You've been in my heart for a long time. Now, keep seeking." Alice's voice was a comforting whisper.

Handing Amadeus a cup of coffee, Tom said, "You look like you need this."

Amadeus sipped the hot liquid, inhaling the light, nutty aroma.

"Troubled spirit? Think you can help?" said Tom.

"I know I can. Been there, sometimes still there."

Hugging Dad, Annie, teary-eyed, asked, "Why are Jennie and Mommy crying?"

"Friends saying goodbye for a few days. You'll see Jennie soon."

"Daddy, she's sad. Does her heart hurt?"

Hugging his girl, her father said, "Yes, it hurts, but it will heal. And we will pray."

Setting the mug on the table, Amadeus stepped over to the sink, and, with his hands gently on Jennie's shoulders, said, "It's time."

Jennie dried her tears and Annie's too. "See you soon, sweetie. Love you."

While Tom held his wife and daughter, Jennie and Amadeus, arms around each other, walked briskly to the truck. Jennie took the middle seat, close to Amadeus, the chocolate lab's head on her lap. The Beast roared its way down Voter Hill, and Amadeus enfolded Jennie's soft hands in his warm calloused one.

A quick trip to the supermarket for a picnic lunch: deli sandwiches, strawberries, vegetables, donuts, dark chocolate, wine, and bottled water. For Rosie, dog biscuits.

At the checkout, no customers in line, Jennie said, "Sharon, so nice to see you."

"Oh, hi, Jennie. Learning anything about your ancestry?"

"Some new information. Have you met Amadeus?"

Amadeus checked the total on the cash register and handed Sharon a fifty. "Nice to meet you. My son, Tim, still talks about you and Rosie."

"He's a curious little boy, friendly and kind, like his two best friends."

Handing him his change, Sharon said, "Thanks for bringing him home."

Amadeus took the plastic bags and said, "No problem. Not out my way at all."

In the parking lot, they packed the woven basket, then went to the drive-thru for three breakfast sandwiches — one for Rosie — and two hot chocolates, as neither felt like coffee.

Amadeus drove across the Sandy River Bridge on the way to the Deane Homestead, Rosie's head hanging out the window. From Route 43 he turned left onto Varnum Pond Road. Up the long hill, pedal to the metal, accelerating downhill, he slammed the brakes, veered onto the logging road, bounced through potholes and over large rocks. Jennie felt the absence of springs. His truck was a real Beast! Rosie snapped her head inside as branches scraped the truck. Crossing over plank bridges, he sped farther up the road. At the clearing, in view of Deane Mountain, he turned onto the old beaten path, set the emergency brake, and prayed silently the brakes would hold.

Amadeus held the door. Jennie and Rosie jumped out and raced across the meadow.

"Wait! Where are you going?"

"The old orchard. I buried it there." Still running, she spied the old crumbling stone wall.

Amadeus caught up, held her eyes in his, and they saw the innocence of youth: the girl — dancing eyes, playful smile, carefree heart, spontaneous; the boy — sparkling eyes, mischievous grin, cheerful heart, impetuous.

"Orchard or stone wall?" he said. Kisses shared tenderly.

EIGHT

In the meadow, Jennie dashed over to the old stone wall. Amadeus raced to keep up, surprised, shouting with laughter. Wild daisies, Queen Anne's lace, and lupine grew between loose rocks. The circus performer, a tightrope walker, a girl in braids thirty years before: she'd walked that wall. Could the woman? Mounting the wall, posture straight and tall, arms spread wide, she balanced on one rock, then the next.

She stepped carefully at first, one, two, three; then more carefree, counting all the way. Amadeus, behind her now, skipping, change jingling in his pocket. On the fourteenth step, the rock slipped out from under her foot. Her oldest friend and her newest stumbled into her, then grabbed her waist, steadying her.

They were of the ballet! Could all but hear the orchestra. She spun. Her hand on his shoulder, she balanced herself. Arms wide, then eyes focused on the truck parked in the old beaten path, the hands of her cavalier about her waist, she stepped backward, five, six, seven, more. Number eleven stone tumbled free under her foot and even Amadeus stumbled. He lost his hold, felt her spiraling, felt then saw the ascension, the descent. Joined her in it. And there she was next to him, hovering just above the wall, carried back to the nineteenth century.

Amadeus pressed his legs against the wall, stood as close to her as he possibly could, and reached up, holding her hand firmly in his grasp.

The Beast vanished. The old beaten path, stone wall, and cellar hole ceased to exist. The logging road, only a tree-lined, well-traveled trail. Wildflowers grew in the clearing, among tall grasses, brush, trees, a few fallen and rotting, insects crawling inside. Cardinals sang, song sparrows too; red squirrels chattered, horses trotted. Wagon wheels crunched over rocks, sticks, and brush, slowing.

A man and a woman rode on the wagon seat, daughters walked alongside, and sons followed behind, herding the farm animals—a goose, six milk cows, and four sheep. A gray-haired, gray-bearded man pulled on the reins. Horses slowed to a walk, then halted. The great Belgians stood still, bent in their traces to graze in the tall grass.

The man helped the woman down from the high wagon seat. Surrounded by young men and women, eight sons and daughters, one daughter-in-law, all members of the Society of Friends, the aging patriarch grasped the hand of the matriarch, viewed the land in its natural wood-scape and looked beyond toward the mountains. Awakening the solitude of this place by settling here, the man stood tall, chest thrust out, shoulders back, establishing a legacy where generations of the Deane family would live, love, and thrive. The man was Cyrus Deane, and his wife was Mary Winslow Deane. The place, the Deane Homestead in the Varnum Pond neighborhood. The year, 1826, late in the planting season.

One son kissed a pretty young woman, grabbed water buckets, and tossed a couple over to a much younger brother. They were John and Abigail Baker Deane, husband and wife, and Abiel, the youngest Deane sibling.

Two older daughters, Rachel and Zibiah, along with Mary, their mother, retrieved cooking supplies from the wagon. Jennie intermingled with the spirits, examining the wares: a stewpot and a skillet with lids, heavy cast-iron; a tin coffee pot, cups, plates, and utensils, much lighter; wooden bowls and spoons made of basswood and maple; and an iron frame with hooks on a crossbar.

Cyrus clasped Mary's hand. She saw his smile, almost hidden by his beard, and the twinkle in his eyes. As always, his twinkle and grin were infectious. She smiled too. Walking away from meal preparation, Mary looked back. Gently, Cyrus pulled her into the trees, past oak, maple, and pine, where he hugged and kissed her, not completely hidden in the woods. Amadeus caught Jennie's attention. His wink, so familiar.

After brushing the horses, Amadeus removed the traces, allowing them to freely graze. Jennie peeked in the wagon and saw stores of food: printed cloth sacks of flour, sugar, coffee, salt, cornmeal, and beans; apple seedlings in baskets; and jars of comb honey.

Joining Thankful, the youngest daughter, and Abigail, the daughter-in-law, Jennie collected firewood and kindling. Amadeus carried rocks and buckets of dirt with three of the sons, William, Samuel, and James. Were they constructing a fireplace?

Jennie inhaled a quick breath. Spiraling, she ascended, Amadeus with her, whirling, spinning, like vertigo. Together they descended; she stood on the wall and he firmly held her hand.

"I saw them!" Eyes sparkling, her face lit up. "My great-great-great-grandparents and their family!"

"The original Deane settlers?"

She nodded. "The day they arrived in Temple."

He grinned. "I thought so. Your people!"

"So, perhaps you *do* see! You were there. I saw you." Still smiling, dimples showing, she said, "You know, it felt familiar, like I'd seen part of it before."

Lifting her to the ground, he said, "It's possible I see only through your eyes, but I do think I was building a fireplace of some sort."

"Our gift! The secret we've always shared! Now we travel together!" Taking both of his hands and laughing, they spun and whirled, their long hair blowing in the wind, until Jennie, feeling dizzy, fell into his arms.

"That we do, past and present, side by side into the future!" He laughed. "Take a walk with me."

"Give me a minute. My goodness!"

He held her hand as she entwined her fingers in his. Their hands fit perfectly together, like puzzle pieces, belonging together.

They hiked in a southerly direction, as if following Cyrus and Mary, past the old apple orchard into the woods and onto a narrow path with maple, oak, and evergreens dense on both sides, far more trees and fewer fields. Noticing the balsam fir, Jennie fondled the cones, the branches, inhaling the balsam-pillow scent. "I made balsam wreaths with a few teachers at school, but I never did hang one on my door. It was a Christmas fundraiser."

"Perhaps this year we'll hang one on our front door."

Our door, he'd said, and Jennie couldn't help but note.

Turning east, they meandered down a narrower path into a stand of tall pines, thickets, dense undergrowth, an abundance of small boughs for feeding. "White-tailed deer lay here this morning, well-hidden," he said. Bending down and laying her hand on the flattened space beneath the pines, Jennie sensed the warmth of sun and deer. In her mind's eye, she saw images of mothers caring for little ones. The fawn nuzzled close, and the doe offered fresh boughs for her baby to nibble, all the while ears and eyes alert, protecting. Jennie's mother lay next to her, smoothing her long hair, humming softly, calming her fears after nightmares. A young mother herself, she held her daughter's hand, teaching her to walk and, later, knowing when to let go.

Amadeus knelt close by, his hand gently resting on her shoulder — a silent presence.

"Tell me about the campout."

"Not much to tell, but let's save it. Today is about you."

"Oh, yes, yes, dear Amadeus, always about me."

"Walk with me," he said, offering his hand.

They hiked farther down the path, through a field of wildflowers, to the Cyrus Deane Stream. Then they hopped across big wet rocks to a massive boulder and rested there, water flowing and splashing around them. Rosie swam, of course — Rosie was a swimmer. Trees bordered the stream, with plank bridges in the distance. The sky, bright blue and cloudless. Hot sun warmed the boulder, and warmed them. Removing their shoes and socks and rolling up their pant legs, they let the cool rushing water soothe their feet.

Drawing circles with her toes in the swirling water, Jennie said, "Up north, the Aroostook River flows by a secluded meadow encircled by trees. I can't hear or see the river water flowing in the current. I only know it does. In my eyes, water is still and stagnant." Amadeus listened as he ran his fingers through her hair. "I can't hear or feel the wind. I can only see branches and tall grass swaying, so I know it's blowing." She paused. "Even the flowers and potato blossoms appear dull. I can't see the brilliance of their colors, but I know they are brilliant." A quick shallow breath, a falling tear. "Once, long ago, I saw, heard, and sensed all of nature."

Holding her close, he dried her tears and asked, "What happened to you?"

The wind and water were still and silent. She said, "It's not all about me. Tell me about the campout."

Current flowing, brook trout holding in the eddies behind rocks, Amadeus thought about eight-year-old boys, and said, "Cub Scouts, best friends. The three amigos attached themselves to me. Great kids, spirited! You'd love 'em!" For a few moments, he held her hand, rubbed her palm with his thumb, and tightened his hold on her. "Tim is a small, thin boy, bullied by the Scoutmaster's son. He has difficulty walking, one leg shorter than the other, one shoulder leans to the side and throws him off balance. He's in a lot of pain."

"Wait, walks with a limp? His name is Tim?"

"Yeah, Tim Bailey. The other two, twin brothers, Mike and Calvin Jackson. Why?"

"I met his mother, the cashier, Sharon Bailey, at church with Alice. Tim was sitting with two boys. He's such a sweetie. But he appears too small, too thin, for eight. Malnutrition, maybe?"

"Like I said, a Cub Scout, but I didn't say this: He's got grit, a determined little boy. He goes to Pastor's house when he's left alone. In the backyard, there were heaps of empty beer cans and whiskey bottles."

As she sat between his legs, Jennie leaned back against his chest, pulled his arms around her, and said, "Well, it's clear you are concerned. And you may have reason to be."

Salmon fry swam upstream—the stocking program was working. Trout sipped at mayflies floating past. An osprey divebombed, caught its prey in its talons, and flew to its aerie high in the trees. They heard its piercing call.

"When I moved into the house on McBurnie Road, my neighbor, Eleanor, an older woman, knocked on my kitchen door and offered me a welcome basket. We became best friends. Eleanor, my Treasure, was a grandmother to Rebecca and a kind friend to Mom."

"May I ask? Who was the ghost and did he hurt your daughter, too?"

Jennie sighed and tears welled.

"Talk to me, honey. You talked to me when we were children."

Gazing at the trees across the stream, she said, "The beating in my dream was the first one. Daniel had demanded alcohol and I'd bought three bottles of whiskey, refused to get the fourth. He needed help, but he wouldn't come out of that upstairs bedroom." Her sweet Amadeus, heart full of concern, love for children, love for her.

Settling in his arms, she was carried back to that time. He shared in the memory of her husband, Daniel Cahill. He had been a gentle, kind boy, a farmworker. Daniel loved God, family, and country. At eighteen, in 1967, he enlisted against her wishes. He had said that in the military he could get an education and build a career, but Vietnam was a war he couldn't possibly survive. Jennie was seventeen and Rebecca an infant. Two years later, a twenty-year-old, battle-scarred soldier returned, full of anger, the rage of trauma, his heart tormented. Holding onto the wobbly railing, he limped up the creaking stairs into the bedroom, shoulders bent, expression empty, and refused to come out.

The memory fading, she said, "He never hurt my baby girl. He didn't even notice her. Rebecca has no memories of her father."

Held in his arms and growing quiet, Jennie saw, in her mind's eye, the upstairs bedroom unlocked, the closet, and the faded-blue floor, just at the top of the stairs. The scent of alcohol filled her senses. Gathering her strength, hands on the railing, she pulled herself up, little Rebecca, next to her. "Please, don't ask me to remember."

Rosie swam by the boulder. A doe and her fawn drank from the stream. A rabbit at the edge of the woods hopped away and hid itself.

He held her hands, softly stroking them, and said, "I see you escaping down a dirt road, fields all around, trees bordering the field. You're carrying a little girl. I see your tears. Hers too. You're frightened, hurting. Close to the trees, you rush into them, and they conceal you."

"You *do* see. You do. We were fleeing to Eleanor's house. Rebecca wasn't safe. That day, I gave my daughter to my trusted friend to keep her safe." Weeping, her voice cracked, and she was almost inaudible. "Then I wandered slowly back to that cold, unforgiving house, without my little one, to Daniel, to more beatings." Another deep breath. "When I left, I heard Rebecca's cries calling to me. I couldn't turn around and look into her sad, frightened face. If I had, I wouldn't have left her." Collapsing, sobbing, Jennie held onto him and Amadeus enfolded her in his arms. Smoothing her hair, he gave her time to weep, as his own tears fell.

"You loved Rebecca, sweetheart, and you knew how to love. Where were your parents, and his? Were you all alone?"

Calming herself, she laid her ear over his heart, listening to its rhythm. With a gentle touch, he massaged her cheek. Her mother had calmed her in that same way, gentle fingers, lilac, delicate and aromatic. "My mother and Eleanor loved my daughter. They cared for her, played and prayed with her, and held her when she was sad or frightened. Rebecca has always loved them dearly."

"What about his parents?"

"They couldn't love him through his pain."

"And your father?"

"He didn't come for me. Deeply saddened, she said, "I wanted to go home, be his child, but my father didn't come."

"Breezes are blowing," he said, like a lullaby. "Sun's still hot, though." Rosie climbed up, with a little help from Amadeus, and shook herself, spraying water over them.

"Who was there for you?" Amadeus said.

"My Treasures: Eleanor, Mom, Pastor Bob, Michael, a police officer, and Doc. He told me to leave Daniel. But I couldn't. Daniel needed help. And he was my husband. So they and others kept a close watch."

"I understand why you call them Treasures." Grinning and splashing her, he said, "The water feels cool. Shall we?"

Rubbing her hand on the boulder, she said, "Why does it sparkle?"

"You see it? It's sunlight on mica."

His grin, his laugh, his wink were infectious, reminding her of Cyrus and Mary. "Well, be prepared to get wet!"

"And you too, my dear!" he said, eyes twinkling.

Knee deep in the stream, splashing, colorful droplets glittered in golden sunlight. Laughing boisterously and grabbing her hand, he pulled her into the middle.

"We'll be soaked!"

"We already are! Come on."

Jennie stood in the middle of the stream, her eyes on him. Amadeus couldn't take his eyes off hers: playful and daring. Jennie, the girl. Unbuttoning her shirt, she took it off and reached underwater to remove her jeans and throw them toward the shore. Missed! Shirt and jeans floated downstream. "Well, it was *your* idea!" Like mica, her eyes sparkled.

Removing and tossing his, too, they floated along behind. Then, stealing a quick kiss, he swam into the current, and she just stood there with a dazed expression.

"Hey, Jennie Girl, are you swimming or not?"

Jennie Girl was his old, sweet name for her. She touched her cheek and dove in.

Paddling upstream, then down in the deep swimming hole, back and forth, side by side, they raced past the rocks. She lost him somewhere under the current, waited, watched, spun around. Oh, where was he? He's still the kid he was! Trickery!

He popped up, startling her, and stole another kiss. They splashed each other. Her laugh was melodious, sweet-sounding; his high-spirited, harmonious.

"Listen!" she said, holding her forefinger to his lips, her eyes darting around. "I hear wind, water flowing! I feel it, too! I hear melodies in the trees!"

Tea-cher, tea-cher, po-ta-to-chip, chickadee-dee-dee, chickadee-dee-dee-dee.

"I know the song of chickadees. What are the other birds?"

"Ovenbird says tea-cher, nests in low branches," he said. "Goldfinch sounds like po-ta-to-chip."

Her face was radiant. Jennie twirled and spun, ripples of water surrounding, flowing around and through them. "Look, over there in the brush, something's moving."

"A rabbit. You see him? He's well-camouflaged."

"I hear him, foot stomping, growling, maybe sensing danger. Now, hopping away. Do rabbits make sounds?"

"Did you know rabbits hum when attracted to a lady?" Holding her face in his hands and laughing, he imitated a rabbit's hum.

"Look at the shore. The mallards, mother and ducklings, waddling and quacking. Frog croaking in the lily pads." She paused, breathing. "In the field, do you see?"

"I do see, yes, the bright light."

"An angel picking flowers, and deer are there too."

Gliding like a cloud hovering above grass and flowers, the light crossed the field to the shore. An angel laid a bouquet on a rock.

Jennie gasped, "Grandma Jennie!"

The bright light faded with the cloud and the deer. The mallards and the frog disappeared. Water, wavy, gracefully flowing, carried along by the wind and current.

"Race you downstream!" she said. "You know, clothing."

And sunlight danced on water.

✳

At the homestead, three of Cyrus and Mary's five sons were leading the farm animals—cows, sheep, and the Belgians—to a place where they could graze. Penelope, the one and only goose, dominated the task. Amid the noise and confusion of scattering sheep, cows, and horses voicing their baas, moos, and neighs, sounding as loud as Penelope's honking, and with goose feathers flying, the three sons chased the overwrought farm animals.

Meandering up the path to the homestead, Amadeus and Jennie were intrigued by sounds of distress. They rushed out of the woods and down into the clearing, among the scattering cows, sheep, and horses. The goose still honked, flapping its wings, a hilarious sight! They joined the chase. Rosie, too, tormenting Penelope.

Jennie saw the other two sons, John and Abiel, leaving to fill the buckets at the stream, laughing at the chaos, as did the daughters, while they prepared a meal.

Amadeus suddenly halted, catching sight of Jennie. Amid the confusion, she stood perfectly still, reached out her arms, her voice melodious, and called out, "Come to me." One cow, then another, cautiously approached, responding to her caresses. "Calm yourself, Kate, and Judy, be still." She crooned softly, hummed and recited Psalm 23:1-2: *The Lord is my shepherd, I shall not want. He maketh me to lie down in green pastures. He leadeth me beside still waters.* "Come, Kate. Come, Judy, to a quiet meadow."

A sheep bumped into Amadeus's leg. Kneeling down, holding its head gently, securely, and stroking its wool, he spoke low and soft, "Come, little sheep, into the meadow, for you are found. Come back into the fold." Then, as Amadeus hummed a low calming baritone, the sheep followed the man, the voice, and three more trailed behind.

"Come Nell, and Rosie, join Kate and Judy. It's so good to see you all again. Pink and Cherry too." Jennie caressed all the cows and welcomed the Belgians, Jacob and Mozark, stroking and patting them. Following Amadeus, the sheep approached her, and she hugged them. "Sturdy, Nimble, White Leg, and Black Leg. All my friends! Do you remember me? The little girl in braids calling to you from the wall."

Wondrously amazed! Chaos turned to tranquility. The sons and daughters looked on as the animals followed the foreigners. Passing by them waddled Penelope, a silent goose, following the man's voice. The playful chocolate lab just behind, nudging her.

Brothers and sisters followed and found their farm animals grazing peacefully in a meadow of tall grass and wildflowers, surrounded by evergreens, mixed with basswood, ash, birch, elm, and a cedar grove. They watched the foreigners saunter, hand-in-hand, their dog alongside, back into the woods and out of the vision.

"I told you my vision was familiar! We walked back into the day they arrived."

"No spiraling? No warning?"

"I saw this from the crumbling stone wall when I was eight. I walked with them to the meadow." Seeing his eyes upon her, she said, "You know that sheep you were serenading? Name's Sturdy. Like you, solid and sturdy."

Wet jeans, shirts, socks, and shoes lay in the grass, drying in the sun. A quilt was spread in the shade of a maple near the old crumbling stone wall with the red-checked tablecloth over it. Amadeus took out the bottle of red wine and popped the cork. It sounded foreign in this solitary place. Jennie held the long-stemmed glasses as he poured.

From the truck, they had retrieved dry clothing, dressed in the trees, hidden from each other, and now sat close together, sipping wine, eating chicken sandwiches, and crunching raw vegetables. "Would you like more?" he asked.

"Are you trying to get me drunk? Next, I'll be skinny dipping with you!"

They laughed.

Water bowl emptied and biscuits devoured, Rosie napped under an oak.

Jennie rewrapped her sandwich and set it in the basket. "I can't eat now."

Laying his palm on her forehead and her cheek, he said, "You're warm. You look flushed. Here, sip some water slowly, then rest."

She drank and lay back on the quilt. He repacked the basket and lay beside her, his arms a pillow for his head. Dozing off, she soon began to toss and turn. Amadeus held her. "Wake up, Jennie. Come back to me," he urged.

Rosie awoke, sniffed the air, and settled next to Jennie, guarding her.

"I'm awake," she said, laying her head over his heart.

In the serenity of the woods, they rested on the quilt in the shade.

Nine

Late that same afternoon, Amadeus, Jennie, and Rosie crossed the clearing to a narrow, steep path, rocks, and roots protruding above ground. Tightly packed tall pines, mixed with other conifers and hardwoods, shaded the way, branches forming a canopy. So as not to disturb this solitary, serene place, hidden from sky and sunlight, they strolled in silence, walking close, down the path through nature's cathedral.

Amadeus, with a canvas schoolbag over his shoulder containing sketchpad, pencils, and camera, led the way up the uneven broken granite steps, a few hidden in tall grass, and through the opening in the iron fence surrounding this hallowed place—the last reminder of the long-ago thriving neighborhood at Varnum Pond, its homes and schools and byways all gone. The Deane–Huse Cemetery remained, timeworn, wild, woods creeping within its borders.

The breeze freshened into an abrupt stiff wind. Trees swayed, dark clouds formed in the west, the summer air was suddenly chilly, and it smelled like rain.

"Storm approaching. Let's hurry," he said.

"Over there on the far side. We'll find them," she said.

Passing by the graves of other neighborhood families and one commemorated with a bronze Civil War marker, they pushed aside tall grass, wildflowers, twigs, and even fallen limbs, looking for hidden small markers. Rosie saw to her own projects, sniffing and shuffling old leaves, alerting the world to the presence of squirrels.

Kneeling in front of a grave, Amadeus pushed aside brush and twigs. "There's a family stone here."

Jennie knelt beside him. The stone was neither cracked nor chipped, only slightly weather-beaten. "The original stones honoring these children sank into the ground years ago. Dad and his brother set this newer stone." She closed her eyes, tracing the indentations, names, and dates. Then she recited, "Anna, sister of Great-Aunt Mary, was the daughter of Cyrus and Fanny Deane. Fanny, Cyrus's first wife, birthed five children, died young, and is buried somewhere here. Cyrus's second wife, Susan, birthed seven children, buried four sons and Anna, her stepdaughter. Their sons were born and died in the years following the Civil War. Grandfather Stephen was their youngest."

She tore pages from the sketchpad, and he held them firmly against the stone. With charcoal pencil, she traced the stone, white spaces forming names and dates.

The wind blew noticeably stronger, and light rain fell from the darkening sky. He snapped photographs of the gravestone, close-up and distant views. Jennie crawled through the grass to the opposite side of the same headstone and knelt in front of her great-grandparents.

Amadeus returned to the children, calculating their ages—Anna, a teenager; Edwin, Augustus, and Oscar, two years and younger; J. Walter, a young adult. He thought about these five young souls, taken from their parents, home with God. Their names faded away as if in a mist, other words materialized. Blinking, he read the familiar message, understanding it in a new way—*Luke 18:16: Let the little children come to me, And do not hinder them, for the kingdom of God belongs to such as these.*

Now surrounded by the mist, Amadeus watched the words evaporate into the atmosphere, visible no more. The children's names and dates reappeared, then vanished. He perceived new, different words, *Matthew 11:28-30: Come to me, all you who are weary and burdened, and I will give you rest. Take my yoke upon you and learn from me, for I am gentle and humble in heart, and you will find rest for your souls. For my yoke is easy and my burden is light.*

Still on his knees, Amadeus watched the words dissolve into nothingness, as if simply erased, names and dates again visible. *Come to Me…Rest for my soul.* His tears mixed with raindrops. *Let the children come to me.* The wind and the rain stilled. A deep voice from somewhere indistinct, in the air or out of his heart, called to him. "Amadeus, it is time…take your last steps to *me*…release your burden." The mist vaporized, the voice stilled, followed by whipping winds, beating rain, rolling thunder, flashes of lightning.

Jennie called, "Amadeus, help me!" That voice he heard in the air or in his heart. He knew who was calling and why. He tore himself from the presence, deserving of his reverence, and rushed to Jennie's side. Holding back tears, he fell to his knees behind her. Hands on her shoulders, he said, "We need to go now!"

She could not hear him or feel his presence.

"The rain," he said.

The sky turned from charcoal gray to black. Amadeus could not hold back his cries. Unaware of him, she remained rigid, as if turned to stone, and he watched her eyes fixed on the monument honoring her family. Then in his heart, he knew the thoughts of her heart: Parents guarding their children. Cyrus and Susan had lived through tragedy. It must be the most devastating grief and loss for a parent to bury a child.

Amadeus could not speak. He held her shoulder, shaking and keening in sorrow and despair. Alerted to his brokenness, she reached out, and he felt her arms holding him tightly. Why was her Amadeus sobbing so? Her hand, so gentle, smoothed his drenched hair as he laid his head on her shoulder. Pressing himself to her, breathing deeply, his chest heaving, his heart crushed, Amadeus sobbed for his lost children.

The storm raged. The wind covered the grave with the old leaves, brush, and twigs, hiding the children first and then their parents. They had seen into lives long past and had felt their grief and loss. Amadeus knew he must face God and face himself.

Weeping, he said, "Pray with me."

Crying, she said, "Yes, I will."

There on their knees under the darkened sky, shivering in the cold wind with sheets of rain pouring down, thunder, lightning, Jennie held him close, while Amadeus prayed, heeding his call into forgiveness and Grace:

"Lord, I can't live with an angry heart any longer. I got in trouble and tried to act responsibly. I was too young, just a teen, too selfish to know how to love. A friend told me that you didn't want to punish me for my whole life, that you would forgive me, that I needed to turn to you, but, Lord, I was angry at you, for I loved them. Now, after years of grief and guilt, I'm listening. I'm releasing Matthew and Elizabeth to you. I know you love them. I know they are safe in your arms. I still love them too. Forgive me. Grant me your Grace. I want to live again. I want You, Lord, to live in my heart. I want to know your peace. Amen."

Rain and wind still raged violently. Amadeus listened to Jennie's prayer, her mouth close to his ear, her voice quavering:

"Lord, Amadeus has lived too long grieving for his lost children and being separated from you. Find him, your lost sheep. Give his heart peace. Show him the way to the fold. Amen."

In that moment of time, the wind stilled, the deluge ceased, the thunder silenced, the lightning vanished, and the storm calmed. Amadeus saw a glowing white beam of light, shining down from Heaven upon him. Jennie was caught in that light as well, but only silence surrounded her. A chorus of angels sang heavenly praises. The Lord's words filled his inner heart—the gift of Grace: *Amadeus, you are home in the fold, for I have found my lost sheep. Now live in my light, my peace.*

The white light and the chorus faded away, and once again the storm raged. Still kneeling, holding her close, Amadeus wiped away Jennie's tears, mixed with falling rain. Calling to Rosie and helping Jennie stand, he said, "Now we must go."

Soaked to the skin and chilled to the bone, holding fast to each other, they plodded slowly, cautiously around the gravestones. No stars, no moon, only flashes of lightning lit their way to the opening in the iron fence and down the granite steps onto the steep path. Under the canopy of water-soaked branches, they trudged slowly, carefully, finding their way to the clearing, the old beaten path, and the safety of The Beast.

Rain continued to pour down, thunder rumbled, and the wind remained blustery, as Amadeus held open the truck door. Rosie jumped in first, settling in the passenger seat. Jennie took the middle. He gave her the dry quilt and, unfolding it, she laid it against the torn leather. Her flannel shirt clung to her, and her stiff, scratchy, wet jeans irritated her skin. Jennie removed her saturated clothing, dropping it behind the seat. Amadeus tossed his shoes and socks there, pulled off his shirt and jeans, too, mixing them with hers and a length of chain, a coil of rope, and a shovel.

Jennie snuggled close to him, enveloping them in the warmth of the quilt. He started the engine and held her closer. Temperature warming, the not entirely disagreeable smell of wet dog permeated the cab. They remained there for a while, giving time for the wind and rain to die down and visibility to clear.

"I am truly sorry, I had no idea," she said with tears in her eyes.

"I need to tell you," he said.

"Later, give your heart time."

"Please listen."

He turned on the light inside the cab and saw comfort and love in her eyes. She saw in his eyes a heart, saddened but growing whole, relieved of long-endured grief and memory, still holding two little souls in his heart, as he always would.

"Remember, I love you."

A tear fell from his eye, "I love you, my Jennie Girl."

He sighed, blinked, and breathed deeply. Smoothing her hair back away from her face, he said, "I was seventeen, my girlfriend, too, Iris. We married in sixty-five, and Matthew, our son, was born. We didn't want to, we didn't love each other enough, but we were expecting a baby. Our parents told us to be responsible adults. I gave up on college, quit school, got a job on a woodlot. Cabin came with the job. Still live there, own the place now, woodlot too. Joined the National Guard at eighteen, earned my GED. Never saw Vietnam, remained in the states serving in national emergencies, and riots."

Rosie sat up and peered at the rain beating on the windshield, the wind, still blustery. She whined softly and lay back down.

"Rosie, you stink," Jennie said.

Amadeus rolled down the window. "Steamy. Old battles with skunks, I'm afraid."

"Such a good dog."

"Our daughter Elizabeth was born in 1970." He wiped his brow, pushed away the quilt. "Jennie, the five children, the boy Oscar—how old was he when he died?"

"They called him Little Pino. I think he lived about eight weeks."

"Not my Elizabeth, my sweet baby girl." He wept.

Holding him close, she dried his tears. "You can stop now, if you want."

"Too early, the doctors couldn't save her." A whispered voice, brittle. "I held my daughter in the palm of my hand. She was too small, and she died there in my hand."

Rain beat on the truck. Amadeus, lost in memory, stared out the open window, his arm extended. Rain drenched his skin. His tears, a deluge.

"Three years later, I lost my son. He was eight."

Jennie laid her head over his heart, her arm draped over him, and stared out the window, joining in his memory. His little boy ran outside, got on his bike, peddled fast down the dirt road, coasting and peddling down the hill. From somewhere, nowhere, appeared a truck loaded with logs. A boy sped into the road. Brakes slammed, tires screeched, the truck swerved, logs rolled off! Then, Amadeus was there on his knees, holding the broken body. Matthew! And how Amadeus raged at God! His cries, his wails, amid sirens blaring, helicopter circling. Too late. His son was dead.

Jennie gasped. Hand over her mouth, she sobbed. He clung to her, and she to him. Their hearts intertwining like creeping vines, summer phlox, they grieved for lost children, their thoughts turning increasingly to children of the present.

Breathing deeply, they felt cool air fill their lungs. Thunder and lightning ceased. "Rain's letting up, but it's still windy," he said.

"It's really dark."

"Still afraid of the dark?"

Her voice almost inaudible, she said, "The hauntings. Hold on to me."

"Always." He held her for a few moments longer, then said, "We should go."

The engine already running, he shifted into reverse. Jennie settled herself next to him, laying her head on his shoulder and unconsciously massaging his thigh. He executed a U-turn onto the logging road, still holding her hand. Visibility was poor. With soggy branches hanging low and some scraping, he navigated the truck around and through potholes, over large rocks, across plank bridges, and onto the Varnum Pond Road. The engine made a dull roar, and it was a slower drive back to his cabin. Windows open, cool, damp air chilled their bodies, quilt loosely covering them.

Home safely, he parked close to the porch and they trotted inside, entering the living space, Jennie still wrapped in the quilt. Wet clothing lay in a heap. Squeezing between them, Rosie collapsed on the kitchen rug. Amadeus led Jennie to the bathroom, a shower against one wall, curtain open, rack behind the door—two towels hung there—a mirror over the sink. Hooks on the wall held two cotton plaid flannel robes, one green, the other blue.

He turned on the shower and offered his hand. "The water warms quickly." She dropped the quilt to the floor, let him lead her, and still held on tightly. He joined her. His beautiful Jennie, naked, wet, streams of water trickling down her body. A woman of strength, a tender, loving heart. She understood his sadness, his brokenness, and for a few moments today she felt joy. Under the spray, he washed her hair, ran his fingers through it, kissed her neck, her shoulders. Jennie felt her chilled body warming from his touch, butterflies fluttering, knees weakening. Her Amadeus, crook in his nose, tall and strong like trees, solid like stone walls, a sensitive heart like crumbling walls, broad shoulders, hands that give warmth. She kissed his lips, and he kissed hers, tenderly, more passionately. Lips parted. She pulled the ends of the leather tie, removed it, washed his hair, smoothed it back from his face with gentle fingers.

Their breathing slowed. Amadeus turned off the water, wrapped a towel around her, and said, "I'll build a fire."

Wrapping a towel around his waist, she said, "I'll make tea." She stood in front of the mirror and wiped away the steam with a hand towel. He combed her long hair, slow strokes calming. She combed his, slow strokes comforting. They put on the plaid flannel robes.

In the small kitchen, Jennie put the tea kettle on, looked through the cupboards, and found two mugs and—wrinkling her nose—a box of teabags. How unpalatable, bland tea bags in hot water. She should have packed her teas, pleasant aromas and smooth delicate flavors, loose herbal tea with a teaspoon of honey, steeped exactly five minutes. She could get them tomorrow.

Honey, where's the honey? Not on the burnt, stained countertop, circles shaped like pots, and not in the two cupboards. He must have honey somewhere. She searched again, opened and closed cupboard doors. Hinge broken on one, the door hung down, held in place by the lower loose hinge. On the shelves sat a few plastic dishes, glassware, and little food—sugar, white flour, two chocolate sugar donuts left in the box. In the lower cupboard, she found a rusty cast-iron frying pan and scratched, nonstick cookware.

She tried to open a drawer, found it stuck, pulled too hard, and dropped it on the floor; several utensils spilled out. Picking up the utensils and putting them back in the drawer, she set it on the counter. She found him in the living room, building a fire, and asked, "Where's the honey?"

"Honey?" He shrugged, then chuckled. "The only honey in the cabin is the one standing in front of me."

"Oh, stop," she said with an exasperated sigh. Back in the kitchen, she opened the refrigerator. Not much there, either, like hers.

Donuts and mugs of hot tea, minus teabags and honey, sat on the tiny table for two. Jennie waited but not for long. Entering the kitchen, Amadeus noticed the loosely hanging door and the drawer out of its slot. "I'm sorry, I pulled too hard," she said.

"No problem. I meant to fix it a few years ago." Pulling out the other hinge, he set the door on the porch and left the drawer. Taking his usual seat at the end of the table, he scooped two heaping teaspoons of sugar and poured some cream into the mug, stirring it. "Have a donut."

She took one, he the other.

"You don't add cream or sugar? Must be flavorless," he said.

"I'll just dunk the donut. Tomorrow we'll get my teas and honey from Alice's."

"You're all the honey I need."

Steam rose from her mug, and she blew on it, dunked the donut, and sipped the hot insipid beverage. Amadeus stirred his again, sipped, then dunked the donut.

Holding his hand, she said, "May I ask? What happened to Iris?"

"The day of Matthew's funeral, she walked out. Haven't seen or heard from her since. Don't know where she went." Jennie tightened her grip. "Soon after, I got divorce papers in the mail from a law office over in Portland, had them checked out, signed my name, and we were divorced. I've been alone for eighteen years."

"Iris didn't stand by you?"

"She was hurting too. We loved our children, not each other." He sighed. "She wanted out, and frankly, so did I."

They left the tea and half-eaten donuts on the table. Settling between the quilts in front of the warm fire, they embraced. Rosie slept, warming Jennie's feet.

TEN

Jennie breathed deeply the warm, spicy, sweet aroma of cinnamon. Snuggled in the quilts, the dryer humming, she thought about Amadeus, her dearest friend, the man she loved. The carefree boy had grown into a gentle, kind, loving woodsman, who loved everything she loved: children, Rosie, music, trees, and all of nature. And he loved her. Could she be the pearl in his life?

Rosie barked, and Amadeus opened the door to let her in. Now, added to the cinnamon, came the scent of bacon sizzling. Jennie rose and stepped into the bathroom. Her clothes warm and dry, she donned an old cotton shirt and comfortable jeans, folding and packing her second set in the one remaining school bag of essentials. The other, containing her sketchpad, pencils, and camera, had been lost in the graveyard during yesterday's rainstorm. She folded the quilts and carried the bedding down the hall. Past the bathroom, she saw two closed doors on the left and on the right two open ones: the first, a small empty room, lit by bright morning sunshine; the second at the end of the hall, a larger room with a small window and little sunlight. Amadeus's bedroom or his library? She deposited the quilts and pillows in a corner. An old, rusty, iron bedstead with wrinkled blankets and the corner of a quilt hanging down to the floor stood on one wall. A worn leather chair sat in the corner. Next to it stood a pole lamp and a small table, layered in dust. The table held two framed photographs. Bookshelves covered one wall: Compendia—forestry, botany, and gardening; wood project manuals; medical reference books; history books and biographies; wilderness stories; children's books; and an old Bible, everything organized by genre in neat rows and dust-free. Reading was something else they both loved.

Selecting a book from the shelf, she curled up in the chair. Distracted by the photographs, she picked them up, wiped away the dust, examined them closely, and wondered if they were his wife and children. Then she opened the book.

Amadeus entered and said, "There you are." He kissed her and checked to see what she was reading.

She looked up at him, dressed in faded jeans and a shirt, and closed the book. Did he wonder if she'd seen the photographs? She touched flannel and gently squeezed the hint of his pot belly. Too many donuts. Too much cream and sugar in tea. Another thing they both loved: soft flannel and natural cotton. "There's a section on nineteenth century medicine. I was wondering what could have caused the deaths of four of the five children. James Walter died of tuberculosis."

Picking up the black-and-white snapshots off the table, he took one last look. "Jennie, honey, it's time for me to put these away. New life begins today." He found a small box, placed them inside, and set it on a high shelf.

Reaching for his hand, she said, "Do you feel different?"

"Yes, I do." Bending down and leaning on the arm of the chair, he lifted her chin and held her eyes in his. "My spirit is free, no more guilt, no grief. My heart is at peace." After a pause, he said, "I saw the white light. I sensed His presence. I heard His words deep in my heart." Touching her neck, he said, "Sweetheart, there is love between us."

The book forgotten on her lap, she traced his lips and said, "Always has been."

"I love you," he said, kissing her. "I am ready to love, share my life with you."

"And I you, but my heart is not whole and free like yours."

"It will be, and your eyes will dance again. Just a little more time."

Gazing into his eyes, she combed her fingers through his red hair. She belonged here with him. She'd always belonged with him and, she knew, he with her. Would her heart ever be like his—at peace?

He led her out of the room, arms around each other, and closed the library door. In the kitchen, two plates of scrambled eggs, crispy bacon, warm cinnamon rolls, and two mugs of hot tea sat on the countertop. On the front porch swing, they balanced plates on their laps and sipped the tea, hers watery, his thick.

"We are definitely stopping at Alice's for my teas and honey."

"You know that skirt and sweater you wore on our first date?"

"Oh, you mean our visit?" She gave him a slight smile.

"Our first date, it was a date." He chuckled.

"It's at Alice's. Why?"

"All in good time. You're still too inquisitive."

He set the plates and mugs on the porch floor. She turned sideways, leaned back against him, drew up her knees, feet on the swing, and he wrapped his arms around her. Songbirds twittered their morning chorus. Rosie napped on the porch.

Entangling his fingers in her hair, he kissed her, and kissing her again, said, "What do you think about children?"

"Actually, I love them."

"Would you want more children? I mean, since you'd be starting over again… or perhaps, you'd rather be teaching."

Relaxing in his arms, she said, "You mean, a baby? Your baby?"

"Our baby. But really it's just too soon."

"Well, my T-Bear, it would have to be pretty soon. We're both in our forties." T-Bear, her old, sweet name for him. Rising from the swing, she held his hand, and they sauntered down the dirt road. It was private at his place, not visible from the road: the field, a stone wall, cabin, sheds, and the dirt road were encompassed by the tree line, the woodlot just beyond. She'd always known he'd live sheltered within the trees.

He asked about her father and she said, "You know I want to forget about him."

"Please tell me anyway."

They walked along, past the woodpile at the edge of the field, and he waited patiently for her to speak. Rosie dashed into the woods, chasing squirrels. Amadeus pulled Jennie right, down a path leading to a secluded meadow. Sunlight glistened on wet leaves and wildflowers from yesterday's rain and sparkled on clear, wind-blown pond water. Rolling up their pant legs and removing socks and boots, they waded in, cooling their feet. "It's peaceful here," she said.

Rosie ran past them, splashing both. "Gotta love that dog," Amadeus said. Then, holding her close, he lowered his voice. "It's time to let go."

Jennie breathed deeply. The birds sang. Just yesterday and this morning she had heard their melodies. "I was lost to him. I lost my home, life as I knew it, and my father's love, or so I believed. Daniel was seventeen. I was sixteen and pregnant. We turned to my parents—his had turned us away. Mom hugged me, cried with me, consoled me. Daniel asked Dad's permission and his blessing on our marriage. Dad put down his newspaper and asked Daniel into the garage. Mom and I stayed inside, and then, through the window I saw Daniel leaving."

Walking slowly back into the meadow, Amadeus held her close. "Stone walls are good places to sit and talk."

Rabbits, a mother and babies, hopped through the tall wet grass. Rosie swam to shore, chased them, and then ran over to Amadeus, dropping a stick, ready to fetch. He threw it across the meadow, and she chased it, tail wagging. Then she was back again with it. Jennie threw it toward the woods and watched the dog chase it.

Remembering that time in 1967, and knowing she needed to share her story, though she wanted to forget it, her memory seized the moment, and Jennie was lost in it.

"Lean on me," Amadeus said, joining her in the memory. Jennie's father had sent Daniel away for one month until his daughter's seventeenth birthday. The family needed time. Jennie had left school and was studying at home. Her father talked more and more about adoption, and their plans for college, but Jennie loved her baby. He would have taken away something else that she loved, the way she had already lost her beloved Temple, her visions, her stories, and Amadeus.

Daniel truly loved Jennie. He quit school and got a job working for a farmer. A house came with the job, the house on McBurnie Road. It was too long for them to be apart. Jennie was home alone on her birthday, Daniel came by, and she went with him. Pastor Bob, her Treasure, the new young pastor at the church on the corner married them. Then they went back. Jennie sought comfort in her mother's arms, a deep love between them. She faced her father's anger: *Then it's time to grow up, Jennie. Your adult life is on that farm.* Dad had spoken quietly, coldly, but Jennie felt in her heart abandoned, lost to him. She had disappointed him and would never again be his child. It was time to leave, time to grow up.

Jennie's tears, the sound of her cries that day, her seventeenth birthday, told the story of a daughter's broken heart. Her father, his own heart crushed, sat in the porch rocker, hiding his face in his hands, his shoulders shaking.

The mallards swam slowly by in the warm sunshine. Rosie sat in front of Amadeus, waiting, panting, tail wagging. He threw the stick into the pond, and the dog retrieved it after swimming after the mallards.

Holding back her tears, her voice a monotone, Jennie said, "My father turned me, his daughter, and his unborn granddaughter away." Deep breaths. "I don't understand," another breath, "how a parent can claim to love a child," sobbing, "but turn the child away." Seeing his tears, she wrapped her arms around him, and he held her close.

"Jennie, I don't understand either." Deep breath. "Children are blessings from God to be cherished. A father must be ready to love and forgive always." Another breath. "When your child is lost, your heart's joy is lost, and your father's joy was lost to him." A sigh. "Honey, did Daniel take care of you?"

"He did, until he enlisted."

"What about your mother?"

"Dad was kind to her. She was determined to remain close to us, and she did. Rebecca loved her and gave Mom joy." Tears sliding down her cheeks, she lowered her head, her voice sad, whispery, "I loved her. I've missed her."

Holding Jennie close, he let her cry and then said, "Did your father ask your forgiveness?"

"He wasn't a man who could easily say he was sorry, but he did, on his deathbed. And I forgave him. He gave me a small card with a picture of a shepherd and words to the twenty-third Psalm, four words underlined—*He restores my soul.*"

Amadeus reached into his pocket, pulled out a small card, and laid it in her hand.

"It's like mine. *He restores my soul.*" She fingered the card. "Where?"

"From your father. The friend in my prayer was him."

Chin trembling, she said, "He showed you how to find forgiveness, but not me?"

"Honey…" his voice was warm. "The words on the card. He showed *us* the way."

Not comprehending his words, she inhaled deeply, exhaled, flexed her fingers, snapped. "He knew my visions were real, and he let me suffer without them. He took all that I loved away from me, even you, but he didn't take my baby!"

Calmly, he said, "Rebecca, a blessing to you and your mother."

Frowning, she said, "How did you meet him?"

He sighed, "He bought wood from Joe Foster, the man I worked for. Your father was here buying from the woodlot owners and a few years later from me."

"Tell me where Joe's woodlot is. Tell me!"

Stroking her palm, he said, "It borders on the homestead. That's where we met."

Holding her chin high, she said, "I knew he wouldn't stay away." Chin quivering, she lowered her eyes. "He found peace there, he always did, but he wouldn't let me come with him to find my peace."

"I'm so sorry for all you faced."

"It's not your fault. If he helped you, that's a good thing." She paused and gazed at the pond, Rosie swimming, catfish jumping, dragonfly hovering. "Your livelihood is here in the trees. As for me, even from the grave he pours salt into my wounds." She held his hand, his eyes in hers. "My dear Amadeus, know this: I truly love you."

"And I you, always have, always will." He smiled, kissed her hand, and entwined his fingers in hers. "Let's get your teas. The skirt and cardigan too."

His grin always brought a smile to her face.

Hand-in-hand, they strolled back down the dirt road with a wet Rosie alongside. Later, at the Murphys, Jennie collected her teas, honey, clothing, and miscellaneous things, packing them in her quilted bags. The ancestry boxes, green boxes, the old book, and the shopping bag remained stacked in the corner of the bedroom.

Annie met Jennie descending the stairs. "Is your heart not sick now?"

Giving Annie a hug, she said, "It's healing, sweetie. My heart is healing."

In the kitchen, Alice watered the herbs in clay pots that hung in the black metal frame. Tom and Amadeus talked at the table with coffee mugs in hands.

Entering the kitchen with Annie, Jennie said, "Oh, Alice, I want to talk with you, but I can't right now."

"Tomorrow, come to Sunday dinner. We'll get the kids too."

"I'd love that. And a walk."

"A walk and a talk, it is."

Amadeus carried her bags and tucked them behind the seat. Rosie sat on the end, head out the window, wind blowing in her face. Jennie, always in the middle, next to him. The Beast roared down Voter Hill, sped back to Temple, and turned onto Cummings Hill Road, passing by Tim's house. The cemetery was up ahead on the right.

ELEVEN

Amadeus pumped the heavy clutch, shifted gears, and slowly steered through the iron gate into the Temple Village Cemetery, stopping by the Deane row. The dirt road, just wide enough for The Beast, extended straight back to the woods, bordering the graveyard. Brown spots marred the grass, and sticks, twigs, and visible roots were scattered about the acreage. Stones, some aged and weather-beaten, others newer, gleaming in the sunlight, spread across the lawn in nearly straight rows.

Beating on the windshield, the sun's rays warmed the cab. Amadeus wiped his brow and hid his eyes. Sensing his sudden pensive mood, Jennie slipped her hand into his and massaged it softly. "Take a walk with me," he said.

Rosie raced past memorials honoring Temple's families, and past tulips, daffodils, and lilies blooming at gravesites, up and over the hill at the back corner. Running by an aged, weather-beaten monument enclosed by an iron fence, she disappeared into the woods that surrounded this reverent place of rest.

Amadeus and Jennie ambled over to the last two burial plots in the second row from the paved road. A gnarled, hardy oak, its roots above ground and green leaves in full bloom, cast its branches protectively over his children. Gray squirrels chattered and scurried through its limbs, and acorns plopped to the ground. Amadeus brushed his hand across the bole. "One of the oldest oaks I've seen, taken root about 1840." A sigh, a pause. "Matthew liked trees, was learning to climb. I'd find him sitting in the branches."

Jennie held his hand, and together they knelt in the shade of the oak, caressing the cool stone, marking the memory of Matthew and Elizabeth.

"I'm ready for life with you, but I'll never forget them," he said. "I love them."

"Of course, you do. And you'll never forget. You have a heart for children."

"You were right, you know. It is the most devastating loss — burying a child."

"You read my thoughts," she said.

"Pushed me over the edge. No choice but to release years of grief."

"We'll plant flowers."

Frowning, he said, "Geraniums?"

"Wild daisies to sway in the breezes and brighten summer days."

"Buttercups and brown-eyed Susans too."

"Any flowers you choose. And others will choose this spot themselves."

Getting to his feet, he helped Jennie up and said, "Let's find your family."

In the maples, the call of the pileated woodpecker rang out. Strolling back to the Deane row and passing by a stone mirroring sunlight, a recipe for ice cream etched upon it, Jennie looked back. At ten she and Grandma Sarah had talked near that oak. "The girl in braids once turned cartwheels here and didn't get caught," she said.

As they walked, he gave her a hug, a quick kiss, and chuckled.

The weathered granite headstone of Grandmother Jennie loomed before them. With Amadeus next to her, Jennie knelt, remembering that long-ago vision. Grandma Jennie: the young woman in love, her alto voice and dancing eyes. If she touched the epitaph, would she see her grandmother again? Jennie held tightly to Amadeus's hand, leaned forward, traced the epitaph, and yes: almost immediately they spiraled like frisbees, spinning, rising, hovering in midair, and landing gracefully in front of a brick church in Farmington.

Snow blowing, wind whistling, temperature freezing. Jennie, her arms folded, shoulders hunched, shivering — no warm coat — and teeth chattering, said, "The organist is playing. Sounds like wedding music." Securely clinging to each other, they slipped and slid across the ice, out of the elements and into the warm church.

Grandma Jennie was beautiful! Dressed in her full-length, high-collared, white gown trimmed with covered buttons and a long veil, the bride carried a bouquet of pine, holly, and winterberries. And Grandpa Stephen, so handsome in his dark suit, a white handkerchief folded neatly in his coat pocket.

Jennie traced the indentations, the etching of a fiddlehead. Was it only an engraving, or did she share Mary's secret?

Instantly, the fiddlehead spiraled, seeming to jump off the stone. They stared, blinked, eyes circling. A mist, a cloud of tiny water droplets, enclosed around them. Jennie felt the wetness, then a touch, a connection! "Great-Aunt Mary, is that you?"

Amadeus, caught in the mist, made a show of listening. He was amazed when a warbling voice said, "My dear Jennie, it certainly is me, and your grandma Sarah loved to hint at my secrets."

"Oh, Aunt! I have your cookie recipe. Dad told me it's in your handwriting."

"I hope you haven't baked them! You know, it's missing an ingredient."

"Delicious. I add nutmeg and brown sugar, not white."

"Oh, yes, hmmm. That could be it! But there's another. I never wrote it down—secret, you know." Mary, white hair, gnarled hands, blue sparkling eyes, laughed in a high-pitched, shaky voice. "I forgot. Maybe another spice. It could be hard to come by!" A soft touch. A puff of wind carried away Mary's words: "Gotta run, sweeties. Nice chatting with ya! Oh, Jennie, loved the cartwheels!" And Mary was gone. The mist evaporated and the fiddlehead was just an etching.

"Kind of daft, isn't she?" said Amadeus.

Laughing, Jennie said, "Check the birthdate. Mary, a mystery."

The stone etchings faded and new words appeared. Jennie knew the source, Isaiah 41:10: *So do not Fear, for I am with you; do not be dismayed, for I am your God. I will strengthen you and help you; I will uphold you with my righteous right hand.*

His word, a lamp, a light. His Peace, He gives. Do not fear, He is with her.

Rosie ran across the field, straight to them. Amadeus stroked her head. Nudging Jennie playfully, Rosie received more affection.

"Would you have dinner with me tonight? A date?"

"A date with you?" She smiled. "I accept."

Amadeus and Jennie, hand-in-hand, strolled across the lawn to The Beast. Rosie pranced circles around them. And the message vanished into weatherworn granite.

At the Kawahnee Inn, they sat at a table for two with a view of Webb Lake, enclosed by woods—Mt Blue looming in the distance, Tumbledown too. Windy on this chilly June evening, with rough water lapping the shore.

The waitress, Irene, a cheerful, older woman, served a cabernet. Setting small plates and a wooden breadboard on the table, she brought them a warm loaf with creamy butter.

"Thank you," said Jennie, ordering their dinner, while Amadeus poured the wine.

"What are you looking at?" Jennie said, taking a sip.

"The lovely view across the table."

"Oh, for goodness' sake!"

Amadeus set down the glass, reached into his shirt pocket, searched his pants pockets, and finally stood and patted his back pockets.

"Oh my, I hope you didn't forget your wallet. I didn't bring my purse."

Laughing, he said, "Well, no need to wash dishes, here's the wallet." He checked his front pockets again and taking his seat, held her hand. "Now close your eyes." Placing a small object in her palm, he closed her fingers over it.

"My bracelet, heart still attached, a gift from Grandma Sarah."

"You gave it to me the day you left."

"You kept it all these years!"

Irene served their entrée — salmon, crisp on the outside, soft on the inside, melting in the mouth, potatoes, vegetables, just the right amount of garlic, pepper, and herbs.

"I planned to give it back," he said. "You've always been in my heart."

"Oh, no! I can't give back your music award."

"What did you do with it?"

"It's buried in the orchard."

They drank another glass of wine. Irene gathered their plates and asked about dessert. Jennie politely declined. He paid the tab, purchased the two wine glasses, and grabbed the wine bottle. She took the glasses. Outside, Amadeus held her hand as they wandered down the wooded path to the lake, to the sand beach.

They set the bottle and glasses in the sand. He kicked off his shoes and socks and she her sandals. Then they sunk their feet into the cool, wet sand, which oozed between their toes. Grinning, he rolled up the sleeves of his blue cotton shirt and his khaki pant legs. Ready for a water fight, she pulled up her cardigan sleeves and tied a knot in her jean skirt, which made it thigh-high. Holding hands and wading into knee-deep, chilly water, Jennie swirled her foot in the waves, splashing him. He splashed her and they splashed again and again. Laughing, she pulled away from him and lost her balance, almost falling. He caught her and held her upright. The sky darkened, the moon rose, the waves splashed at their legs. They embraced and kissed, slow and sizzling.

"Your eyes were dancing," he whispered.

"As if you could see," she whispered, knowing it was true.

Hand-in-hand, they strolled onto the sand, picked up the wine bottle, glasses, shoes, sandals, kissed, and meandered to The Beast.

Amadeus turned up the dirt road, parked by the cabin, and tuned the radio to the mellow, orchestral sounds of love. Lingering there, they shared warm, inviting kisses until she said, "An eventful day."

"Not over yet," he said. "May I have this dance?"

Eyes brightening, dimples showing, she said, "When did you become such a romantic?"

Opening the door of the truck, he held her hand, and they stepped out. "Last Monday, in a rowboat." Enfolding her in his arms, they slow danced, cheek to cheek.

The unpaved driveway; the ballroom floor. The full moon and an array of glimmering stars; a ceiling of skylights. Imaginary walls; a tall maple and a solid oak, branches spreading far and wide, and tall pines, some aged.

The strings with the distinctive sound of a violin then played an old-timey. Waltzing gracefully, he held her waist, and she leaned her head on his shoulder, swinging and swaying, twirling and a few dips. One last song, alluring for lovers, a duet. Pressed together, their bodies swayed where they stood.

"Hey, Jennie Girl," he said, tracing her nose, lips, and neck softly. His fingers felt warm and roughened. Under the stars, in the moonbeam, they kissed lovingly, long, and passionately. He reached into the truck, turned off the radio, grabbed the wine bottle, and handed her the two glasses. Embracing, they strolled up the steps onto the porch. Amadeus opened the front door—Rosie was snoozing on the kitchen rug—and Jennie entered the living room first. Holding each other close, they shared a kiss or two, while ambling over to the fieldstone fireplace. Amadeus halted instantly, stared at the wood floor, and said, "Where are the quilts and pillows?"

"Folded, piled in the library."

"How about you get the quilts and I'll build the fire."

In the darkened hallway—thoughts of him, their closeness to come—she opened a door, flipped the switch, not the library, the room on the left, not the right. Storage: tools, grease buckets, a skidder chain, and under it all, a kid's bed frame, a baseball, and a glove. Sensing his presence, she heard him whisper, "This room was Matthew's."

Closing the door, she caressed his face, and he kissed her palm. From the library, they gathered the quilts and pillows and together made their bed by the fireplace. Her eyes held his, and with deeper breaths, he pulled her close, and their lips met.

The fire provided the only light, its crackling the only sound. Dreamy-eyed, Jennie slowly removed her clothing. His eyes upon her, he did the same. "Hey, T. Bear." Hands roamed over shoulders and down spines. His scent pleasant, woodsy. Her scent fragrant, vanilla. Her skin, her breasts soft and silken. His skin soft, not like his hands. She reached behind him, untied the leather string, entangled her fingers in his red, shoulder-length hair.

Naked, they lowered themselves to the quilts.

"Ouch!" she said. "Your knee is pinching my thigh."

"Sorry," he said, moving it. "Better?"

She moved her leg, wiggled around, adjusted the pillow. "Now it is."

"Your feet are freezing."

She pulled him down. "Rosie warms my feet." Their lips touched. Kisses deepened, intensified. Chests rose and fell with each breath. Hearts raced, skin prickled, and they loved each other, they really did.

In the twilight, naked bodies slept comfortably on a bed of quilts, a chocolate lab at their feet. The fire had died out. A quilt had slipped off. He held her close, warm hand flat on her lower back. Legs entwined. Her head lay on his chest, hand over his heart, sensing a resting rhythm.

Dreaming, she saw them gliding around the ballroom, kissing, waves splashing, and a gold bracelet with heart attached. She was home, loved by him.

Suddenly, naked bodies pressed together, hearts raced, postures tense, eyes alert. His arm long down her back, his hand strong on her hip, protective.

A second arm stretched its full length, the hand just short of grasping her shoulder, pulling her back. Daniel's ghost! Willing herself to melt into Amadeus, to hide, she saw a mother and a child, afraid, crying, concealed by trees.

Alarmed, Rosie, ears perked, sniffed the air, and lay close to Jennie, guarding her.

From above, a third hand reached down. A gentle open hand with a hole in the palm. It was close enough, just there, above her head. She could grasp it—salvation. Words flooded her mind: *lamp, light, Peace, His Peace,* and, words from Isaiah*: Do not fear for I am with you.* A gentle voice, kind and welcoming, spoke to her heart. "It's time. Release your burden. Come into the fold."

Crying, clinging to Amadeus, she repeated in her sleep: *He restores my soul.*

Awakening, he turned on his side, still holding her close to him. Smoothing her hair, drying her tears, Amadeus whispered, "Wake up, wake up. Jennie, honey, wake up."

"I'm awake," she said.

"Talk to me, my Jennie."

"The hauntings. I need to tell you and then find God."

"I'm listening."

"Not here. I don't want Daniel's ghost in our bed."

Frightened, she melted in his arms, preparing herself for the heart-wrenching truth she must tell. Would God offer her Grace? Would Amadeus still love her?

Twelve

In the Murphys' backyard, the storytellers sat on the stone wall, shaded by a clump of white birch—mountains in the distance, a duvet of treetops below, a sea of blue above. Down the hillside lay the old Parkhurst farm. Sitting either cross-legged or on their knees in the grass, Rosie in the middle, the six friends, all wiggles and jiggles, looked up, anticipating the story. Blades of grass decorated their sticky fingers. Popsicles!

Jennie said, "Tell me what you know about cemeteries."

"Dead people live there!" said Tim.

"It's spooky!" said Calvin.

"Scary!" said Mike and Annie added, "If they're dead, they don't live."

"There's one near our street," said Gracie. "It's not scary. Flowers grow there."

Jennie began the telling: One summer when I was five and he was seven, we played hide-and-seek almost every day. We needed to find new hiding places. So we ran down the street. It was a long way, but we got there and ran through the gate into the cemetery. The lawn was mowed and flowers were growing. A chain link fence surrounded it. We climbed the oak tree, and he told me scary stories.

Calvin said, "What stories?"

Amadeus said, "Ghost parties in the moonlight. Boo! Haunting sounds, like branches creaking, owls hooting, black cats screeching."

Annie said, "Were you scared, Jennie?"

"No reason to be afraid in the daytime. The sun was shining. Well, at least no reason until the black cat jumped out of the oak. Meooooooow!"

Instantly, Maggie crawled onto Jennie's lap. Tim moved next to Amadeus, tapping his friend on the shoulder. Rosie crept near Tim.

Amadeus said, "We climbed down out of that tree real quick."

Jennie said, "Hiding behind gravestones, we crept silently from one to another, hiding and sneaking up on each other, calling, *Boo*! Good hiding places in cemeteries."

And he continued: *Amadeus, come quick*! Jennie screamed. She was hopping, jumping, shaking her hands, like this. *Hurry up!* Jennie was scared! I ran as fast as I could run. And I saw it—on the ground, next to a tombstone. A bone! A round bone!

Gracie and Annie hugged Jennie. Maggie still sat on her lap. Mike and Calvin, on their knees, drew even closer to Amadeus. And Tim's face paled.

"Now, can you guess what it was?" said Amadeus.

"A leg," said Mike.

"Somebody's arm," said Annie.

From Tim, "A head-bone."

"It was a soup bone!" Laughing, he said, "A dog must have left it there."

Giggling, the kids slapped their hands on their cheeks. The boys rolled in the grass and the girls tumbled down the grassy incline.

Jennie turned to Amadeus and frowned. "A soup bone?"

Kissing her hand and grinning, he said, "My dear, you wandered there. You were sitting in an oak tree, waiting, afraid to climb down. Sweetie, you said it felt like being lifted, like flying."

"Oh, I never remembered the wanderings."

"I lied to your dad that day and saved you," he said.

She patted his thigh. "You were a convincing liar. Saved me many times."

"So I seem to have forgotten ever playing hide-and-seek," he said.

"Oh, that was fiction." She laughed, her eyes sparkling.

Holding hands, they crossed the yard, inhaling the scent of charcoal. A backyard Sunday afternoon picnic with best friends. Juicy burgers and crispy fries served on paper plates, and Kool-Aid and iced tea in paper cups. Condiments made their way around the table. Silly jokes and antics brought giggles, as the kids filled their hungry tummies.

Friendly conversation among the adults touched on the whereabouts of Emilie, the archivist: touring Quebec City. She and her old high school sweetheart, James Foster, an attorney, had rekindled their love from forty years ago. With Jennie's arrival, their time had come. Jennie's vision, Emilie's telephone call. The male voice, James.

So while Alice and Jennie spoke of loving relationships, Tom and Amadeus wandered into the garage, burgers in hands. Tom had purchased a new tractor, top of the line, multi-use—plowing, hauling, mowing, digging, and more. Amadeus admired the hum of the engine. A woodsman could put this machine to good use.

Their plates cleaned, the children wanted dessert. Annie passed around Alice's Famous Chocolate Chip Cookies with double the chips, some M&Ms, and a secret blend of crunchies.

"Delicious," said Jennie. "What are the crunchies?"

Alice laughed. "Whatever you have in the cupboard."

When the men returned, Alice set the cookie jar in front of them and said, "How about a walk and a talk, girlfriend?"

Tom smiled at Alice, "Go ahead. We'll clean up and watch the kids."

Amadeus said, "The Cubbies will help, and then we'll run a game of Simon Says."

Tim said, "Amadeus, the Cubbies. You need the Cubbies help?"

The girls chatted. The women walked. The men and Cubbies cleaned up.

Strolling down the hillside, Jennie and Alice disappeared behind the trees. Pushing aside branches and stepping over fallen limbs, they followed a narrow path into the overgrown Parkhurst apple orchard. The solid stone wall seemed to welcome them into a world of memories. Sitting there, the friends reminisced about the hill, where they'd once played, as had their mothers: sliding in winter, climbing trees, walking stone walls in the pastures. They talked of friendship, three generations, beginning with grandmothers, who met on the day Sarah walked up the hill to her new job—housekeeper at the dairy farm—the place where she met Grandpa Harold, a farmhand.

That faraway look—no spiraling, only seeing—anchored Jennie in a vision: In the cool winds of autumn, her grandparents, a younger Sarah and Harold, climbed the ladders, hand-picked apples, one at a time, and carefully set the delicious fruit in woven reed baskets. Young girls, their mothers, jumped off the stone wall, skipped to the trees, climbed into its branches, and plopped apples into small baskets.

"Where are you, girlfriend?" said Alice, holding her hand.

Blinking twice, Jennie smiled, "What do you mean? Where am I?"

"A million miles away, like the child you were." Squeezing Jennie's hand, Alice said, "Do you remember the tea party?"

Their grandmothers had sewn new dresses and mailed them in boxes with fancy invitations. On Sarah's porch one afternoon in early autumn, grandmothers and granddaughters gathered around the table, set with a white tablecloth, china cups and saucers, fancy cookies from the bakery, and a silver teapot filled with peppermint tea.

They'd talked about school, books, and boys, until the girls had grown too fidgety. So Sarah had turned on the radio, that big console, and grandmothers taught granddaughters how to dance.

Jennie said, "They said we'd need to know how in just a few years."

Alice laughed. "I was twelve, invited to my first dance with Tom."

Jennie jumped up and stood in front of Alice, still laughing. "Well, I'm not your Tom." Bowing, she extended her hand. "May I have this dance?"

"Why, certainly," said Alice, accepting the offered hand.

There in the old Parkhurst orchard, Jennie took the lead, played the part of the boy, as she had on the porch that day, and they waltzed around the stone wall, weaving in and out of the apple trees. The breezes were an orchestra, the trees and wildflowers swayed to the music, the setting sun frolicked on the stone wall, and the spirits of their grandmothers smiled sweetly, laughing in soft silvery tones.

The pale crescent moon climbed from behind the mountains. Strolling up the hill, they held hands like young girls, best friends. "I think tonight I'll remind Tom of that first dance." Wrapping Jennie in a hug, Alice said, "Thank you for the memories, especially the presence of our grandmothers. You've still got it, girl, the magic!"

"Such happy times in those days, when our friendship took root. Now, it flowers."

Meeting the kids on the hillside, they finished the climb, hugging the children.

"Jennie, wake up! Wake up!" said Amadeus, sounding alarmed. In the darkest hours of night, he bent down and touched her face. "Wake up!"

His touch, gentle, his voice, urgent, Jennie said, "It's still night. You're dressed, why?" Rosie wasn't covering her feet.

"Sheriff called. A housefire and a lost child. I need to go."

"Who? Where?"

"I need something with Tim's scent for Rosie."

"Tim is lost?" Throwing back the quilt, she said, "My sweater. He hugged me today." Darting into the bathroom, she dressed and, with the sweater over her shoulder, met him at the truck, tying back her hair.

At the roadblock in the Intervale, they waited. An ambulance, lights flashing, siren screaming, turned onto Route 43 and sped toward Farmington. Allowed to pass through, Amadeus parked on Cummings Hill Road as close to the burning house as he could. Bright yellow flames lit the interior, escaped through burned-out doors and windows, shot out of the roof, and gray black smoke curled into the atmosphere.

Firefighters battled the enemy in sweltering heat, water and hoses their weapons.

With an emergency backpack on his shoulder, flashlight and sweater in hand, Amadeus held Jennie's hand, as they raced with Rosie toward the conflagration. Amid bright flashing lights, they weaved around emergency vehicles: state and local police, sheriffs' cars, fire engines, ladder trucks, pumpers and tankers from neighboring towns. He caught the attention of the fire chief and the deputy sheriff. "Anyone found the boy?"

The fire chief said, "No idea where he is. They found two adult bodies inside, severely burned. The man didn't survive. The woman was frantically calling for someone named Jennie."

"I'm Jennie! Where's Sharon?"

"In the ambulance that just left," said the fire chief. "You need to hurry."

"I'll take you," said the deputy sheriff.

After a glance at Amadeus, unspoken words between them, Jennie hurried with the deputy to his vehicle. Blue light flashing and siren blaring, they sped away.

Firemen dashed out of the blazing inferno. Everyone stood motionless, stared, felt the scorching heat, as walls of bright yellow-orange flames engulfed the house. The roof caved in, charred beams collapsed, walls crumbled, flames lit the night. Still the firefighters battled until the flames died down into small fires, into smoldering embers, and then died out. Only the solid stone fireplace and the stone foundation stood as monuments to the generations who had lived in that home built at the turn of the century.

Amadeus felt a hand on his shoulder. "Need some help?" said Tom.

He exhaled long and hard, and his voice cracked. "Let's go. Need to find Tim."

He turned to the chief. "Get someone to go door to door through the neighborhood. Tim knows people."

The chief nodded.

Amadeus held Rosie's collar, pressing the sweater against her nose. "Find Tim!" She sniffed the ground, circled around, caught the scent, and sped through the backyard into the woods behind the pile of burned timber and the mountain of cans and bottles. Tom and Amadeus followed closely behind Rosie, searching the woods for what seemed to be hours. Rosie lost the scent, circled and circled, sniffing, no scent. They moved forward slowly, picked up the pace, slowed down, backtracked, moved forward again, searched in and under trees, bushes, and undergrowth, everywhere a small boy could hide. They called out over and over again, "Tim! Timothy! Tim!" and then listened in the silence. Only silence. They shined their flashlights in an arc, a panoramic view until, finally, Amadeus accepted what he already knew: Tim did not run in this direction. Amadeus, Tom, and Rosie trudged back, fearing for Tim's whereabouts, his life.

At the hospital, Jennie stood over Sharon's severely burned body with Pastor Andrew by her side. She heard Sharon's painful whimpering. Jennie lightly touched the white sheet and spoke in a gentle, soothing voice, "Sharon, it's Jennie. You were calling for me. I'm here beside you." Sensing slight movement of Sharon's fingers and hearing unintelligible words, Jennie gently took Sharon's hand. "I'm here. Jennie is here, beside you."

The room was filled with the monotonous humming of machines, the quiet movement of nurses, the whispers between doctors and nurses. Jennie repeated over and over again, "I'm here. You called for me. Sharon, I'm Jennie."

Agitated, shallow breathing, Sharon's cries were weakening. Jennie offered comfort, hummed softly hymns of love, of Grace, of peace. Sharon, more agitated, struggled to breathe, to speak. Then, as though God Himself interceded and gave her strength, in a voice strong enough to be heard by all present, she clearly and slowly spoke her last words, the words of a loving mother. "Jennie, I give you my son. Love Tim. Take Tim home. Amadeus, love Tim."

"I promise," said Jennie, tears flowing, her voice cracking. "We will love Tim, raise him to be a strong, loving man. Tim will know that you loved him."

"Nobody else to love Tim," said Sharon, her voice whispery, "Only you."

Within seconds, Sharon's body relaxed, the machinery flat-lined, and the beeps were silent. Sharon journeyed home to God. The only sound was Jennie's soft cries and her whispered words, "Safe journey, my friend."

The fire engines and all but one sheriff's vehicle, the bright lights, blaring sirens, the flurry of activity—everything gone. Amadeus stood alone, unmoving in the yard under the moonlit sky filled with twinkling stars, holding tightly to a small toy he had found in the grass. It must have belonged to Tim. Tom gave him space, held Rosie, bent to his knees and prayed. Amadeus stared at the charred beams, the stone fireplace. Looking down at the burned rubble, he kicked a small object, picked it up, burned his fingers—knob and tube wiring. He threw it back. Ashes scattered in the wind, blowing past him, through him. The scent of smoke, of burned wood, filled his lungs. Tears flowed down his cheeks as he prayed for Jennie, Sharon, and Tim. Lifting his eyes to Heaven, he sought divine guidance, the still small voice, and prayed: *Lord, where is Tim. Show me the way.*

"Amadeus!"

Turning, he saw the deputy sheriff hurrying toward him. "I've canvased the neighborhood. No luck. No one has seen the boy."

Amadeus lifted his eyes, still praying: *Lord, guide my path to this lost child.*

In that moment and in that place, one light among billions glimmered brilliantly, illuminating the way. Inspired, his prayer answered, Amadeus said, "Follow the light." Racing down Cummings Hill Road with Rosie alongside and the men following, he dashed through the gates of the village cemetery. Darkness prevailed inside the graveyard. Halting, he scanned the darkness and held the sweater against Rosie's nose. "Find Tim!"

Quickly catching the scent, Rosie barked and, nose to the ground, weaved around a maze of stones over to the gnarled oak tree. The three men followed closely, and beheld a wondrous sight! Behind the headstone of Amadeus's children, the bright light shone on Tim hugging tightly to Rosie, her tail wagging. Only Amadeus saw the angel perched on the headstone. *Thank you, God, and Great-Aunt Mary.*

Falling to his knees, tears flowing, Amadeus opened his arms wide, and the sobbing Tim fell into them. Hugging Tim, he said, "With God's help, Rosie and I found you."

Popping up his head and still crying, Tim said, "I knew you'd come for me. I knew you'd come, but what took you so long?" He sniffled. "The light, the angel, they been shining on me the whole time I been here."

"Tim, how did you get here?"

"The fire. Mommy carried me." Sniffling, he said, "to the road, told me, run, hide, wait. Then she went back to get Quinn out."

"Quinn?" said Amadeus.

"Yeah, her boyfriend, not my daddy. I don't got one."

"Why all the way to the cemetery?"

His voice shaky, Tim said, "I was scared. I didn't know where to go, and Jennie, she told us, 'Good hiding places in cemeteries.'" Tim leaned on Amadeus's shoulder.

Rosie nudged the backpack. Rubbing her head, Amadeus said, "You're the best tracker." He pulled out treats and gave them to Tim, who offered them to Rosie with his small hand.

Still crying, Tim said, "Where's my mommy?"

"Jennie's with her." Carrying Tim out of the cemetery and down the road with proud Rosie alongside, her head held high, Amadeus and the two men praised God for keeping Tim safe and still held Jennie and Sharon in prayer.

Amadeus ran through the emergency room doors with Tim in his arms. "Where's Jennie?"

"In the chapel," said a nurse. "Let me take the child."

"Not until we see Jennie." Amadeus walked on. Opening the chapel door, he saw her in the front row near the altar, her head bowed in prayer. Pastor Andrew prayed next to her. He strode down the short aisle, bent down, and covered her hands with his own. "Honey."

Jennie raised her head, and he saw her tear-stained face. Throwing her arms around them, she hugged and kissed them, crying in sorrow and joy. "Thank you, God."

"Where's Mommy?" said Tim, tears flowing.

Jennie took Tim into her arms, sat in the pew, held him close, and with Amadeus's arm around her, said, "Oh, my sweetie. Your mommy loved you." She held back tears. "Your mommy saved you. She's a hero, but she's not here now."

"Where is she? Did she die?" said Tim.

"Yes, honey, she did," said Jennie, tearfully.

Holding his hand gently on Tim's shoulder, Pastor Andrew said, "Yes, son, Mommy is in Heaven with Jesus."

Lowering his head, Tim cried out, "I love Mommy," and dissolved into sobs.

Enveloping Tim, Jennie held him close to her heart, smoothed his hair, and hummed softly. Amadeus enfolded both of them in his strong, gentle arms and let them cry as his own tears fell. Pastor Andrew quietly slipped into the hall and waited nearby, his heart in sorrow.

When Tim had calmed a little, he sat up and asked, "Did Quinn die?"

Amadeus said, "Yes, little one. They couldn't get out in time. Your mommy was brave, and she got you out."

"They're gone and my house is gone. Where do I go?" Tim asked.

"With us. To our home. We love you. I promised your mommy," said Jennie. "Her last words were about you, about loving you, about giving you a home and love."

Once Tim had been examined by the doctor and released, Amadeus carried him, an exhausted, saddened boy whose legs and back ached, through the double glass doors into the waiting area. Pastor Andrew met them there, as did others.

The police officer stood, the woman, too, and the officer approached Amadeus. "We need to speak with you."

Holding Tim, protectively, Amadeus said, "What can I do for you?"

The woman, her identification in hand, stepped forward, and the police officer took Tim out of Amadeus's arms. "Come with me, little boy."

"Wait! No! You can't take him! I promised his mother!"

Amadeus enfolded Jennie in his arms. Pastor laid his hand on Amadeus's shoulder.

"You'll need to consult with a caseworker," said the social worker. "The office opens at nine."

Then they turned and left, carrying a frightened, heart-broken, screaming, kicking, sobbing little boy with his arms stretched out, reaching for Amadeus.

"A-ma-de-us! A-ma-de-us!"

PART TWO

THIRTEEN

Seven-year-old Jennie slumped down in the back seat of Dad's blue Ford station wagon, quiet, queasy, hands over her belly and eyes pinched tight. She didn't even want to look at Amadeus, who at nine was the big kid in the car. Route 17 in Roxbury was hilly, up and down, up and down, long, steep hills. Conifers and hardwoods, tall grass and wildflowers, undifferentiated shrubs lined both sides of the two-lane road, fused together—the effect of vertigo. Jennie tasted vomit rising in her throat as they barreled over hilltops, sudden braking, slowing, then accelerating downhill and up the next. The sun warmed the inside of the Ford—too warm, not enough fresh air—Grandma Sarah would only open her window halfway. Suddenly, Jennie clasped her hands over her mouth.

"Stop! Jennie's sick!" cried Amadeus.

"Again!" said Dad and looked at Charlotte. "How many times must we stop?"

"Now, Henry, she's carsick. Please stop!" said Mother.

Dad braked precipitously, pulled over onto the gravel, and set the emergency brake. Amadeus flung open the door, grabbed Jennie, tugged her out, and watched her stagger into the ditch, hands still over her mouth.

Jennie's mom climbed down next to her, held her braids back, and softly massaged her back, forming circles, in a futile attempt to soothe her. Eggs, bacon, and soured orange juice splattered the grass, shrubs, and flowers. Mother washed Jennie's face and hands with one of the wet washcloths she always carried in a plastic bag on long trips, as motion sickness was a common occurrence.

"That's right, honeybee. You're okay."

Cars and trucks sped by on the paved road, kicking up dust at the Ford, at Mother and the children. Not before she was ready, Mother and Amadeus helped Jennie back into the car, and Mom pressed a wet clean cloth in her hand.

"You feeling okay, sugar pop?" said Dad.

"Are we there yet?" said Jennie.

"She will be fine, when we arrive at your father's," said Mother.

"Few more hills," said Dad.

Jennie sighed, fell back into the middle seat, covered her face with the wet cloth, leaned her head against Amadeus's shoulder, and plopped her hand into Grandma's. Amadeus opened his book and read aloud to Jennie, as Grandma held her hand tightly.

At the top of the last hill, near the Byron town line, Dad turned left and gunned the engine up the steep drive to the tarpaper camp, the home of Stephen and Florence Deane.

Jennie and Amadeus followed Mother past the old plow and the grindstone where Grandpa used to sharpen his ax. On either side of the porch steps, gladioli in mixed colors bloomed in Grandma's flower garden. Clay pots filled with a mix of geraniums and petunias in bright hues, a neat stack of wood, and two old wooden rockers with peeling white paint sat on the porch, the chairs rocking gently in the breeze and a view of the mountains beyond. Oh, how Grandma Florence loved her flowers!

Inside, Grandma Florence gave Jennie a cup of hot tea and some salted crackers. Amadeus had tea and two molasses cookies, baked early that morning. Scents of cinnamon and ginger still lingered.

In the center of the room, the gathering place, sat the round table with mismatched high-backed chairs pushed underneath. On the yellow, gingham-checked tablecloth sat white china cups and saucers, salt and pepper shakers, and a sugar bowl.

Mother and Grandma Sarah sat with the children. Father and Grandma Florence joined them. At the back wall, as he always did, Grandpa Stephen relaxed on the old cot, covered with a gray wool blanket; a pillow lay there too. The adults conversed, laughing, even Dad smiled. The temperature was very warm inside the cabin, to keep the old people warm.

Henry said, "Dad, have a restful nap? Are you taking your medicine regularly?"

"Don't need you checking up on me! Is this a friendly visit?" asked Stephen.

Through the one window over the black, cast-iron sink, maple counter, and water pump, sunshine illumined a naturally darker room. In a cast-iron pot, chicken stew simmered on the dual-purpose woodstove that both cooked and heated the two-room camp. Biscuits were baking in the oven, the coffee pot perked, and the tea kettle whistled. In this crowded stifling room, a sick feeling rose in Jennie's stomach.

"Mom, may we go outside?" she said.

"Yes, get some fresh air; you'll feel better."

Jennie and Amadeus stepped politely outside, then giggled and ran like the deer on the windy hillside. A ladder leaned against an outside wall. Climbing onto the flat roof, they sat on the edge, legs dangling. From there, they had a sweet view of Ellis Pond, its wavy blue water sheltered by trees. Tumbledown and Little Jackson Mountains, carpeted in evergreens and hardwood, loomed before them. The sun warmed the roof and the sky encased their world of woods and mountains.

Amadeus said, "Read some more?"

"What's it about? Your big fat book? In the car it just sounded like words."

Amadeus flipped back to the first page. Reading aloud, Jennie grabbed his hand, held tightly, as they spiraled, spun, and whirled, ascending high above the camp roof. The book fell into the day lilies. Descending, they landed on a stone wall by an unfamiliar paved road, a forest, and a lake, mountains in the distance. Traffic flowed past, up and down the winding steep hill: a blue roadster, a Coca Cola delivery truck, and a farm truck with side rails, loaded with hay.

"Jennie, the cars and trucks, they're old, from way past, like when our parents were kids!" said Amadeus. "What happened?"

"I don't know. Where are we? It's never been like this before."

"Usually you just wander. Look, there's a sign."

He grasped her hand and she said, "You always find me." They rushed to a plaque secured to a big rock and a newly painted sign beside it.

"Height of Land," she read.

He read the sign, "Rangeley, Maine. Moose-look-me-gun-tic Lake."

Wide-eyed, they repeated, "Mooselookmeguntic Lake" and laughed.

"Jennie, the lake, its way down there!" A logging truck, fully loaded, brakes grinding, headed down the hill. A green Chevrolet pickup followed.

Marching down the grassy slope and waving batons, they led the parade. Reeds, percussion, and brass instruments sounded the rhythm in the syllables—Moose-look-me-gun-tic Lake. Halfway down, the parade forgotten, the band silenced, they raced past sparse evergreens, climbed on rocks, jumped off, and raced past lupine, buttercups, and dandelions. As they descended, the conifers and hardwoods grew denser, concealing the lake from their view.

Jennie collapsed in tall grass, tired, breathless. Amadeus rested beside her, catching his breath. "Almost there, just through those trees," he said. Lying still, they gazed at snow-white puffy clouds, like giant cotton balls against an azure sky.

"What's that tree called, the one over there?" she said.

Amadeus pulled off a twig and a cone, giving them to her. "Tamarack."

"Is it like pine?"

"A conifer, except see how the needles grow in clusters, and in autumn they turn yellow. Winged seeds fly off them."

"Pine cones are long, and these are small," she said.

"You ready to hike through the trees?"

Stepping into the thick woods, Jennie felt the spiraling, the vertiginous feeling. She grabbed onto him, and he clung to her. They gyrated, swirled, shot up above the trees, over water, and beyond, descending on a ledge in the Longfellow Range of the White Mountains. Below, the rushing river, white water, flowed between ledges, past densely populated maple, pine, and spruce. Trout swam upstream. On a hillside with far fewer trees and many more stumps, Jennie saw a woman standing among the cut logs, viewing the river. "Look, down there," she said.

"I see her," he said. "Come on."

Blazing their own trail, pushing aside low branches, and climbing over fallen logs, they emerged on the hillside. Jennie darted toward the lady and stopped in her tracks. A man, his forehead sweaty, his face reddening, approached the lady. "Truck's loaded! I've been waiting for fifteen minutes! Told you not to walk way down here!" He inhaled, exhaled slowly, then said kindly, "Dinner date at the Chicken Coop?" Holding the woman's hand, he helped her over the logs, and they strolled up the hill.

Jennie gasped, "That's Mom and Dad!" She raced behind them, tugging Amadeus along. Popping out from the trees, they stopped at the side of the logging road. Mom and Dad were seated in the truck, loaded with logs: a half-ton green Ford with a V-8 engine and siderails. Starting the engine, Dad pushed heavily on the clutch, shifted gears, and drove slowly down the dirt road toward Route 17, avoiding potholes and large rocks, with a wood delivery for Oxford Paper Company.

"Hey, Jennie, let's explore. I mean, since we're already here."

"Mom and Dad didn't even see me," she said, teary-eyed.

"Well, do they see?"

"No, Grandma Sarah said they don't." She wiped her tears and followed.

"Go slowly, look carefully. We might discover artifacts," he said.

"What are artifacts?"

"Old things that teach us history."

Her Amadeus sure loved the woods!

Traipsing back into the trees, they climbed over logs, some rotting, moved aside brush, twigs, and fallen limbs. Amadeus jumped off a log, turned his ankle, and dropped to his knees. "I found something," he said. Together, they dug with sticks and hands, tugging on a partially buried length of heavy rusted chain. "Probably used to pull logs along the ground."

"Horses did that job," she said.

They trudged farther down the path, and she stumbled. Digging again under old, dry, crumbled leaves, twigs, and dirt, they found a rusty ax blade. "An artifact," he said. "Woodsman cut trees with axes and two-man saws."

"Like my grandpa," she said.

Wandering off the path into a grove of towering trees, they happened upon a monumental stone fireplace and chimney, perfectly intact. Sunlight shimmered on the stones.

"Wow!" they said, dashing over to investigate. Jennie gazed at the sparkling, wavy light, and Amadeus examined the fireplace, searching for signs of a camp. There were no old boards, no rusty nails, roofing shingles, or a rock foundation; only the fireplace, standing tall and solid. "There was a camp here, but it's gone," he said.

"Maybe a house," she said.

"I think a logging camp. How can the fireplace still stand?"

Jennie shrugged her shoulders. "Well, stone walls are solid for a long time; even after they crumble, we walk on them."

"Yeah, you're right. What a discovery!"

Rabbits hopped out from the piney undergrowth. Birds sang in the trees. Squirrels and chipmunks scurried across the ground.

Jennie looked around and said, "Where's the path?"

Amadeus surveyed the area and peered up at the sun. "This way."

"But that's not the path. I think we're lost."

"Not lost. The path is far back. This way is shorter to the road."

Was it really shorter, the way to the road? She didn't care. Exploring with Amadeus was always fun! Jennie followed her best friend, weaving around trees, through bushes, and ducking under branches. Halting, he scanned the woods and listened for nature's sounds. Were they lost?

"Are we lost?" she said, a tear running down her cheek.

"Quiet," he said, listening. "Not lost, I hear the river. That way!"

Jennie didn't hear water sounds, but she plodded along behind, certain he could find the way. Soon they were out of the woods and back on the hillside.

Feeling again that same dizziness, that circling, she took hold of Amadeus. Immediately, they spiraled, twisted, ascended above the woods, and descended, landing with a bump back on the roof above Grandpa's camp. On Route 17, a line of cars and trucks moved along like crawling ants. Beyond, Ellis Pond, Tumbledown, and Little Jackson Mountains. Her best friend always knew the way home.

"Jennie! Amadeus! Come inside!" called Mom from the grindstone.

"Coming, Mom," her voice echoed.

Climbing down the ladder, they rushed over to the porch. Mother was there, waiting. "Oh, my, you, two, are a mess!" Brushing off her daughter and Amadeus, too, and pulling twigs out of their hair, she said, "It's a mystery to me how you two get so dirty, just sitting and reading."

"Sorry, Mrs. Deane," said Amadeus, "but dirt is just the world's way."

"No matter, whatever you were doing, you had fun." Mother laughed—she always found Amadeus amusing—and picked up his book out of the day lilies. "Well, dinner's ready, come along. Stop in the privy and wash those hands and faces. Use soap and water. You, too, Amadeus, world's way or no!"

Gathered at the table, Grandma Florence said grace. Chicken stew and hot biscuits with butter and honey were offered. Florence baked the best biscuits, topped only by her molasses cookies.

Desperately hungry, Jennie ate and ate. Wiggling in the chair and bored by noisy adult voices, she whispered to Amadeus, "I still don't know where we went."

"We'll figure it out."

During a lull in the conversation, Jennie asked, "Grandpa, are you coming outside with us? Can we ride the horses?"

"I wondered if you were going to ask," said Dad, chuckling.

"Sure, you can ride. I mean, if you're feeling okay," said Grandpa.

Up and out of their chairs, the kids were ready to ride! "Dad, can we go now?"

Dad nodded and the friends darted outside, but turned and ran back through the door, squeezing past Dad and Grandpa to thank Grandma for dinner. "In the bedroom, there's something for each of you on the bookcase," she said.

In her grandparents' bedroom, a cross-breeze from windows on both front and back walls cooled the room. There was no evidence of dust in the sunlight. A hand-sewn quilt—a flower garden—covered an iron bedstead. A dresser, a mirror, a vintage Singer sewing machine, and a chair stood on opposite walls. Jennie and Amadeus headed straight for the bookcase with glass doors, filled with

Grandma's treasured old tomes. On top lay an opus for each of them—*Pollyanna* and *The Call of the Wild*. Inside the covers, Grandma's script: *Florence Deane*.

"Grandma, these are your books," said Jennie.

"Don't you want to keep them?" said Amadeus.

"It's about time I shared, so enjoy them," said Grandma.

"Thank you, I'll keep it forever," said Jennie, hugging her.

"Thank you, Mrs. Deane, I've wanted to read this story, and I'll keep mine too."

"Now you go on, time to ride," said Grandma.

Books abandoned on the table, they hurried outside. Flying past Grandpa and Dad to the pasture, they climbed the rail fence and called to Polly and Theo. The Belgian draft horses, who in past years had pulled plows, heavily loaded wagons, and logs out of the woods, had aged, and were now weaker, slower, content inside the rail fence.

Walking slowly through the small barn, Dad and Grandpa took a moment to remember. Old rusty farm tools, a scythe, an ax, and a two-man saw hung from nails on an inside wall, surrounding two framed photographs—a testimony to a man who had worked hard all his life, farming and logging.

In the pasture, Grandpa gave the kids each an apple and a carrot. "They'll come now." While the horses partook of the treats, Grandpa and Dad rubbed their heads and necks, spoke softly, and held them near the fence. Climbing over it, Amadeus and Jennie balanced on a rail near the top and leaned in, hoisting themselves up on the great beasts. Swinging their legs over, they rode bareback. Jennie wrapped her arms around Polly's huge neck, her head resting on the mane, and Amadeus sat up straight holding onto Theo's. The Belgians walked slowly, lazily, stopping frequently to consume blades of tall grass and wildflowers.

Amadeus said, "Jennie, sit up straight like me and hold the mane."

"Think I don't know how to ride," said Jennie, kicking gently at Polly's sides.

Suddenly spry, the old horse trotted ahead. Theo soon caught up, and they trotted around the pasture fence. The kids bounced up and down, held on, and kept their balance, laughing, as did Grandpa and Dad, who recalled other children in bygone days riding the good-natured Belgians.

Grandmothers Florence and Sarah, along with Jennie's mother, Charlotte, strolled around outside admiring the gardens full of blooms: bright colors by the porch, rose bushes behind the camp, a variety of wildflowers inside a rock border near the barn. Noticing the Belgians trotting and the kids bouncing, they too, laughed. Mother ambled over, leaned on the fence, and watched the children fondly. The two grandmothers, returning to the porch rockers, chatted among the flowers.

In sun and breezes, enveloped by mountains, woods, and sky, the Belgians still trotted, and the kids still bounced, joy on their faces and two sets of eyes, one brown and one blue, danced. Too soon, the old Belgians grew weary, trotting turned to dawdling with numerous stops to consume more grass and flowers.

Dad said, "Jennie, Amadeus, time to let the horses rest."

"Okay," they said in quiet voices, chins tilting downward.

Dad and Grandpa held the horses by the fence. Amadeus swung his leg over and slid to the ground. Jennie swung hers over and hung there, clutching tightly to Polly, her legs swinging. "Help, it's too far down!"

"Same distance as up," said Dad, chuckling. He stepped closer to her, still rubbing the horse's head. Polly moved away from the fence.

"I can get her down," said Amadeus. "It's just like getting her out of a tree."

The two men chuckled, and Mother laughed.

Amadeus held tightly to Jennie. "Okay, let go, but don't knock me over."

"Okay, I won't." She slid down, feet on the ground, both kids still upright.

Climbing onto a fence rail, she said, "That was fun!"

Amadeus agreed, "Lots of fun!"

"I haven't seen those horses trot like that in a long time," said Grandfather.

"Come on, you two," Dad said. "Let's do the barn chores."

Dad, Jennie, and Amadeus raked and shoveled out the stalls, filling the wheelbarrow, while Grandfather sat in the old wooden chair by the barn door, resting to catch his breath. Mother sat on the old bench, talking with him. Jennie noticed that his heart was not as strong as it once was. Grandpa had aged over the years, like the Belgians.

Jennie plugged her nose and said, "Polly and Theo sure poop a lot!"

Grandfather and Dad chuckled. Dad said, "Fertilizer."

"It's all cleaned up now," said Amadeus.

The kids pushed the wheelbarrow out to the manure pile and dumped it.

"Henry, Son, your little girl is a delight, such spunk, and those eyes like your mother's, my Jennie's eyes," said Grandfather. "So, enjoy time with her now. She'll be grown and on her own, before you're ready to let her go. That's the way with kids."

"Like you enjoyed time with me?" said Dad.

"You don't need to bring that up," said Grandfather sharply.

The kids pushed the empty wheelbarrow back into the barn. The squeaky wheel bounced over the rough floorboards.

"Stalls look good," said Grandpa. "How are you at pitching hay?"

"We can do it!" said Jennie.

Amadeus noticed the wall of tools and two framed photographs. Hurrying over for a closer look, he said, "Jennie, come here."

"What is it?" asked Jennie, standing next to him.

"The truck, it's loaded with wood."

Dad set aside the pitchfork and took down the pictures. Giving them each one, he said, "That was my truck. It's loaded with rock maple."

"Dad, is that a river and Mom?" asked Jennie.

"It's the Swift River, up by Height of Land. Grandpa and I logged there, cutting spruce, maple, and pine."

"Wow, did you live in the woods?" asked Amadeus.

Mom said, "Near Byron. A house with a woodstove for heating and cooking, a privy, and a well pump."

Dad hung the photographs back on the wall. "Now let's pitch hay."

Amadeus said, "Did you saw with that two-man saw?"

Grandpa said, "To fell the trees. Farm tools there too."

The kids and Dad climbed onto the bales and pitched hay into the stalls. While Dad filled the feeding troughs, the children fetched water from the well. Amadeus lowered the wooden bucket, turned the handle, drew water, and poured it into the pail. Next time, it was Jennie's turn. Several more trips back and forth, racing down the steep slope and trudging up with full pails, water sloshing, and the galvanized tubs were filled with fresh cool water.

Jennie and Amadeus plopped down next to Mother on the wooden bench. Barn swallows flew around. Theo and Polly stomped into the stalls, chewed their feed, and drank from the tubs. Their tails swatted flies, and mice scurried.

Dad said, "Jennie, Amadeus, it's time to head home. Now hug Grandpa and find Grandma."

Jennie said, "Can we say goodbye to Theo and Polly?"

Dad and Grandpa led the kids into the stalls. Stroking the horses' backsides, Dad said, "Always be sure the horse knows you're there." The two friends petted the horses and smoothed their manes, and the Belgians whinnied.

Everyone gathered near the Ford. Mother carried the books. Grandma Florence gave the kids a paper bag of cookies and Grandpa Stephen gave each a penny. "Buy yourselves some penny candy with that," he said. Hugs shared all around. Then, with everyone settled in the car, Dad drove down the steep drive and turned right onto Route 17.

Jennie's heart was happy that day: her father had smiled, not upset with her, not even once; molasses cookies and two books from Grandma; shiny new pennies from Grandpa; trotting on the Belgians; a secret shared. And best of all—her two best friends she could ever hope to have in all the world sat on each side of her in the backseat, Grandma Sarah and Amadeus.

FOURTEEN

Monday morning, just hours after the past night's fire, Amadeus and Jennie sat in the two straight chairs across from the caseworker's desk at social services. The office was small and clean with sterile white walls and one window. A desk, filing cabinet, and three chairs filled the room. The caseworker's degree and certifications hung on the wall.

Mrs. Greene rushed through the office door, set a large coffee on her desk, and dropped her shoulder bag behind it—folders spilling out. Sitting in the chair and scanning several messages, she said, "Well, Mr. and Mrs. Amadeus, you didn't need an appointment with me. Pick up an application at the front desk."

Amadeus uncrossed his legs and sat up straight. "Stuart, my name is *Amadeus Stuart*—s-t-u-a-r-t—the old spelling of Scottish kings."

"Oh, Amadeus," said Jennie, turning to Mrs. Greene, "I have the same problem with my name *Deane*. Most people leave off the *e*, but it's my family name, the old English spelling with an *e*. You must see your name misspelled, without the *e*."

"Not that I recall."

"Mrs. Greene," said Amadeus. "Timothy Bailey was taken into your care after last night's house fire—fully justified—in Temple. Jennie and I want to be his foster parents, leading to adoption. And for his good, we want that to happen now."

"Mr. Stuart, do you have a connection with Timothy's family?"

Amadeus cleared his throat to speak.

Suddenly, Mrs. Greene seemed to have had second thoughts. She jerked her chair back. "No! No! No!" A breath. "You live way out in the woods with your new girlfriend, correct? No! I would not place any child in that environment."

Interrupted by the phone ringing, Mrs. Greene answered it, sighed, and said, "I'll be only a few minutes." To Amadeus and Jennie, she said, "Please excuse me, I have a meeting."

"Mrs. Greene, we waited over an hour for a scheduled meeting with you," said Amadeus, his voice low and calm. "We were on time. You were late. Our business is not finished." He held Jennie's hand. "And furthermore, you will address Ms. Deane respectfully. She is also a professional. And she's of the community, with deep roots, a very old friend, and now my life partner." He continued politely, "Let's begin again, please."

Mrs. Greene dialed the receptionist and explained the situation. To Jennie, she said, "Ms. Deane, is it? All right. I apologize for my rude remark."

"Apology accepted," said Jennie.

"Please tell me what can you offer Timothy? Why should I consider you? That's all I'm saying. You'd be an unconventional choice, and here we are proudly conventional."

Jennie folded her hands over her lap and spoke confidently. "I am a certified special education teacher, have taught for almost twenty years, and I'm qualified for therapeutic foster care. Tim has special needs—academic, literacy, and definitely medical, leg length discrepancy. Walking is painful for him. At present, he's grieving his mother's sudden death. Everything was lost in that fire: his only parent, his home, and his belongings. Nothing left. His precious heart is broken. He needs parents with time to devote to him, and we have the time."

The caseworker looked dumbfounded.

"Mrs. Greene, are you unaware of Tim's needs?" asked Jennie.

"I've just this morning received his file. I heard he put up quite a fuss."

Amadeus said, "I'll bet he did. He trusts and feels safe with us, as he does with Pastor Andrew and Jill Griffin."

"Visit with him. You'll see what I'm talking about," said Jennie. "We can offer Tim love, home, time, and understanding. We have no children. We can give him a family and a life within his own community, among existing friends. Why take that away, too?"

Amadeus said, "We know Tim through scouting, church, and friends. Jennie promised his dying mother that we would love and raise Tim; it was her last request." A breath. "Tim would choose to live with us. His mother did choose us."

"Yes, his mother," Mrs. Greene said, pleasantly. "So sad, losing her life and leaving a son. It won't be easy. You have little time and no guarantee."

"Tell us what to do and we'll get it done," said Amadeus.

"Once I receive the applications and references, I'll do the background check. If that comes back positive, I'll schedule a home visit. However, the process will not be completed in time for Timothy."

Jennie uncrossed her legs, back straight. "Why not in time for Tim?"

"He's in a crisis center. Within the week, he'll be moved to a home. There are approved families, waiting for children." Mrs. Greene pushed back her chair and picked up a notepad, file, and a pen. "I am very late for another meeting. Please excuse me."

"Please, wait, Mrs. Greene," said Jennie. "Amadeus found Tim last night and brought him to the hospital. I am the one who told Tim of his mother's death. He needs to be with familiar people who knew his mother, know him, and understand his loss and grief. Healing takes time and love."

"Well," sighed Mrs. Greene, "ask the receptionist for an emergency appeal. That and the home inspection would be your only chance. Now I really must go."

"Thank you," said Jennie.

At the front desk, phone lines were ringing, and the receptionist juggled calls. Jennie and Amadeus waited patiently, but nervously.

The child-friendly waiting area was furnished with tables and chairs in bright primary colors, buckets of toys, coloring books, and storybooks. Jennie spied an old college friend, a professional colleague and now director of social services, building block towers with the children. She stepped over to greet her. "Ellen Baker!"

"Jennie! It's been ages since we've seen each other," said Ellen.

While sharing a short personal conversation between friends, Jennie introduced Amadeus, and they explained the purpose of their visit.

"Mrs. Greene is cautious about placement," said Ellen. "Come with me."

In the conference room, Jennie and Amadeus sat at the polished table. She crossed her arms and tapped her foot. Bouncing his knee, he checked his watch multiple times. A spider plant and manuals sat on a bookcase. Large windows allowed for natural light. Finally, Mrs. Greene entered. "Okay, here's the paperwork. This room is available for your privacy, if you wish to complete the forms now."

"Definitely," said Amadeus.

"Home inspection, Monday one o'clock. I'm squeezing lunch hour to pull it off. You'll get one chance, though it's probably a waste of your time." She gave them a copy of the regulations and a long list of requirements, and turned to make a hasty retreat.

"It's our time. We'll decide how to waste it," said Amadeus in a monotone.

"Thank you," Jennie said, smiling.

Mrs. Greene nodded, turned, and left the room. They completed the forms, gave them to Ellen, and left, stopping at the supermarket. Jennie silently remembered Sharon, an employee, and prayed for Tim, lost, alone, and frightened. "I'd like to have had time to be Sharon's friend."

"She saw a friend in you. She entrusted you with her son," said Amadeus.

"Us. She entrusted *us*."

After collecting several empty cardboard boxes, they stopped at the drive-thru for lunch and headed home. Jennie read the requirements for children in state care.

"Oh, sweetie, please be more careful when speaking to Mrs. Greene. She already doesn't approve of us and our goal is to give Tim a home."

"I was being funny. You smiled," he said, holding her hand.

"I appreciate your humor. She doesn't."

"Okay, I'll be more careful."

Amadeus sped up Voter Hill, engine roaring all the way, passing fields, stone walls, and an old, barbed wire fence before he spotted Alice's husband, Tom, on the hill mowing his lawn. Tom Murphy was Amadeus's longtime best friend, a log home builder with an experienced crew. Parking in the drive next to Jennie's Jeep, they trekked downhill to the front yard.

Tom shut off the mower, removed his glasses, cleaned them on his sweaty shirt, and wiped his brow. "What's the hurry, tree lover?"

Jennie said, "Alice and Annie home?"

Tom said, "At Pastor's. Hearts are broken, losing Tim."

Amadeus said, "You got time this week to help me fix up the cabin?"

Tom said, "I can push the schedule, you know that. Why this week?"

"Home inspection next Monday. Hope to bring Tim home."

"Meet you at the cabin after mowing. I'll make some calls, free up some crew. No special orders though. Forget the Jacuzzi and steam room."

Up at the house, Jennie collected her belongings; the ancestry and memorabilia were stacked in the corner of the bedroom. They packed boxes and the shopping bag in the Jeep on top of the slab of marble that once belonged to her great-grandparents. For years it had sat in her kitchen next to the old creaking rocker by the potbelly stove. She would store these things in the Jeep while fixing up the cabin. At home they again reviewed the inspection requirements and made a list.

In the library, they packed up the books displayed on the tall bookcases and the small box containing two framed photographs of his children. He thumbed through the pages of his old Bible and noticed a white envelope addressed to him still tucked inside. A corner of folded paper slipped out of a wood projects manual. Unfolding it, he glanced at the old forgotten plans, refolded it, and slipped it into his pocket.

Amadeus carried the taped boxes to the storage shed. Then Jennie folded the old musty bedding, and he loaded it, along with the worn mattress, box spring, old bookcases, pole lamp, and small stand into the truck bed. They kept the leather chair and the bedstead.

Jennie picked up her quilted bags and a school bag and noticed a white envelope, addressed simply Jennie. How did that get in here? No time to read. She stuffed it back into the bag and stored them in her Jeep.

Next, they cleaned out the smaller room, loading the child-size bed onto the truck and moving the grease bucket, chain, and work tools into a shed. He picked up an old mitt with a baseball tucked inside; he had played catch with his son, Matthew. Jennie swept the floors, cobwebs too. In the kitchen they emptied cupboards and drawers, saving only Jennie's ceramic teapot, the mason jars of tea and one of honey.

Tom walked into the cabin, calling out, "Hey, Amadeus." Jennie and Alice chatted in the yard, while Annie threw Rosie's chewed frisbee, and the dog chased it. Laughter and barking filled the air.

On the kitchen table, Amadeus laid out yellowed drawings of his renovation plan from twenty years before, the pencil markings smudged and creased folds cemented. Tom leaned in, reviewed the familiar designs, all within the existing foundation: a new and expanded kitchen, bathroom, and laundry; closets; improvements in other rooms; and construction of the tower, whose concrete slab had been poured years ago before he lost his family. The tower would have a dining room on the main floor and a library on the second floor with a south wall of windows. The library would be converted to a master bedroom with French doors facing east, and a pantry cupboard built on the long kitchen wall.

Laying his hand on Amadeus's shoulder, Tom said, "Welcome back, my friend. You've got Jennie to share your life and a boy to love."

"Jennie, for sure. Tim, we're hoping and praying."

Outside Tom and Amadeus checked the old concrete, covered with a tarp and a woodpile. They removed several sticks and found the slab still in perfect condition.

Tom inspected the structure of the cabin. Old rock foundation, still solid. Shingles old, some broken—new metal roofing on the cabin and detached garage. Stone chimney, straight and solid. Add new flashing. He examined the windows and doors.

"I got all the windows in the storage shed, just missing French doors."

"Got several sets, real high-end," said Tom. "I got some beautiful long, narrow windows. They'd look real nice flanking the fireplace and a woodstove. You'll need one in the tower."

"Add it to the estimate," said Amadeus.

"My crew chief and a few guys are on their way over here right now."

"Are you sure this is doable in less than a week?"

"My guys work fast; they know what they're doing. Be done in a few days," said Tom.

"Well, then, let's build a home for Jennie and Tim."

After relocating the woodpile to a spot between the sheds, with everyone's help, Amadeus left his cabin in Tom's capable hands. With Jennie and Rosie, he rushed into town.

First, they stopped at the dump, and next shared a quick dinner at the truck stop. Then they went shopping for two mugs, an electric teapot, a picture frame, smoke detectors, and sundries. At the local appliance store, they purchased floor models, straight into the truck, no boxes—refrigerator, upright freezer, stove, washer, and dryer—and a kitchen fire extinguisher. Finally, at the furniture store they purchased mattresses and box springs, a one day sale, buy one set and get one free. They chose two sets—a more restful night's sleep than a few quilts piled on the wood floor—and scheduled delivery on Thursday. Invoices would be mailed.

Arriving home, they were met by the Murphy family waiting on the porch swing. The crew had left. Tom helped unload the new appliances, lined them up in the drive and tossed moving blankets over them. He shook his head, turned to Amadeus, laughed, and said, "Meet me at the barn at five a.m. I've got milled logs, lumber, pre-built kitchen cupboards, and a pretty damn nice countertop from that big lake house that fell through. Most anything else we'll need is left over from other projects. You can help me with the inventory write-off!!"

"Don't forget the estimate."

"I'll get you one. Good night."

In the yard sat the old stove and refrigerator, cupboards and countertop, tiny table and chairs. Old exterior logs lay on the ground. Huge tarps covered the open space, secured in place with staples and duct tape.

On the front porch swing, they sipped hot herbal tea, Rosie asleep at their feet. Just two nights ago, they had danced in the moonlight and loved each other, knowing their hearts and lives belonged together.

"There is something laid upon your heart," he said, holding her close. "When you're ready, I'll listen and love you through it."

Her late husband came to mind. "Not now," she said. "Let's think about Tim and all we need to do." Sharon had told her there was no one to love Tim but them.

"If you decide to tell only God, that's okay too," he said.

"God already knows all," she said.

He held her close as they rocked on the swing under the night sky.

Fifteen

Precisely at six thirty Tuesday morning, trucks lined the dirt road. The Beast—loaded with a refurbished white claw-foot tub, lavatory fixtures, and a cast-iron woodstove from Tom's inventory—was parked under the maple. Tom's flatbed and his pickup—both loaded—sat in the tall grass. Rosie wandered around the yard, barking friendly greetings.

Cases of bottled water—some in ice buckets—hot coffee, and donuts were stacked on the front porch, with more to come each morning. Lunches would be delivered from the supermarket's deli and bakery and from local eateries.

Pre-stained, milled, kiln-dried, twelve-inch logs and lumber were piled near the concrete slab. Saws, drills, other tools, and supplies sat in the front yard. And so began construction of the tower, a two-day project. Building the subfloor and the elevated log stack on the concrete slab, the crew then raised and insulated log walls, two stories high, with dovetailed corner notches. They framed in cutouts for windows and doors. After securing studs in place for the interior walls with open arched doorways from the kitchen and mudroom into the dining room, they laid the second story subfloor and installed windows on the south wall.

Late in the afternoon, the crane would arrive and set engineered roof trusses in place. Roofers would secure them, drill plywood to the trusses, and lay gray metal roofing. By day's end, the tower would be closed in, and the roof—a high-pitched square-based pyramid—would resemble a turret on a medieval castle.

Over the next three days, Sadie Jackson, a finish carpenter on Tom's crew, built closets in the bedrooms and a linen closet in the hall, all fine wooden built-ins with naturally stained bifold wood doors and glass knobs. She'd also construct the Shaker style pantry cupboard in the kitchen along with benches and hooks in the mudroom.

Sadie toted her tools and supplies into the library, where she found three women assessing the iron bedstead. "You're not thinking about saving that old bed, are you?"

Alice laughed. "Jennie's considering it."

Jill smiled and said, "You're welcome to have Tim's bed."

A wire brush in hand, Jennie said, "Thanks, but it's only rust. Okay, mostly rust."

Entering with his son, Jack examined the bedstead. Towering over Phillip, his hands clamped on the boy's shoulders, he ordered, "Make restitution. Clean it up for Tim."

Phillip cringed, "Yes, Sir, spit shine and polish."

Jennie smiled at Phillip. "Thank you."

Phillip said, shyly, "It's not so hard." Disassembling the frame Father and son carried it outside to a grassy spot, where Rosie napped. Phillip de-rusted and cleaned, with materials from his dad's truck. Rusty particles sparkled in grass.

Hal, the crew chief, Amadeus, Pastor Andrew, and Jack installed new windows and doors on the main floor: French doors on the east wall of the library (soon to be the master bedroom); tall, narrow windows in the living and dining rooms, flanking the fireplace and the new woodstove; and six-pane windows facing the front porch. Standard size replacements, stored in Amadeus's shed, were installed throughout, and last, insulated exit doors on the west and north walls.

Tom caught up with the women in the library helping Sadie, and said, "Jennie, how quickly can you choose paint?"

"We haven't even talked about colors yet!"

"Well, painting begins tomorrow. Buy primer, too, please." Turning back down the hall, Tom joined the volunteers installing windows.

Alice laughed. "Come on, you two. I'm driving," she said. "We have our assignment."

Arriving at the hardware store, which was swamped with serious shoppers and hobnobbers, the women wove through the crowd to the paint section. Jill and

Jennie chose paint chips in nature's hues, while Alice located Tom's Uncle Willy. He dominated the counter area—his beer belly occupying most of the work space—and took over the paint mixers, apologizing in his booming but friendly tone for the delay while other frustrated customers waited in line. An employee stacked the cans on a cart and loaded them in Tom's pickup. Uncle Willy would send Tom the invoice.

Alice stopped at the dairy bar and Jennie treated her friends to guilt-free indulgence—two scoops on cones. Then they headed to Temple.

Jill said, "Alice was telling about her new business plan."

"Well, share," said Jennie.

"We're opening a gallery in the barn for independent artisans to sell their wares."

"That's exciting!" said Jennie.

Back at the cabin, the ladies worked alongside the others until sunset. Tom's pickup was unloaded and all left. The first day's work of a three-day project was completed. Quiet now, Jennie stood outside, viewing the colossal tower. Amadeus held her hand and walked with her to Tim's bedroom. The last rays of sunlight beamed through the west window and danced on the polished gold-tone, antique iron bedstead. Jennie brushed her hand across the smooth footboard. "Like sun on glass."

Clomp. Stomp. Scraping shovels. Cloudbursts. Old broken shingles, roofing nails, and damp sheathing board littered the tall grass around the cabin's old section and detached garage. Roofers laid new plywood, screwed into place gray metal roofing, and installed new flashing around the stone chimney—not all the old would go.

The electrician installed new outlets and switches, overhead lighting with ceiling fans in the tower's library and dining room, and two ceiling lights with glass globes in the kitchen. The electrical box certified, she handed Tom the invoice. The inspector was right behind—her dad!

In the tower, carpenters insulated and installed pre-stained tongue-and-groove pine ceilings and laid new flooring of curly maple. After stacking quarter logs on the inside elevated log stack and stone on the outside, they built interior beadboard walls.

Hal and a volunteer built a small porch outside the French doors.

Giving the cabin's old section a fresh new look, Amadeus, Pastor Andrew, Tom, and Jack laid and insulated a plywood attic floor. They installed ceilings of beadboard and assembled an attic access with a pull-down ladder in the hall-way. Once the new ceilings were whitewashed, Alice, Jill, and Jennie primed and painted the interior bedroom walls.

The primer dry, Jennie rolled blue paint — the shade of a frosty morning — in their east bedroom. She stared out the elegant French doors, the paint roller hanging down at her side. A fog surrounded an angel: she was very thin and frail, and her long stringy white hair hung down. Her dress of pure white waved in the breeze. Jennie opened the doors and welcomed Great-Aunt Mary. "Are you here to visit or to help?"

Wafting her way inside, Mary held her head high, and her pointed, bony chin stuck out prominently. "My help, dear one," she said, her voice a warbling whisper, "is not the help of your world." She scowled and shook her long, thin finger toward the floor, as Jennie looked down, dripping paint. "My dear, you must go. Oh, dear! Oh, dear! Oh, where is it?" Mary tapped her forehead with one curled forefinger. "Iisal…Iisalo Road. That's the place. Today. Now, mind if I take a look?"

"Please do, but why? Can't it wait?"

"Today, my dear." As Mary's cloud glided into the hallway, Jennie rolled paint.

Later, Amadeus and Jennie peeked into the bedrooms, admiring the colors: grayish-blue, like a gentle rain, in Tim's bedroom; lavender, a reminder of Grandma Sarah's scent, in the next room; in the smaller bedroom, yellow, like moonlight. And Jennie shared Mary's visit and her self-guided tour.

"Seriously." He laughed. "Could the spirits use the front door?"

While Amadeus painted the beadboard walls in the tower's main floor, dining room and mudroom a fern green, with Phillip's help, and volunteers removed bathroom fixtures, the three women left in Tom's pickup.

"Jennie, where do you need to go on Iisalo?" asked Jill.

"Oh, I'll know when I see it," replied Jennie.

Few homes along that stretch. Evergreens, bushes, and wild daisies lined the roadsides. Jennie scanned both sides. Where was she supposed to go? Why? Then, she saw the angel in a mist. Aunt Mary. "Turn left now. Looks like a yard sale."

Alice pulled into the drive at a small white farmhouse. Furniture was scattered around the front yard and firewood stacked on the porch. The barn roof was caving in. A rusted antique tractor sat in the field. An old leather chair, the match to Amadeus's, caught Jennie's eye. This could be a money-saver! Hurrying over, she examined it closely. An elderly gentleman approached. "That's real leather. Say a hundred?"

"Real, but old and faded. How about fifty?"

"Deal," he said.

Scouring through other pieces, Jennie noticed a gray sofa. Pulling up the three cushions and scrutinizing the fabric, she found no stains, little wear, and stitching like new. She sat down on firm springs, no sagging, comfortable, a high back, and solid arms. Probably priced too high. Alice and Jill joined her there. "How much for the sofa?" said Jennie.

"Seventy-five is what I'm askin' and seventy-five's what I'm takin'."

"Are you sure? It's worth more."

"Take it," whispered Alice, elbowing her.

"Well, I really could use a sofa. So I'll take the chair and the sofa." Jennie reached into her pocket and then her other pockets. "Oh, no," she sighed. "I forgot my wallet." Thinking for a moment, she said, "Would you trust me? I live not far from here."

"Well…" said the old man, drawing out the *well* and rubbing his chin.

"Fred," said Jill, "Jennie lives just over to Amadeus's place."

"I got a guy coming by later. He'll help me load your stuff. Cash on delivery?"

"Deal and thank you," said Jennie.

The ladies returned to the cabin. Another day's work done—the project right on schedule for completion tomorrow—the third day.

At dusk a pickup backfired its way up the dirt road. The old gentleman backed up to the porch where Amadeus and Rosie met him. While Jennie held the door, the men carried the furniture inside.

The old gentleman glanced around at the renovation. "Well, Amadeus, lots of changes."

"Yeah, Fred, you could say that."

Jennie offered payment to Fred, said, "Thank you."

Fred held her hand and closed her fingers around the bills. "Miss Jennie, you have already paid in full." He closed the door on his way out and the rusty pickup backfired as the old man drove down the dirt road.

Frowning, Jennie said, "We made a deal."

Shrugging his shoulders, Amadeus chuckled and grasped her hand. "Come with me." In the kitchen, a ladder leaned against the open wall. Up they climbed into the library. Jennie gazed at log walls, maple flooring, a tongue-and-groove pine ceiling, and overhead lighting with a fan. Bookcases of cherry stood on the north wall.

"Exquisite! Where did you find these?"

"My passion," he said. Steering her to the wall of windows, Amadeus showed Jennie Deane Mountain and enfolded her in his arms. Together, they viewed their world—nature's world.

Her voice high and whispery, she said, "How I have missed my beloved homestead, the mountain, spirits, and you, all those years."

"Not missing it now," he said.

Held in each other's arms, her head on his shoulder, they waltzed above the trees, in the clouds, to their own music, baritone and sweet alto.

Old shingles, damp boards, roofing nails, scrap metal, old exterior logs, and torn-out bathroom and laundry fixtures littered the yard. Board lengths lay on sawhorses. A table saw and new appliances stood in the yard and scaffolding surrounded the tower.

Troop 79, along with Jack, cleaned up the yard and, with help, stacked old logs.

Electric drills whizzed. Carpenters screwed the black metal railing into the library floor and wall, overlooking the kitchen, and the staircase to the dining room wall.

Heavy plastic covered furniture and floors. Volunteers painted a sunny yellow in the kitchen, bathroom, and laundry.

The Shaker pantry cupboard built, Sadie worked in the mudroom.

Everyone with a free hand hefted white Shaker cabinetry with glass knobs and a quartz countertop, white with grayish markings, into the kitchen for installation and then, set appliances and fixtures in place. In the lavatory and laundry, a pre-built counter with sink and cupboards and the claw-foot tub were ready to be installed.

Jake, from the woodstove shop, studied the tower's layout and spoke with Tom before installing two woodstoves, one from Tom's inventory on the main floor, and a second, from Jake's shop upstairs in the library. He, also, installed fire-resistant flagstone hearth pads and wall panels. Finished, he handed the invoice to Tom.

Midday, Pete, the master plumber, arrived with Kenny, his young apprentice, and met Tom on the porch. "Got a real nice sink, refurbished cast-iron with drainboard."

Tom said, "Thanks. They'll appreciate it."

Pete said, "Real heavy, beautiful white sink."

Trucks filled the yard, two with signs, Murphy's Log Homes and Pete's Plumbing, and by late afternoon, two more arrived: Flooring by Gus and the furniture store truck—a mattress delivery—followed by a red Chevrolet Blazer.

Mrs. Greene got out of her SUV. With posture straight, bag on her shoulder, and a scowl on her face, she observed the yard: a table saw, board lengths, saw-horses, scaffolding, and trash loaded in pickups.

Awakened from her nap on the front porch, Rosie instantly barked and paced. Tom and Alice darted through the door and walked with her to the pond. Amadeus and Jennie, who were cutting crown molding, quickly crossed the yard. "She's three days early," said Jennie.

"She'll see love for Tim, for us, and community," said Amadeus.

Meeting Mrs. Greene in construction-scape, he said, "What can we do for you?"

"I found time for a pre-inspection," said Mrs. Greene. "May I enter?"

"Certainly, come inside," said Jennie. "Has something happened to Tim?"

Kenny came out of the lavatory and said, "Amadeus, laundry and bathroom are done. Suppose you could find me a couple guys to help carry that sink?" Volunteers stepped forward.

"Plumbing in need of repair?" asked Mrs. Greene, staring at Amadeus over red-framed glasses. "Looks like a big renovation."

"Not so big, and it was already in progress," said Amadeus.

"This way, Mrs. Greene." Jennie escorted the caseworker through the living room and down the hall, where painters had primed interior walls and applied a summer sky blue.

Entering Tim's room—bedstead sparkling, smell of fresh paint and new wood, windows, ceiling, a closet, all new—they saw Gus, the floorer, leaning down to study an enormous floor stain in plain sight. Jennie's heart fell through that floor.

"Oil spot! Was this some kind of workshop?" said Mrs. Greene.

"It's on the list for repair," Jennie said.

"This room exceeds the required dimensions," said Amadeus.

"Please, has something happened to Tim?" asked Jennie.

Mrs. Greene, an edge to her voice, said, "I'd like to see that monstrosity."

"This way," Jennie said, calmly, leading the caseworker back down the hall to the tower.

"On the main floor are the dining room and mudroom. The library is upstairs."

Frowning, Mrs. Greene pointed, "Stairs! Do you think it's safe for that boy to climb stairs?"

From the doorway, Amadeus, quietly, but firmly, said, "Tim, his name is *Tim*, not *that boy*. Yes, it's safe. He climbed Potato Hill with the Cub Scouts."

"This simply will not work! A construction site is not the best placement!" Mrs. Greene barged out the cabin. Rushing to her Chevrolet, she turned the ignition.

Jennie and Amadeus bolted through the door and Jennie called out, "Stop!" Her voice was too strong, and Mrs. Greene clearly had a heart of stone. Calming herself and catching up, Jennie said, "This *is* the best placement. These people and businesses have given time and work to bring Tim home. You see a construction site. We see love and community."

Amadeus said, "Tim has lost everything but this community, his home."

"Well," Mrs. Greene sighed. "It's probably a waste of time, but I'll see you Monday." Speeding down the road, her tires kicked up a trail of dirt.

On the porch swing sat the angels, Grandmothers Sarah and Jennie. In the road, Amadeus held a teary-eyed Jennie. "Come on, we've got molding to cut."

Tom's crew, plumbers, the floorer, and volunteers labored to beat the clock: time ticking away. The Boy Scouts left to cook stew for a crowd. Tom, Alice, and Rosie returned, and Tom said, "Jennie, go shopping. I'll help this guy."

Amadeus said, "Jennie, please buy what we need for the kitchen."

The women left. Everyone else worked, finishing the renovation and cleaning up the yard. Tom collected more invoices. Best friends hung a blue glass front door. The rustic cabin had been transformed into a loving, welcoming home.

Floodlights shone over the gathering. The crew, friends, volunteers, and business owners mixed and mingled. Maxine was tucked warmly under a quilt, while Madeleine, her devoted sister, and their friend, Fred, the old gentleman from the yard sale, sat comfortably in lawn chairs.

Boy Scouts arranged pots of camp stew, hot biscuits, and a sheet cake on folding tables. Disposable bowls and plasticware too. Bottled water cooled in ice buckets.

"Jennie! Jennie!" called the five friends, running to her. One was missing tonight. *Lord, keep Tim safe. Let him know he is loved.* She opened her arms and hugged them.

"Oh, my sweeties." Rosie nudged her way to Jennie.

"We been inside," said Mike.

Calvin said, "Amadeus told us we can't tell you what we saw."

From Annie, "It's a secret!"

Gracie asked, "When is Tim coming home?"

"Soon, honeybees. Keep Tim in your prayers. We miss him too."

Amadeus held out his hand. "Hon, Tom and Alice are waiting."

Packing themselves close around Amadeus and Jennie, the kids and Rosie climbed the steps onto the porch, ready to share the spotlight.

Tom rang the dinner bell, catching everyone's attention. "From my family to yours and from all of us, may God grant you love, peace, and joy in your new home. May He bring Tim to you soon. We're all praying." A deep breath. "A few gifts for you: the dinner bell, a bottle of champagne, and an envelope of invoices."

Best friends hugged and Tom said, "I've waited a long time for this day."

Amadeus whispered, "Thanks for always being there."

They shared hugs with the Murphys and the children. Jennie, her eyes watering, said, "Thank you, Tom, for a lovely home and friendship."

Hugging her, Tom said, "Welcome home, Jennie, where you belong."

Amadeus and Jennie smashed the bottle, wrapped in a towel, on the porch railing, and as champagne poured on the ground, they kissed softly. The crowd's cheering—hands clapping, kids grinning and bouncing, Rosie barking—woke the silence of the night. From the porch, Pastor Andrew offered grace:

"Lord, Thank you for the blessing of Amadeus and Jennie and for the community that renovated this home. Give Tim comfort and love. Bring him home to us soon. Thank you for the scouts who prepared this delicious meal. Amen."

"Now, let's eat!"

The scouts served the stew, and Jennie served Maxine, Madeleine, and Fred.

Voices from the crowd called out. "Delicious stew!" and "Who baked the biscuits?"

"Phillip baked them!" said one of the scouts.

Amid sounds of joy, Treasures created closer ties to a community that had banded together and generously given time and talents to renovate a home for a little boy in need, for a man who had once been lost, and, without quite realizing it, had welcomed home a sojourner.

Amadeus shouldered his violin and played hits from the sixties. Voices sang along. Some simply hummed, others listened, hands clappin' and toes tappin'. Couples held hands, lost in memories of their youth. Jennie danced with the children.

All too soon, the celebration ended. Friday, the next day, was a work day. Amadeus and Jennie gave everyone a heartfelt thank-you, as did Tom and Alice. Amadeus had helped all of them over the years. That's just the way it was. Nothing was owed, nothing expected.

Once their guests had left, Alice backed the truck up to porch. Amadeus and Tom unloaded the purchased items for the kitchen. The floodlights were turned off and laid in the flatbed. The friends shared hugs, and then Alice, Tom, and Annie left with Maggie and Gracie for a sleepover. The flatbed and the pickup were soon out of sight down the dirt road.

Cabin lights glowed in the darkness. Strolling up the porch steps, Amadeus held Jennie's hand. He opened the front door, and Rosie squeezed by. He waited for Jennie to enter first. "You're home now with me, where you've always belonged."

Summer sky blue and log walls. Glass lamp lit. A log cabin quilt lay over the gray sofa. Jennie gently rubbed the soft natural cotton, the exquisite stitching, the blues, greens, yellows, and browns of nature's hues and the red centers—hearth and home.

"A gift from Jill," he said.

"She's a master quilter."

Moonlight streamed through the long, narrow windows and shone on maple end tables, an oaken coffee table, two maple rockers, and the sofa—the gathering place for family and friends.

On the mantel lay two books—a faded pink cover with gold letters stacked on top of a faded gray cover, *Pollyanna* and *The Call of the Wild*—gifts from Grandma Florence on the day best friends rode Grandpa Stephen's Belgians.

"You remember that day?" she asked.

"I do, every detail," he said.

She held two old black-and-white photographs: Grandma Sarah with five-year-old Jennie and, in a new frame, a boy and a girl. Tears sliding down her cheeks, she whispered, "The boy and the man have always known the way home."

Replacing the photographs on the mantel, Amadeus turned Jennie toward the blue wall.

"Oh, my goodness!" she said. "Where did this come from?" Stepping over to the 1940s Baldwin-Hamilton school piano, she lightly brushed her fingers across the walnut stain. The piano on which Emilie had given her lessons held many memories. Teary-eyed, Jennie played a simple song on the pure white keys, only a few yellowed with age.

"Mom loved you and hoped that one day Emilie and I could give this to you."

In a high-pitched, whispery voice, she said, "I loved her. I missed her. She was so kind to me. I'll treasure this, as I do my memories of her."

"Your books are inside the bench," he said, escorting her to the sofa. Reaching into his pocket, he pulled out a small box. Jennie's breath quickened. No, no, not now. She hadn't yet shared what lay on her heart.

"For you," he said, setting a small box in her hand and taking a seat beside her.

As she opened it, more tears flowed. It was a necklace, one single pearl set in gold, strung on a fine gold chain. Grandma Sarah's ring. Her mother's string of pearls. Could she be his pearl? "A pearl. It's beautiful. Thank you."

Kissing her, he said, "For the pearl of my life."

"I never thought I would ever be anyone's pearl, made with spit inside a shell."

"You are mine, always have been, and always will be."

"Partners, not possessions," she said.

"Definitely partners."

Weeping softly, Jennie closed the box, hugged him, and laid her head on his shoulder. "Not tonight, but soon, I have a story to tell you, as well as God."

"When you're ready. Whatever it is, you'll still be my pearl." He stretched out his legs, resting his feet on the coffee table, and held Jennie close. For a while, they stayed there, kissing and caressing, until Amadeus said, "Would you like to see our bedroom?"

Holding hands, they ambled down the hall, stopped at Tim's room on the west side, just across from theirs. Turning on the light, she said, "We'll need to add some things. Create a boy's room."

"I'll unlock the workshop doors tomorrow."

Moonlight and a glass lamp lit their east room, showing the bed covers turned down. In the center against one wall stood a four-poster maple bed with a hand-carved headboard and a low footboard. Jennie traced the carved maple tree, its branches and fissures.

"I made one leg too short, so I added a piece," Amadeus explained. "You can see the seam there."

"Oh, my! The wood looks aged, and the posts are turned like table legs. It's art, sweetie." Jennie set her pearl necklace in the top drawer of the matching dresser and turned out the light. "I'm ready for bed, are you?"

In the moonlight, they lay under pre-washed cotton sheets and the new white comforter. Resting her head on his chest, she embraced him. With gentle fingertips, he traced her spine.

"It's aragonite and conchiolin. Not spit."

"My pearl? So lovely, spit or no."

They soon slept, home together in their log cabin in the woods.

SIXTEEN

The morning sun streamed through the French doors, flitted on frosty blue walls and maple furniture, and fluttered around a white comforter. They lay like spoons, entwined, relaxed, easy breaths on this serene Friday morning. Just beyond the French doors and the porch, a doe and twin fawns stood silently. Tall grass mixed with wildflowers waved in the breeze. Songbirds welcomed the day.

Pacing back and forth by the bed, her nails clicking, Rosie barked. The deer vanished. Amadeus donned his clothes and headed outside with the dog.

Jennie lazily slipped into a flannel robe, made the bed, and threw the towels in the washer. In the doorway of Tim's room, she closed her eyes and prayed silently: *Are you watching over Tim this morning, Lord? Help him not to be afraid and bring Tim home.*

She smelled pancakes! He must have found the new cast-iron fry pan. In the kitchen, Jennie set the oak table, while munching fresh blueberries from the wooden box. Watering the herbs in clay pots hanging in the black metal frame, she said, "Our quilt, the piano, hand-tatted doilies from Sadie, and these herbs from Alice. Precious gifts from true friends." Morning sunlight nourished the herbs. As he served the pancakes, he said, "After breakfast, check out the dining room." The old mitt with the baseball tucked inside lay on the table. Jennie caressed it, and he said, "I'll oil that today. Get it ready for Tim." Holding hands, they shared the same wish, that soon the loud voice of a little boy would interrupt the quiet.

In the dining room, a china cabinet with glass doors sat against a wall. Sliding her fingers along the smoothness of the wood, Jennie said, "Luxurious, rich-looking."

"It's rock maple, like the table."

"And plenty of space for family and friends." She could see the grain. "Exquisite!" In the center sat the silver teapot. Caressing it, she said, "Grandma Sarah and journeys." Pausing for a moment, she remembered the quest and Grandma's words: *Come home. It is time.* "Where did you get these beautiful pieces?"

"I've been building them for a while, Jennie. Somehow, I knew, even before there was a place to put them, even before you came back. In my workshop, I built them from trees in my woodlot. They're imperfect."

"Every flaw a testament. Not that I see a single one." Jennie opened the glass doors, held the silver teapot lovingly, and set it inside the china cabinet.

"My secret devotion is now public knowledge."

"It should never have been hidden in the first place." Leaning into him, she laid her head on his shoulder. Hugging him tightly, tears in her eyes, she prayed silently: *Lord, let this be where I belong in this lovely cabin with this man. I truly love him.*

He held her close, knowing she needed time.

Then, together, they opened the boxes and bags from yesterday's purchases, and washed, dried, and placed in an upper cupboard the set of four white porcelain dishes and the glassware. They laid the silverware with the tiny rose pattern in a drawer. Arranging small appliances on the quartz countertop, Jennie looked down at the remaining bags full of bakeware, cookware, and stainless steel pots and pans. Washing utensils, she filled the sand-colored ceramic jar.

He took the dishcloth from her hand and said, "Walk with me? We'll finish later, then unpack the books and the ancestry."

"We really should get Tim's room ready."

Startled by the loud rapping on the front door and Rosie's barking, she said, "Didn't you say your place was private?"

Chuckling, he kissed her quick. "Our place. It was, before you moved in."

"I should probably get dressed." She ran into their bedroom just before he opened the door, admitting a pack of Cub Scouts with Mike and Calvin in the lead. "Mr. Amadeus." " Mr. Stuart, Is Tim home yet?" Rosie next, and all the boys followed, standing in the living room, wiggling and wondering.

Bob Adams, behind them, asked, "Amadeus, would you mind if we mowed your lawn?" Bob laid his hand on a Boy Scout's shoulder and said, "Phillip volunteered."

"Yeah, sure, and thanks."

The boys and Rosie filed outside. Hurrying to meet their company, Jennie said, "Hi, what's going on?"

"Good morning, Jennie," said Bob. "Please give this gift to Tim from the pack. I'm sure his was lost."

She thanked him and peeked into the bag. "Oh, my, he will love this!"

The monotonous groaning of the lawn mower—background white noise to the chattering Cubbies—cut through thick tall grass and wildflowers, creating a coverlet of green lawn surrounding three sides of the cabin: east, beyond the French doors, the tool and storage sheds, and the workshop at the edge of the field; south, from the front lawn to the dirt road; and west, to the tree line. On the north side, over the years, weeds and bushes had invaded and grown up the sides of the detached garage with its new gray metal roof.

The Cubbies chattered happily as they worked, scooping potting soil into planters and acquiring dirty hands, fingerprints on T-shirts and jeans, and grins on their faces. Amadeus poured soil from the heavy bags. "Now, you can plant."

Jennie removed flowers from the plastic trays and laid them on the ground. Small hands dug holes in the soil and transplanted them: colorful petunias into hanging planters; geraniums, mixed shades, in clay pots; and a mix of flower seeds in two more clay pots. Potting soil spilled on the ground. Bob and Amadeus set the pots of flower seeds on the porch by the French doors, the geraniums on the front steps, and hung the petunias above the porch railing.

"Boys, come with me and bring the watering cans," said Amadeus.

They followed, carrying assorted sizes on the way across the yard. Amadeus filled the cans from the hose. Then he sprayed the boys. They whooped, hollered, laughed, ran away, then sneaked back to be sprayed again. Puddles formed in the mowed grass. Jump! Jump! Splash! Splash! Sneakers and jeans soaked and pasted with cut grass.

He's still a big kid. They had soaked each other many times in childhood. Creeping up behind him, Jennie wrestled the nozzle out of his hand and, with her thumb over it, pointed the hose to the sky. Water rained down over Amadeus. He burst out laughing! Holding her close to him, he released the nozzle from her hand. A cloudburst rained down over Jennie. She laughed that melodious sound of girlhood.

The boys toppled over, rolled on the wet ground, and giggled in fits of laughter. Bob roared. Phillip had finished mowing the east and south sides and begun raking the grass. He laughed, too, the wet spray soaking him. Calvin and Mike grabbed the hose and sprayed Bob.

The faucet finally turned off and cans filled to the brim, the boys watered seeds, flowers, grass, steps, porches, and each other.

Jennie disappeared inside, changed into dry clothing, and towel-dried her hair. In the kitchen, she searched through the cupboards and the refrigerator, finding small amounts of flour, white sugar, four eggs, butter, and baking powder, but no peanut butter, brown sugar, or chocolate chips. The missing ingredients meant no cookies. Spying the can of cocoa, she opened it. There was just enough to make brownies.

The groan of the lawn mower was replaced by the grating of the tiller. Bob tilled the ground, a flower bed by the front porch steps and another, circular, on the east lawn, visible from the cabin and the workshop. Amadeus dumped bags of peat into the dirt, raked, and hoed, mixing it into the soil. Cubbies sat on the front porch, elbows on knees, chins rested in palms, anxiously watching and waiting.

Brownies baked in the oven.

Phillip mowed the west lawn, past the tower near the tree line.

Jennie glanced out the window over the sink. A white GMC Acadia was parked in the shade of the maple tree. Ellen Baker. Rushing onto the porch, she squeezed by the boys and grasped Amadeus's hand—their hearts racing. "Oh, no! The kitchen is a mess! The boys are still soaked!"

"Calm down. She'll smell baking chocolate. See boys having fun. See love."

Hurrying to meet Ellen, Jennie said, "Where's Tim? What happened?"

"Nothing to worry about. Still in the crisis center. Who are the boys?"

"A gift. Tim's Cub Scout pack, planting flowers."

"Oh, Jennie, let me visit with them, please."

Jennie knew Ellen loved children, so she returned to her task of cleaning up the kitchen. Amadeus caught up with Phillip, emptying the wheelbarrow in the field. Then, a second trip. "The lawn looks well-maintained, like home."

Phillip shrugged his shoulders. "I mow our lawn. Who's that lady?"

"Ms. Baker from social services. She says not to worry. She's nice."

Phillip dug a hole and transplanted a young lilac tree.

On the porch steps, Ellen sat comfortably among the Cubbies, introduced herself and said, "Beautiful flowers."

Calvin said, "Do you know Tim?"

Ellen smiled, "I do. Tell me about him."

Mike said, "Tim's mine and Calvin's best friend and a Cubbie."

Calvin said, "His house burned down and his mommy died."

One boy said, "He likes trees and Rosie." And another said, "Rosie likes Tim."
Calvin said, "He goes where Mr. Amadeus goes."

Mike said, "Do you know he don't walk good?"

"Yeah," said the others. "Can you help him?" one boy asked.

Ellen smiled. "Yes, I can!"

"You know what?" said Mike. "The bullies hurt Tim. Mr. Amadeus stops them."

Walking slowly to the porch, Bob interrupted. "Boys, it's planting time."
Turning to Ellen, he said, "Nice to see you, Ms. Baker."

The Cubbies picked up flats of daylilies in shades of orange, yellow, and
white. Around the porch, they dug in the soil with trowels, plopped the flowers
into the holes, covered the roots, watered the garden, and spread mulch.

"Ms. Baker," said Bob, "this is the best place for Tim. Amadeus and Jennie are
the right parents. Tim is loved."

"Thank you, Mr. Adams, but I'm not really here to interview you!" She
stepped through the front door into the living room.

Jennie said, smiling, "To what do we owe this visit?"

Ellen smiled. "I smell brownies!" Glancing around the room, she said, "Your
home is certainly not a construction site!"

"Who said it was?" Jennie said. Of course, they both knew.

"Mind if I look around?"

"Sure, go ahead."

The kitchen timer buzzed. Jennie removed the brownies from the oven. Amadeus entered through the mudroom door and sat at the oak table.

The Cubbies followed Mr. Adams and Phillip into the field, trowels in hands,
to dig up daisies, black-eyed Susans, and purple coneflowers, Rosie at their heels.
The boys carried the flat cardboard boxes of flowers with their roots attached
back to the circular garden and transplanted them. A few lay in the field missing
their roots.

Several boys trod behind Phillip, making multiple trips back and forth, collecting rocks, and creating a circular border. Rosie barked as she chased rabbits
and squirrels.

Mike and Calvin ran back into the field, collected the rootless flowers and
picked a few more. Racing back to the cabin and up the porch steps, they knocked
on the door, bouquets in hands.

Jennie opened the door. Grinning from ear to ear, they presented their gift,
colorful flowers with stems of various lengths and dandelions mixed in.

Jennie smiled. "Thank you very much. You're such sweeties."

Mike and Calvin, still grinning, blushed and ran back to the wildflower garden.

Jennie arranged the bouquets in water glasses and set them on the windowsill. The mixing bowl, measuring cup, and spoons dried on the drainboard. A few full bags still lay on the floor. Brownies cooled on the counter.

Ellen descended the stairs and said, "A bright, warm, welcoming home. And the quartz counter sparkles."

Amadeus said, "All the windows and doors are new, the roof, too, and it heats efficiently. Electrical certified and fire safety requirements met."

"How did you manage it in three days?" asked Ellen.

Amadeus chuckled. "Friends, neighbors, local businesses, community volunteers. All hoping Tim comes home. The Cubbies, our youngest volunteers, are anxious to see their friend. Have you met Tim?"

Ellen smiled, "I've spent time with him."

"Ellen, do you have time for tea and a chat, for old time's sake?"

"Actually, I don't, Jennie. Brownie-to-go for old time's sake?"

Cutting and loosely wrapping one, Jennie gave it to her former colleague. Through the window, she watched Ellen hurrying to her GMC. Phillip approached and they exchanged a few words. Then Ellen headed down the dirt road, and Phillip helped the boys pick up the tools, plastic pots, cardboard boxes, and empty bags.

Ellen had visited for a reason. Jennie knew her old friend and colleague well.

Amadeus found a galvanized tub in the storage shed, carried it out on the lawn, and filled it with cold well water. Jennie tossed a bar of soap to him and sat on the porch steps with a pan of cooled brownies next to her. Rosie lay under the porch swing. The boys scrubbed their hands. Amadeus inspected them for cleanliness, sending only two back to wash again. Gathering around, Mike and Calvin next to Jennie, they munched on brownies. Amadeus, Bob Adams, and Phillip stood nearby.

"Is that lady gonna bring Tim home?" said Calvin.

"She can help Tim walk!" said Mike.

"We hope very soon," said Jennie. "I love the flowers and the lilac tree! Thank you for the beautiful gardens. You all worked hard."

The Cubbies' faces beamed, bits of chocolate sticking to the corners of their mouths.

Calvin said, "These are real good!"

"Yeah! Real good!" said all the boys, licking their fingers.

Jennie held out the pan, "Seconds, anyone?"

Mike said, "Tim will be real happy, you cook good!"

The adults laughed as the boys reached into the pan for more.

Hanging planters displayed white, pink, or purple petunias, sorted by color, none mixed. By the porch were lilies, again sorted by color and lined up almost straight. In the circular garden, wildflowers were mixed and clumped together with bare spots of earth inside the rock border. The lilac tree could be seen from the kitchen window.

Amadeus and Jennie, hand-in-hand, crossed the mowed lawn to the workshop with Rosie alongside. "What a fun morning," she said.

After unlocking the barn doors of the red building with the dirt-covered windows, Amadeus opened them wide. Sunlight hit the space inside: tools hung neatly, some lying on shelves, a jig saw, more saws, a planer, wood carving tools in a case, stains, and varnishes. A table saw stood in the center. At the far wall were unfinished pieces of furniture. He removed old blankets and quilts. Small dressers, bookcases, chairs, so many pieces. A four-door cabinet with a drawer in the middle, wood knobs, a natural stain. Jennie opened the doors. "Exquisite!" The scent, the hues of cedar.

"For us, for our home," he said. "That cabinet is for our living room."

"Perfect," she said. "And these two chairs by the French doors."

"Have you decided what to put in Tim's room?"

"Red oak."

"Wait here."

Backing the truck up to the open doors, they loaded the furniture. He balanced the cabinet on a dolly and pulled it up planks into the truck. First stop was the east cabin wall, where they unloaded outdoor chairs. A lovely porch with French doors, cedar chairs, and clay pots.

In Tim's room, Jennie made his bed with soft cotton sheets, a blanket, a blue cotton bedspread, and fluffy pillows. Folding a light gray blanket, she placed it at the foot and laid the gift from the Cubbies neatly, with no wrinkles, on the bed.

Amadeus set a bookcase on the long wall, the storage bench under a window, and the dresser in the corner. He laid the mitt with the baseball tucked inside on a bookshelf.

Tim's room had grayish-blue interior and log exterior walls, a white beadboard ceiling, polished bedstead, new vinyl flooring, and red oak furniture built with loving hands and prayerful thoughts.

In early evening, Amadeus opened and closed the cupboard doors, the refrigerator, the pantry cupboard, and the refrigerator once again. All were nearly bare. What's for dinner?"

"Grilled cheese, I guess."

He grabbed Jennie's purse, guided her out the door and to The Beast. Rosie followed, tagging along for the ride.

"We need to stay by the phone," said Jennie. "I know Ellen."

Amadeus frowned. "Grilled cheese for dinner?" Sighing, he said, "Besides, it's too late. The office is closed for the weekend."

In the western sky, the setting sun beamed over the treetops straight into Tim's room, glittering on the bedstead. On the porch swing, white light surrounded Jennie's grandmothers, and Great-Aunt Mary, enveloped in her foggy cloud, hovering above the roof. In that moment of time, in that eerie silence, there were no branches swaying, no grasshoppers and no crickets chirping, no coyotes howling, or creatures moving about, only Rosie's uneasy whine in an unnatural stillness. Jennie followed his gaze toward the sky—nature's sudden storm.

Suddenly, Rosie barked and ran onto the porch. They hurried inside and Jennie grabbed the phone. She listened with tears running down her cheeks. Amadeus held tighter to Rosie, his eyes upon Jennie.

"Thank you." She hung up the phone. A bright smile, dimples showing, on her tear-stained face, she said, "Trust me when I tell to you to stay home!"

He stood and said, "Tell me!"

"Tim's coming home on Monday!" Hugging and kissing, they danced around the kitchen, hearts filled with joy. Rosie pranced in circles. Instantly, he held Jennie at arm's length. "The inspection?"

"Ellen did it, and the appeal was approved!" They hugged and kissed.

"Ellen's our new caseworker and..." she kissed him again, "she's spending time with Tim this weekend."

"Oh, thank you, God and Ellen!" He kissed her, then said, "Dinner out?"

"Let's stay home. A whole day at home together."

While she made some calls, he made dinner—grilled cheese, served with chips, hot herbal tea, and cupcakes. Amadeus pored through the invoices and found they just didn't add up. "Look these over, please."

Jennie thumbed through the stack. Murphy's—*Inventory Write-off, labor, paid in full.* All invoices showed no dollar amounts, simply the words *paid in full.*

Amadeus leaned on the counter and said, "People deserve to be paid for the work they do. I'll speak with Tom."

"Sit next to me." She sipped her tea and held his hand. "Tread lightly if you do, for you have Treasures of your own. And Tom Murphy is one." She paused. "Humble yourself, accept the gift, and pass it on as you always have. There will be others in need."

"A whole renovation? Sweetie, I can pay for all of this."

Squeezing his hand, she said, "My dear Amadeus, you are a Treasure too."

"And so are you." He kissed her softly.

Each had given from what they had—time, talent, possessions. Treasures—gifts of love, kindness, and generosity for Tim, Amadeus, and Jennie.

SEVENTEEN

The university campus dominated High Street where Amadeus parked The Beast between two out-of-state vehicles whose license plates read Virginia and Ohio. Trucks, campers, SUVs, and sedans displayed both Maine plates and plates from elsewhere in New England.

On Saturday, two days before Tim would come home, Amadeus and Jennie entered the fairgrounds, the Trash and Treasure Fair, with crowds of spectators and shoppers. Swept up in a swarm of deal seekers and treasure hunters, they passed by artisans and antique dealers. Pulling the dolly behind them, they hurried to the flea market.

In the summer heat, sellers sat in lawn chairs under umbrellas, coolers next to them. Some read, others did needlework and whittled, and still others chatted with passersby. The scent of hot dogs, fries, and doughboys permeated the air.

Amadeus and Jennie disregarded displays of old furniture, used camping equipment, tables of puzzles, games, tools, and more, heading straight toward the hovering foggy cloud. In the middle of the books—hardcovers, paperbacks, and children's stories—piled on and under plywood, balanced on sawhorses, and in no particular order, Great-Aunt Mary's gnarled, wrinkled hands dug through a partially hidden cardboard box. One treasured book fell through her crooked fingers.

Rushing past book lovers scavenging through stacks, they knelt by the vanishing spirit. Jennie picked up the dropped book. "Agatha Christie. Aunt Mary was a fan of murder mysteries."

"A great find," he said, thumbing through the box. "Books published in the nineteen twenties and thirties—Hemingway, Fitzgerald, Steinbeck."

Inspecting them, Jennie said, "The covers are worn, but clean. Spines are creased, the pages not torn, corners folded over, and notes penciled in margins. Treasured tomes!" Seeing the old gentleman nearby, she smiled, "Hi, Fred. How much for the old books?"

"Five bucks," he said, chuckling. "Probably worth less. Readin's a waste a time. Picked up this stuff from a yard sale."

"I'll take the box." She paid with a Lincoln. Now the dolly held classic literature.

"That was a steal," Amadeus said.

Farther down, kitchenware was displayed on folding tables. Jennie spied a white china plate edged in blue. No chips, no cracks, no flaws. It was one of a set of twelve place settings, serving bowls, a platter, and other pieces. This would enhance the beauty of the china cabinet, but two hundred dollars was a lot for used china.

Jennie approached the seller, an older woman with gray hair and a kind smile. "I'm interested in the set. Would you accept one hundred?"

The seller caught a glimpse of Amadeus, who was eyeing a vase. "One seventy-five. Excellent condition, rarely used."

"One twenty-five. I'm taking a chance there are no flaws."

"One fifty. I'll throw in the vase. That's my final offer."

Jennie glanced at the vase and at Amadeus. "It's a deal."

The seller repacked the plate, marked the three boxes "Sold," wrapped the glass vase in old newspaper, and boxed it. Jennie paid cash, while Amadeus piled the four boxes on the dolly, the vase balanced on top. "Go shopping, Jennie. I'll catch up with you," he said.

Jennie wandered around, window-shopping. She negotiated for an old stained-glass pole lamp and saved another fifty. The seller tightly packed the glass globe in a box stuffed with newspaper. Then, finding a bench in the shade, she rested and waited…and waited. Where was Amadeus?

Finally, he appeared, rushing toward her, a new cardboard box on the dolly.

"Where have you been?" she asked.

"Got sidetracked. Ready for lunch, hot dogs and fries?"

"Doughboys, too?" she said. "What's in the box?"

Grinning, he said, "For Tim." Opening the box flaps, he showed her metal construction equipment. "A bit rusty. Just needs cleaning and paint."

"Tim and his friends will have the dirt road all dug up."

He stacked her box on the dolly and pulled it along, while she carried the pole. Strolling through art kiosks, against traffic, and weaving around buyers and bystanders, they stopped to watch a potter at the wheel. Following her gaze to a lamp, he said, "Here, take this," handed her the dolly, and slipped away.

Buyers and admirers of pottery closed in on Jennie, as though she were invisible, blinding her view of Amadeus. There was no space, no fresh air; she couldn't breathe. Too hot. Voices too loud. Pushing along the dolly and carrying the pole above the heads of the crowd, she said, loudly and repeatedly, "Coming through. Excuse me," inching her way through the mass of people. She finally rested on a nearby bench, breathing deeply, waiting again, and observing passersby: a young mother, a canvas bag over her shoulder, pushed a stroller with twins and held the hand of a small boy who dragged a plastic grocery bag along the pavement. "But, Mommy, I want to play with my cars," the boy protested. Tim would like Matchbox cars.

An elderly man and woman walked by slowly. He held a cane in one hand, and the woman's hand in the other. They must have shared a lifetime of love, still loving, like she and Amadeus, a journey that began in childhood.

"Jennie, is that box fragile?" said Amadeus. "Jennie? Jennie?"

"Sorry, just people watching." She lifted the box, and he stacked on more, replacing hers on top. Then he sat next to her.

"You must have spent a fortune," she said. "That's art!"

"Not a fortune," he said, chuckling. "How about lunch?"

"Long lines at the food trucks. It's hot. Hordes of people," she sighed. "Let's get the groceries, stop at the 'Everything Place,' and home for lunch in cool breezes."

Weaving around buyers and spectators walking toward the exit, Jennie spied a kiosk containing handcrafted Christmas ornaments: blown-glass bulbs with detailed paintings. They watched the artist paint fine lines with a steady hand and chose one, a shiny blue bulb with a snow scene and a horse-drawn sleigh—a keepsake of their first Christmas together. They paid full price, for this was art, this was love.

The Beast, full of art and treasure, heaps of plastic grocery bags, and several more bags, roared home. Parked in the drive, Amadeus switched off the engine, gave Jennie a kiss, and said, "Wake up, hon. Let Rosie out. I'll carry everything in."

When Jennie opened the door, Rosie rushed outside, streaking past Amadeus. He made numerous trips between cabin and truck until grocery bags covered the kitchen floor, spreading into the dining room. Some bags concealed the top of the washer and dryer, and a few lay in Tim's room. Treasure boxes and a pole lamp were scattered on the living room floor. In the kitchen—an awesome task—they organized the abundant supply into the pantry cupboard, refrigerator, and freezer. Soon they would have a hungry little boy to feed.

"Lunch? I'm starved," he said.

Flashing her enticing smile, she grasped his hand. "Come with me."

Holding hands, they ambled along the dirt road to the pond as Rosie ran ahead. Time for a skinny dip.

A candlelight dinner at the rock maple dining table—roast chicken, baked Caribou russets, grown in Aroostook County, steamed mixed fresh vegetables, and a warm baguette—served on white porcelain. Red wine in long-stemmed glasses. Candles burned. The radio sat on the stairs, playing old recordings of sentimental songs.

"A toast to your dancing eyes," he said. Glasses clinked.

"A delightful day with you," she said.

"Home cooking, so delicious. We may never eat dinner out again."

She laughed, "I'd like to open those boxes."

"Dessert first." He kissed her and served a large bowl of vanilla ice cream with two chocolate French macarons and two spoons.

"Deliciously sweet," she said. "Is now a good time?"

Relaxing in a maple rocker, Jennie opened boxes, and to her surprise, found a white lamp shade, a set of three blue mixing bowls, and a larger matching bread bowl.

"I hope you like to bake bread," he said, smiling.

"I love kneading dough; it warms my hands. And the scent of bread baking."

"Fresh from the oven, butter melted on a center slice. Heavenly," he agreed.

In the last box was the table lamp in gradient blues. "So beautiful. So costly."

"Those were tourist prices." He laughed and said, "I deliver wood to the potter. Bartered art for art. Two matching porch rockers for the pottery."

She carried the lamp to their bedroom and set it on the maple dresser with the white tatted doily under it. She moved the glass lamp to an end table in the living room and set the bowls on the kitchen counter.

They emptied a few bags in Tim's room, placed the blue ceramic lamp on the red oak dresser, and arranged toys on the bookshelf with old and new books.

Amadeus washed the china, and Jennie arranged it in the rock maple cabinet with the silver teapot, the glass vase, and the keepsake Christmas ornament. There were no flaws in anything.

"The vase," she said, "is crystal, pricey. She gave it to us."

Setting the construction vehicles on the front porch, he smiled, "We'll deliver an extra load of firewood." Then he carried the pole lamp and the box of old books upstairs.

In the library, the stained-glass pole lamp glowed, reflecting its many colors over the two leather chairs, sitting side by side next to the marble slab, supported on a solid oak table. Behind the chairs, Amadeus's book collection and Jennie's ancestry, Bible, and memorabilia were displayed in cherry bookcases. On the top shelf sat Grandma's pearl ring, Mother's string of pearls, the small box containing the photographs of his children, and his old Bible.

New clothes for Tim agitating in the washer, Jennie ascended the stairs. Through the wall of windows, she viewed the night sky, its moonlight and starlight enveloping them in its world of tranquility.

Jennie unpacked and dusted the old tomes, read titles, and flipped through the pages: *Their Eyes Were Watching God, Arundel, and Rabble in Arms.* She passed them to Amadeus, who organized the bookshelf, reading each title aloud: *The Hobbit, Ben of Old Monhegan.* "Good reads with Tim."

Jennie held *The Good Earth* and opened it to the flyleaf. A quick breath. "Oh, my goodness. I didn't notice this before." She passed him the opus.

Reading the name, *Florence Deane*, he said, "Your grandmother! These books are first editions. Could these have been the set in the bookcase?"

Jennie shrugged her shoulders and said, "treasure at the flea market." Brushing her fingers across the cherry desk and chair, she remembered his words: *You have many stories to tell and more to come.* On the desk of Amadeus's craftsmanship, he had placed a journal, sketchpad, pens, and charcoal pencils.

Sliding her hand across the desk to the top drawer, she opened it and removed the sealed white envelope. He held his breath, glanced upward to the old Bible, his white envelope concealed within its pages.

Jennie had had a marvelous day with him, and her heart had felt free. She stuffed it back inside and closed the drawer.

He exhaled slowly and quietly. They descended the stairs. Time for evening tea.

A face—a child's face—flashed in his mind. The man's arms reached out to the boy, but he was too far away. The boy ascended into Heaven, caught up with the angels. The man on his knees, glued to the earth, keening, his hands reaching upward to the sky. Boy gone. Angel's wings.

Images of a second boy flashed. Tears fell down the boy's face, and his voice called out, "Amadeus! Amadeus!" Boy's arms reached. Man's arms stretched. Hands almost touched. Too far away. Boy toppled over. Man could not see or find boy, but heard boy calling, "Amadeus!"

Sweat poured from his brow, tears from his eyes, as he tossed and turned, calling out, "Tim! Tim! Where are you, Tim?"

Whining, Rosie nudged him. Someone wiped a cool cloth gently across his face. Soft hands caressed his shoulders, and one held his calloused hand. "Amadeus, Amadeus, wake up! Wake up!" That hand. That voice. Jennie. He opened his eyes, saw her worried face. "Tim, I can't find him! I lost him!" He wept. "Jennie, I can't lose another child!"

"Calm down, sweetie. It was a nightmare. Tim is safe, and he will come home."

"He called to me. I couldn't reach him. I lost him."

"Tim is not lost to us. God will not take another child from you," she said, wiping his brow. She lay next to him, rested his head on her heart, and smoothed his hair.

Rosie settled at their bedside.

EIGHTEEN

At noon on Sunday on Deane Mountain Road, Amadeus and Jennie sat on the front porch swing, holding each other close, their eyes peeled to the dirt road. Rosie sat next to them, whining. The last few minutes had seemed like an eternity. Amadeus checked his watch countless times. The aroma of baking chocolate drifted through the window.

"They're twenty minutes late," he said, his knee bouncing.

"Calm down, relax. They'll come."

That morning, just as they were leaving for church, the telephone had rung: Tim would be home today! Jennie's promise was now on the path to being fulfilled.

"In a couple hours," she had said. "Got things to do!"

"What's to do? Cabin's done."

"Well, boil macaroni!"

The hours had passed by in a flash. Macaroni and cheese baked. Green beans snipped and boiled in the pot. Salad sat in a bowl. A chocolate cake baked in the oven. Telephone calls to Pastor Andrew, then to Alice: *Tim's on his way home.* Dishes washed and drying on the drainboard. Nothing else to do, but say a word of thanks and wait.

Church bells pealed jubilantly, their joyous sounds praising and soaring through the air, carried by the zephyr from Grace Church to the front porch.

Five more minutes passed before the white GMC came into view. Ellen parked under the maple, stepped out of her vehicle, opened the door, and extended her hand to a smaller one. Tim slid off the seat, and grinning, stood next to Ellen.

Rushing down the steps, Amadeus held Jennie's hand. Tail wagging, Rosie raced past them, sniffing and licking Timmy's face. He giggled and hugged his pal. Laughing, Amadeus and Jennie knelt near Tim. Opening his arms, Amadeus said, "Hey, Buddy, got a hug for us?"

Tim's steps were slow, sluggish. He was exhausted. His leg and back hurt. His limp was more pronounced. Falling into open arms and held securely in them, Tim laid his head on Amadeus's shoulder, his little arms glued to the big man. "I was worried. I was scared." He cried, and his thin little body shook.

"You are home, my boy." Comforting words from Amadeus.

Jennie wiped their tears, her own, too, and hugged both of them. "Oh, sweetie," she said, gently drawing circles on Tim's cheek. "We love you, little one." To Ellen, she whispered, "Thank you."

Leaning down, Ellen touched Tim's face. "I see love here. I'll catch up with you in a few days." Hugging Jennie, she whispered, "Remember, this is foster care. We're searching for a relative."

"We must listen to Tim!" Jennie said.

Ellen nodded and left, drying her eyes.

"Oh, no! The cake!" Jennie rushed into the kitchen. Amadeus carried Tim inside. Rosie followed. Tim's head popped up and he said, "Where you and Jennie go, I go?"

Meeting Tim's eyes, Amadeus said, "That's right. Where we go, you go."

In the kitchen, he set Tim on the floor. "Explore, if you want."

Tim touched the cool, sparkling quartz, peeked through the arched doorway, saw the rock maple table, a woodstove, and stairs. Holding tightly to the railing, he climbed slowly, cautiously, with Amadeus and Jennie following and Rosie tagging along.

"Is this a castle?" said Tim.

"What do you think?" said Amadeus.

Looking through the wall of windows, he saw mountains. Treetops, a long way down. Tilting his head, he looked at the sky. "Yup, a castle, and this is a tower." He turned and saw chairs, a lamp, and books in neat rows. "You got a lotta books."

"Jennie and I like to read," said Amadeus.

"Not me!" said Tim, shaking his head.

"We shall see about that," said Jennie.

Stepping slowly down the stairs, Tim took his time, his hand grasping the railing. "You got a TV?" he asked.

"No, Jennie and I like to read and spend time in the woods."

"Mike and Calvin's got a TV."

Downstairs, Tim peered into the mudroom. A man's jacket hung on a hook. Work boots and hiking boots sat near the door. "Sadie built the nooks and bench."

"Mike and Calvin's mom?" said Tim.

Amadeus nodded.

Shrugging his shoulders, Tim said, "Well, I don't got a coat."

"Neither does Jennie. We'll have a shopping day!"

"I hate shopping!" Tim said brightly and wandered back through the kitchen into the living room. More books, a piano and a violin. He touched the quilt. "Mrs. Andy?"

"A gift from Jill," said Jennie.

Wandering down the hall, he peeked through open doors: bathroom, yellow room, purple room, and stepped into the room with the French doors. "Who sleeps here?"

"Jennie and I," said Amadeus.

Through the French doors, he saw a field, a woodpile, bits of green breaking through dirt in clay pots, chairs on the porch, and sheds. "You got a lotta sheds."

"Can't have too many," said Amadeus.

"Where do I sleep?"

Taking his hand, Amadeus guided him across the hall. Rosie lay on the floor, eyes following Tim. Sunlight gleamed through the window, danced on bluish-gray walls and new vinyl flooring and glittered on the big old bedstead. Bookcases held toys and books. Tim dropped to his knees, touched the Lincoln Logs, the Legos, saw the books, and picked up the mitt with the baseball tucked inside. Setting it back in its place, he picked up a Matchbox car. "I used to have these at my house."

"The cars, everything is for you. It's your room," said Jennie.

"And good stories in those books. Some were mine," said Amadeus.

In the dresser drawers, new clothes were folded. The blue lamp felt smooth to his touch. And that big shiny bed! Climbing up, he bounced on the thick mattress, laughed, fell to his knees, and hugged the new Cub Scout uniform. "You got me this?"

"Mr. Adams and the pack gave it to you," said Jennie.

"I like Mr. Adams. I'm a Cubbie?"

"You're still a Cubbie, like Mike and Calvin," said Jennie.

"O-kay!"

Tim held Amadeus's offered hand as he slid off the bed, and said, "You got peanut butter? I'm hungry."

"We got mac 'n' cheese too. Would you like both?" said Jennie.

Tim nodded, "I'm real hungry!"

In the kitchen, they sat at the oak table. Jennie set a glass of milk and a plate in front of Tim—mac 'n' cheese, a peanut butter sandwich, and green beans. Tim was very quiet, concentrating on his fist holding the fork. Rosie lay by his side, quickly swallowing any bites that Tim dropped. He switched to the spoon, held in his fist, and got more in his tummy and less in Rosie's. The plate almost clean, Tim said, "Do I have to eat the green strings?"

"They're green beans. Help you grow strong," said Amadeus, eating one himself. Tim picked up one with his fingers, bit into it, ate the whole piece. Picked up another, ate it too, and yawned.

Jennie said, "Use your fork, like this."

He tried and lost the bean on the floor. Rosie ate it. The next one he ate with his fingers.

"We'll work on it," said Jennie, smiling.

Tim yawned again.

The warm breeze blew through the window over the sink. Dishes soaking, Jennie packed the leftovers in the refrigerator. She served up chocolate cake, confectioner's sugar sprinkled on top and covered with whipped cream, and poured a little more milk in Tim's glass. Rosie lay quietly, waiting for crumbs. Between yawns, a few fell off the spoon, but most of that piece of cake went into Tim's tummy. His eyelids drooped.

"Come, little one, you and I need a nap." Amadeus carried Tim into his bedroom, chose a book, and carried him back to the gray sofa. He settled himself, put on his reading glasses, and stretched out his legs, resting his feet on the oak coffee table. Tim snuggled close, his friend's arm around him, legs curled, his head over Amadeus's heart—home safe and tummy full. Listening to the rhythm of Amadeus's heartbeat and his voice reading *My Side of the Mountain*, Tim soon fell sound asleep.

Jennie cleaned the kitchen. The phone rang several times, calls from inquiring friends. Climbing the stairs, she retrieved her sketchpad, journal, charcoal pencils, and a pen.

Again, Jennie drew circles on Tim's cheek, kissed it, and covered him with

Jill's quilt. "Sleep, little one." Removing Amadeus's glasses, she placed them and the book on the end table by the glass lamp, smoothed his hair, and kissed him too. "Rest, my love. Our boy is home." Turning the rocker toward them, she opened the sketchpad and, with charcoal pencil, drew a portrait of father and son, their hearts entwined.

Dear Lord, We are blessed to have Tim in our lives. Guide us as we parent and love our boy. We long to keep him in our family. Lord, Amadeus and I, our hearts belong to each other, and we would like children born of our love too. Amen.

The quiet afternoon passed, and the living room darkened. The sun shone from behind the treetops through the west windows. Tim and Amadeus still slept, or so Jennie thought. She closed the journal, carried her things upstairs to the desk, and returned to the kitchen to find Amadeus leaning on the sink, drinking water. He pulled her into a hug and said, "Sorry, I slept all afternoon."

"You both needed the rest."

"Amadeus!" called Tim.

"In the kitchen, hugging Jennie!"

The patter of Tim's feet, the click of Rosie's nails, and they stood before the huggers. "Oh!" said Tim, hands over his eyes, blushing and giggling.

Jennie held out her hand. "Come, make it a threesome." Tim hurried to them and Amadeus held him in one arm and Jennie in the other. Soon, they heard a knock.

"Tim, would you like to greet our friends?" said Jennie.

Tim's body stiffened, and he shook his head. With fear in his eyes, he said, "No, the mean people took me away." He clung to Amadeus. "They might come after me again."

Jennie smoothed his hair and Amadeus said, "We're together now. You're safe here. No one will hurt you or take you away. Besides, you made a friend, Miss Ellen."

Another knock.

"She brung me back to you," said Tim.

"Come, let's all open the door together," said Jennie.

"Pastor Andy!" said Tim.

Swinging Tim high over his head, Pastor held him there, and Tim laughed. "I missed you, my boy! Our checker games, too!"

"Come, see my room! It's a nice room, like at your house." Holding their hands, Tim led them down the hall and said, "Mrs. Andy, what's in the bag?"

Jennie and Amadeus gave them time alone and prepared dinner—salad, a warm baguette, and Jill's chicken casserole.

All gathered at the rock maple table. Tim said, excitedly, "They brung me stuff, my star quilt, my teddy, peanut butter cookies. Lotsa stuff."

"For you, Jennie, recipes on the counter. Tim's favorites," said Jill.

"Thank you so much."

All held hands and bowed their heads. Amadeus squeezed Jennie's and Tim's a little tighter. Pastor Andrew said a heartfelt grace for Tim's return home. Good food, close friends, and joyful conversation filled the room.

Later Sunday night, Tim, tucked into his bed, hugging the bear, story read and prayers said, fell asleep, covered with the star quilt—brightly colored stars shining in the blue night sky. Rosie lay on the floor next to his bed.

On the porch swing, as they sipped tea, Amadeus held Jennie's hand, massaging it softly with his thumb. "I'm even more convinced now that he belongs with us. We love him."

"We'll always love him. That's what he needs, our love, and we will freely give it to him." She squeezed his hand. "You need to know this. Social services is searching for a relative." Her voice whispery, a tear fell as she said, "That night Sharon told me there's no one else to love Tim."

Holding her close, he said, "I haven't told you this: I called James Foster and retained legal services for Tim's adoption. Spoke to Emilie. They're on the way home."

"Of course you did. And it's good to have an attorney in the family."

Holding hands, they stepped inside. Checking on Tim, sound asleep, they entered their bedroom, and he closed the door. There was that idea of babies to consider and so they did.

NINETEEN

On Independence Day, The Beast, loaded with firewood, Amadeus, Jennie, Tim, and Rosie, bumped and heaved from Deane Mountain Road east on unimproved road to Mitchell Brook Road, turned north onto the Intervale and east onto Day Mountain Road. Emilie's yellow cottage with white trim was located within walking distance of the little red schoolhouse, now the Temple Historical Society.

In Emilie's front yard, planter boxes filled with herbs, hostas, and other greenery bordered a walkway of old flat stones found in Temple's woods and fields. Two Adirondack chairs and a small table sat on the open wraparound porch.

Jennie, Amadeus, and Tim threw the last few logs onto the pile in the driveway. "Where'd Rosie go?" said Tim.

"Exploring the stream behind the house," said Amadeus. "She'll be back."

Amadeus jumped down and assisted Jennie. Next, Tim fell into his arms, a spin and dunk, feet on the ground, and laughter. Inside the shelter attached to the small garage, they stacked a mix of maple, oak, and birch. Tim stepped slowly, cautiously, around the woodpile, tripped and fell a few times. Amadeus set Tim upright and brushed him off. "Stand here. Help Jennie stack. I'll bring the wood to you."

"Okay, I can do that."

Tim needed to see a pediatrician and an orthopedic specialist. Jennie would contact Ellen.

Emilie and James stepped onto the porch. She carried a plate, a glass, and a sealed cookie container. He helped the wood stackers. She sat in a porch chair, eyes on Tim, smiled, curled her forefinger, and patted the seat next to her.

He'd seen Emilie at church before. Tim dropped a piece of wood. Amadeus lifted him free of the scattered sticks, and Tim took his time climbing the steps. He sat next to Emilie, and she passed him the plate and the glass. "Thank you. Peanut butter sandwiches are my favorite. And I love cookies."

Rosie, a wet dog, darted out of the trees through the backyard. Squeezing between flower pots and settling within range of falling crumbs, she waited. Tim devoured the snack, sharing bread crusts. Peanut butter and strawberry jam stuck to the corners of his mouth, and a milk mustache lined his upper lip.

"Are you my grandma or something?"

"Not grandma, aunt, Aunt Emilie. I'm Amadeus's big sister."

"I have an aunt! You're my aunt?" Tim grinned. "Do I have to say both names? I like *Auntie.*"

Emilie laughed and gently mussed his hair. "Auntie, it is."

"Auntie, why do you hang your glasses around your neck?"

"So I don't lose them."

"Well, if you keep them in front of your eyes, you can see where they are."

The wood stackers laughed. Amadeus piled the last few sticks, filling the shelter, and joined the others on the porch. "Hey, buddy, it's time to go."

"Okay," Tim said. "Auntie, I gotta go now. My friends are coming to my castle."

Emilie gave Tim the container and said, "Share the cookies with them."

"Thank you, Auntie. They love cookies." Tim passed the container to Jennie, called to Rosie, and slowly climbed down the steps with Amadeus.

The women hugged, and Emilie said, "Oh, Jennie, to be an aunt again. Such a sweet boy." Hugging a moment longer, Jennie said, "See you soon," and hurried to the truck.

Amadeus shifted into gear and headed home. He enfolded Jennie's soft hands in his, and she turned to him. His heart was whole and free, but hers was still broken. And their Tim—how easily he'd connected with this family.

✴

At the small white house on Maple Street, Maggie, Gracie, and Annie sat on the green front steps, knees bouncing, elbows poking into their legs, chins resting in their hands, waiting, while Jennie visited with Maxine and Madeleine. Maxine's condition had worsened quickly, and her skin, a pale grayish hue, felt cold to the touch. Her voice was weak, her breathing now rattled. She had no appetite and slept most of the time. With the thermostat set above eighty degrees and tucked under quilts, she still felt cold.

Jennie softly touched Maxine's hand. "How are you today?"

Maxine roused, "Oh, tired. Can't get warm." She paused, took some shallow breaths, and said slowly, "My girls have fun with you."

"They're sweet girls. They can visit anytime."

Maxine fell back into sleep, and Jennie sat next to Madeleine who, in her eighties, was fatigued, just worn out, caring for her younger sister and her lively great-nieces.

"How can I help?" said Jennie.

Madeleine squeezed her hand. "You already are, my dear. Give the girls a fun sleepover. They need time with friends to laugh and be happy."

Hugging Madeleine, Jennie left and, with the girls, crossed the uncut lawn, blanketed in dandelions, to her Jeep. Gracie and Maggie carried their bags filled with pajamas and toys. Annie's was already in the Jeep. It was time to pick up the boys.

At the cabin, Tim pushed the construction equipment around on the front porch. Amadeus stood by Pastor Andrew's Jeep, conversing with him in quiet tones. Then Pastor waved to Tim. "Hey, buddy, great checker game. See you soon." Tim waved as Pastor drove down the dirt road.

Amadeus sat on the front steps, his arms resting on his thighs. Tim sat next to him, elbows on his knees, propping up his chin. "I like the construction trucks."

"This winter, we'll de-rust and paint them."

"That will be fun. When's Jennie coming back?" It was a never-ending wait for an eight-year-old boy, excited to play with his friends. Finally, Jennie's Jeep appeared.

"They're here!" Tim jumped up, excitedly, almost toppling down the steps. Catching him in his strong hands, Amadeus said, "Slow down, buddy."

The kids jumped out of the Jeep to an echo of, "Tim!" "Timmy!" "We missed you!"

"Want to play with my trucks? We can build roads," said Tim.

Annie said, "Can we see your room?"

"Yeah, it's a nice room. I got toys, and I live in a castle."

All six chatting at once, bunched together, they climbed the porch steps and squeezed through the wide-open screen door, proceeding as a tight pack down the hall to Tim's room. Amadeus held the door for Rosie to follow, her tail wagging.

Gracie said, "You got a big bed for a little kid."

Calvin said, "You got toys like mine."

Mike said, "Mine too."

Annie, hands on hips, said, "Timmy, how do you get into that bed?"

"I climb, like this." He put his foot on the side rail, held tight to the headboard, hoisted himself up, and fell onto the bed. "I slide down like this." Taking turns, all the kids pulled themselves up and slid down several times.

They settled themselves on the floor, where there was plenty of play space for six: Matchbox cars, Legos, Lincoln Logs, and more scattered about. Only the mitt, baseball, and books remained on the shelves. Annie checked the titles, then joined the group. Rosie lay nearby, eyes darting from child to child, but always keeping a close watch on Tim.

Amadeus and Jennie peeked around the corner and saw a bedspread full of wrinkles, corner hung down, star quilt, teddy bear, and pillows mixed with toys. Smiles and giggles—music to their hearts.

On the sofa, shoes kicked off, feet resting on the coffee table, and books lying in laps, they settled in for reading time. Alastair, the heirloom violin, lay on top of the old piano. "It's time to hear you playing again," Amadeus said.

Her head on his shoulder, Jennie opened Agatha Christie's book. A postcard fell out, and Jennie noted her daughter's comment: *Worried. Did you arrive safely or take time to think?* She'd hoped Rebecca would have accepted her decision. Climbing the stairs, she sat at the desk and penned a note:

July 4th

Honeybee,

So sorry I didn't write. Met old friends. Amadeus too. Staying at his cabin in the woods. Digging up the past. Will I see you in Temple?

Love you, Mom

Placing the postcard on the stack of outgoing mail, she settled next to Amadeus. It wasn't long before Maggie wandered down the hall, carrying her baby doll and a big storybook. Laying them on Jennie's lap, she climbed up, squeezed between them, held her doll, and patted the book.

"*Make Way for Ducklings*," said Jennie. "Look, Maggie, ducks."

Jennie read the story, turned the pages, and Maggie turned them back, pointing her finger at the illustrations. "Ducks. See baby ducks."

"You have a sweet voice, little one."

Most of the toys were now tucked inside the bench, a few on the shelf, the star quilt, teddy, and pillows tossed back on the bed. The friends soon sat quietly at the coffee table, waiting, staring. Jennie was still reading.

When she closed the book, Gracie said, "Will you tell us a story?"

"About you and Amadeus, when you were kids?" said Annie.

"Let's take a walk," said Jennie.

Jennie, holding hands with Maggie, led the way across the lawn, past the wildflower garden, past the sheds, and into the field with the girls trudging along. They crossed through tall grass almost to the tree line and stopped at a stone wall, shaded by maple, white birch, and oak mixed with hemlock and pine.

Inside the workshop, the boys watched Amadeus move boards, sandpaper, and chisels aside. Gathering up three old quilts and three sawhorses, he enlisted their help, carrying or dragging these things to the stone wall. Lining up the sawhorses next to the wall, Amadeus covered them with the quilts.

And Jennie began the telling of a memory: "In my grandpa Deane's barn, there were two huge, chestnut-colored Belgians named Theo and Polly. One day Amadeus rode Theo, and I rode Polly."

"What's a Belgian?" said Gracie.

"What's a chestnut?" said Calvin.

Tim, his elbows on his knees, tilted his head and said, "What's huge?"

Amadeus said, "Chestnut is reddish-brown. The horses were old, had some gray hairs mixed in with chestnut, called roan. Belgians are big, gigantic, like friendly giants. The horses work, plow fields, pull loaded wagons, and haul logs."

"Can we ride the Belgians?" said Mike.

"How do we get on? They're giants!" said Gracie.

"Hmm. When you packed your pajamas, did you pack your imaginations?" asked Jennie.

The children nodded excitedly, and Calvin added, "We take them everywhere."

Climbing on the wall, the kids reached out and held tightly onto the horses, swung a leg over and straddled the Belgians—riding double, bareback.

Jennie said, "The tree line is the pasture fence. It goes way down by the maples, past the pines and the clump of white birch. It goes along the woodpile and back to the stone wall. If you go on the dirt road, you have to jump the fence. Today is a sunny day, blue skies, breezes blowing, purple mountaintops in the distance. A perfect day for riding!"

Wiggling, the kids sat up straight and held their heads high.

"Gently kick your horses to keep them moving. If you want them to stop, say 'Whoa!' and pull back on the reins. Now ride!"

And the children took off. "Giddy up!" they yelled and "Whoa!" at the turns. No stopping to nibble flowers! Round and round the pasture fence they rode, laughing, bouncing, racing. Cowboys and cowgirls roped cattle. Gracie's horse jumped the fence, jumped back into the pasture and flew to the stone wall. Jumped it! Maggie held tightly to her sister and, bouncing, laughed her sweet sounds. Annie's horse danced and pirouetted, then raced through the pasture, as Calvin preferred the wind in his face. Tim and Mike, English riders, bounced, a steady cantor, followed Rosie, and chased a fox. Tally-ho! Wild imaginations!

Laughing with him, Jennie slipped her arm around Amadeus and leaned on him.

He held her close. "Those kids are such fun. The innocence of childhood."

"Believing, the magic of childhood."

Toward the dinner hour, the boys played catch and built roads to everywhere. Annie and Gracie jumped rope. Maggie climbed the steps into the cabin. Finding Jennie in the kitchen, she hugged her tight, laying her head just below Jennie's waist.

"Hi, sweetie," said Jennie, gently drawing circles on the little one's back. "Would you like to help me set the table?"

Maggie looked up, nodded, her blue eyes shining. Hands and face washed, they laid a wipe-clean tablecloth on the rock maple table and set the plates, glasses, tableware, and napkins, one at a time, in place.

Pots of water boiled on the stove. Amadeus snipped beans, peeled and sliced carrots, and added them, turning down the heat. The children ran into the kitchen, and Tim said, "We're hungry! Is the spaghetti done?"

"Yeah, we're real hungry," said Calvin.

"Go, wash up. It's almost dinnertime," said Amadeus, adding spaghetti to a pot.

Rushing to the bathroom, they banged the door shut. Jennie shooed the girls down the hall. They lined up at the door and listened to the silly boys and running water. Arms folded, foot tapping and scowling, Gracie knocked and said sweetly, "Spaghetti's ready."

Bolting out of the bathroom, Calvin threw the towel at the girls, and the boys hurried to the dining room, only to come to a halt, their mouths open. "Where's the spaghetti?" said Mike.

"In the cooking pot," said Amadeus. "Have patience, Horatius."

"Huh?" Mike and Calvin shrugged their shoulders. Tim scratched his head, nose twitching.

The girls marched in just behind the boys. Annie and Maggie, hands on their hips, frowned. Gracie held up the towel. "Jennie, look at what the boys did to your pretty towel!" Sweaty hands, too long in leather mitts; dirty hands, too long in the dirt road; and dirty faces, too, were imprinted on a background of white.

Jennie sighed. "Sweeties, it will wash. Set it on the washer and get a clean one."

"Okay, but boys get really dirty. Wait until you see the bar of soap and the sink!" said Gracie, as all three marched back to the bathroom.

Amadeus's shoulders shook with laughter, and Jennie gently patted his bottom. "Get the spaghetti on the table."

Five minutes later, all were settled. Plates of steaming spaghetti, covered with sauce, cheese, and meatballs, were ringed with carrots, green beans, and garlic bread. There were glasses of milk for the children. All held hands while Amadeus said grace.

The kids dug into the spaghetti, and Jennie said, "Don't forget to eat the vegetables."

"Really?" said Calvin, "You mean it?"

"Yes, we mean it," said Amadeus. "You'll grow strong like Paul Bunyan."

"Huh, who?" said the boys, staring at Amadeus.

"A lumberjack. We'll tell you the story about Paul and his blue ox at story time."

"We love stories," said Gracie, placing her hand in Jennie's. Gracie's deep brown eyes gazed into her friend's brown eyes. Jennie squeezed her hand.

*

Outside in the summer sun and breezes all day, ice cream and Emilie's cookies in their tummies, and the story told, the three boys piled into the big bedstead. Rosie settled on the floor. Pushing together new twin beds in the lavender room, the three girls snuggled. The children soon slept, but Tim tossed and turned.

Relaxing on the porch swing, rocking slowly, Amadeus and Jennie sipped hot herbal tea and gazed at the stars. In the humid night air, the citronella candle burned.

"We need to talk," she said, holding his hand.

"Pastor stopped by. The end of Maxine's life is probably near," he said.

"Alice wants to be close to Maggie and Gracie, as Annie's friends."

"Tom and Alice dreamed for years, and finally planned to share the business."

"Once you asked me about teaching. I want to spend my days with you and love our children, including Tim, Maggie, and Gracie. The girls know of the loss they'll soon face, and they're reaching out to us."

Creak! The screen door opened, and Tim stood on the porch, teddy in one hand and Rosie next to him. Jennie opened her arms. "Come here, sweetie." Tim walked slowly over, his head lowered, and sat between them. Rocking the swing, Amadeus smoothed his hair. "Why are you crying?"

Tim pulled up his knees, hid his face in his folded arms, and sobbed. Jennie softly rubbed circles on his back, "Cry, little one, cry the sadness away."

The katydids and grasshoppers sang nature's lullabies. Rosie lay at their feet, whining. Tim sniffled, his voice muffled. "I want to see Mommy."

"Oh, my honeybee," said Jennie, teary-eyed. "Look up at all the twinkling stars. Choose one and let your heart remember. Mommy lives there in your heart, in your memories." Jennie pulled Tim close, his head on her heart. "That's what I did, when I was a girl and my grandma Sarah died. And she still lives there with my memories."

Still rocking the swing back and forth, Amadeus reached into his pocket, opened Tim's hand, and placed a small object in his palm.

Sniffling, Tim said, "My little truck. Mommy bought it for me. Where was it?"

"I found it that night in the yard, far away from the fire. Maybe you left it outside. Can you tell us the memory?"

"Mommy and me went to a big store. I liked the truck, and she bought it for me. Then we went someplace and had chocolate milkshakes."

"Such a good memory," said Jennie, teary-eyed.

"If you want, we can clean it up and paint it," said Amadeus.

"Yup, like the construction trucks," said Tim.

Quiet now, they rocked. Tim leaned on Jennie, his eyes on the stars. She softly stroked his cheek, and Amadeus sang lullabies until Tim fell asleep.

Twenty

On Sunday, July 7th, Jennie sat in the pew next to Amadeus, surrounded by friends—Alice and Tom and all six children. The organ sang the melodies of hymns, the notes clear and crisp. Lyrics mixed with children's voices flooded Jennie's mind. She loved the notes of music, the words of hymns, and the sounds of children.

Oh, why had she forced Tim to wear that ridiculous dress shirt and tie! The little guy sat there suffering, fidgeting, constantly pulling the sleeves, collar, and tie. He'd told her it was too tight and scratchy. Her mother had understood the need for comfortable, soft fabrics, pre-washed and no tags. Tim had told her that Mike and Calvin wore T-shirts.

Jennie leaned around Amadeus. "Timmy, sweetie, come here."

Stepping on Amadeus's feet, Tim held onto the pew and to Amadeus's hand. Standing in front of Jennie, pulling at the tie, he said, "Can I take this off?"

Jennie untied the necktie, unbuttoned the top two buttons of his shirt and, untucking it, let his shirttail hang out, "Now, you'll be more comfortable. Next Sunday, you can wear a T-shirt."

His face beaming, Tim hugged her tight, and she said, "Now, sit with the boys, it's time to sing."

The congregation stood, hymnals in hands, a joyous sound. The organ and piano played fortissimo. A chorus of angels praising joined with Amadeus's baritone. The notes, the lyrics reverberated off the walls and straight into Jennie's heart. One word cemented itself: *healing.* A tear escaped, and Amadeus hugged her close, smiled, and kissed her cheek. Oh, how she loved him! Would he still love her when he learned the truth?

Pastor Andrew led the congregation in quiet prayer. Folding his hands, Amadeus bowed his head. Jennie leaned against him. Then, the hymn—pianoforte, softer, louder, softer, prayerful. One word: *hands. Healing hands.* Her dream flashed in her mind: three hands and the need to grab hold of the one that heals. Jennie slipped her hand into Amadeus's, and he turned to her, tightening his grip. His hands were warm, strong, calloused, and fit perfectly with hers.

Pastor Andrew shared the message. Jennie listened to every word, *Matthew 5:8. Blessed are the pure in heart, for they will see God.*

Her mind pondered more words—six words: *healing hands, pure hearts, see God.* She repeated those words silently over and over again, while her tears softly fell. Alice slipped her hand into Jennie's. Amadeus held her close to him, and she listened to the closing hymn, piano and organ, the voices, his baritone. Quiet notes and lyrics resonated in the sanctuary, giving her the gift of one more word—*Grace.*

Parishioners filed past the third pew from the back. Jennie and Alice hugged, and Jennie said, "Could Tim go home with you for a while, please?"

"Sure, I'll take all six, a playdate." said Alice. "You take all the time you want."

Turning to Amadeus, her hand in his, Jennie said, "Would you stay with me?"

"I'll stay," he said, squeezing her hand.

"And give me a moment with Tim? I'd like to talk with him."

Amadeus nodded, giving her hand another squeeze.

Outside, Jennie and Tim sat on the church steps. Jennie said, happily, "All the kids are going to play at Annie's house, even Mike and Calvin!" She held his hand. "Voter Hill is a fun place. Alice and I played there as children."

"Are you coming?" said Tim in a low timid voice.

"Later." Hugging him, she said, "I need to talk to Amadeus and God. My heart is broken, like yours. God and Amadeus will take my hurt away. Then we will come."

"But those mean people might come," Tim said, fearfully, teary-eyed.

"Sweetie, don't be afraid. No one will take you away. You'll have fun with your friends. Tom and Alice will take good care of you."

Amadeus interrupted, "Are you ready, buddy?" He held Tim's hand, and they walked slowly to the Murphys' caravan. Turning around, Tim stared at Jennie, sad eyes pleading, fearful, tears falling. Jennie waved, gave him a smile, and blew him a kiss. He turned, crying, and walked away with Amadeus. Her Amadeus would calm Tim's fears.

The worshippers had gone, and Alice and Tom, all the children in tow, were the last to leave. A Sunday afternoon of play in sunlight and summer breezes on Voter Hill for the six little friends.

Jennie and Amadeus, his hand holding hers, walked slowly back into the church to the second pew from the front and sat nearer to the altar and the towering stained-glass window—Jesus among the sheep with open arms. Just outside the still and silent sanctuary, Pastor Andrew said to Jill, "One lost soul will soon be home in the sheepfold." He closed the double doors quietly, leaving Jennie and Amadeus alone with God.

"Tim was afraid to leave us," she said, teary-eyed.

"He was chatting with Mike and Calvin when they left. He has found his place in our hearts and he's learning to love us."

"How will we ever let him go?"

"We'll leave it to God," he said, tears welling. "And do what's right for Tim."

"We should pray. We will need His strength. So will Tim."

Amadeus covered her hands with his and bowing their heads, he prayed:

"Lord, Tim has been with us now for one week, and we love him. He fills our hearts, but we are your instruments in his life. Help us to serve his needs first. Guide us daily as we love and teach our little boy. Thank you for giving him to us and grant us the strength to face what may come, but know we love Tim, and losing him will break our hearts, and Tim's also. Fill Tim's heart with Your love and give him Your strength. He will need it. Amen."

His hand still covered hers. "Now tell me, what is laid on your heart."

Jennie sat silent, hands folded in her lap, tears flowing. "Healing hands, pure hearts, see God—Grace." A deep breath. Looking into his eyes, she said, "I pray you will still love me, still want me, when you hear the last chapter of Daniel's and my story."

"I'll always love you." He touched her necklace. "You are a blessing to me." With his fingers under her chin, he gently turned her eyes to the stained-glass window and said, "He loves you, always has, always will."

And at long last, Jennie shared the burden that held her heart captive. "Daniel lived only six weeks after returning from Vietnam. Near the end, he asked to see Pastor Bob and Doc. They talked in that upstairs room. Doc prescribed medication to ease trauma, rages, flashes in his mind—*My Lai, My Lai.*"

"My Lai, the massacre, the shame of our intervention in Vietnam."

A deep breath. "One day I tried to leave him. I couldn't take the beatings, his pain and rages anymore. I packed my bag and walked out the door, but I couldn't step off the porch. I tried, but I couldn't. Without me, he would have been alone. I remembered Pastor Bob's words: *It will all be over soon.* I didn't know when soon would come." And Jennie cried.

Amadeus tightened his hold on her hand. "Take your time. I'm walking beside you down the path."

Another deep breath. She clasped her other hand over his, fingers tight, holding on. "The medication. I had a full bottle of pills and whiskey, the last bottle. No money to buy more. No more money. That bottle was left on my porch. I could help him die, it's what he wanted—to die." Still crying, she looked back into his eyes, "Please understand! I had a child to love! And I missed her! I could take away his pain."

Her head lowered, she avoided his expression. "More and more beatings—I was so frightened of the monster in him, and I feared he would kill me. I was alone. I was nineteen, and I had a little girl, whom I loved, and a husband I feared. And my body was racked with constant pain, and the beatings, the rage never stopped. I didn't have the faith or the strength to help him. I wanted it all to end."

Jennie hid her face in her hands, sobbed, her body shaking, and cried out, "I can't go on, I can't! I'll never have a pure heart!"

Amadeus's tears streamed down. He wrapped her in his strong arms and called out, praying, "Take her guilt away, Lord, release her from all of it." Then holding her as close as he possibly could, images flashed before him. "I see a mortar and pestle, an open bottle of pills beside it. Hands poured a few into the mortar and with the pestle crushed and ground the pills." Breathing deeply, he said, "Jennie, tell me your story."

For a few moments she sobbed and shook in his arms. His comforting hands smoothed her hair. Words flashed in her mind: *Embrace your quest. You will find what you seek. Trust in his love. Do not falter.* A deep breath, then another. She sat up, looked into his face, saw love there, and wiped his tears. Hers still flowed. "I crushed a few until they were like powder. There was an egg sandwich on the plate. His lunch. I mixed the powder into the sandwich and carried it upstairs. I was going to kill him, Amadeus!"

"Just tell me, please, tell me this truth."

"I always left it by the closed door, then I would leave before he opened it. That time he flung the door open, banged the wall, kicked the plate out of my hands, pulled me inside, and beat me. He demanded the pills, the whole bottle, and the whiskey. It was in the hall and the pill bottle in my pocket. I tried not to give them to him, but to get away, but the monster kept on beating me."

Jennie collapsed in his arms, sobbing, "I can't tell you anymore, I can't!"

He still held her tightly. "You were afraid for your life. Jesus is waiting for you. A few more steps. I'm walking beside you. Finish the story."

Again, she sat up and hung her head low, crying still, her voice cracking, almost inaudible. "I threw the pills at him, crawled to the whiskey bottle, rolled it into the room, and screamed at him, 'Kill yourself! But you won't beat me again!'" He lifted her chin, and she saw love in his eyes. "And I know he did."

"Oh, Jennie, know you are forgiven. How did you save yourself?"

"I crawled down the stairs and out the door, hid under the maple, and waited."

"Did he follow you? That wasn't a safe hiding place."

"He was afraid to come out of that upstairs room. The maple was the only place I could go. Farm workers drove into the field all day. My Treasures came by every day. I needed to be seen. I needed help. And then Michael, the police officer, saw me and took me to Doc's. Later that day, Michael, Doc, and Pastor Bob went back to the house and found Daniel in the upstairs room on the floor, dead, an empty whiskey bottle, broken glass around him, and the empty pill bottle in his hand. The death certificate was signed, and it was over."

"And through your Treasures, His instruments, God took care of you, protected you. Now, your dream…"

"Don't you understand? I almost succeeded. When I was seventeen, I stood before Pastor Bob in church and promised to love and honor my husband, but I could have killed him. My heart cannot be healed. There's no Grace for me, no mercy."

He held her hand. "You promised to love a kind, gentle boy, the boy he was until he faced war, and it changed him. War killed your Daniel, not you. And a few crushed pills would not have been enough. He released himself from his pain." A moment of silence. "Honey, remember the kind boy who loved you and the young man who had the courage to serve his country."

"I should tell my daughter about her father."

"She needs to know the boy and the man he was. Her grandfather too." Holding her eyes in his, Amadeus said, "Jennie, honey, our God is a loving, forgiving God. Jesus paid the debt and God has already forgiven your sin—Grace, Mercy, Love, for you." He wiped a tear from his eye. "Now, it's time for you to seek God and find your peace."

For several moments he simply held her, let her heart feel peace. "About your dream, the hands. Which one will you grasp hold of?"

"The hand with the hole in the palm, a wooden stake driven through it."

"He'll restore your soul. He's waiting for you by the altar. Go to Him now, and the nightmares and the ghosts will be gone forever. Your heart will be whole, pure, and free."

Jennie nodded, rose from her seat, stood in the center aisle, and set her eyes on the stained-glass window. Amadeus stepped silently to the piano. As tears flowed down both their faces, the melodies of hymns filled the sanctuary. The lyrics flooded her mind, her heart, and she walked straight into the open arms of Jesus.

And Jennie knelt in prayer:

Lord, I am lost and still wandering, and I am tired of wandering. My heart is broken. I need to come home. I want to come home and live in your peace, your love. Let me come back into the fold. Heal my heart. Forgive me for my sin and grant Your Mercy, Your Grace on my soul. Amen.

She remained there on her knees, sensing warmth and seeing brilliance from the glowing white light beaming through the stained-glass window, as though it were reaching out to her straight from His hands, and she listened to the music and the words in her heart. Gentle hands touched her: Grandmothers Jennie and Sarah knelt beside her with love in their eyes.

And in her heart, Jennie heard the Lord's words: *Welcome home, my child, my lost sheep is found. You will wander no more. Live in My Peace and My Love. You are home.*

The glowing white light faded, her grandmothers were gone, and the notes of the piano silenced. Another touch, a familiar one, Amadeus lifted her and looked into her eyes. "I love you, always have, always will."

They walked, arms around each other, back down the aisle, and out of the church into sunlight, united in love, new life, renewed faith, and seeking purpose.

On Route 43, Amadeus drove straight past the right turn that led to Voter Hill.

"Where are we going? Tim may be missing us."

"Taking the pearl in my life out for ice cream. Tim will learn that he is safe and loved. Besides, he's playing with the other kids."

At the ice cream stand, Jennie sat at a table in the shade of tall maples. Amadeus stood in line, his turn next, and ordered two ice cream cones, or so she thought. Minutes later, he presented her with a banana split and two spoons—three scoops, two chocolate, vanilla in the middle, hot fudge poured all over it, whipped cream piled high, and covered with colorful jimmies like a quilt.

Jennie savored the taste of sweet chocolate, the mixture of cold and hot. Digging her spoon into the bottom of the dish, she said, "Where's the banana?"

"Who wants fruit when you can eat ice cream?" Devouring some himself, he said, "Tell me, how did you ever get through college? You had no money."

"I earned my high school diploma through homeschooling and marched with my class. Pastor Bob orchestrated a miracle—full scholarship in special educa- tion—and I had only three hurdles to jump—transportation, balancing work and raising Rebecca, and maintaining a three point eight average."

"You are an accomplished woman. And I love you."

Jennie held his hand, entwining her fingers in his. "I love you, but I simply cannot eat anymore!" She stuck the spoon in the dish.

They arrived quietly at the Murphys, as he drove the Jeep today. No roaring Beast announced their ascent up Voter Hill. No children ran across the lawn to greet them. They walked hand-in-hand, to the front door, Jennie lagging a little behind, her eyes and heart lifted upward to the sea of blue with mountainous cumulus clouds. Here, on top of Voter Hill, above the world—the treetops below, a blan- ket of mixed green hues, distant mountains, brilliant colors—she had always thought she could reach up and touch the sky, where God lives. Today, God had reached down, welcoming a lost sojourner home.

Jennie let go of his hand, stepped out of her shoes, and spread her arms wide. Dancing eyes turned upward, she twirled, whirled, and laughed with joyous abandon, her heart free and whole, at peace, and loving.

All six children, bunched together, squeezed through the front door, Alice and Tom at their heels. Down they ran, two holding hands with adults. Alice grasped Jennie's hands. They spun, they waltzed, they laughed the sweet melo- dies of girlhood, while twirling ballerinas and bouncing boys giggled, encircling them. Tom and Amadeus laughed wholeheartedly. Alice and Jennie, their knees buckling, lay in the grass, holding hands, catching their breaths, children collaps- ing around and on top of them.

Alice said, "Not seeking now, my friend. You have found your way home."

"My name, Jennie, from Swedish, means *God is gracious.*"

"Jennie, your heart, is it all better?" asked Tim. "I was worried."

"Yes, little one. My heart is well. It is healed." She pulled Tim into a close hug. *Thank you for this child, Lord.*

Leaning down, the men helped the women and children to their feet. Togeth- er, all climbed back up the hill, the children packed around Jennie.

That night, Tim climbed up the big bedstead and snuggled under the star quilt. "Jennie, can God and Amadeus make my heart happy?"

Jennie held his hands. "Yes, God can give you a happy heart. Amadeus will guide you along the way. He knows the way home. We'll keep praying."

Kissing his cheek, she said, "Did you know that Amadeus, from Latin, means *Love of God?*"

Yawning, Tim said, "Does my name have a nice meaning, too?"

"Yes, Timothy, from Greek, means *to honor God.* Now close your eyes."

Amadeus smoothed Tim's hair. "When you're ready, I'll walk beside you."

Rosie settled herself next to Tim's bed. A boy and a dog, the truest of friends.

In their bed, he held her close, whispered, "Feeling different?"

"Once, long ago, when we shared childhood, I saw, heard, and felt all of nature. I do now, with you. And today, on Voter Hill I saw brilliance."

Snuggling under the comforter, moonlight shimmering on French doors, they kissed, loving and passionate. She breathed the scent of him. Held by him, loved by him. It was an hour or more before they slept, wrapped in their own thoughts, until she interrupted the silence. "I'd like to open that envelope now."

"Not tonight. This moment feels like perfect peace."

PART THREE

Twenty-One

Several days later—family time at the old homestead—Tim held tight to Rosie, giggling, as The Beast bounced up and down on the logging road, through potholes, over large rocks, and across plank bridges—still in need of springs, shocks, tires, and brakes. Abruptly, Rosie pulled her head inside as branches scraped the truck.

At the clearing, Amadeus parked off the beaten path. They climbed down and carried their things across the meadow to the old crumbling stone wall: Jennie, a new sketchpad and the oversized quilt; Tim, the shovel, dragged along behind him (one hand on proud Rosie, her head held high); Amadeus, the rake, and the woven picnic basket.

At the stone wall and the cellar hole, day lilies and lilacs remained, their blooms like historical markers—once this was a homestead—their colors not as bright on this overcast day. Close by, Deane Mountain, a timeworn monument to Jennie's ancestry—a portrait of wisdom and grace gained through ages of time past—abides a friend of her childhood while overlooking the homestead. Even more than the trees, the mountains possessed the secrets of this land and of the ancestors who lived here long ago.

Amadeus noticed Jennie—standing taller, straighter, shoulders back, her past not weighing her down, the wind blowing her long hair—observing Deane Mountain, shades of purple where it met the sky. Taking his long stride, he walked purposely over to her and wrapped his arms around her. "One day, we'll marry, and our wedding should be here."

"Do you call that a proposal, Amadeus Stuart?"

"Well, no, not proposing yet."

"We already have love and family, so take your time."

Laughing, he took her hand, shifted gears, and said, "Let's show Tim how to walk a stone wall."

"First, your music award." Jennie raced toward the orchard, passing by Tim, still slowly crossing the meadow. "Tim, follow me! Help me find what I lost long ago!" The words: *marry, wedding.* Perhaps she could marry him, but put that aside for now. Tim was here. Tim was happy.

His hand on Rosie, the little boy followed Jennie, as fast as he could without falling, not too fast, still dragging the shovel, the world's heaviest security blanket. Amadeus caught up, grabbed the handle, held Tim's small hand in his large hand.

"What are we doing?" said Tim.

"We're going on a treasure hunt for a little gold pin. It belonged to me, and Jennie buried it when she was ten."

"Why would she take your stuff? Did she steal it?"

Amadeus laughed, "Long story for later."

"Long story now," Tim said, but Amadeus tugged him along.

In the overgrown apple orchard, Jennie was kicking brush in her hiking boots. How would she pinpoint the spot of her heart's burial? It looked so different now—bushes everywhere, fallen limbs, sticks, and twigs scattered. It had been thirty years since she had seen it, and a decade at least since anyone had trimmed the trees.

Next to her at last, Tim kicked at the brush, and even Rosie was digging. Falling to his knees beside the dog, Tim scattered brush with his hands.

Amadeus said, "Okay, Jennie, where did you bury it?"

Tim said, "Okay, Jennie!"

Jennie said, "Under an apple tree. I covered it with brush."

Amadeus said, "Oh, under an apple tree. There's only two hundred trees."

Tim said, "No, only twenty-three."

Jennie said, sounding doubtful, "Well, we have to start somewhere."

All three on their knees combed through the brush, crawling from tree to tree and removing sticks, twigs, and grass. Amadeus moved fallen limbs.

"Dig here, Amadeus, next to this tree," said Tim. "Right here, it might be here."

Jennie sat back on her knees, sighing. "I dug a little hole with my hand, covered it over, set a rock on it, and then the brush."

"Maybe it's under *this tree,* Jennie," said Tim, slapping the tree trunk.

Amadeus raked, cleared away undergrowth, exposed countless rocks of various sizes, shapes, and hues of gray, under several trees.

Tim played dog: picked up a stick, put it in his mouth, and shook his head, growling.

"Oh, Tim," said Jennie. "It's dirty. Don't put sticks in your mouth."

"Woof! Woof!" said Tim.

Jennie grasped the stick and said, "Let it go, little pup." He did, and she threw it. Rosie fetched, brought it back, dropped it in front of Tim, tail wagging—one of Rosie's favorite games. Tim threw it again and Jennie said, "Help me look! I put it under a rock. Small, round, smooth, and gray."

"They're all small, round, smooth, and gray," said Tim, following her. He picked up many, showed them to Jennie, asking repeatedly, "Is it this one?" Some were tiny, others too large, still others too rough or not perfectly round. Together, they chose five, and Amadeus dug small holes under the rocks. On their knees, Jennie and Tim sifted through loose dirt. Fetch forgotten, Rosie dug, too, dirt flying. Nothing! No gold pin shaped like a double clef.

Tim said, "What are we looking for?"

Amadeus said, "When I was eleven, I won a music award for playing my violin in competition. Jennie was in the audience. She was proud of me and she really liked the pin, my award, shaped like a double clef. It was gold and looked like leaves."

"Is that the long story?" said Tim.

"Our story is a chapter book, but it's why we're digging," said Amadeus. "And Tim, she didn't steal it. I gave it to her."

Amadeus bent down. "Honey, I think it's gone, swallowed by the earth." Hands in his pockets, a man with big thoughts. "You didn't bury your heart. It's free and loving."

"I know that! I just wanted to get the pin back!"

Tim and Rosie wandered, but not far. Picking up sticks, Tim threw them, and Rosie playfully retrieved the sticks. "Wait!" said Tim, pointing his finger, "Look! Look! I saw a lady! I saw her put it there! Over there!" He hurried back, Rosie beside him. "Jennie! Jennie! On the leaf, a hand! I saw a hand!" Grasping her hand, he said, "Come!"

Jennie and Amadeus followed. Gold lay upon straw. Nearby on the leaf, sparkling bright light spread golden rays around the tree, transforming its hue to straw. Jennie gently touched the leaf, delicately removed the double clef, and placed it in Amadeus's hand. "Not lost, but found." For a moment they remembered the day in the maple, when ten-year-old Jennie gave Amadeus her bracelet and Amadeus, two years older, gave her his music award. Then best friends parted: Jennie across the state and Amadeus deeper into the forest. This summer, thirty years later, they found each other.

"Wait!" said Jennie. "Tim, what did you see?"

"The lady. She put that on the leaf. I saw her hand!"

"Tell me about the lady."

Tim shrugged his shoulders dramatically. "Just a lady. And then just her hand. Then nothing at all!"

Jennie and Amadeus bent down and she said, "What lady? Tell me about her."

"She was there. She smiled like you. Where did she go?"

"Maybe we'll find her. Tell me about her hands."

"Hands were wrinkled, like in a bathtub. Can we find her now?"

She pushed his hair out of his face. "Oh yes, a treasure hunt!"

A murder of crows flew out of the trees. Branches wavered and bent. A flash! Someone or something breezed past the orchard, just beyond the trees.

Jennie took Tim's dirty hand and followed Amadeus, walking stealthily toward the edge where the orchard met the meadow. Rosie too. Still hidden, Amadeus laid his rake and shovel in the grass just beyond the trees. Pushing aside limbs, they spied the old vegetable garden.

"Do you see?" she said to Amadeus.

Finger to his lips, he nodded, said to Tim, "What do you see?"

"The lady! Right there!" He pointed his finger. "It's her! In the garden! The lady with your pin."

"Jennie, Tim said he sees the lady."

"Oh, how wonderful that you see her!" Jennie brushed leaves, twigs, and dirt off Tim's face, hands, and clothing. "That's Mary Deane, my great-great-great-grandmother, with her daughters, Zibiah, Rachel, and Thankful." Jennie glanced back at them. "What else do you see?"

"An old man runnin'!"

"Oh my, how delightful that you see him. That's Cyrus Deane, my great-great-great-grandfather. Look at him go!" To Amadeus, she said, "Do you believe he's sixty, and Mary's fifty-seven?"

"He sure is spry for a man that age."

"Yeah," said Tim, "he runs faster than Mike and Calvin."

The passage of time, apparently, had been kind to Cyrus and Mary. And here he was, not quite in the flesh: Cyrus Deane pacing at the edge of the garden.

Mary rubbed her aching back, wiped her brow—it was a hot summer day in 1826—and viewed rows of plowed earth where mounds of soil sheltered seeds, green shoots sprouting in sun and rain.

Cyrus waved his arms, and Mary trudged over to him. They walked across the meadow to the edge of the orchard where Jennie, Amadeus, and Tim knelt. A southern exposure. Cyrus set seedlings on the ground. Spying gardening tools, he reached out next to Amadeus, not seeing him, and grasped the shovel and rake. Digging holes, he carefully planted the chance seedlings—apples fallen from trees—covered them, and raked over the soil. Standing straight, shoulders back, his arm around Mary, they admired the beginning of the Deane apple orchard.

Cyrus's chance seedlings—Nine Ounce or the Deane apple, one of Maine's heirloom varieties, originated on the Deane Homestead in Temple, Maine. Its color is light red with pink stripes on greenish-yellow. Its shape is roundish with a flat base and flat at the stem. Its weight, nine ounces. Its taste, juicy and tart.

Farming in Greene (1790-1826), Maine's fruit basket, Cyrus may have raised an orchard and brought with him to Temple chance seedlings, among them, Northern Spy and Duchess from which the Deane apple may have propagated.

In 1858, two years after Cyrus's death, it was first exhibited, perhaps by his sons William and James, before the Franklin County Board of Agriculture, named Nine Ounce, and again in 1859 with the name Deane apple.

The Deane Orchard grew from the 1800s to the mid-1900s, but has over time disappeared, encroached upon by various species. Deane trees grow in the yards of a few Temple and Phillips residents. One has been planted at the Temple Historical Society.

Suddenly swirling, like vertigo, Jennie pulled Tim close. Amadeus held them both, and Rosie too. Spiraling! Spiraling! Ascending above the treetops, they descended—Jennie saw to it with unbidden powers—at the Cyrus Deane Stream, the water's edge. Rosie jumped in.

A young man held the hand of a young woman, helping her onto the wagon seat. Lingering there, their eyes saw only each other, until she took the reins from his hand. Tipping his hat and giving her a slight grin, he watched as the young woman drove away—the horse a slow trotter—down the well-traveled path that would become the Varnum Pond Road. Could they have been William and Louisa, her great-great-grandparents? William Deane: BY HIS LOSS ALONE WE KNOW. She'd seen those words before.

Sensing motion, Jennie clutched Tim. Amadeus called to Rosie. Swimming to the edge, Rosie shook and sprayed a giggling Tim, just as Amadeus pulled the dog into a one-armed hug. Rising! Twirling! Ascending! The four descended, spinning downward and landing near the old crumbling stone wall.

"Oh, Mom! I mean Jennie! That was fun! Twirling around in the sky!" Arms spread wide, Tim spun around, once, twice, thrice, fell in the grass, and laughed. "Annie and Gracie twirl all the time."

They all laughed.

Sitting on the wall, Jennie opened her sketchbook and roughly drew the faces, the orchard, and the Cyrus Deane Stream. "Amadeus, later, let's walk down to the graveyard. Perhaps I could find the words I seem to have forgotten about William."

"Lunch first. Tim and I are starved." Spreading the quilt in the grass, the red-checked tablecloth neatly on it, Amadeus and Tim unpacked turkey sandwiches, carrot sticks, strawberries, small bags of chips, peanut butter cookies, and bottled water.

Tim set Rosie's water bowl and dog biscuits in the grass. Then, sitting next to Jennie, a sandwich in one hand, he looked at her drawings. Touching one, he said, "That's Mary," and another, "That's Cyrus. She gave you back the pin. He planted the trees." One finger pressed against his chin, he stared at the overgrown orchard. "Why did they plant trees that were already growed?"

Amadeus and Jennie glanced at each other: *How to answer.*

"Tim, this place has stories to tell. Some Jennie's dad told her. When we are with her, we see the stories too. It's fun, don't you think?" said Amadeus.

Tim nodded, biting into a sandwich, said, "like imag…imag."

"Imagination," said Jennie.

Tim nodded, excitedly.

Jennie squeezed his cheeks. "Mine is wild!"

Chewing carrot sticks, Tim said, "Why did Cyrus plant trees that were growed?"

"The story happened a long time ago, before the trees grew, before the orchard was there," said Amadeus.

"Oh," said Tim, "before Adam and Eve and the apple tree?"

Amadeus chuckled. "Not that long ago."

Strawberries consumed, everything repacked in the basket, they carried their things to The Beast. Tim lagged behind, munching a cookie, more in his other hand.

"Jennie, I'm missing my tools! Cyrus still has my shovel and rake!"

"Perhaps, Tool Man, he'll return them someday."

Reaching for Tim's hands, they waited as the little boy, still chewing, stuffed half-eaten cookies in his pockets, wiped his hands on his pants, and clasped theirs. Heading down the rough steep path, a slow walk, rocks and roots exposed, they veered right through the woods to a solid stone wall. Rosie sniffed woodsy scents.

"Tim, have you ever walked on a stone wall?" said Amadeus.

Shaking his head, Tim said, "I'll fall down."

Sheltered by tall pines, light seeping through branches, the solid stone wall seemed to invite the three to sit, to walk, to simply enjoy its seclusion. Amadeus helped Jennie as she hopped up, balanced, and with posture straight, arms spread wide, stepped slowly, carefully, across the wall, bowed, and curtsied. Tim's eyes grew big, his mouth shaped liked an O. Jennie could walk on walls!

Next, Amadeus, arms to his sides, took quicker steps, a little heel and toe action. Giggling, Tim toppled over. These grown-ups acted like kids!

"Now, Tim, it's your turn," said Amadeus.

Tim shook his head.

Amadeus grinned. "Want to try?"

"You'll hold onto me?"

"We both will," said Jennie.

Tim nodded. Amadeus lifted him onto the wall. Taking slow, cautious steps, almost toppling over, they held Tim secure in their strong, steady hands. Still clutching their hands, Tim jumped off. "That was fun! Maybe someday I can do it by myself."

"One day you will," said Amadeus.

Plodding downhill through the woods, not as treacherous as the path for Tim, they slowly climbed up cracked granite steps into the Deane–Huse Cemetery. Holding tightly to Tim's hands, they passed small hidden markers in tall grass and crossed to the far side.

Observing the headstone honoring five lost children, Jennie remembered the rainstorm—their last visit here and Amadeus's release of his grief-stricken heart. On her knees in front of two sunken stones, William and Louisa Deane, who had raised five children and farmed the homestead, Jennie wiped away dirt, twigs, and grass, and then traced engravings, recalling Louisa's story. At six the little girl from Wilton had been farmed out to the Varnum family of Temple after the death of her mother, Mary Gibbs, wife of Isaac Chamberlain Noyes—a veteran of the Maine troops in the War of 1812. Digging deeper around William's gravestone and brushing away dirt and debris, she discovered the hidden epitaph. Tracing, she read aloud: BY HIS LOSS ALONE, WE KNOW HIS WORTH AND FEEL HOW TRUE A MAN HAS WALKED WITH US ON EARTH.

The bitter east wind whirled through the wooded graveyard. Daylight turned to twilight. Amadeus held Tim close, protecting him from the wind and gloom. Hands pressed against the epitaph, eyes closed, shivering, long hair fanning, Jennie waited to spiral back to the ten-year-old she once was—back to a long-ago unfinished vision.

"Jennie, where are you?" called Amadeus, blinded by swirling debris.

"Where is she?" called Tim, crying.

"Here with you. Nothing," she said.

"Perhaps you should not seek, but accept what you are shown," said Amadeus, clasping Jennie's hand. "Come. You and Tim are freezing in this raw wind." They trudged slowly, vigilantly, leaning into the wind, back to the gate, as twilight gave way to darkness.

Suddenly, Jennie halted. Rosie whined. A presence held a lantern, light in darkness. The air, bone-chilling. "Who are you?" she said. "Is it you, William?" She shivered, feeling light pressure on her cheek.

Sticks and twigs snapped. Old, crumpled, dead leaves shuffled. Jennie turned. The dark-skinned boy in tattered clothing ran ahead of a man and a woman, out of the woods, out of hiding. She turned back, but the spirit was gone.

Beyond, heading up the path, the spirit of William Deane ambled along, carrying the lantern. The family followed, seeking safety and freedom.

The air warmed. The wind calmed. Jennie's hand was still held in Amadeus's.

"Where are you?" he said.

"I am here beside you."

"Come, walk carefully. I've no flashlight again."

"Follow the lantern and Shoofly."

Outside the iron gate, Tim said, "Jennie, who was that boy? I weared shirts and pants like him."

"Do you mean clothes with rips?"

"Yup, but now I don't. You got me new ones. Will that boy get new ones?"

"Yes, Tim, he will. Like you, he'll be a handsome boy in his new clothes."

Up the steep path they walked, keeping the lantern in sight. From under the canopy of branches, they stepped into the clearing, into the late afternoon light of day.

When all were settled in the truck, Amadeus held the clutch to the floor, his right foot on the brake, and released the emergency brake. The manual shift in neutral, he turned the ignition. The familiar roar sounded like a jet engine in this solitary meadow.

As they accelerated down the logging road, Tim bounced up and down—jolly fun for a boy—and then Amadeus sped down the long hill. Turning onto Route 43, the paved road, much smoother—not so merry for a boy—soothed Tim into sleep.

Amadeus stopped at the town hall, where the post office was located. They hadn't checked their mail all week. He hurried inside and then back to the truck. They browsed through the stack: monthly bills, her credit card statement, a tool catalog, and a one-page letter from Rebecca. While Jennie deciphered the quick scrawl, he scanned through the local newspaper. One blocked item in bold print seemed to lift itself right off the page before his eyes—Accepting Bids for Land. Deadline end of July.

July 10

Dear Mom,

Yes, I plan to visit, okay? End of month, Friday the 26th? Come to your hillbilly's palace? You have room? We could spend a few days exploring before we head north to normal life, assuming your little fling is over. I'm intrigued by the old family homestead and cemetery.

School opens August 14th. I hope you have reconsidered your resignation. You need to be at home where I can be of help.

Love,
Your daughter

Amadeus got out of the truck and folded the newspaper under his arm. "Back in a few."

"Where?" she said, but he was gone.

At the town clerk's window, he inquired about the location of the tract of land—up near Varnum Pond. Just as he thought. Completing the form, he put in a bid without hesitation—fifteen thousand dollars—sealed the envelope, and passed it to the clerk. Too much for wooded land, but worth every penny.

Jennie smoothed Tim's hair while he slept with his head on her lap. Amadeus slid into the driver's seat, and she said, snappily, "Where did you go?"

"Just talking to a man about a horse. You sound a little angry."

Jennie sighed, "Rebecca's letter. She'll be here soon. It won't be pleasant."

"Tea time, we'll talk." He started the engine, shifted gears, put his arm around her, and backed up the truck.

Twenty-Two

Late that same night—was it already July 15th? Upstairs in the tower's library, whose cherry bookcases were filled with volumes, the old stained-glass lamp glowed. Jennie sat in a worn leather chair, wrapped in Amadeus's flannel robe, pages held in her shaking hands.

Awakening, Jennie not beside him, Amadeus quietly donned his pants, the other robe, and checked on Tim, sleeping soundly with Rosie next to him. From the kitchen he heard Jennie's cries and climbed the stairs, two at a time. Seating himself on the marble coffee table, he said, "Sweetheart, what's wrong?"

Handing him the pages, she said, "I opened the white envelope."

"Why in the middle of the night?"

"It's quiet. I couldn't sleep."

"Tell me more."

"For Rebecca to embrace her own life, I need to show her that I am totally free of the past and capable of making my own decisions."

He read the letter silently:

Dear Jennie,

I am truly sorry for not accepting the child you were. I denied your identity by taking away all that you loved, the things that gave you strength, joy, peace: your visions, stories, Temple, and even Amadeus. How I wish I had not driven that wedge.

Your visions were real. I feared you were becoming too connected with our ancestral spirits; for the present and future belong to you, not the past.

How I hurt you. I forced you to choose between home and family and love for your unborn child. Later, I should have come for you and Rebecca. By ignoring Daniel's abusive treatment of you, I, too, became the abuser.

I did not act as a loving father. I broke your mother's heart, also. I hope that you three will forgive me. Not seeing your dancing eyes, not hearing your sweet alto, and not loving my granddaughter has broken my heart.

Jennie, you are a courageous, loving woman, mother, and teacher. I am proud of you. I love you. I know you live in darkness. Find your roots and live in the light. Go to Temple. Your Amadeus is there. Safe journey, my child.

Love,
Dad

Amadeus glanced at the second sheet:

Dear Jennie,

Your father did not allow me to share this. The day you left, he vowed to watch over you, and he did. Attached are only two of the receipts he saved in his account book.

Love,
Mom.

July 21, 1969 — one bottle of whiskey.
A bill of sale — a Ford Maverick. Jennie's going to college!

Laying them on the table, Amadeus glanced up at the top shelf of the bookcase: his letter was hidden there, withheld from her. Her heart had not been ready before now, and neither had his.

"If I had read this letter years ago, I would have come to you."

"You arrived at the right time, in God's time. Any sooner you would have found a broken, angry man—not the boy who was your friend or the man you found a few weeks ago." Caressing her hair, he said, "Your journey began when our hearts sought healing."

Jennie knelt and wept, held in his arms. Would she understand why he withheld his letter and did not fulfill her father's request? Would she forgive him, or would she lose her? "Jennie, the receipts?"

"The car was one of my hurdles to jump, but I never knew who gave it to me. The bottle I found on the porch. Dad gave Daniel the means to die."

"Oh, my sweetheart." Still holding her close, he gave her time to cry. He couldn't have shared his letter before now. He needed to know, first, that she had released her burden and truly loved him. Was their love now strong enough to acknowledge yet another revelation and grant forgiveness? Oh, how he loved her!

Amadeus stepped over to the bookcase, reached onto a high shelf, pulled down his old Bible, and flipped through the pages. Finding the white envelope addressed to him, he set it in her hand. "Please, forgive me for not sharing this. Until now, I didn't believe you were ready. Truthfully, I wasn't ready either."

"Wait, you've got a letter from him too?"

"Written the year he died. I'm sorry for withholding it."

"If I am to convince Rebecca, then you and everyone else must stop treating me as *poor pitiful Jennie*." She wasn't happy with him, but then she had let herself become *poor pitiful Jennie*. Clutching the envelope, she adjusted her robe, pulled out another letter in her father's familiar hand, and read:

Dear Amadeus,

I pray that by this time your heart has healed from the tragic loss of your children. If not, please heed the lesson I learned: the longer one waits to seek forgiveness, the harder the heart grows.

I have one request of you, since the end of my life is near. Find my Jennie. She lives in darkness with a broken heart. Help her heal, help her find her way into the light and back to you. I regret separating the two of you.

Jennie: my daughter with the big brown dancing eyes; music in her heart and her voice; the inquisitive, curious girl with joy in her heart; the daughter who confused, puzzled, and perplexed me; the daughter I love and miss.

Find her and her eyes will dance, and her heart will sing joyously.

Your friend,
Henry

Silently waiting for Jennie to speak, he lowered his head, unable to look into her eyes. Leaning his elbows on his thighs, he folded his hands in prayer. He had fallen from her graces. He'd not been the boy who always found her, but instead, the man who allowed her to remain lost.

Jennie held his hand and said softly, "Did you search for me?"

Raising his eyes to meet hers, he said, "No. I prayed for you night and day. That's when I started building furniture. In my workshop I prayed."

Pulling away from him and sitting back in the chair, she said, sharply, "Furniture! Why didn't you come? You knew where to begin searching."

"Please, hear my story. Listen with your heart."

Through the wall of windows, Jennie gazed at the moon, stars, and Deane Mountain. Grandma Sarah had told her to love him through his story and to trust in his love. She nestled his hand in both of hers. "I'm listening with my heart."

"I was still grieving. I couldn't help you. So, I prayed for others to care for you, and a few friends here also prayed. My heart was hard as stone. I couldn't forgive God. I hurt deep in my soul and waged war against God. I was lost. I needed to find my way into forgiveness, into Grace, before guiding you." Hiding his eyes, he breathed slowly.

"Look at me. Tell me how you found your way."

"It took years. I stayed in the woods as much as I could, trying to find solace in trees. Nowhere could I find rest, not even in music, so I stopped playing. Emilie and Tom stayed close, meeting me here. A new pastor arrived: Andrew guided my way."

Holding her eyes in his, he said, "A strange thing happened. While praying for you and working with wood, I saw you, the girl: climbing trees with me, loving my music and books, wandering. I saw gravestones, Belgians, our maple tree. Memories flooded my mind. I saw your smile and your tears, heard your laugh." Caressing her face, he said, "I found joy in you, in our childhood days, and my heart softened. I played my violin again, saw you in the notes and listened to your angelic voice."

Drying Jennie's tears, he said, "A light in the workshop appeared pure white with a brilliance I'd never seen before. In those moments, I felt enclosed, safe, at peace with the smells, textures, hues of wood, and the sounds of tools were like music. Always you beside me."

"My angels!"

He nodded. "Yes, I met your grandmothers there. I was finding my way, so I kept on crafting. Not knowing exactly why, only knowing it was what I needed to do. I still grieved, but my anger was falling away, and my heart was forgiving God. Then I saw you that day, walking up Voter Hill. I knew it was you, and I knew why you had come."

"My quest to renew my heart. Grandma Sarah's words: *Come home. It is time.*"

"I knew you would lead me to a renewed heart and spirit."

"I couldn't have done that. I needed you to walk with me." *Let me walk beside you on your journey.* His words in the maple tree.

Stroking her palm gently, he said, "At the gravestone of the five lost children in the rainstorm, you told me their story. Then I met Jesus there. I saw Him, I heard His words, and I knew your thoughts. In that moment, I came face to face with a choice: to be lost forever or to be found and live a new life. Only then, could I walk with you down that path to renewal." He caught his breath. "Up on Potato Hill, Grandma Sarah told me, *The time has come.*"

"Grandma Sarah told me, *This journey is not yours to walk alone.* My path was our path and Tim's. He belongs in our family." Kneeling again, she enfolded him in her arms. She had been in their hearts for a long time. "Who prayed for me?"

"Tom and Alice, Pastor Andrew and Jill, Emilie and myself. They knew only your name, and I alone knew the reason for prayer, a broken heart." Lifting her chin, he held her eyes in his. "Does it make a difference, not coming for you?"

"No, no difference. Our love is precious to us, for we have lived without love."

Gently tracing her face, he sought her lips, and they kissed. Helping her stand and holding her close, they viewed Heaven's lights, the moonbeam illuminating Deane Mountain.

"With you, my eyes dance, and my heart sings." One more loving kiss shared and they descended the stairs, leaving the letters lying on the marble table.

Nails clicking in the hallway, Rosie met them in the kitchen, whining. Tim tossed and turned in his sleep. Sitting on his bed, Jennie laid teddy in the crook of Tim's arm, pulled the star quilt over him and drew circles on his cheek. Amadeus knelt by the bed, held Tim's hand, and sang lullabies until the boy relaxed into undisturbed sleep. Kissing his cheek and petting Rosie, they retired to their bedroom.

Cozy under the comforter, he caressed her soft skin with his warm hands. She roamed over his body with cool fingers sinking into his chest hair.

"Honey, Maggie and Gracie belong in our family, just as Tim does. I've prayed about this. All three are seekers on our journey."

"They are helpers, too," she said, her voice cracking and tears sliding onto his chest. "We'll call Pastor and set Maxine's heart at peace."

Soft, tender kisses grew more intense and they shared their true and precious love.

The letters still lay on the marble table in the library. Truth had been told, forgiveness granted, love had grown more precious, unbreakable, and purpose had been found—loving the children.

Twenty-Three

On Friday, July 26th, ten days after Tim's mother's funeral, friends, family, and members of Grace Church gathered at the village cemetery to lay to rest Maxine Simmons, grandmother of Maggie and Gracie Simmons. Sunlight encircled the polished casket adorned with an array of lilies, supported above an empty grave, next to the headstone of Maxine's daughter, Margaret Grace Simmons, mother of the two girls.

Jennie swayed slowly, smoothed Gracie's long light brown braids, stroked her cheek softly, heard her cries, and felt her tears slipping down her face. Gracie hugged Jennie tightly. Amadeus held a teary-eyed Maggie, light blond braids hanging down to her waist. Maggie laid her head on his shoulder, arms hugging his neck. Tim, posture tense, hair tied back like Amadeus's, held hands with Auntie Emilie and Uncle James. Dressed in their Sunday best, the family stood in prayerful silence. Others stood close by: Tom, Alice, and Annie; Jill and Great-Aunt Madeleine; Sadie with her sons, Mike and Calvin. Jennie caught a glance at her family from the elderly gentleman who had sold them a box of books and had attended Tim's mother's funeral.

While a group of Maxine's friends and former colleagues crossed the cemetery and gathered around, Jennie remembered assembling here ten days ago with a smaller group of coworkers and church members to honor Sharon Bailey, loving mother and heroine, saving her son's life. Sharon had found her way back into Grace. Jennie had sung a hymn of peace, accompanied by Amadeus on his violin. Pastor Andrew had spoken from *Luke 15:6: Rejoice with me for I have found my lost sheep.* And Tim had stood tall and silent, like a tin soldier, tears running down his cheeks, his hands clasped securely in Jennie's and Amadeus's.

Today, Pastor Andrew carried Jennie back from memory by speaking these words: "Welcome, everyone, to a celebration for our sister in faith. Maxine—mother, grandmother, sister, teacher, friend and God's faithful servant...."

Jennie whispered, "Amadeus, look there."

"I see," he said.

A bright white light shone on the casket: Grandmothers Sarah and Jennie and Great-Aunt Mary gathered by Maxine's grave, as they had for Sharon's.

Standing behind the podium, Tom Murphy cleared his throat, glanced at Alice, and introduced a time of shared memories, first, telling his and Amadeus's: Maxine Simmons had told them: *True lasting friendship comes from the heart, not from being like everyone else.* Tom and Amadeus had met in Maxine's eighth grade classroom. As preteen boys, they'd become friends and taken some teasing because of their differences. Tom was a basketball player and Amadeus a violinist and a pianist. They'd shared their different interests—movies and building things for Tom, and for Amadeus, books and the woods—and found their commonalities were greater than their differences. So the gift of lifetime friendship had been planted and tended in boyhood by Maxine.

Friends and colleagues and church members approached the podium, sharing special thoughts and memories.

From where they stood, with children clinging and friends close by, Amadeus and Jennie sang Maxine's favorite hymn, a cappella. Resting his hand on her back, Amadeus offered comfort, as Jennie's sweet alto chimed clear strong notes with articulated lyrics. His baritone gave her the strength to sing, despite tears streaming down her face. In her heart she saw thirteen-year-old Jennie clinging to her mother at Grandmother Sarah's funeral: the solo then, she now sang. Yet her heart knew Maxine was at peace with God, the battle with cancer at its end. No more tears, no more pain, and her granddaughters were loved.

Pastor Andrew Griffin spoke from God's Word, *John 3:16: For God so loved the world that he gave his only begotten son, that whosoever believes in him shall not perish but have eternal life.*

A final word of prayer, and all departed, sharing comfort and memories of Maxine.

During the last two weeks, James Foster, the attorney Amadeus had retained for Tim's adoption, had filed court documents for the private adoption of Gracie and Maggie. Maxine had entered hospice, and the girls had moved into the lavender bedroom at the cabin. Madeleine had moved into a senior apartment complex, close by friends and the family who had welcomed her—a gift of love for an elderly woman and memories told in life stories for the girls.

That afternoon at the homestead, Amadeus and Jennie sat on the old crumbling stone wall, holding the girls with Tim squeezed in between. In tall grass and wild-flowers, Rosie spied movement, and the chase began.

Hearts were sad. Tears flowed. Maggie sniffled. "Where's Mam?"

They turned the children's heads upward to the sky, and Amadeus said, "Look up, my dear little ones, look up. See the sky. See Heaven. Mam is there, just up there with Sharon, looking down, watching over you and all of us. Mam and Sharon are with Jesus."

"But how can she take care of Maggie and me?" said Gracie sadly. "I miss her."

"Mam gave you to us, to love you and be your family. We'll take care of you. We love you," said Jennie, caressing their braids. "Mam watches from Heaven, and she's very happy we are all together."

"Mommy gave me to you, too," said Tim.

"Yes, sweetie, she did, and we love you," said Jennie, hugging Tim close. "We love all of our honeybees."

"Mam is where you are. She lives in your heart, in your memories, in the life stories Aunt Madeleine tells you," said Amadeus.

Tim sat listening quietly. A tear fell, and then he said, "Mommy stays in my heart."

Amadeus pulled him close. Jennie kissed him on the cheek and then jumped up. "Anyone want to hike down to the stream?"

Climbing off the wall, Tim said, "Come on, let's go! Maybe Cyrus will be there. It's his stream. Got his name on it."

"Sounds like fun." Amadeus called to Rosie, and the chase forgotten, she sped to the stone wall and bumped into Tim, knocking him over. Laughing, he rolled in the grass, and the chocolate lab playfully nudged him.

They crossed the meadow back to the beaten path and into the woods. Maggie held Jennie's hand, and Gracie followed. Tim, just behind them, held onto Rosie. Amadeus led them down the same path he had walked with Jennie several weeks before, past the stand of pines and into the field by the Cyrus Deane Stream.

"Who is Cyrus?" said Gracie.

"An old man that likes apple trees," said Tim. "He plants them."

"Oh, like Johnny Appleseed?"

Shrugging his shoulders, Tim said, "I don't know Johnny Appleseed, just Cyrus Deane." Loudly, he called to Amadeus. "I still don't know why Cyrus planted trees that were already growed."

Gracie turned and faced him, hands on her hips. "Timmy! Cyrus wanted a bigger orchard!" Palms up, she said, "More trees, more apples!" Abruptly turning around, braids swinging, she followed Maggie down the path.

Tim halted. "Yeah! That's it! More trees, more apples!" Then he followed.

Jennie reached for Amadeus's hand, and they shared a quiet laugh.

In the field, Jennie, still holding Maggie's hand, ran to the water's edge. Kicking off her hiking boots, she pulled her jeans above her knees, Maggie's too. "Come, sweetie, splash with me." In the warm flowing water, sparkling in sunshine, Jennie and Maggie splashed. Their joyous sweet sounds mixed with melodies of songbirds and quacking ducks, carried downstream by the current. Rosie barked, jumped in, and splashed them both! Amadeus, Gracie, and Tim followed. More giggles and laughter. Acting silly, Tim toppled over, soaking wet, and the girls intentionally followed. Jennie and Amadeus hugged.

An elderly Quaker couple strolled by, picking a bouquet. Pointing to the field, Tim said, "Look! It's Cyrus, our friend! I see him and Mary, too!" Gracie frowned, stared at the field, unseeing. Maggie giggled, splashing her sister and Tim.

Standing still in the water, looking at the sky, trees, and spirits, Tim said, "Amadeus, will Cyrus let us put something here for Mommy?"

Gracie said, "For Mam, too?"

Amadeus said, "Like what?"

Tim said, "Flowers."

Gracie said, "Mam liked flowers."

Jennie said, "A remembrance garden. Sharon and Mam would like that."

Grinning, Amadeus said, "Cyrus and Mary would enjoy the garden too."

The sun dipped toward the horizon. Still chattering happily, they trudged back across the field and up the trail in soggy clothes but dry shoes. Back on the path, Amadeus chuckled, seeing the rake and shovel leaning against the truck. He laid them in the truck bed. The family, including a wet Rosie, piled into The Beast for the ride home.

Gracie said, "How come I didn't see Cyrus? Is he an imaginary friend?"

Tim said, "He's a real friend, like Mike and Calvin."

Jennie said, "Perhaps next time, Gracie, you will see."

Wiggling in her seat, Gracie said, "Timmy, can you move over?"

"No, I can't. Rosie will be squished against the door."

"I'm too crowded. Tim, move over."

"I told you, I can't."

Amadeus said, "Quiet down. Sit still. We'll be home soon."

Jennie pulled Maggie onto her lap. "Now Rosie won't be squished."

Driving down the logging road, the children bounced and giggled. Amadeus slammed the brakes and the bald tires slid on dirt and rocks. A black bear coaxed her two young playful cubs across the road into the woods. Like children exploring their world, the cubs ignored their mother's gentle but firm nudges, rolled in the dirt, wandered away, and scratched on tree trunks.

Up on their knees, elbows on the dash, faces peeled to the windshield, breaths fogging it, the children watched intently. Rosie barked.

Amadeus said, "Rosie, quiet," and Tim petted her head.

"Why don't they move out of the road?" said Gracie.

"Because the babies want to play," said Tim. "Move, you're in my space."

"No, I'm not. You're in mine. You're touching me," said Gracie.

Maggie, her knees poking into Jennie's thighs, fingerprints on the windshield, counted. "One, two, three. Three bears," and giggled.

"Stop shaking your head, Gracie," said Tim. "You're whacking me with your braids."

Finally, mama bear got her little ones headed in the right direction. After gentle pushes from behind, they disappeared into the trees. The kids settled down for the ride. Several minutes later, Amadeus turned up the dirt road, parked under the maple, and Gracie said, "There's a girl on the porch."

"Not another one," said Tim, hands over his face.

"It's Rebecca, but who's the man?" said Jennie.

Running down the porch steps and over to the truck, Rebecca opened the passenger side door. "Mom, I've missed you." Rosie, Tim, and Gracie piled out and Gracie said, "Did you find treasure?"

"Yes, I did. Lots of cool stuff, like bones."

The young man hurried over to Amadeus, and they hugged. Annie caught up to Gracie, and the girls giggled, jumped, and twirled.

Lifting Maggie out, Amadeus offered a hand to Jennie. Mother and daughter hugged tightly, and all four children gathered around. Amadeus introduced Isaac, and Jennie said, "You're the Murphy who digs holes."

Isaac laughed. "You're the Jennie in the magical stories my mother told me."

Rebecca said, "Mom, who are the children?"

Jennie glanced at Amadeus and pulled the kids close. "Meet Maggie and Gracie, your sisters, and Tim, your brother, all best friends with Annie. There are two more friends, but they don't live here. They've all been waiting for weeks to meet you."

Amadeus said, "Rebecca, welcome to our home. Come inside."

"Wait, Mom? What's this all about?"

Linking her arm in Amadeus's, Jennie said, "Meet the boy in the photograph, the father in our family." Taking Rebecca's arm, she escorted her inside their beautiful home and said, "Tell me about the dig, honeybee." The girls ran into their bedroom to play with Annie. Amadeus, Tim, and Isaac walked to the workshop.

That evening when all was quiet and stories had been read, prayers said, lullabies sung, children tucked into bed, Rebecca reading in the yellow bedroom, and Rosie pacing, guarding through the night, Jennie and Amadeus sat at the rock maple table and opened the beautiful blue box. The lid displayed a painting of wild daisies against a blue sky.

Inside, fine script read *painting by Margaret Grace*.

Madeleine had given it to Jennie: memories from Mam for the girls. On the table, Jennie set photographs of Maggie, Gracie and three others in small frames: one of the girls and Mam on the steps at their house; a second of the girls' mother; and a third of the sisters, Maxine and Madeleine. Other treasures included a white porcelain music box and a folder of their mother's childhood drawings and paintings.

Amadeus found a large manila envelope containing birth certificates, medical records, and newspaper articles. One reported a show by an aspiring artist named Margaret. The other, an obituary. Margaret, the victim of a car accident, had given birth to Maggie before dying. Gracie had been two at the time.

Amadeus sipped his tea and, seeing Maggie and Rosie in the arched doorway, he opened his arms. "Come, sweetie." She ran to him and he held her. When Maggie saw the music box and the framed photograph, she pointed and said, "Mam."

Jennie said, "Mam, Maggie, and Gracie." She set the photo in Maggie's hand, and the little girl laid her head on Amadeus's shoulder and cried softly. Jennie wound the music box, lullabies in soft chimes. They listened until Maggie quieted, and Amadeus carried his daughter to a rocker, leaving the photograph on the table.

Jennie packed up the blue box, minus the manila envelope. Carrying it to the lavender bedroom, she set the music box and the framed photographs on the dresser and the beautiful blue box on a bookshelf. *Lord*, she prayed, *the girls will treasure these memories, but, what of Tim? After the fire, only ashes, nothing left but a little toy truck.*

She listened to the soft baritone. Amadeus—a gentle kind loving father.

Gracie stirred, whimpering in her sleep. Jennie lay close beside her daughter, held her, and smoothed her hair, while humming, her alto with his baritone, until Gracie relaxed into quiet rest. While they kept watch over the girls, Rosie slipped quietly down the hall to Tim's room.

Sisters asleep in their beds, Amadeus and Jennie heard Tim's cries. Amadeus lifted his boy into his arms, held him close, and the three of them cuddled on the sofa. "Hey, buddy, calm down, talk to me."

Jennie laid her hand on Tim's cheek, "Did you have a bad dream?"

Shaking his head, Tim sniffled. "Mommy's gone, and I don't have a place to go."

"Look at me," said Amadeus. "Tell me why you think you need to go."

Tim said, "Well, you know I worry. You got Maggie and Gracie and Rebecca, so maybe you don't want a boy anymore." Sniffling, he wiped his nose on his sleeve. "Did I do something bad?"

"Tim, we still want a boy. We love you. You've done nothing bad. Even if you make a mistake, we still love you, but you didn't."

"This is home, a home for all of us in our castle," said Jennie. "Sweetie, you always have a home with us. And Tim, Rebecca's only visiting." She kissed him on the cheek, and Tim thought about wiping it away, but he didn't.

My Side of the Mountain lay on the coffee table. Jennie picked it up, opened to the first page and read, her voice lulled him to sleep, while Amadeus held him.

With Tim snug in his bed and Rosie at his bedside, a tired Jennie and Amadeus fell into bed themselves. "Three have broken hearts, and Rebecca's heart is in turmoil. Watch out, my dear Amadeus, the storm is brewing."

"Give it time and patience. The storm will pass, and the sun will shine."

TWENTY-FOUR

On a breezy Sunday afternoon, mother and daughter walked down the dirt road, past the woodpile, the pine, maple, birch, and wildflowers blooming in the field. "Hang a right. There's a lovely pond down here and a stone wall, a good place to think, pray, and talk. I've sat there myself a few times, seeking answers."

Rebecca thrust out her chin, stared critically into her mother's eyes, veered off the dirt road, and traipsed down the path. Deer lapped at the water's edge. Alerted by limbs pushed aside, footsteps crunching twigs, and strange scents, the deer fled.

Following behind, her chin trembling, Jennie thought about the broken relationship between her father and herself. Would building a new life free Rebecca to lead her own, or would it drive a wedge? They'd always been too close, too interdependent.

Sitting on the stone wall in the sun's warmth, Jennie gave her daughter a few quiet moments. Rebecca, leaning against an oak tree, arms folded, shoulders drooping, turned away from Jennie and lowered her head.

"Sit next to me, honeybee. Please, sit with me."

Rebecca sat down, giving her a wide berth, crossed her arms and legs, and swinging one leg, said accusingly, "Really, you actually took time to think and pray?"

"Did you check out those letters from the colleges?" asked Jennie in a quiet, calming voice. "I saw them on the seat of your car."

"They were just applications inviting me to apply to graduate programs. They send them out by the millions."

"Any of interest?"

"Mom, let's drop the grad programs, okay? How could you do this? Really! In seven weeks—seven weeks—you hook up with this guy and take on three troubled little kids. You give up your career to shack up in the woods with a guy in a ponytail who delivers wood. Wood! I thought this was a quest of self-discovery."

"Yes, dear daughter, I fulfilled the purpose of my quest." She kept her voice even. "It's now time for you to step out into the world. Now, any of interest?"

The breezes silenced and the current stilled, stagnant. Meadow grass and wildflowers slumped in the heat of the sun. Rebecca's posture stiffened, her expression sullen. Jennie waited out the silence and her daughter's obstinance. "Only one."

"And?"

"Okay," Rebecca said, sharply. "I received an acceptance letter from a prestigious college in Boston to study archaeology. They offered me a scholarship and a paid position in the research department."

"That's fantastic!" Sliding closer, Jennie hugged her daughter. "I'm proud, so proud of you. Will you take this opportunity?"

"It doesn't really matter." Chin quivering, Rebecca said sadly, "I signed a contract. School opens in two weeks. How could I do grad school? It's quite obvious that I can't leave you!" she snapped.

"Contracts can be broken, sweetie. Just resign. They'll find a teacher." Jennie held her daughter's hand. "My life with Amadeus is the life I chose. And furthermore, missy, if you turn this down, you'll be miserable in the classroom."

Rebecca said brusquely, "Okay, Mom! I'm going back. I have a date with Isaac."

Leaving the meadow, where the grasses and flowers now swayed in the breeze and the current flowed, Rebecca trudged up the path, her mother just behind. At the dirt road, Jennie linked her arm in Rebecca's, but her daughter pulled away, jogged, then raced ahead. Thunder and lightning, floods, limbs falling, Hurricane Rebecca whirled, gyrating around the cabin. For a time, the winds would blow, and the cabin would need to stand solid and strong, waiting out the storm.

*

When Tim left the health clinic on Monday, he carried a balsa wood airplane, a thing of timeless beauty, that he had chosen from Dr. Michelle Peterson's treasure box.

Dr. Michelle had listened to the foster parents' concerns: Tim's vision; a fist hold on objects; slow academic progress; issues with balance, falling, and motor coordination; small size and stature. And, possibly, malnutrition and truancy. Examining the leg length discrepancy and feeling Tim's bones and joints, she had said, "Well, Mr. Tim, think you can handle plenty of healthy food, outside playtime in the sunshine, and ten hours sleep at night? Naps too, if you want?"

"Okay, I can do it. But, no naps!"

Amadeus said, "Will do and thank you. Naps and all!"

And Tim had scowled at Amadeus.

Dr. Michelle had agreed with Jennie and recommended that Tim see a team of medical and educational professionals. She'd also recommend an immediate referral to physical and occupational therapy. (At the girls' check-ups, a week earlier, Dr. Michelle had recommended the same therapies and educational evaluation for Maggie.) A more serious diagnosis, other than malnutrition, truancy, and the discrepancy in leg length, could be the root of these issues.

After Jennie scheduled the follow-up appointment, they left. Tim's mind was now occupied with the next stop—lunch at the fast food restaurant—and Amadeus had told him that he could take a burger home to Rosie.

While Tim was at his appointment, Rebecca and the three girls entered the local independent bookstore. Browsing through publications, novels, biographies, and nonfiction, displayed on tables and shelves, two items had caught Rebecca's interest—historical archaeological digs and Boston's colonial history. Scanning through the pages, she didn't see the girls fidgeting. Standing on one foot, then the other, Gracie said, "May we look at the children's books?"

"Please," said Annie. "They're just over there by that chair."

"Of course, go ahead. I'll be right there." Flipping pages and reading short passages, Rebecca did not notice the woman approaching. "Excuse me, are you with those three girls?"

Startled, Rebecca said, "Yes, yes I am."

"I'd appreciate it if you'd keep an eye on them."

Rebecca peeked around the bookcases enclosing the small space. "Oh, my goodness! Well, I'm sure they'll be careful. They're just reading."

"And pick them up, please." The store manager returned to the checkout counter, where customers had formed a line.

The space where the three girls sat, cross-legged or on their knees, surrounded by a stack of books, held a comfortable leather chair, an oversized teddy bear, and a brightly colored thick carpet. Annie and Gracie talked noisily about cover art, turned pages, and read aloud. Maggie built a tower with books of various shapes and sizes.

Sitting in the chair, books on her lap, Rebecca held back laughter. "Maggie, the book in your hand? Would you like me to read the story?"

Maggie plopped *The Very Hungry Caterpillar* on Rebecca's lap and, turning the pages, pointed to the pictures as Rebecca read. "Do you like the story, sweetie?"

Smiling sweetly, blue eyes shining, Maggie nodded.

"Let's buy it." To Gracie and Annie, she said, "And yours too."

"Thank you," they said, holding up *Charlotte's Web* and *The Secret Garden*.

"Mom read those books to me. I loved the stories," said Rebecca.

Gracie said, "We have story time every night."

Rebecca said, "So did I. We didn't have a television."

Gracie said, "Maggie and I watch TV at Annie's."

Annie said, "I have story time and TV time."

"I watched it at Eleanor's house. Now find a book for Tim." said Rebecca, catching a glimpse of Maggie, wandering around the corner.

From the shelf, Annie chose *The Sign of the Beaver.*

"Perfect choice," said Rebecca.

Hurriedly replacing the dozens of scattered books neatly back on the shelves, Annie and Gracie found Rebecca and Maggie sitting at a child-size table, looking at a puzzle of farm animals in a frame.

Rebecca said, "What do you see?"

Maggie pointed, "Ducks, pigs, sheep, cows."

With permission, the older girls selected one of kittens, five hundred pieces.

Rebecca added two puzzles to her purchases and paid with her credit card, a rather hefty charge for a recently unemployed teacher, but worth every penny.

Then, with the girls settled in the Mustang, Rebecca turned on High Street, passed by the college, and left on Main Street, parking at the fast food restaurant. Time for lunch with family.

*

That evening, the children, all bathed and in pajamas, their story read, stomped loudly up the stairs and across the maple floor to hug their mother and their big sister.

"Good night, my sweeties," said Jennie.

Hugging Rebecca, Tim said, "I like the story. It's Calvin's favorite."

"It's a good story. Good night, little ones," said Rebecca.

Another hug for Rebecca from Gracie, and the kids headed to the stairs. Maggie ran back, patted Rebecca's cheek, and said sweetly, "Love you." A bear hug shared between sisters. "Love you, too, Mags." And Maggie ran straight into Amadeus's arms.

Jennie said, "Did you enjoy your day with the girls?"

"I really did. They're so lively. They seem genuinely happy with the two of you."

"All three bring joy to our hearts."

A lull in conversation made the library too quiet, like the eye of a hurricane. Jennie inhaled slowly. "What about your opportunity?" she asked and waited silently for the storm to bash against the cabin walls.

Rebecca said, sharply, "You already know, I resigned. If you won't come home, I'll need to move here. Mom, you need my help."

"Well, sweetie, I do love you, but we'll see about that."

Rebecca sighed gloomily, "Maybe I could find a teaching position here." Rising from the chair, she headed toward the stairs. "I'm tired. Good night, Mom."

Curling up in the chair, Jennie gazed through the window, her eyes watering.

The children tucked into bed, Amadeus climbed the stairs with a tray of tea and cookies. Setting it on the marble table, he leaned down, kissed Jennie, and gave her a mug.

"Does she see only *poor pitiful Jennie*? Yes, of course. Did I do that to her, make her see a mother dependent on her daughter?"

Sitting in the other chair and holding her hand, he said, "Give her time to sort it out." He gave her hand a squeeze. "She loves you, Jennie, and there is another issue."

"Wait, what?" Jennie frowned.

"Love is in the air, sweetheart. Isaac's headed for grad school, MBA, in Boston. What will Rebecca do? Now she's unemployed and five hours closer."

"Amadeus! Jennie!" called Gracie from below the stairs. "Maggie's puking!"

Hurrying down the stairs, they squeezed into the overcrowded bathroom. Rebecca, already there, spoke soothing words and tenderly cleaned Maggie's face and hands with a cool washcloth as Gracie hugged her little sister. Jennie stepped toward her daughters, but Amadeus caught her hand.

Wednesday brought a pleasant, tranquil morning to the cabin. On the porch, Gracie jumped rope, and Maggie hopped past the swing to the steps, back and forth. Tim and Amadeus played catch, and Rosie chased the ball. Rebecca was somewhere with Isaac.

Pulling open the junk drawer, Jennie removed the calendar and set it on the counter. Turning to the month of July, she marked off days with dots in red pen.

Tim hurried, as fast as he could, not too fast, through the mudroom door. Passing by Jennie, he tossed his glove on the counter. "I have to go to the bathroom!"

Amadeus followed more slowly, stopping at the counter when he saw the calendar. "Wrong month. It's the first of August." Staring into her face, a slow smile grew on his.

"Oh! I turned to the wrong month. School opens soon."

"School! I'm not going! I'm never going back to stupid school ever again!" Tim stamped his foot. "You can't make me!" Tears streaming, he wailed and rushed to his room, fell twice, slammed the door, and hid his head under the pillow, sobbing. Rosie had followed but had the door slammed in her face. Barking, she ran to the kitchen, whining and prancing.

Flying through the screen door, Maggie just behind—door slammed—Gracie yelled, "What's Tim screaming about?"

The calendar forgotten, Jennie said, "School. He says he won't go."

Gracie said, "Oh, that! I know why. Annie, Mike, and Calvin too."

Amadeus said, "Jennie, let's talk to Tim first."

"This isn't about losing summer playtime. It's serious."

Entering the bedroom, Amadeus lifted Tim, sobbing, shaking, and clutching teddy. Tim's body was stiff, tense, his head erect; he could not relax and hug his trusted friend. Enveloping his boy in secure, gentle arms, Amadeus said, "Let's read a story." In the blue living room on the gray sofa with the log cabin quilt draped over the back, Amadeus held Tim close. Listening to that comforting voice, Tim laid his head on Amadeus's heart, its beat steady. Jennie softly drew circles on his cheek.

Maggie and Gracie, both weeping, sat next to Jennie and Gracie said, "It wasn't nice, what they did. They hurt Tim."

Hugging her girls, Jennie said, "Calm yourselves now."

For the next hour, Amadeus read again *The Sign of the Beaver*, then turned back to the first page. Sobs turned to whimpers and then to sniffles, as Amadeus read on until the sniffles stopped, the tears dried up, and Tim's body lay limp in his arms. "Now, buddy, can we talk?"

Tim shook his head, still resting on Amadeus's heart.

Gracie said, "Timmy, you can tell them. They'll help you. Please, tell them."

Jennie said, "Sweetie, tell us why you don't want to go to school."

Clutching teddy tighter and tears flowing, Tim said, "The bullies, they call me names, push me down, hurt me, take away my food. I was hungry." He sniffled. "That Phillip kid pushed me off a log. He hurt me at school. I can't run and play. I fall down. I can't do the work." He stuck out his shorter leg. "It hurt all the time." Crying, he said, "Those mean people got me at the hospital, and they might get me at school. I'm staying home. I'm safe here." And Tim sobbed.

Carrying Tim to the workshop, Amadeus gave him a piece of wood and sandpaper and showed him how to sand. They sat there—Tim on the worktable and Amadeus on a tree stump—sanding pieces of wood and talking about trees.

On the sofa, Jennie hugged a crying Gracie. "Did anyone help Tim?"

"Some kids were nice, and teachers too."

Here's the heart of the matter, as told by Gracie: Mike and Calvin helped Tim all the time. They got teased because Tim's their friend. Mr. Adams protected Tim from the bullies. Tim spend time in his classroom, a safe place. He'd often given Tim his lunch and helped him do his work. The bus driver helped. The three boys sat in the front seat. Frequently, Tim was excused from school, and Pastor Andy and Mrs. Andy took him to their house. Tim's heart was sad.

Jennie enveloped her daughters in her arms, giving them time to cry, as her own tears fell. "Thank you for telling me this. You and your friends know how to be kind." Then she found Tim and Amadeus in the workshop—the scent of wood, the scraping of sandpaper, unfinished projects, and a pile of plans on an old desk—and hugged Tim tight. "I love you, sweetie. Miss Ellen's coming later, and we'll talk about school."

"I won't go," Tim said, shaking his head and tears falling.

"I understand, okay?" Brushing her hand across the sanded block, she said, "You do good work. This wood is smooth."

Late that afternoon, at the rock maple table, Ellen gave Jennie the list of appointments, her support for homeschooling, and one last piece of information: social services had located a living relative.

TWENTY-FIVE

Several days later, Jennie parked at the side of the old Temple–Wilton Road. Jennie and Rebecca walked briskly up the steep dirt road with Annie and Gracie running ahead and Maggie following them. They climbed the embankment into the hidden Quaker Mott Cemetery, a small burial ground for the family of Cyrus and Mary Deane, and other Quaker families at the corner of what had been the Friends Meeting House, now only scattered foundational rocks. Headstones faced east, as it was believed that the deceased met their Savior at sunrise.

The small, sheltered graveyard, shaded by tall trees at the edge of the woods, is a remembrance of Temple's Quaker families from post-American Revolution years to just before the Civil War. By that time, many Friends had journeyed west.

Some headstones had been carved from natural fieldstone—the Deanes' crafted of white marble—and all showed their age, weather-beaten by more than a century's exposure, cracked and worn and chipped, inscriptions fading. Cyrus Deane's headstone leaned almost flat on the ground.

On her knees, Jennie touched the stone of Thankful Deane. It had once lain flat, broken into three pieces, and now stood in its place—cleaned, polished, pieces cemented together. Close by, the stones of Rachel and Zibiah. Three sisters who never married and who lived out their lives on the Deane Homestead.

Rebecca followed her mother—the younger girls just behind—to each of the family graves. James, a son, a bachelor, a teacher, known as *the learned Quaker gentleman*, had been a favorite among his students at the Deane–Huse School. Every morning he opened school with prayer. His stone, weathered and reshaped by time and the elements—camouflaged among a pile of rocks—appeared to have engravings shrouded in the darkened marble.

Jennie led them to another grave: Abigail Baker Deane, John's wife, who died in childbirth. Their daughter, given her mother's name, became a teacher in the Temple schools and later with her husband, Thomas Gipsen (Jepson), left the homestead and her grandparents, Cyrus and Mary, emigrating to California. So far away.

Linking her arm in Rebecca's, Jennie guided her to the two remaining Deane family graves: Cyrus and Mary, born before the American Revolution and passed away in the decade before the Civil War, were the parents of eight children. Three sons, Abiel, John, and Samuel, were buried in the Midwest; one son, James, and three daughters, here at Quaker Mott; and the remaining son, William, at the Deane–Huse Cemetery.

Kneeling, Jennie caressed the marble stones of the old Quaker couple she had met in visions. Rebecca bent down next to her, and the girls wandered around the graves.

A Deane descendant heard family stories of those seeking freedom from slavery, arriving and leaving the Deane Homestead. Night sounds: leaves rustled, twigs snapped, rocks kicked underfoot, tree limbs pushed aside, and whispered voices.

From Brunswick, an abolitionist city, those seeking freedom followed the Androscoggin River through Lewiston, Auburn, and Jay and to the Deane Homestead in Temple, a seventy-mile journey. Cyrus and Mary Deane and their family were operators, Quakers, and thus abolitionists. Their home was a safe house. It was another seventy miles to the border, traveling to Phillips, Kingfield, and on to Canada by way of the rivers, either northwest along the Carrabassett, or east, following the Kennebec.

Suddenly, the wind roared, dirt and dust, airborne, formed a whirling spiral. Long hair fanned in the wind, veiling faces, braids whipped around. Jennie and Rebecca caught the three girls, carried toward them on a powerful current of air.

Huddled together, the girls wrapped protectively in their arms, the twister carried them away, among flying debris, twigs and branches, twirling, spiraling, ascending above the trees. Descending, they dropped straight down into the dark-ness of the earth, surrounded by rock walls.

"Mom, what happened?" said Rebecca.

"That was fun! Twirling and twirling," said Gracie.

"Where are we?" said Annie.

"Well, my sweeties," said Jennie. "It appears to be story time in the old Deane family cellar hole: *Once upon a time in a root cellar....*"

Footsteps lumbered, and furniture slid across the floor. Hinges creaked, as someone opened the trap door. A lantern shed its light downward. A ladder was propped against the opening. Zibiah slowly climbed down, the lantern in one hand. Rachel followed, carrying folded clothing in one arm.

Lantern light exposed walls, concealed in darkness. Old tools, a mallet, an auger, a hand saw, rakes, and shovels leaned against one wall. Canning jars, filled with vegetables, fruit jams, and applesauce sat on shelves. Bushels of apples, pota-toes, squash, other root vegetables sat on the dirt floor. In dim, wavy light, Rachel handed folded clothing into hands concealed by a false wall.

Jennie's breath quickened. Three people, dressed neatly, emerged into lan-tern light: a mother, a father, and the boy she had seen twice before in tattered clothing—visions in the Deane–Huse Cemetery. Climbing the ladder, Quakers reached down, grasped their hands, and pulled them up out of sight.

Jennie and Rebecca rushed to the ladder, pulled the girls along, and climbed. Rebecca first, the girls in the middle, and Jennie, last, took one more look at the sisters. At the top, Rebecca climbed out, and the girls rolled across the puncheon pine floor. Jennie accepted Rebecca's offered hand, the spirits on her heels.

In the warm, cozy cabin, lit with flickering candles, a stew simmered in a cast-iron kettle hung in the brick fireplace. Corn bread baked in a cast-iron Dutch oven set in ashes. Quilts were draped over two rocking chairs. Jennie and her daughters admired the artistry of bold, bright colors, mixed with lighter shades, the intricate piecework and patterns, the codes of the Underground Railroad. Flying geese led the way north to waterways, safety and freedom. Shoofly, a guide, signaled with a lantern in woodsy cemeteries. Log cabin, black center squares, identified a safe house—the Deane Cabin.

Gracie said, "Jennie, can we make a quilt?"

Annie said, "Yeah, can we?"

Jennie said, "The patterns, the colors, it's art, sweeties."

William covered the hole, concealing it with a braided rug, and his brothers replaced the table and benches. Mary gave the woman a basket of food for the journey. Cyrus shook the man's hand and held onto the boy's hand, leading them into the night. It was now 1840, a new decade, and Cyrus and Mary had aged.

That vertiginous feeling came over Jennie and she rushed her girls outside into a blustery wind. Crushing Gracie and Annie against her, Rebecca held Maggie securely. They whirled and twirled high above the logging road, above Varnum Pond Road and descended at Quaker Mott, in time past.

In the corner of this small Quaker cemetery, Jennie saw the meeting house, supported on its firm stone foundation. As a child, she had seen only a small section of crumbling foundation rocks. Holding hands with the younger girls, Jennie and Rebecca walked slowly past gravestones and up the steps into the meeting house.

In awe their eyes darted around the room, a different place of worship than they attended. Plain bare walls, no stained-glass windows, no religious creeds, and no paintings of Christ or biblical events. Friends sat on benches, facing each other. Worshippers prayed in silence, seeking the *still small voice* of God (1 Kings 19:12).

Sitting together on a bench, little girls in the middle, Jennie recognized the Deane family opposite them. Silently reciting Psalm 46:10: *Be still and know that I am God,* she prayed: for God's guidance and presence in her and Amadeus's life, their place in Tim's life, her new family, and for Rebecca.

The service ended in conversations and hand shaking among the Friends. Jennie whispered *Amen,* unfolded her hands, and opened her eyes. Rebecca, her head bowed, hands folded, still silently prayed. A tear rolled down her cheek. The girls watched. This evening Jennie would find time to chat again with her daughter. Departing, they mixed in with the Friends. Skipping along, hand-in-hand with the girls among the Deane family spirits, they followed other Friends down the wooded path, the Quakers to their wagons and Jennie's entourage out of the vision and to her Jeep.

In the late afternoon at the rock maple table, Rebecca, Gracie, and Annie opened the jigsaw puzzle box, a picture of kittens, and noisily assembled the puzzle. Maggie and Jennie put together the thick cardboard pieces of the framed farm animals.

Jennie said, "My little girl loves puzzles."

Maggie fit two more pieces together, beamed up at Jennie, and said, "I like cows."

In that moment, seeing Jennie through Maggie's shiny blue eyes and sweet smile, Rebecca slowly climbed the black metal stairs, stopping halfway, and glancing back, tears sliding down her cheeks. In the tower, she gazed through the wall of windows at Deane Mountain formed during the glacial age, shaped and molded by time—a periphery of Jennie's world, but a barricade to Rebecca's.

Hurrying upstairs and hugging her daughter, Jennie said, "It's time to begin your journey, my honeybee."

"You see Deane Mountain and you are content. I see beyond mountains and oceans. I wonder about life, its secrets, stories of ages past, and I want to know. Mom, I heard the still small voice."

"What did it tell you?"

"Your quest brought you home. It's time to dig out the old maps and see where they take me." She dried her tears. "I love you. I'll miss you, Mom."

"And I you," said Jennie, teary-eyed. "Follow your heart and always remember the way home."

As daylight turned to twilight, they sat in the old leather chairs, reminiscing about those days on McBurnie Road, surrounded by potato fields and the great sweeping, rolling blue sky, when Rebecca was the little girl with shiny brown eyes.

Story time with Rebecca that evening, upstairs in the tower: four children, already in their pajamas, sat cross-legged or lay prone, chins on palms, feet swinging in the air, shadows in the moonbeam. Rosie lay next to Tim.

Gracie said, "What's spiraling?"

Rebecca said, "Twirling, like you girls do."

Gracie said, "We twirled today. Tim, we saw Cyrus."

Annie said, "Gracie, Jennie told us it was a story."

Tim scratched his head and frowned, nose twitching. "Where'd you see Cyrus?"

Gracie said, "At his house. At church, he was praying."

Turning to Rebecca, Tim said, "Can you tell me the story?"

Crawling onto Rebecca's lap, Maggie wrapped her big sister's arms around her, and Rebecca began the telling: *Once upon a time in a root cellar, Cyrus and Mary....*

Downstairs in the quiet kitchen, mugs of hot herbal tea with honey, cupcakes, and one tapered candle, the only light, sat on the oak table. Holding his hand, massaging his palm, Jennie gazed into Amadeus's eyes and saw love, home, a mountain. She really could marry him.

The story told, the children stomped noisily down the metal stairs with Rebecca and Rosie. Giving good night hugs, Maggie, Gracie, Annie, and Rebecca twirled, like dancing ballerinas, to the lavender bedroom. Tim remained next to Jennie, and said, "Are you gonna eat that cupcake?"

Jennie pulled out a chair. Tim sat down, ate the cupcake, and between bites, said, proudly, "Cyrus helped that boy we saw in the cemetery. The boy with the rips in his clothes. Yeah, he gave him food, new clothes, and showed him the way to be free."

"Yes, he did!" said Jennie, wiping frosted crumbs from the corners of Tim's mouth and kissing his cheek. "Now, sweetie, it's past bedtime."

Amadeus said, "You were a big help today stacking wood."

Tim said, "Well, I got time tomorrow to help you work."

Amadeus chuckled. "I can use your help."

Tim walked slowly to his room, climbed onto the iron bedstead, and Rebecca tucked him in. Then, joining tea time, she said, "Mom, tell me what happened today."

Jennie explained: childhood wanderings and visions; lifelong connection to her ancestors; Grandmother Sarah who also could see; and her best friend, Amadeus—the boy and the man who always found her and to whom her heart had always belonged. She spoke about the years when everything had been taken away and her sense of feeling lost, abandoned, without an identity.

"Grandma Sarah's cryptic message on the photograph?" said Rebecca.

Amadeus said, "Yes, please keep her secret. Those who do not see do not believe and may not accept the seer."

"It's safe with me," said Rebecca. "It was thrilling, an eye-witness to history, and I'd like to go with you again." Rising from the table, she kissed her mother good night and said, "Sometime, could you tell me about my father and grandfather?"

"Tomorrow, honeybee, a walk and a talk and an old crumbling stone wall."

Then, checking on the kids, Rebecca settled in the smaller yellow bedroom with a good book. In a week or so, she and Isaac would share her final journey to Presque Isle.

Asleep under the carved maple tree and wrapped snugly in the white comforter, Amadeus held Jennie in his arms.

Dressed in the fashion of the Gilded Age—the Gay Nineties—she wore a yellow silk gauze shirtwaist with pleats and darts, puff sleeves, and a dark blue tie. Her gray woolen skirt, of natural fibers, wool and silk, felt like cashmere. It was snug at the waist and hip and full at the hem. White side button gaiters covered black shoes with a chunky square heel. Her long brown hair was tied back with a dark blue bow.

Amadeus was decked out in his dark gray tweed, knee-length breeches. Wool socks stretched to his knees. A starched shirt, a bow tie, and a matching tweed blazer completed his fashionably sporty outfit.

Both wore straw hats: hers adorned with a bright yellow ribbon, and his plain.

Humming a happy tune, they pedaled the tandem down the dirt road past the field and the woodpile on the left and past the maple, oak, and pine on the right. Unexpectedly, he turned a sharp right and they bounced over rocks down the path to the stone wall by the pond. The tandem leaning against a tree, Amadeus invited Jennie to sit on the wall. He reached into his pocket and dropped to one knee.

In the predawn hours, as the moon descended behind the horizon and the sun began its ascent, lighting a new day, Amadeus listened to Jennie's sweet alto, not humming, but singing in her dreams. Awakening to his low, deep voice, accompanying her, she said, "What? You see my dreams now?"

"Not see, hear. Honey, your sweet alto sounds angelic. You've still got it, the music in your heart."

They kissed lovingly, tenderly.

TWENTY-SIX

The crickets were speaking, and the children were nestled in their beds. Faithful Rosie paced quietly from room to room keeping watch through the night. Jennie relaxed in the soaker tub—lavender-scented bath oil mixed with hot water. All was quiet, perfect timing, on this Sunday evening in mid-August.

Amadeus collected certain items: a bottle of red wine, two wine glasses, a large white envelope, and a small blue box tied with a white satin ribbon. He removed Alastair from the piano, tuned earlier that day, and carried these items upstairs to the tower, arranging them on the white marble table—the first trip. In the kitchen he placed a baguette in the oven to warm, arranged chocolate-covered strawberries on a plate, sliced white cheddar, and poured olive oil into a dipping dish. A second trip upstairs; he held the radio in one hand and strawberries in the other, a book under his arm. The bread warmed, he sliced and set it on a plate with the cheese and the dipping bowl. His third trip upstairs and Jennie was still soaking.

In their bedroom, he dressed in his light blue dress shirt, dark blue tie, and a new pair of comfortable dark gray dress slacks. Never would he don tweed breeches, even if he had lived in the 1890s—it was not his style. He re-tied the leather string around his shoulder-length red hair, rummaged through the closet, removed the blue dress he had seen only once, and laid it neatly on the bed with a note.

Opening the door, he stepped into the hall, and Tim opened his on the opposite wall. They met in the middle and Tim said, "Did she say yes?"

"Shhhh!" Comically, Amadeus shooed the little scamp back to his room. "I haven't asked the *question* yet. Go back to sleep, you nut." He turned to leave, then closed the door quickly and hid in Tim's room, as Jennie hurried down the hall. Waiting for her to close the door, he sighed. "That was close."

Laughing, Tim climbed into bed and covered his head.

On his way down the hall, Amadeus stopped at Gracie and Maggie's door. They'd been waiting for him. To Maggie's giggles, Gracie nearly shouted: "Did Jennie say yes?"

"Ixnay!" Amadeus said, grinning despite himself. He tucked them back into their beds. "I haven't asked the *question* yet! Good night, nosy ones! Enough of your giggles!" Dashing upstairs, he sat in the leather chair and read the last pages of *Arundel*.

Jennie saw the dress on the bed. The stylish store associate had said that shade of blue was her color. Reading the note, she laughed: *Wear the dress if you will, my lady, and meet me in the castle tower. A.*

Jennie dressed, clasped the pearl necklace around her neck, tied back her hair with a big blue barrette and dug in the closet for her black dress shoes. She checked on the children, sleeping peacefully, or so she thought, and kissed them good night.

Amadeus heard her footsteps in the kitchen, pushed the book under the chair and stood at the top of the stairs, playing his violin. Jennie floated on air up the black metal staircase, smiling and eyes dancing, letting the soft, slow notes flow into her heart. At the top, she spied Amadeus's handiwork: two glasses of wine, snacks, an envelope, and a small blue box. Stepping slowly toward the wall of windows, she gazed into the starry night — lights twinkling, moonlight beaming on the floor — and listened to Alastair express their true and precious love.

Downstairs, three pairs of feet crept slowly, noiselessly in a line — Tim first and Gracie last, Maggie in the middle — from their bedrooms into the living room. Tim constantly turned around, checking on the girls, finger to his lips. *Shhh!* On tiptoe, they crept through the kitchen to the stairs, carrying pillows. Rosie followed, nails clicking. Sitting on the steps, they leaned on their pillows, silent and still. Rosie lay at the foot.

Amadeus laid the violin on the table and tuned the radio, the volume low. Turning to Jennie, he held out his hand. "May I have this dance?"

She took his hand, and he held her close. They waltzed around the room to the slow, romantic sounds, then kicked it up a few beats, danced the twist, rock n' roll, in and out of the moonbeam, to the music of their youth.

He leaned close to her. "You look stunning in that dress."

She leaned closer to him. "You're looking handsome yourself."

Was that the sound of children yawning?

Music still playing, Amadeus escorted Jennie to the old leather chairs. He sipped some wine as she caressed the glass. They shared a strawberry and a slice of bread.

"Are you planning to tell me what's in the envelope and the box?" she said.

"Why would I tell you?" he said. "It's your job to open!"

Yawning, she said, "Lazy, I guess."

Turning on the old stained-glass lamp, he said, "Envelope first."

From the envelope she pulled out documents. "A contract?" she said, clearly disappointed, but amused at the same time. "Are we celebrating because you bought land?"

"Read it," he said, chuckling.

She read silently, turning the pages. "The Deane Homestead?"

"The Deane Homestead, nearly eighty acres."

Jennie's breath quickened, her eyes shone. "The cellar hole, the orchard." Her voice grew higher and whispery. "Stone walls and the cemetery. All those beautiful old trees."

"For you, for your descendants. You love the land, and it's your home, your history."

"Thank you, sweetie. Oh, thank you, but it should be ours, not mine. You love it too." Here she paused, a heat coming over her. "And my descendants will be yours."

Amadeus didn't miss her tone. The heat was washing over him too. His voice belied his businesslike words: "The title is forthcoming."

Jennie held her wine glass to her lips, breathed the scent of mocha mixed with vanilla, and set it down with an extra caress. Stroking the small blue box, she untied the white satin bow and said, "My family's home." She held his hand. "So thoughtful." Opening the box, she caught her breath. "Oh, my love! It's beautiful!" A gold locket with two hearts entwined. Holding it delicately in her hand, she turned it over and, eyes watering, read the inscription: *Life, Love, Purpose.*

"Here, let me put it on you." He set down his wineglass with that same extra caress, stepped behind her, turned off the radio, and fastened the locket around her neck. One hand still at her nape, he removed a white box hidden behind the first editions, slipped around to be in front of her, and dropped to one knee.

A quick breath. "What are you doing?"

"Jennie Abigail, I love you, always have, and always will. I promise to guard, protect, and keep you safe; to honor and respect you every day; to treat you as my equal in our home and our life; to put you before myself; and to be the man, the husband, the father God expects me to be. Sweetheart, we are building our life on the Cornerstone. You will always know that I love you and you will live in warmth and peace. We've been brought back together to share our life, love, and purpose. In good times and not so good times, we stand together as one."

Amadeus gently dried Jennie's joyous tears and showed her the ring. "This is true Maine tourmaline, light blue, a rare color. It stands for healing, tranquility, living in truth. Live now, my love, with a peaceful heart." Her hand in his, he breathed and said, "Jennie Abigail, will you marry me?"

Tears streaming, Jennie nestled his hand in both of hers. "Amadeus Aaron, I love you, always have, always will. I love the kind, gentle, and solid woodsman you are. We belong together, and my heart has always belonged to you. We've already bonded as one. I promise to honor and respect you every day; to guard and protect our hearts; to treat you as my equal at home and in our life; to put you before myself. I will be the woman, the wife, the mother God expects me to be. You will always know that I love you. My answer was best said by Ruth to Naomi: *Wherever you go, I will go/ Wherever you lodge, I will lodge/ Your people shall be my people/ And your God, my God.*"

Jennie's face glowed in the light of the stained-glass lamp, her eyes danced and her heart sang: "Oh, yes, Amadeus Aaron! I will marry you and live in the light, for with you I am home."

Placing the ring on her finger, they sealed the proposal with a kiss.

Footsteps and giggles, a vibration up the metal stairs! Three children and a chocolate lab tumbled over onto the maple flooring. Tim cried, "Did she say yes?"

"Did she, did she?" the girls cried.

Amadeus hugged them all, laughing and pulling Jennie into the scrum. "She did."

"Yes, I did."

The ring dazzled, sparkling in the light. "So beautiful," said Gracie. Maggie patted her face and said, "Pretty, like you." Jennie hugged her daughters.

"You were dancing," said Gracie, shyly.

"Why, yes, I was. A family habit! May I have this dance, my daughter?"

Gracie smiled, nodded, her deep brown eyes sparkling in the light of the lamp.

Timmy stuck his head through the black metal railing and stared down into the kitchen. "Tim, dance with Maggie," said Jennie.

The girls nodded, excitedly. Tim blushed, tilted his head, and shaking it, looked up at Amadeus, but he nodded. Pulling his head out, Tim took Maggie's hand. While Amadeus played the violin, the children and Jennie danced around the room to the joyous sounds of Alastair. Gracie twirled and twirled while holding Jennie's hand. Maggie and Jennie held both hands and turned circles, sharing sweet giggles. Jennie then tapped Tim's shoulder. Placing his right hand on her waist, her left on his shoulder and palm to palm, they waltzed slowly in a square in the moonbeam—Jennie graceful and Tim unsure, hesitating. Looking up at beautiful Jennie, Tim stood as straight and tall as he could, grinning his best and widest grin, and the girls danced around them.

"Now, my sweeties, it's time for sleep, but, first, share strawberries with us."

Grinning and wiggling, the children balanced on their knees at the marble table, bright eyes darting from Jennie to Amadeus to the strawberries. Amadeus laid Alastair next to the book under his chair, and Jennie placed napkins in front of each of them. Passing the plate, the honeybees each chose one and bit into the sweetness of chocolate wrapped around the plump, red, juicy, scrumptious taste of summer strawberries—sticky chins reddish with juices trickling down the corners of their mouths and chocolate melting on their fingers and faces.

"I love strawberries!" said Gracie.

"Yeah, and chocolate, too!" said Tim.

Maggie held up her sticky fingers and said, "I like strawberry."

"Kiss, kiss! Mom and Dad, kiss!" Gracie said, blushing to have called them those names. And Jennie kissed Amadeus, and Amadeus kissed Jennie.

"Now, little ones, it's time for sleep," said Amadeus.

"Come, we'll tuck you in," said Jennie.

Tim said, "We can do it ourselves. You two need quiet time!"

The children and Rosie slowly descended the stairs, stopped in the bathroom, washed their faces and fingers, and hurried to their bedrooms trailing fits of giggles.

Jennie laughed, "It will be a chocolaty strawberry sticky bathroom when those three are finished."

Amadeus offered his hand. "May I?" Embracing, they swayed slowly, barely moving, kissing softly, to the music of love.

"You will be a beautiful bride. Plan our wedding, as you must have dreamed."

"It's our day. We should plan together."

"It is our day. Yours to plan." Kisses, soft and slow. "Mine is the wedding night."

"Rebecca leaves for grad school on September second."

"Then we'll marry on Sunday, September first. What do you think?"

"A lovely day for a wedding on the homestead." She slid her arms tightly around him. "You must have spent a great deal of money for that land."

"Not really, back taxes plus my bid, only fifteen thousand dollars."

Stunned, Jennie let go of him, stared. "What?"

"Yup, Fifteen K! That's, that's nothing!"

"Well, it's something."

"Just not the extravagance I thought! My thrifty bear!" He laughed, held her waist, lifted her, and whirled around. "Worth every penny and more." She stiffened, clutched his shoulders, closed her eyes, and breathed slowly.

He set her down. "Sorry. Sit for a few moments."

"Let's not whirl again," she said. "I'm serious about it being our land."

"Okay, and thank you," he said, sitting in the chair and pulling her gently onto his lap. "We could build a home there, if you want."

"Kindness and generosity built this home for us. We fell in love here and brought children to our home. Could we revive the orchard and beautify the cemetery?"

"Yes, we could." He reached for the last strawberry and offered it to her. "Perhaps a small cabin, a foothold with a warm woodstove."

One bite and Jennie offered the berry to him. The strawberry devoured, their kisses deepened and grew sensual. Removing his tie, Jennie draped it around her neck and slowly unbuttoned his shirt. He unzipped the back of her dress. Their hands wandered softly over skin, his warm, hers cool, increasingly heating.

Twenty-Seven

At the Cyrus Deane Stream, the current ran fast. Trees displayed the beginning of seasonal change. Leaves still mostly green, but some were already dressed in autumn hues. Gardening tools, a wire mesh cage, and pails of peat and mulch sat in the grass. The children dropped bags of flower bulbs on the ground and, with playful Rosie, jumped, rolled in the grass, and frolicked in the field, waiting to plant the remembrance garden.

Once Amadeus had dug up clumps of dirt and grass and raked peat into the soil, he and the children bent to their knees. Wearing gardening gloves, that dwarfed their small hands, the children dug holes with trowels and Rosie's help. "Dig deeper," Amadeus said. "Keep the bulbs warm through winter." The children dug deeper and then planted yellow daffodil bulbs, pointy side up, and crocus bulbs in shades of purple. With miniature rakes they filled the holes, smoothing the dirt.

While Amadeus raked mulch onto the garden, the kids searched for small rocks, not too small, not too heavy, at the edge of the stream. Finding two short fat sticks, Tim hurried back to Amadeus. "Can we make a cross?"

Running after him, Gracie said, "Us, too?" and Maggie added, "For Mam?"

"Would you like their names on the crosses?"

The kids nodded and Tim said to the girls, "Come on, we got to find two more sticks." Rushing back to the stream, they found more sticks and plenty of rocks. Toting stones—many trips, stream to garden, garden to stream—they lined them up around the garden's perimeter, while Amadeus sat on a tree stump, carving names. In his pockets he found leather strings and helped the kids wrap the sticks.

"Look! By the stream it's Cyrus and Mary!" said Tim, waving to the spirits.

"Where? I don't see them," said Gracie.

"Ducks! See ducks swim!" said Maggie. Rosie splashed into the stream, swimming after the mallards, and everyone laughed.

The garden planted, they knelt, and the children stuck the crosses in the dirt.

Amadeus said, "Perhaps you'd like to sing a song."

Gracie said, "Maybe the one we're learning in Sunday school."

"Yeah," said Tim. "I like that one."

"Me, too," Maggie said.

Together with Amadeus's baritone, the children sang softly and loudly on and off key—heavenly music. The words and notes flowed through the air into their hearts, up into the sky and along the current—a gift for their loved ones.

Looking up at the puffy clouds, tears welling, Tim said, "I love you, Mommy. It's okay that you had to go. Jesus is taking care of you. Amadeus and Jennie are taking care of me." He threw his arms around Amadeus in a tight hug.

Gracie said, "I love you, Mam."

From Maggie, "Love you, Mam."

And from Gracie again, "We miss you. They love all of us." Their arms wrapped around Amadeus, he hugged all three. A gentle woodsman—his arms full of children, of blessings.

Before leaving, the kids watered the garden. Amadeus dug a trench outside the rock border and set the tight mesh wire cage deep into it, securing the posts. The kids then piled clumps of dirt, grass, and rocks around the edge of the cage.

Collecting tools and pails, they followed the path back to the logging road and The Beast. Tim waved to Cyrus and Mary, as the spirits glided nearer to the garden.

In the spring, daffodils and crocuses would grow in sunlight among a field of wildflowers where Cyrus's stream flowed by. The family would visit the garden to remember a loving grandmother, Maxine Simmons, and a loving mother, Sharon Bailey.

＊

Churn dash, flower baskets and maple leaf quilts lay folded on a chair. Shelves overflowed with quilting magazines, patterns, tins of scissors, pins and needles, baskets of thread, mason jars of buttons, and piles of folded fabrics. Dresden plate squares lay on a Singer sewing machine. African violets sat on the windowsill.

That same August day, five days before the wedding, upstairs in Jill's sewing room, Jennie waltzed in front of an antique full-length mirror, humming her melodious sweet sounds. Her wedding dress was of soft, creamy, natural cotton, full-length, an overlay of intricately woven lace and long sheer sleeves. The skirt, smooth at the hip, flowed into a gentle sweep at the hem. "Exquisite!"

Laughing, Jill said, "You'll be a lovely bride. Now, stand still." With a pin cushion on her wrist and a few pins between her teeth, she marked and basted the hem.

Dresses of lavender, blue, and light pastel green hung on a wall-mounted rod. For the flower girls, Gracie and Maggie, full-length cotton dresses with ruffles in place of sleeves, lace, and wide satin bows tied in back, long ties hanging down. For Rebecca, her maid of honor, the green would enhance her brown eyes. "My girls will love their dresses. How did you manage so quickly?"

"Rebecca sewed your dress, her gift to you."

"Oh, my goodness! Beautiful stitching and sewn with loving thoughts."

Jill's task completed, she presented Jennie with two quilts: wild geese for Rebecca and the other, a wedding gift.

Admiring the prints, colors in rich hues on an ivory background with detailed stitching, Jennie said, "Oh my, but you've already given us one."

"I keep my double wedding ring on the bed. I hope you enjoy yours."

"I'll treasure this. Rebecca will love hers too."

They descended the stairs. A cello and violins sat in the corner of the living room. Jennie hugged and thanked Jill, leaving through the front door.

As she lay the quilts on the back seat, a sudden foggy mist filled the Jeep. "Aunt Mary, what are you doing here?"

"We need to hurry. Could you give me a lift?"

"Oh, Aunt, our wedding day is Sunday, and you are invited."

"Get this contraption going," said Mary, pointing her gnarled finger. "That way."

Jennie backed onto Route 43 and, singing love songs, hit the accelerator. Her venerable great-aunt Mary fiddled with the gadgets. "How do you open a window?"

Still singing, Jennie pushed the button on the door handle. Aunt Mary pulled out her bun, letting her long thin white hair sail around in the breeze, adding camouflage to her already foggy appearance. Jennie rounded the bend and sped past Day Mountain Road.

Aunt Mary called out, shakily, "Stop! Stop!"

Jennie slammed on the brakes, and tires screeched, leaving skid marks, as the Jeep swerved, crossed the shoulder, and stopped inches from a stout hemlock trunk! Shaken, hands gripping the wheel, Jennie breathed deeply. "Please, Aunt Mary, give me a warning when you need to stop. Where are you going, anyway?"

"The little red schoolhouse. You need to go there now," said Mary.

"Can't it wait?"

"It's time," said Mary. "Remember the yard sale and the book sale. It's time."

The misty cloud vanishing, Jennie slowly backed the Jeep onto the road, sped back to the schoolhouse, now the Temple Historical Society, and walked in.

Emilie said, "This is a surprise. What can I do for you?"

"I'm not sure." Jennie's face flushed as she took a seat.

"Let me get you a cup of tea. You rest."

The map of Temple tacked to the wall, old-fashioned school desks and the old woodstove reminded Jennie of her first meeting with Amadeus. He'd stood by the window in sunlight. She'd had no idea what they would encounter on that journey together.

Pulled from memory, she saw a hand—an angel's hand, gnarled and arthritic—reach into an old sewing box and lay a photograph, one corner creased, in front of her. Jennie examined it closely.

Emilie entered the room with a cup of tea. "Feeling better?"

"Do you know the people in this photograph?" said Jennie.

Emilie studied the picture. "The older woman, Lucinda, died years ago."

"The man, Fred, lives on Iisalo Road. I purchased the sofa from him. Correct?"

"Yes, Lucinda was his wife, but I don't remember the others." Emilie turned it over but found no writing on the back. Jennie rose quickly, kissed Emilie on the cheek. "Gotta go, love you." And she was gone. The tea, untouched and steaming, sat next to the box.

Speeding back to the Intervale, Jennie parked at Grace Church. Spying Pastor Andrew crossing the lawn, his Bible in hand, she met him on the steps. "I think I found Tim's living relative. May we talk?"

Holding the door, he said, "Come inside."

Nearly two hours later, Jennie turned onto Iisalo Road, sped past a few homes, and turned into Fred's driveway. His words: *Your debt is paid in full.* With a heavy heart, Jennie walked up the path to the front porch. The elderly gentleman sat in an old rocker.

"Hello, Miss Jennie. Sit for a while. Thought you'd be right along."

Pulling the other chair closer to Fred, she held his hand. "I know a boy who now has no connection to his family. Children need connections to family: it gives them an identity, roots, a place of belonging, of knowing where they came from."

A tear rolled down Fred's cheek. "How did you know?"

"Ancestry. Sharon Bailey is your granddaughter, correct?"

Fred nodded. "She is. Her mother, Lucy, was my only child."

"Tim needs his great-grandfather. He needs his family stories, his history, and only you can share it." Jennie sighed and said, "We love him. Tim loves us. He's happy with us. We are petitioning the court to adopt him, Sharon's last request. But he also needs you, and you need him."

"Lucy and her husband died young, an accident, black ice, leaving a five-year-old daughter. Lucinda and I raised Sharon. When Lucinda died, it all fell apart. Since Sharon came home, we talked some, mostly with Pastor present. I offered to help, but she turned me down, kept me away from Tim. All I could do was watch from afar."

"Please, tell me, was that man Quinn Tim's father?"

"No, he's not. He ignored Tim. They met up only a couple of years ago. Don't know who Tim's father was, not sure Sharon knew either. I'm sure Amadeus saw the evidence in the yard. Quinn was an alcoholic."

"Now you are free to love your great-grandson. You're welcome in our home and family, just as Madeleine is. Don't be afraid: Tim will welcome you with open arms."

She squeezed his hand, walked to the Jeep and glanced back at an old man, close to tears, rocking on the porch, lost in memory.

*

At home Amadeus cooked dinner and set the table. The kids hurried into the kitchen. "Where's Jennie? Is dinner ready?"

Tim added, "I love chicken pie."

Glancing out the window over the sink, Amadeus said, "I'll be back in a minute, kids." He quickly walked through the front door and down the steps, past the flower gardens to the Jeep. Opening the door, he said, "Why are you sitting out here? Come inside." Holding her hand, he helped her out, and she hugged him warmly, thankful for the gentle woodsman in her life.

Embracing her, he said, "What happened? Where have you been?"

"Aunt Mary handed me the shovel and I've been digging."

"Jennie, Jennie, you're home." "We missed you." "Time to eat." The kids and Rosie rushed down the steps, clinging to Jennie.

"Did you plant the flower bulbs?"

Tim said, "Yup, we did. We sang a song too. We can sing for you."

Amadeus steered his family back inside for dinner at the family table.

Later that evening, the children sleeping soundly, Jennie sat on the porch swing, next to Amadeus, humming the song the children sang. She smiled at their joyous voices. Handing her a cup of tea, Amadeus waited silently.

"Timmy, our precious child. So sweet and kind. We love him." In tears, Jennie told Sharon's story: a teenage girl stood over the grave of her beloved grandmother, Lucinda and, too young and broken-hearted, Sharon ran away from home. She wandered down the wrong path, one that led to alcoholism, homelessness, and multiple relationships. She became pregnant and found love in motherhood—a love that sustained her through the battle with addiction, but Tim may have suffered from the effects of fetal alcohol syndrome. Sharon had sought help from AA, but no one knew when she stopped drinking. Was it before or early or late into her pregnancy, and did she suffer setbacks? A few months ago, she had come home, faced her mistakes with help from Pastor Andrew, continued recovery, found a job, and loved Tim.

Frowning, he said, "Lucinda Grey? Fred is the relative?"

"Another heartbreaking story."

Setting the mugs on the floor and holding her hand, he said, "That explains all the appointments, the therapy and testing."

"Our sweet boy." Jennie laid her head on his shoulder. "Oh, Amadeus, what if Fred doesn't sign those papers? What will happen to our Tim?"

Embracing her, he said, "Tim belongs with us. A judge would surely see that. Sharon knew that…her dying words."

Sharon had told her there was no one else to love Tim. And they do love Tim.

Twenty-Eight

Deane Mountain, a witness to generations of life and love, of changing cultures through the ages, stored Sunday, September First in its centuries-old memory. The ancestral spirits in time-honored history on the Deane Homestead kicked up their heels and celebrated in the land of the living with family and friends who gathered at the wedding of Amadeus and Jennie.

Goldenrod, Queen Anne's lace, and wild daisies mixed with tall grass bordered the perimeter of a mowed and trimmed meadow. White satin ribbon defined the aisle from the beaten path through the meadow to the crumbling stone wall. The Deane family spirits intermingled with the guests gathered there.

Annie, Mike, and Calvin stood in a zigzag line in front of the white satin ribbons, holding woven reed baskets of torn blossoms. Annie, pretty in a long, lacy pink dress, French braid, gold locket, and daisy crown, bounced excitedly. The boys, fidgeting and grinning, looked smart in slacks, white shirts, ties, and gold tie pins.

Gathered in the meadow, the quintet—Emilie Stuart, keyboardist; Pastor Andrew Griffin, violinist; Jill Griffin, cellist and violinist; Ellen Baker, harpist; and Bob Adams, guitarist—viewed the canopy of branches sheltering the steep path, the way through the woods to the old Deane–Huse Cemetery.

Sadie captured photographs of the wedding party, guests, and scenery.

Maggie in blue and Gracie in lavender, so cute in long, lacy dresses and shiny, black Mary Janes, quivered happily, baskets of wildflower blossoms in their hands. Rebecca, who once was Jennie's lively little girl and now a beautiful young woman in pastel green, held a bouquet of hydrangeas in mixed colors. The bride and her daughters wore French braids, gold lockets and crowns of daisy chains. Jennie's locket, two hearts interwoven, was a gift from Amadeus. The bride's bouquet of white hydrangeas burst with splashes of color.

Tim, squirming like the boys in the aisle, was well-dressed, like Amadeus, handsome in gray slacks, a light blue shirt, dark blue tie, and stiff black shoes. Gold tie pins adorned their ties, Amadeus's, a gold double clef shaped like leaves, the music award.

Next to Tim, always with Tim, her tail wagging, sat faithful Rosie, pretty in a chocolate lab sort of way with a piney scent and daisies entwined in her collar.

Jennie brushed a smudge of dirt off Tim's face, smoothed his hair, and straightened his collar. "You are a handsome boy with your new haircut."

"Jennie, you are beautiful."

"I feel beautiful. Do you have the rings?"

Tim, proudly, patted his pants pocket. "Yup, right here, where Amadeus told me to keep them safe."

Joining the quintet, Amadeus shouldered his violin for a solo. With his eyes on Jennie, his elegant bride in creamy natural cotton and lace—all loving heart, dancing eyes, and wildflowers—he drew the bow across the strings of Alastair. That beautiful old hymn, its mellow, sweet notes, airborne, sailed along treetops to Deane Mountain, and settled in Jennie's heart. Her Amadeus—a man with a loving joyful heart.

A flash on gold lockets and tie pins! Beams of light frolicked like children at play. In the sunny sky Jennie saw her angels and Tim followed her gaze.

The musicians joined Amadeus in that lovely hymn. Laying down his violin, he crossed the meadow to the beaten path and Jennie.

"They're here. Did you see?" she said.

"I saw. Now, if you'd turn your attention to the stone wall?"

"Jennie, look," said Tim, pointing to the wall, "the angels."

"I see."

"That one in the cloud," Tim said, "I seen her before. She comes to me in the nighttime, even when I was little. I saw her at the cemetery and that bad place."

Jennie bent down. "You have a guardian angel. And she's my great-aunt Mary."

The music silenced. Pastor Andrew and Tom Murphy, the best man, stepped over to the stone wall, and the guests and spirits turned toward the path.

The quintet performed the processional as though the homestead were a cathedral of evergreens and deciduous trees — the low, rich notes played slowly, then quickened to a walking pace. Rebecca, the maid-of-honor, strolled across the meadow to the stone wall. Now a lively melody, and flower girls in cotton and lace, adorned with daisy crowns, bright smiles and shining eyes, skipped and hopped, dropping petals along the way.

Tim weakened for a moment, eyes watering, and turning to Jennie and Amadeus, said, "I don't want to fall."

"Go ahead, walk slow, hand on Rosie," said Amadeus.

The music slowed, flowing now, like water in a lazy current. A presence, a gentle pressure, a hand on Tim's arm. "My friend!" Tim walked slow and sure across the meadow, seeing water flowing gently down Cyrus's stream with Rosie on one side and Cyrus Deane of the apple orchard on the other.

Jennie said, "Do you see?"

"I see, and so does Tim."

Mike and Calvin, silly boys, giggled and tossed blossoms at Tim.

The melody, the harmony now graceful, Jennie linked her arm in Amadeus's and they stepped from the path onto the meadow. Suddenly, Jennie hesitated, glued to the earth, and gazed up at Amadeus. She saw the boy who always found the lost girl and today, thirty years later, the man and woman, both found, would walk into a shared life full of love.

"What?" he said.

"You didn't need to cut your hair, but you look really hot."

Amadeus chuckled, held her close and kissed her softly. They viewed the homestead, music in the air: friends, family and spirits, the stone wall, trees, the meadow and the cellar hole. The Deane Apple Tree stood in sunlight, alive and growing. Deane apples, greenish with light red and pinkish stripes, red around the stem, hung from its branches. Turning their gaze to Deane Mountain, they both knew that Jennie was home, enveloped in all of generational time, where she'd always belonged.

Jennie shivered. Gentle pressure, like a hand, a tender grip on her elbow. Sensing the coolness of Great-Great-Grandfather William Deane, she also felt the warmth of Amadeus.

He saw too. "Ready?"

With Grandfather, they stepped slowly down the aisle, a leisurely pace, as though it were one of their quiet walks in the woods.

The children—grinning, giggling, bouncing—tossed petals in front of the bride and groom. At the stone wall, holding hands, they listened to Pastor Andrew's words: *But the fruit of the spirit is love, joy, peace, patience, kindness, goodness, faithfulness, gentleness and self-control.* (Galatians 5:22)

When Pastor called for the rings, Tim reached into his pocket and, grinning, handed them to Rebecca and Tom. He had been entrusted with these most important rings and had kept them safe. In this moment of sharing vows, those spoken at the proposal, and symbols of belonging to each other for a lifetime, the sun, at its highest, shone down on Deane Mountain, the homestead, and this couple, shimmering on golden rings.

Pronounced Mr. and Mrs. Stuart, Amadeus and Jennie kissed softly, enfolding each other. Joyous cheers, words of congratulations, and applause filled the meadow.

The quintet played selections from contemporary composers, and Amadeus, a twinkle in his eye, held Jennie as they waltzed and spun down the aisle to the brisk tempo followed by twirling ballerinas and dashing boys. Still grinning, Tim held onto Rosie and Cyrus. The guests followed Rebecca and Tom, dancing as well.

While choreographing their own foxtrot, Amadeus and Jennie called for the children to whirl and spin to the melodies. The little girls caught the hands of the little boys and bopped, boogied, and twirled their own improvisations. Rebecca and Isaac, and Tom and Alice danced.

Great-Aunt Mary strutted to the beat, shaking and whirling. Laughing, Jennie said, "She's certainly having a good time, and look at Tim watching her so closely!"

"She's comical," said Amadeus, laughing. "Your grandmothers are sitting with Madeleine, Fred, and James and Joe Foster. I wonder if they know angels are listening."

The tune was a waltz of times past, and William and Louisa, lighter than air, floated by the Stuarts and the children. Cyrus and Mary, that old Quaker couple, love written on their faces, glided above the meadow. Sadie, camera in hand, caught the special moments, but not the spirits, who were seen only by Jennie, Amadeus, and Tim.

The tables, now laden with food, wedding cake, and champagne, the bride and groom, children encircling them, and the guests and musicians gravitated to the tables. It was time to raise their glasses.

Tom offered the toast, "To true lifetime love."

Rebecca said, "To lovers and soulmates."

From Alice, "To journeys."

Amadeus stood, helped his bride stand, and holding her eyes in his, said, "To Jennie, my love, who walked the journey with me into life, love, and purpose."

Glasses raised once more, the couple kissed, and he wiped a tear from her eye.

Then Pastor Andrew offered grace:

"Lord, we come to you with grateful hearts for the miracles of healing we have seen in the lives of Jennie and Amadeus. We ask your blessings on their life, home, and family. We ask, too, that you bless and guide safely Isaac and Rebecca, as they begin a new journey. We thank you for this delicious meal, for those who prepared it, for fellowship and friendship. Amen."

Conversations and laughter among family and friends resonated through the air, above the trees, and to the mountains. Grins and giggles spread among the children. Jennie stood, took note of where Rebecca was sitting, turned, and threw the bouquet straight into Ellen's hands. Laughing, she grasped Amadeus's hand and together they cut the cake. Another memory stored.

As the sun set behind the mountain, Amadeus and Jennie thanked their guests for celebrating with them as they strolled onto the logging road to their vehicles. The angels and spirits departed: Great-Aunt Mary, Grandmothers Sarah and Jennie; and the Deane sons and daughters. Cyrus and Mary, airborne, disappeared into the overgrown apple orchard. William and Louisa, hovering above the steep path, vanished under its canopy.

Noticing Tim and Rosie alone by the stone wall, Amadeus hurried across the meadow, while Jennie shared a few moments with Rebecca. Releasing the string of pearls into her daughter's hand, Jennie said, "For you, from Grandma Charlotte."

Rebecca closed her fingers around the necklace. "Thank you. I loved Grandma. I'll treasure this and the memories. And I love you, Mom."

Jennie held her daughter close. "I love you, my honeybee. Now, embrace your journey. And remember, your family, past and present, is always here, waiting to welcome you home."

Sitting on the stone wall, Amadeus watched Tim dragging his feet in the grass, eyes cast downward, his face tear-stained, Rosie, next to him. "Crumbling stone walls understand hearts. Come, sit with me. Tell me."

Tim pulled himself up on the wall. "Do I really have to stay at Sadie's all night?"

Stroking Rosie's head, Amadeus said, "You like sleepovers with your friends."

"Well, yeah, in my castle." Tim sniffled. "You know about those mean people."

"You'll be safe with Sadie. It's only one night. Rosie's going with you."

"Well, I probably won't sleep."

"I'm sure you will, but if you don't sleep, there's always naps."

Tim scowled, and Amadeus said, "Can you keep a secret?"

"I'm a good secret keeper."

Turning Tim to face the mountains, Amadeus pointed. "That's Deane Mountain. Named after Jennie's family. We're going to climb it tonight."

"Are you crazy? You a nut? All the way up there to the sky?" said Tim, loudly.

"Shhhh! Don't tell her. It's a surprise."

"Okay, but Jennie would probably rather go home, like me."

"When you look up at the stars tonight, we'll be looking at the same stars."

Hand-in-hand with her flower girls, Jennie crossed the meadow to the wall, and Amadeus said, "I was just telling Tim how responsible he was holding onto the rings."

Smiling down into Tim's face, Jennie smoothed his hair, hugged him, and kissed his cheek. "That's our boy."

Then together, the Stuarts strolled over to the cellar hole, joining the Murphys. It was time to send Isaac and Rebecca on their way.

Hefting backpacks, the soulmates hiked up logging roads, ascending Deane Mountain. Moonlight was darkened by thick stands of hemlock and undergrowth encroaching upon the dirt roads. They walked slowly, cautiously, hand-in-hand. Flashlights shone down on the trail, obscured by slippery leaves. A maze of twitch roads with twists and turns: inexperienced hikers could easily become disoriented, but Amadeus had climbed this mountain many times in light and darkness.

"I hope Tim's all right. I feel more comfortable leaving the girls," she said.

"I know, and he's become our son," he said.

"This thing with Fred weighs on my heart."

"Honey, he does love us. But he needs to trust that we'll not leave him. He'll only learn if we do and return." Still holding hands, they climbed higher.

"I know you're right, but I can't help how I feel."

Some roads narrowed to the width of a trail. In wet, muddy areas they crossed corduroy roads, logs laid close together, rough and uneven. Roots, rocks, and deep ruts were embedded in the dense, compacted soil.

"Are we going in circles?" she said. "We've been hiking forever."

"Find the Little Dipper. Now, the North Star on the handle. Keep it in front of you. Look for Cassiopeia and Orion to the east. We're heading north. Not far now."

At the summit, the sea of night sky illumined with the brilliance of billions and billions of twinkling stars. Jennie dropped the backpack, turned circles, arms spread wide, viewing the universe. Embracing him, leaning into him, soft kisses quickly deepened. "Hey, T-Bear, how about stargazing with me on that boulder."

The double sleeping bag under his arm, they carried their backpacks to the boulder. Unzipping one, he handed her a gift bag. "If you like it, you can put it on."

Hiding behind a clump of trees and slapping at a few insects, she said, "It's lovely, so silky! So soft!" She emerged from the trees, appeared in front of him in a cream-colored gown and robe. His eyes upon her, he caressed her face, her lips. "You take my breath away." He kissed her tenderly. "An angel in the moonlight, and a sexy one." They kissed again and, holding her waist, he helped her onto the boulder. Snuggled together on the sleeping bag under brilliant starlight, kisses hot and sizzling, he untied her robe, gently pushed it off her shoulders, and caressed her skin. "You really should exchange my flannel for this one."

Jennie unbuttoned his shirt. He removed it. Her soft hands roamed over his chest, shoulders, and down his back. "Soon I'll be wearing your flannel shirts too. Reaching for her backpack, she pulled out a small gift bag. "For you, for us."

The bag—lighter than air. Inside—an empty box. Squinting, too dark to read, he turned on the flashlight. "You're pregnant?"

"Surprised?"

"Thrilled!" Laughing through tears of joy, stars in his eyes, he said, "I didn't know that loving you would bring the blessing of children, but I suspected."

Jennie sat up. "How? I was careful, keeping my secret."

"Red marks on the calendar, accepting a glass of wine, but only caressing the glass, and nature's signs, the fawns, bear cubs, and rabbits. You saw them too."

They kissed lovingly, long and lingering, caressing, kisses intensifying. Breathing deep and fast, hearts racing. On the boulder in the cool mountain air under Heaven's lights, they loved each other.

Later, Amadeus passed her the glasses and poured the champagne. "To our life." They clinked. He sipped, she didn't. "I'm carrying our baby."

He took her glass, poured both on the ground, the bottle too. They ate the cake.

Jennie shared her sketches: Tim walking next to Rosie, Maggie's shining eyes and sweet smile, and Gracie jumping rope.

"This is art. I see love," he said.

What's in the envelope?"

"A gift from Joe Foster. He gave me my first job in the woods, a place to live, and he taught me about trees and forest management. Joe helped me through hard times." Pulling out the documents, he read aloud the note by flashlight: *Take care of the trees, and the trees will take care of you and your family.* "Joe has deeded us his woodlot."

"What a wonderful gift! Why me?"

"You love the trees too. It's home and borders the stream and the homestead. We own nearly two hundred acres now. A mix of hardwoods, some softwood, and conifers."

"Oh, my goodness! Our life together—children and trees."

Lying there in the quiet, feeling blessed, he embraced her and sighed. "Tim's staring at the stars tonight. Let's hike down. Take the kids home."

"I'm missing our little ones too. We'll leave at first light."

Gazing at the constellations, they thought of blessings—three children and the one conceived in love. Not far away, throughout the night, Tim stared through the living room window at the same stars, frightened, waiting. Sadie and Rosie next to him.

As night faded and the sky showed its first signs of light, they hefted their backpacks and, flashlights in hand, descended slowly, cautiously, down the trails to The Beast. As they pulled into Sadie's driveway, the front door opened. Exhausted and tears flowing, Tim stood on the front porch. Taking his long strides, Amadeus lifted his boy into his arms. Tim laid his head on the shoulder of the man he loved and trusted. "I was worried."

Jennie, teary-eyed, softly stroked Tim's cheek. "We've come to take you home."

Thanking Sadie, they collected Tim's things, and headed to Voter Hill.

At the Murphys, while Annie slept on the sofa, Alice and Tom sat in the rockers by the woodstove with Gracie and Maggie, who were sleepless, crying, and missing home.

Knocking softly, Amadeus and Jennie stepped inside, Tim in the middle, and the girls ran to them. While hugging their daughters close and calming their cries, they thanked Alice and Tom, collected the girls' bags, and settled the children into The Beast.

At home they put their little ones to bed, kissed them, covered them, and they fell fast asleep. Later, they would all gather on the sofa and talk. Rosie lay next to Tim.

In their bedroom, Jennie stood in front of the French doors, sunshine on her face, her hands covering her womb. Water droplets slid down her cheeks. The journey she'd embarked on only a few months earlier had given Rebecca the freedom to follow her dreams. Boston would not contain her daughter. One day, Rebecca would see the world. So far away.

Amadeus drew her into his arms, and under the carved maple, he held her close. The double wedding ring quilt lay folded at the footboard.

TWENTY-NINE

Tim, his jeans too short and the knees worn out, scuffed along, kicking crumbling leaves, and crossed the yard following Amadeus to the workshop. He stopped, spread his arms wide, stood on his right leg and, losing his balance, instantly placed one hand on Rosie. Stretching the left, his toe almost touched the heel of Amadeus's footprint. A few more steps, and Tim tried leaping, footprint to footprint. He fell, picked himself up, lowered his head, and continued on.

Rosie barked, and Amadeus and Tim halted and, hands in pockets, looked high above autumn's brilliant colors. Wearing his new glasses—so cute with his boy's haircut and gold metal frames like Amadeus's—Tim saw Canada geese flying south. In past seasons, he'd heard the honking but had never seen the migration.

The geese would not rest at the pond today: the first week of October, and a chill in the air. Amadeus had already seen nature's signs of an early winter: an abundance of acorns, the height of the hornet's nest, the halo around the moon.

"Why do they fly like that?" said Tim. "Looks like a V."

"It's called V-formation. Each goose flies just above the one in front to save energy and lessen wind resistance. So they can fly longer hours and longer distances before resting."

"Why so much honking?"

"To keep the flock together. They're encouraging each other to keep flying."

"Why do they fly away?" said Tim.

"Winter's coming. It'll be cold here but warm in the south. No ice on the lakes. No snow hiding the feeding grounds. They'll be back in the spring."

"Doesn't the first bird get tired?"

"They take turns." Laying his hand on Tim's shoulder, Amadeus said, "Come on, son."

"Where's south?"

"We'll dig out the map."

In the workshop, a red oak stick with a tapered end lay on the workbench. Tim had whittled it, creating a nail, like in the old days. With an auger and mallet, Tim and Amadeus had drilled and pounded pegs into dovetail corner notches on the tower. Today, Tim smoothed the rough spots on a maple desk and chair with fine sandpaper, while Amadeus stained a cedar cabinet, both special orders.

It was already mid-October, and they had heard nothing from the elderly gentleman, Tim's only relative, and neither had Ellen, Tim's caseworker. Fred had simply remained aloof. What would they do without Tim, and Tim without them? What would happen to their boy? Jennie's and Amadeus's hearts grew heavier every day. Amadeus had said they'd challenge Fred in court, if he petitioned for guardianship. Tim belonged with them, and they had become a family.

Since September, a homeschooling program had been in place for all three children: daily lessons at the rock maple table; science and nature studies in the woods, fields, and homestead; history, including life stories of the Underground Railroad; piano lessons with Auntie Emilie; art, cooking, and woodworking; ballet and tap at the recreation center and quilting with Jill for Gracie, Maggie and Annie; Cub Scouts and Lego Club at the library for Tim with Mike and Calvin. Tim and Maggie attended physical and occupational therapy each week. Today, they'd all walk down to the pond, collect colorful leaves for an art project, and search for green ones for a science project on chlorophyll.

Midweek, a day off from school, Amadeus drove the Jeep down the narrow streets of Freeport—the promised city shopping excursion and, later, Tim's appointment with the orthopedic specialist in Portland. As he drove slowly, he kept a careful watch on pedestrians weaving around vehicles, disregarding traffic lights and crosswalks. Turning right, he parked behind a department store.

They shopped first for shoes, winter boots, work boots, and soft wool blend socks, like his, for Jennie and the kids. Then, winter wear. Amadeus soon found himself sitting alone on a bench in children's clothing, repeatedly checking his watch, as Jennie entered and exited dressing rooms with her arms full and the kids following single file. He chuckled at the image of a mother mallard, followed by her waddling ducklings, wearing new work boots. Tim, the last in line, fell behind. With pleading eyes, bent knees, and hands held prayerfully, Tim drew out the words, "Help me! Save me!" Laughing, Amadeus shook his head and pointed toward Jennie.

Eventually, Amadeus managed to get Jennie's attention, informing her that he was taking a walk. Carrying their purchases, he added one more item he'd seen her admiring. Descending the stairs, he walked briskly toward the double doors and stopped short of the exit. A window display in the sports department caught his interest. After a few more secret purchases, he hurried to the Jeep, unseen by his family.

Reentering and imagining the Jeep filled with shopping bags, leaving little to no room for the kids, he spied his family coming down the stairs. Carrying one small bag, with Jennie next to her, toting a larger one, Maggie securely held the railing and watched her feet. Behind them, Tim took in the sights of shoppers and brightly colored items on racks and decorating walls. He, too, carried a bag, as did Gracie. Bored with the slow movement, Gracie cut in front of strangers, excusing herself politely—as she was a girl with manners—and ran straight down into Amadeus's arms.

Finally, his family in tow, he escorted them to the Jeep. Packing their bags in the cargo space, he hid his own purchases, and noticing room for more, said, "Jennie, where would you like to shop now?"

Frowning, Jennie said, "Are you sure you're comfortable with more shopping?"

"Definitely," he said, an image of their cabin in the woods in his mind.

Holding hands with the children, they walked through parking lots, crossed the narrow street, and entered a toy store. Following bright, happy faces up and down aisle after aisle, they gave permission for each child to choose one thing. Tim selected a brown model truck, resembling The Beast; Gracie, a stained-glass art kit; Maggie, Playdough; Jennie, a memory game; Amadeus, checkers.

"Tim, you want to play?" said Amadeus.

"Okay, I'm a pretty good checker player, you know. Pastor Andy told me so."

"Yeah, so am I."

Leaving the checkout counter, they headed down the street toward the restaurant on the corner, stopping along the way in a bookstore, a candy shop, and a women's clothing outlet.

In the crowded, noisy, family-style restaurant, Amadeus ordered at the counter, paid the cashier, and sat with his family in a corner booth.

Gracie said, "Lots of fun things in a toy store. Hard to choose."

Maggie said, "And dollies too."

Tim said, "You know, me, Mike, and Calvin want to play baseball."

Amadeus said, "We'll keep throwing and catching the ball. Practice batting too."

"I can see now with my new glasses, and when I can run, I'll be a good player."

"You'll be a Babe Ruth," Amadeus said.

Tim scratched his head, "Huh?"

Amadeus said, "We'll borrow a book from the library."

Tim said, "Rosie might not have any balls to chase. I might catch 'em all."

Jennie said, "Perhaps, you can miss a few for the chase."

The waitress served their lunch—chicken burgers, fries, and bubbly, fizzy soda pop—no milk today.

"Jennie," said Amadeus. "Do you have more shopping to do?"

"We've spent enough. We have what we need and a few wants."

Lunch devoured, they headed for Portland.

In Dr. Nichols's office, a spacious room with an antique desk and an examination table, the foster parents sat in comfortable chairs. A skeleton—dressed in a black suit coat, a tie, and a top hat, and wearing orange glasses—hung from a pole. Standing near it, looking up, Tim, Gracie, and Maggie stared, and Tim said, "Must be for Halloween."

"These are bones," said Gracie.

"Gotta be Halloween. It's black and orange," said Tim.

Dr. Nichols entered. "You're right about Halloween. My friend, Sid, Sid Skeleton, likes to dress for the holidays. Which one of you is Tim?"

"That's me." Tim stared up at the doctor, taller than the skeleton.

"Nice to meet you. Could you climb up on the table? I can't check out your legs from way up here."

Tim climbed up. "My friends and I want to play baseball, so I need to run."

Dr. Nichols had previously studied the CT scan and report. Today, he checked Tim's bones and joints, the shoulder tilt, and compared the lengths of his legs, concluding that a lift in his shoe would alleviate his back and joint pain and straighten his spine with no shoulder tilt. Since he was in a growth spurt, the pediatrician would monitor the growth of his legs. If the difference did not increase, orthotics could be the answer. A technician measured and took the molds of Tim's feet to shape the inserts.

Giving Tim a pamphlet, Dr. Nichols said, "Do these exercises every day to strengthen your legs and keep going to therapy. You're getting stronger. Wear your orthotics, and you'll run like the wind." He patted Tim's new work boots. "These are perfect for you."

Following a short discussion with Amadeus and Jennie, Dr. Nichols offered the kids lollipops from Sid's Halloween candy bowl.

Leaving, they crossed the parking lot to the Jeep and settled the children in the back seat—packages piled in the cargo space. Jennie had turned north, heading for I-95. Since they'd been up shortly after sunrise, the kids soon fell asleep. Amadeus tuned the radio to the oldies station, reached across the console, and massaged Jennie's thigh. She held his hand.

October 22nd was a cold evening with a fire in the woodstove. Gracie and Maggie crawled under the rock maple table, pulled out cards and gifts, and set them in front of Tim and Jennie. Racing to the kitchen, they carried bowls, spoons, and ice cream. Amadeus carried the cake, while the girls sang along with his baritone. Ten burning candles, nine for Tim and one for Jennie, forty-one today.

Eyes closed, secret wishes made, and candles blown out, Jennie and Tim opened their gifts. A new camera for Jennie—time to preserve memories. Hers had been lost in the cemetery in the rainstorm.

Tim read all the names on the handmade card, which depicted a boy on a Belgian.

Open your gift carefully, so it doesn't break," said Amadeus.

Sitting next to Tim, Jennie waited until he tore away the birthday paper. "You drew these for me!"

"This drawing is the first time I saw you, walking away from church with Mommy."

"And this one, Mommy and me are happy."

"Look here, the day you came home. Napping on the sofa, curled next to Amadeus."

"Thank you. Now I have a memory." Tim hugged Jennie and Amadeus, too, and said, "Thank you for making the frames."

"We'll hang them in your room," said Amadeus.

"Can we cut the cake now?" asked Gracie.

"The ice cream's melting," Maggie chimed in.

Plates full, they savored the taste of sweet chocolate and vanilla.

Jennie and Tim opened their cards from Rebecca. For Tim, a five-dollar bill, and for Jennie, a note: *Happy Birthday! Loving my journey! Love and miss you, Mom.*

THIRTY

Coffee filters with bands of green, red, yellow, and orange pigments, extracted from leaves—a science experiment about chlorophyll—decorated the refrigerator.

The next evening, Jennie cleaned up the kitchen and, wiping the quartz countertop, moved the stack of new books—accounting, finance, and taxes. After yesterday's birthday celebration Amadeus had snuggled with Jennie on the sofa and shared with her a business proposal—*Stuarts' Fine Furniture and Cabinetry*. No more long days and nights plowing snow. For Jennie, no long nights in darkness without him. He would be home, as he'd rather cuddle with her by the fire and enjoy time with the children than be alone in the cold and dark. They'd study together, share the accounting, the decisions, and the tools.

While she cleaned, Amadeus sat at the oak table, reading the educational team's reports for Tim and Maggie. For Tim, they had diagnosed learning disabilities, dyscalculia (mathematics) and dysgraphia (fine motor and writing). For Maggie, with Down syndrome, they had recommended she begin her education in the pre-school curriculum. Both children should continue in occupational and physical therapy.

In their rooms, Maggie and Gracie colored pictures, and Tim piled log upon log, raising cabin walls with Lincoln Logs. Seeing fog enclosing the cabin, he looked out the bedroom window at the misty form of Great-Aunt Mary.

Hearing a rap on the front door, Jennie and Amadeus welcomed company. Racing down the hall, the girls grasped Great-Aunt Madeleine's hand. "Come, play with us!"

Fred Grey cleared his throat. "Amadeus, thank you for stopping by." A deep breath. "Miss Jennie, Amadeus, I signed the papers. Tim belongs here with you."

Laying her hand over her heart, Jennie inhaled deeply, exhaled, and teary-eyed, threw her arms around Fred. "Thank you, a million times, thank you."

Startled, Fred jerked his head back and stared at Amadeus, wondering what to do. Then, politely, but stiffly, he patted Jennie's back. "I know you love him."

Amadeus shook Fred's hand. "Welcome to the family, Grandpa. Time to get acquainted with your great-grandson." Laying his hand on the elderly man's shoulder, Amadeus led him down the hall to Tim's room and tapped on the door. "Tim, this gentleman is Fred Grey, and he has a story to tell you. Please listen with your heart." Returning to the kitchen, Amadeus hugged Jennie. "We'll talk later."

"Want to sit on my bench?" said Tim.

Fred sat on the bench, a small, framed photograph in his hand, and laid a paper bag on the floor next to him. The cabin walls were complete, and only the green roofing boards lay scattered on the floor. The neatly folded star quilt and teddy lay on the bed. Shelves held toys, books, and the little truck. Framed drawings hung on the grayish-blue wall.

"That's a nice cabin you're building," said Fred.

"It's like the old cabin at the homestead. See here at the corners, it's a dove tail notch, like on the tower." Tim picked up the whittled peg and showed it to Fred. "This is red oak. Hardwood. They whittled these into nails and pounded them into corners and floors."

"You know lots about cabin building," said Fred.

"Amadeus taught me. What story do you want to tell?"

Fred sighed, his head downcast, eyes on the photograph, silent for a few moments. "Well," said Fred, his voice shaky, "I have this picture to give you. It's a picture of your family taken a long time ago."

Tim held the photograph as Fred pointed. "That man is me, and this woman beside me is Lucinda, my wife. We're your great-grandparents. This woman is our daughter, Lucy, your grandmother, and the little girl is our granddaughter, Sharon."

"My mommy! You know my mommy? And you're my great-grandpa? How did you find me?"

"Well, Tim, Jennie found me," said Fred. "I know this is your home, and they are your new mom and dad. So if you want, I'd like to your grandpa."

"Want to see my truck? Mommy bought it for me."

Fred nodded. Tim laid the truck in his hand. "Amadeus found it at the fire."

"That's a nice truck and a good memory," said Fred, passing it back to Tim. "I have a memory to share with you." From the paper bag, Fred removed a small violin and bow, just the right size for a boy. Giving it to Tim, he said, "It belonged to your mother."

Tim fell to his knees, held it in his lap, and softly touched the smooth walnut-stained spruce and maple, the ebony fingerboard, and the strings with his fingertips. He stood as straight and tall as he could, positioned it on his shoulder, and drew the bow across the strings—like fingernails scraping on a chalkboard. A tear slid down his face.

"This was Mommy's? I can have it?"

"It's yours. She would want you to have it," said Fred. "When your mommy was a girl, she loved music. She played this violin and later, a cello. In the meadow, she played prayerfully, like an angel. When I get real quiet, I hear the music in my heart."

His eyes upon the violin and fingers sliding gently over the wood, Tim said, "I used to hear Mommy's music. She played for me on her cello. Maybe, someday, I'll hear her music again."

Jennie and Amadeus stepped quietly down the hall. Peeking into Tim's room, Amadeus said, "Tea and cookies on the table. Perhaps Grandpa would like to join us."

Tim stepped over to the window, waved, and watched, as Great-Aunt Mary gave him a wink and then vanished. Setting the truck and the oak peg on the shelf and the photograph on the dresser, he walked down the hall beside Grandpa. "You can sit next to me." In front of the piano, Tim balanced on tiptoe, and laid the violin next to Alastair.

Gathered at the table, the family held hands and Jennie prayed:

"Lord, we are so blessed with family and children. In times of sadness and broken hearts, You offer us peace. Bless our family, friends, Treasures, those nearby and faraway. Amen."

Poster-sized leafy trees of red, green, and blue washi tape decorated the ferngreen wall. Branches displayed autumn's colors, and a few green leaves dried in waxed paper were mixed with brightly painted leaflets—the children's art.

"Grandpa, have a cookie. It's real good," said Tim.

"I think I will." One bite carried Fred back to another time, to another kitchen, to his wife, Lucinda, who baked his favorite ginger cookies. "Lucinda's mother got this recipe from a lady up near Varnum Pond."

"She knew my great-aunt Mary?" said Jennie. "That woman is a mystery."

Tim's mouth fell open. Wet cookie crumbs dropped into his lap. "She's my angel!" Gulping milk, he grinned at Jennie. "What's this? You know, soda pop's real good."

While Maggie blew bubbles, her milk frothy, Gracie said, "Yeah, we could buy bubbly pop instead of milk."

Jennie laughed. "Milk is the preferred drink of healthy ballerinas and baseball players."

Madeleine said, "Friendly lady. My mother got that recipe too. Mary liked to tell folks about the missing ingredient, a secret she'd forgotten."

"Grandpa, Jennie tells interesting life stories. It's history. Will you tell me life stories too?" asked Tim.

Gracie said, "Us, too?"

Maggie added, "I like stories."

"Sure will, kids. Got lots to tell all of you," said Fred.

Darkness had fallen on the gathering. Fred and Madeleine hugged the little ones and thanked Jennie and Amadeus for a warm welcome into the family and into the roles of grandparents. Under the porch light, Fred held Madeleine's arm, helping her down the steps and to the truck. "It's getting late. Guess I need to get you home, dear, unless you'd like to stay at my place."

"Are they a couple?" said Jennie.

"Good for them, if they are," chuckled Amadeus. He stepped inside with Jennie and his children, as the rusty old pickup backfired down the dirt road.

Later, with Rosie guarding the sleeping children, Amadeus stood outside, staring at the starry sky and breathing deeply the fresh, crisp, cold air. His thoughts were on family.

Jennie donned her jacket and sat on the swing, holding two mugs of hot chocolate.

Joining her, he said, "A bit chilly to sit outside, isn't it?"

"Still time to stargaze before winter sets in."

"Read the reports. Tim and Maggie will be fine. They're already making strides." Leaning forward, arms resting on his thighs, mug in one hand, Amadeus sighed. Jennie's soft touch drew circles on his back and he began the telling: out there in the woods the other day, he'd thought and prayed about the situation with Tim's adoption. Fred was grieving too. Like, Amadeus, he'd lost children, his daughter and granddaughter.

In that time of fearing they'd lose Tim, Amadeus hadn't considered Fred's broken heart. So, while rocking on Fred's porch, they'd talked about what they both understood, the brokenness that goes with the loss of children. They'd talked about healing, about forgiving God and Sharon, and about the gift, the blessing of a child, Tim, a boy to love.

Jennie kissed Amadeus and laid her head on his shoulder. "Now, Tim's heart will heal. Family stories will give him roots to grow and flower. Fred will know a child's love."

He set the mugs on the floor. Embracing, they gazed at the stars, swung slowly, until Jennie's hands turned icy, and she melted closer to him, seeking warmth.

THIRTY-ONE

Home from a Cub Scout meeting and a furniture delivery from Amadeus's inventory to Alice's gallery, whose grand opening was the following week, in mid-November, Tim hurried up the porch steps and rushed through the front door, carrying a small box in his hands. "Jennie, where are you?"

"In the kitchen kneading bread dough."

Tim set the box on the oak table. "Look! It came in the mail. It's from Dr. Nichols."

Entering and kissing Jennie, Amadeus said, "He's anxious to open the package with you."

Jennie set the smooth gluten-y ball in a bread pan and covered it with a cotton dish towel—the beery scent of fermenting yeast.

"Amadeus, look at me and Gracie," said Maggie, holding up her hands and smiling sweetly. Their faces were smudged and their hands coated with flour and dough. Aprons wrapped snug around them with big bows tied in the back and shirt sleeves rolled up, the sisters stood on kitchen chairs rolling warm, multi-grain dough into balls, pushing their hands into it, flattening and rolling it. When the dough stuck to their hands, they added more flour into the gummy consistency, flattened it, and rolled it again. The stoneware mixing bowls and four greased bread pans sat by the breadboard. Heat from the oven warmed the kitchen.

"My pretty snow lassies," said Amadeus, kissing giggling girls on blotchy cheeks, handprints on his shirt.

"Tim, what's in the package?" said Jennie, wiping dough off her hands.

"What's Tim got?" said Maggie.

"The things to put in his shoes," said Gracie.

Inside the box were Tim's new orthotics molded to his feet. "Wow! Look at them!" Pulling on his sleeve, Tim brushed flour off the oak table, lifted them out of the box, and laid them in that clean spot. Elbows on the table, chin in hands, Tim closely studied them—the red one for the right foot and for the left, the thicker one in red, blue, and green layers. Squeezing the firm absorbent material, he traced the ups and downs, from the toe, high over the arch, and the dip down into the heel. "There's not much to 'em."

Jennie said, "Put them in your shoes."

Pulling out a chair, Amadeus said, "Sit here, Tim, and take off your work boots."

Amadeus inserted the orthotics. Tim pulled up his socks, put his boots back on and stood—spine straight, shoulders back, no tilt, hips and knees even, and a grin on his face. Holding his head high, he walked slowly around the kitchen, around the rock maple table, up and down the black metal stairs twice and back to the kitchen. Jennie gave him a hug, held him close, said, "My tall handsome boy," and kissed him on the cheek. Tim didn't say, *Yuck*. Tim and Amadeus hugged. "You look real good, son, standing tall."

"Come on, Rosie," Tim said, dashing out the front door, down the porch steps, across the yard to the dirt road, and over to the maple tree.

From the porch, Tim's family watched as he ran around the yard with Rosie by his side, barking happily. Instantly, Tim stopped, hopped, jumped on both feet and then on one foot, right and left. He picked up a stick, drew a line in the dirt, and with his arms spread wide, stepped slowly, heel to toe, eyes cast upward as the wind blew in his face.

Gracie said, "Why's he doing all that?"

Laughing through her tears, Jennie hugged her daughter. "Because he can."

Grasping Jennie's hand, Amadeus said, "Maggie, Gracie, keep him company."

The girls dashed down the steps, the adults just behind. Tim darted away, running, and his sisters, laughing, chased after him, but didn't catch him.

Zooming towards Amadeus and Jennie, he extended his arms, leaped as high as he could and soared in midair for a moment or two before landing in Amadeus's open arms. Rosy cheeks and sparkling brown eyes, Tim stretched his arms upward. "I can run! I'm as fast as Mike and Calvin!"

"You run like a deer," said Amadeus, choked up. He hugged Tim tight.

"I can walk a stone wall and someday I'll climb the mountain!"

A tear sliding down her cheeks, Jennie held his hand, said, "We'll climb together."

"It only hurts a little," said Tim.

"That'll pass," said Amadeus.

"Stay right here," said Jennie, walking briskly into the cabin. With her camera, she preserved a memory on the day before Halloween—The day Tim soared.

A few evenings later, the children, tucked into bed for the night, listened to Jennie playing the piano while Amadeus made tea. A fire burned in the stone fireplace. Footsteps and clicking nails proceeded slowly down the hall. Tim sat on the bench next to Jennie and watched her fingers slide along the keys, creating the melodies and harmonies.

Tim said, "You play real good. Even Gracie and Maggie play better than me." He lowered his head. "I don't play good, but I don't like the piano. I've played forever, and I still don't get it."

"Are you practicing?" said Jennie.

Tim shook his head.

"But you like music. Are you interested in a different instrument?"

"The violin. Mommy's cello burned in the fire, and I can't hear her music now."

"Oh, sweetie." Jennie hugged her son. "Talk with Amadeus. He plays both, and maybe you can still learn piano with Auntie."

"He does."

"Think you have time to practice, along with your studies, Cub Scouts and helping Amadeus?"

"Yup, I've got lots of time," said Tim.

Jennie held his chin and caught his eyes in hers. "Your fingers will learn to do what your brain tells them—with practice. Eight weeks is not forever. Even Amadeus sounded like howling cats and bleating goats when he was learning to play the violin."

Tim giggled. "He did? He really did?"

Jennie nodded, laughing at the memory.

Setting the mugs on the oak coffee table, Amadeus settled on the sofa, put on his reading glasses and picked up his opus by Hemingway. Tim curled up next to him, drew up his knees and hid his face in his hands. "I made a deal with Jennie."

Closing his book, Amadeus said, "What's the deal?"

"Well, I want to play the violin. If you could teach me violin, I'd still learn piano with Auntie." Tim sighed, shaking his head.

Amadeus chuckled. Taking the violins down from their place, he set them next to Tim. "There's a life story to my violin. It was crafted in the nineteenth century, which means the eighteen-hundreds, when the ancestors were active." He told the story to Tim: In Scotland, a man stopped at my great-great-great-grandfather's farm. The man, tired and hungry, had been walking across the moors and needed a horse to continue on his journey. He was a poor man and couldn't pay for the horse. So my grandfather, Alastair Stuart, gave the man food and a night's rest in his barn. Then they made a deal for the horse. The poor man gave this violin to my grandfather as collateral. When he traveled back that way, passing by the farm, they'd trade the horse for the violin. You know, that man never returned, and neither did the horse. My grandfather kept this violin and learned to play, and in every generation since, there has been a violinist. My father passed Alastair to me, and, someday, I'll pass it to you, if you become a violinist.

Positioning the weighty Alastair on his small shoulder, Tim grinned and, eyes sparkling, said, "You'll teach me to play this special one?"

Amadeus said, "I'd be proud to teach you. We'll begin playing your mother's violin. It fits your shoulder. And there are rules to obey."

"I will! I will! I'll pay real good attention."

"Rule one: You can only take it off the piano for lessons and practice. Rule two: Always put it back on the piano. Rule three: Practice. Rule four: Allow time for your hands to learn what your brain tells them to do. Rule five: Practice some more."

"Okay, I can do that. Someday, I'll be like you, a violinist and play the piano too," said Tim. "Maybe tomorrow, I'll have my first lesson."

Setting the violins in their place, Dad tucked Tim into bed and, joining Jennie on the sofa, he gave her a slight smile. "Howling cats, bleating goats?"

"Oh, my violinist," she laughed, "you've come so far since your first lessons."

Warmed by the fire, they sipped their tea and studied accounting.

Thanksgiving Day. Inside, the cabin was warm and cozy. Outside, a storm was brewing. Light powdery snow swirled and drifted. Peering through the windows, the children jumped and cheered, "It's snowing!" "Yay!" "Look at the deep snow!"

In the kitchen, apple, pumpkin, and pecan pies, baked yesterday, sat on the quartz counter.

Turkey, roasted the day before, and this morning mixed into a stew with vegetables, potatoes, herbs, and spices, simmered in the cast-iron stewpot, hanging from the fireplace spit. Corn bread baked in the cast-iron Dutch oven near the fire covered with ashes. In the soup pot, cider mixed with orange slices, cinnamon sticks, and whole cloves simmered on the wood stove, the aroma permeating the dining room.

Tim said, "Why don't you use the stove?"

Jennie said, "Power's out, sweetie. No electricity, no stove, no lights. We're cooking dinner like Cyrus and Mary."

Tim said, "Thanksgiving dinner, like at Cyrus's house. That will be real good."

At the oak kitchen table, the children cut, glued, and folded decorations—construction paper turkeys with wiggly eyes and red wattles and assorted colored pumpkins in a row connected with leaves and vines. A poster-sized chart with multicolored printed letters read *Thankful For.* Gracie wrote—*quilting on Saturday and family.* Maggie traced dotted letters—*I like cows.* Tim, in deep thought, printed his list, meticulously, checking the spelling with Jennie—*Home, Family, Mike and Calvin, Aunt Mary, Cyrus, Rosie, Oh, everybody.*

"I never want to have power again," said Tim.

Gracie said, "Jennie, your turn."

Jennie wrote—*my Amadeus, my children, stories, angels, and love.*

They hung the poster and the decorations on the wall in the dining room.

The high winds subsided but the feathery snowflakes still fell. Amadeus, with the kids and Rosie in the truck, plowed the dirt road and the way to the garage and sheds. The heap of pure, white snow grew monstrous.

Through the living room windows, Jennie saw Tim and Gracie cleaning snow off the steps and porches. Maggie and Rosie romped and rolled near the walkways as Amadeus shoveled. He'd be shoveling again by nightfall. A tractor, for plowing, gardening and mowing would be the perfect gift.

Trucks and Jeeps arrived. Jennie grabbed her jacket and hurried outside, greeting their guests: Aunt Madeleine and Grandpa Fred, Auntie Emilie and Uncle James, the Murphys, Pastor Andrew and Jill, Ellen Baker and Bob Adams, and Sadie with her sons.

In the yard, the men talked and laughed, seeing the six friends scramble up Snow Mountain and roll down, dethroning kings and queen.

Inside the cabin, the ladies set the white china with blue edging and four white tapered candles on the rock maple table. They filled glasses with warm cider. Jennie brushed ashes off the Dutch oven, removed the cover, and stuck a knife into the golden-brown corn bread. The top cracked. Kneeling and laying a plate on the floor, Jennie scraped around the crusty edge and tipped the Dutch oven so the corn bread slid onto the plate. Carefully pulling the rod, she swung the stew pot out of the fire, stirred the turkey stew, and filled the bowls. The ladies carried the food to the table.

Alice admired Jennie's charcoal sketches, now framed and hung. One more had been added: Amadeus sat at the wheel of The Beast and Rosie's head hung out the window.

"Jennie," said Alice, giving her a hand, "there's a market for your sketches."

"Really, they're just drawings, like I've done since childhood."

"You convey emotions in art," said Alice.

The table laden with Thanksgiving dinner, Jennie rang the dinner bell: a cast-iron farm bell hung on brackets screwed into the log wall by the front door. It had been one of the gifts from Tom and Alice at the celebration of the cabin's renovation. Best friends had hugged, and Tom had said that he'd waited a long time for that day. What else had Tom said? *Welcome home, Jennie, where you belong.*

Piling into the mudroom, the noisy children removed wet, snowy boots and snowsuits, hung them on hooks or left them on the floor in puddles of melting snow.

Gathered at the table, everyone held hands, bowed their heads, and Amadeus said grace:

"Lord, we are so blessed with family, friends, and many children among us. We thank you for this delicious dinner that Jennie prepared with loving hands, like her grandmothers of bygone days. We thank you for winter's snowfall, nature's pure white world, and Your Love and Grace offered to us all. Amen."

Amadeus said to his friends, "Our children would like you all to add your blessings to the chart."

Poking the spoon into the stew, Mike said, "Where's the turkey?"

"Eat your stew and you'll find the turkey," said Jennie.

"It's real good," Tim said, chin resting in his hands. "Jennie got the recipes from Mary, my friend Cyrus's Mary. She knows how Mary cooked it."

Tasting the stew, Calvin said, "Yeah, it is real good."

Gracie said, "Mary makes pretty quilts in lots of colors."

Jill said, "You know, girls, I'm really enjoying our quilting circle."

Annie said, "Quilting's lots of fun, and even our moms help us."

Maggie swung her legs under the table, waved her spoon like a baton, and sang, "Santa, Santa, Santa's in the barn."

Everyone laughed.

Jennie whispered to Maggie, "What barn?"

Maggie shrugged, "Annie told me."

"Missy Magpie," said Amadeus, chuckling. "Where's the barn?"

Smiling innocently, Maggie said, "A barn where the cows are."

"Oh, okay, now eat your dinner," said Amadeus.

The children quieted down, ate dinner, and listened, as Great-Grandpa regaled his audience with stories of long-ago Thanksgivings.

Later, kettles of melting snow sat on the woodstove. Glassware, china, tableware, and the soup pot sat piled on the quartz counter. Everyone added their blessings to the chart and gravitated to the warm, inviting living room. Then the kids watched Amadeus write his entry. They hurried over, and Tim read aloud: *Jennie, my children, Rosie, trees, music, etc.* "Huh? What's e-t-c spell?" he asked, and all the kids shrugged their shoulders.

The empty stew pot hung on the spit. The Dutch oven, crusts of corn bread stuck to it, sat on the hearth. Adults gathered near the fireplace, sitting in rockers, kitchen chairs, and on benches. Fred and Madeleine sat comfortably on the sofa. The children played noisily in the bedrooms. Rosie napped in Tim's room. Animated voices and laughter seeped under the doors and drifted like melodies down the hall.

Snowflakes floated down. The fire crackled. With Emilie's accompaniment on piano, Amadeus shouldered Alastair and performed a few favorite classical selections.

Yawning, Tom said, "How about playing something more upbeat?"

Maggie ran down the hall and poked her elbows in Amadeus's leg. Her chin, resting in her hands and her eyes shining on Amadeus, Maggie said, "Can we go?"

Was that muffled laughter coming from the hall?

"Go where, sweetie?" said Amadeus.

"Santa, the barn, the cows," said Maggie.

All six children and a barking Rosie raced into the living room, encircling Amadeus.

"Can we go?" said Annie.

"Please?" said Gracie.

From Tim, "Well, it would be fun."

Amadeus said, "Not today. We have company."

"But everybody can come," said Mike.

Tom said, "Annie, where is the barn?"

Annie, her palms open, said, "Daddy, the Elliots' barn."

Calvin said, "It's just down the road."

Amadeus said, "Well, no promises, but I'll see about it."

Bouncing, hopping, hands clapping, the kids sang, "We're going to the barn!" "Yeah!"

"Come on," said Gracie. "Let's get our jackets and boots on."

Amused, Jennie whispered, "How are you making this happen?"

Laying his violin on the piano, Amadeus stepped into the kitchen and dialed the telephone to the giggles of children and the laughter of adults.

Later, at the Elliots' farm on Route 43, light snow still falling, the Stuarts, Murphys, Sadie, Ellen, Bob, and the children followed Hazel Elliot, the farmer's wife, and their old English sheepdog, Milo, to the barn. (The other guests had elected to remain by the fireplace.) Plodding up a knoll to the open barn doors, they met Farmer John, a white-haired, round-bellied, bearded man dressed in red.

Maggie, holding Jennie's hand, suddenly stopped and stared. "Santa!"

"Ho! Ho! Ho!" laughed Farmer John. Bending down, he said, "What's your name?"

"Maggie!" And all the children stared, wide-eyed, and told Santa their names.

In the big red barn, the children huddled close to Jennie, all chatter ceasing. They gazed at the animals, listened to the moos, baas, cluck-clucks, whinnies, oink-oinks, and honks—the barn was a tower of Babel. Rabbits occupied a corner pen. Chickens strutted around. Sheep crowded at the fence of the fold. Jennie stroked a gray miniature donkey named Wilbur. Cows chewed their cuds. Horses accepted apples and carrots from Hazel.

The men lifted the kids onto the Morgans, and Amadeus said, "Some are race horses. Others are stocky. They work or are riding horses. Like Belgians, they're gentle, just not as big."

Stroking Nellie, a chestnut mare, Jennie said, "Beautiful horse."

Maggie said, "I see cows."

"Yes, sweetie," said Jennie and, with Ellen, they stepped into a stall occupied by a gentle Jersey. Stroking and crooning to the cow, Jennie nodded to Ellen, and she sat Maggie on Molly. Listening to the soft mooing, Maggie happily stretched out her arms, petted, and laid her head on Molly, hugging the gentle milk cow.

Ellen laughed, "Jennie, you've always worked magic with children."

Five of the kids had followed the other adults into the rabbit pen, where they held white ones, black ones, and angoras. In the sheepfold, they touched the wool. Tossing feed to the chickens, they giggled. With a long-handled brush they scratched the pigs' backs. They fed hay to the cows.

While ambling over to Jennie, Amadeus spotted Phillip Warner mucking out a horse stall. "Are you working here now?"

"Ya, I like the job," said Phillip.

Tim watched Amadeus and listened, drying his cheeks on his sleeve.

"What's Jack up to? Haven't seen him around."

"He got a promotion and travels now," said Phillip. "Got more stalls to muck out."

As Phillip pushed the wheelbarrow toward the barn door, Amadeus called out, "It's good to see you."

Everyone followed Farmer John and Hazel to a large, penned area at the back of the big barn. The children's faces lit up, hands tingled, and hearts pounded. The men lifted the kids onto the middle rail and, on tiptoe, they stretched their arms, fingers wiggling, and touched Santa's reindeer.

Back home with power restored, they tucked sleepy children into bed, and Rosie paced from room to room. Intending to wash the dishes, they turned on the kitchen light. The quartz countertop shined. Glassware, tableware, china, and cookware were stacked on the table.

With Rosie alongside, Tim padded into the kitchen, sat in a chair, folded his arms, and frowned at Amadeus. Rosie stared too. Jennie checked on the girls and went to bed.

Taking a seat at the table, Amadeus said, "What's on your mind?"

"You know that big kid, that Phillip, pushed me off a log, and you got mad." Tim sniffled and wiped his nose on his sleeve. "Now you're being nice to him."

"I know he treated you badly, and he knew it too. So he helped to bring you home."

"Like how? Why?"

"He de-rusted your shiny bed. It took him all day. He did other work around here and helped the Cubbies. I think he talked with Ellen about your coming home."

Tim scratched his head, his nose twitching. "Why?"

"It's about growing up, and Phillip's doing some growing."

Tim rested his elbows on the table, chin in hands. "Maybe the horses help."

"Could be. Maybe you can do something nice for him one day," said Amadeus.

Tim sighed. "Well, probably I can, but it might be awhile."

"You'll know when the time is right." Dad turned out the kitchen light. They walked down the hall, and he tucked Tim into bed. Then he joined Jennie, holding her close.

THIRTY-TWO

Late afternoon on December 17th, with presents, decorations, cake and ice cream, the mail, and one classic Christmas tale piled in The Beast—now outfitted with new brakes, tires, shocks, and a bench seat with springs—Amadeus turned up the dirt road, parked and dimmed the headlights.

Smoke curled lazily out of the chimney. The cabin lights glowed. Snow blanketed the roof, covered bare branches and evergreens, and carpeted shed roofs like overgrown mushrooms. The stack of firewood stood tall and wide at the end of the porch. A balsam fir wreath—uneven ends, too many tips bunched together in places and too few in others, clusters of silver balls, and a crooked blue bow—decorated the log wall by the blue front door. Amadeus and the children had made it for Jennie with love.

Warm and cozy in The Beast, he held her close, and she gently stroked their little miracle. "An ingenious idea, sitters at the cabin," he said. "Time alone with you." With calloused fingers he traced softy over her womb, entwined his with hers and kissed her softly.

"Perhaps in a few years, maybe twenty, we'll be able to leave overnight," she said.

"I'm not waiting that long for time alone with you."

The front door opened, and blue eyes and brown eyes peeked outside. Scurrying down the porch steps, the kids and Rosie welcomed them home, just as Amadeus turned off the engine and opened the truck door.

Amadeus carried the cake, the girls, ice cream and one gift bag with a big silver bow to the rock maple table, set with the best china, a plate of decorated sugar cookies, herbal tea, and milk for the children. Tim carried the new book with Rosie alongside. Auntie Emilie and Uncle James, always happy to babysit, joined the celebration—Amadeus's forty-third birthday.

The kids presented their hand-drawn stick figures on cards: small hand cradled in a big one; large and small hands petting sheep, made of cotton balls; Tim and Dad, sanding wood. Another, from Jennie, showed a boy and a girl sitting in a maple tree. All with messages of love for Dad in traced block letters, curlicues, neat print, and cursive.

The excited kids crowded around Amadeus. Gracie asked, "What's in the bag?" Tim said, "Yeah, open your present." From Maggie, "I can help you."

He kissed giggling Maggie on the cheek and hung the silver ribbon, a long necklace, around his daughter's neck.

Small hands reached into the bag and pulled out three sets of folded documents. "What's this?" said Tim.

Dad grinned and declared, "We are the Stuart family now!"

"You're our mom and dad for real?" said Gracie.

"We are. Remember we talked about your names?" said Dad.

The kids nodded, excitedly. Tim said, proudly, "I'm Timothy Blessing Stuart!"

"Blessing is my name and Maggie's, too," said Gracie. And Maggie hugged Dad.

"Yeah," said Tim. "Wait until I tell Mike and Calvin that we're the Blessin' Stuarts."

They all laughed and Dad said, "That we are! And no more worries, son." He pulled the giggling kids and a teary-eyed Jennie into a big family hug.

Emilie dabbed her eyes with a tissue, her voice weepy, and said, "Oh, well, let's cut the cake. Ice cream's melting." James and Emilie served the family. The kids dug into sweet chocolate with thick peanut buttery frosting and vanilla ice cream. They'd waited all day for cake!"

Amadeus and Jennie kissed. He whispered, "Best birthday ever! Time with you, our three blessings and more to come." Jennie squeezed his hand.

That evening, with Rosie asleep by the warm crackling fire and a plate of decorated cookies on the coffee table, the children, ready for bed, cookies in hands, nestled close with Mom and Dad for story time. Dad put on his

reading glasses — gold metal frames, just like Tim's — and began the reading
of *A Christmas Carol*.

Scents of peppermint, citrus, cinnamon, ginger, and chocolate escaped from the
kitchen and hovered throughout the cabin, as Jennie baked and filled sweet sam-
pler tins — gifts for family and friends. The children practiced Christmas carols
on piano and violin. The family attended evening performances: Gracie's, Annie's, and Maggie's ballet recital; and the church play, where Tim, Mike, and
Calvin were shepherds. Gracie played Mary, Annie, a wise man, and Maggie, an
angel. The family delivered and stacked firewood. Tim and Amadeus delivered
the special orders, a cedar cabinet and the maple desk and chair. Finally, the week
passed, and Christmas Eve arrived.

The balsam fir stood tall, full, and straight in the tower's wall of windows and
cast its white light across the starry sky and through snowy woods, reaching back
centuries and generations to the Deane Homestead and Deane Mountain — a
gift from the Stuarts to their beloved family angels and spirits on Christmas Eve.

Mom and Dad sat in the old leather chairs. Gracie and Tim, snug and warm
on Dad's lap wrapped in shoofly and star quilts, and Maggie, curled under her
four-patch on Mommy's lap, listened to Dad's low voice articulating every word,
continuing the reading of *A Christmas Carol*. (In Jill's quilting circle, the girls had
made their quilts.)

Cuddling with Maggie, feeling fluttery movements, and viewing white lights
and silvery, golden sparkles, Jennie faded into memory. Just three days ago, they'd
set the tree in front of the windows, strung the lights, and wrapped the garland.
She'd handed him the blue, hand-blown glass ornament with a painting of a
snow scene and a horse-drawn sleigh. He'd hung it on a high branch where white
light reflected in the blue. Then he'd enfolded her in his arms and said, "Merry
Christmas, my love." They'd kissed softly.

She'd said, "Merry Christmas, my dearest." Once the glassy bulbs adorned
the tree and the children had awakened from their nap, they'd led them into the
tower of twinkling lights.

"Oh!" exclaimed the kids, their eyes wide and all aglitter.

"Pretty, shiny!" said Maggie.

"Sparkling!" said Gracie.

Tim, skin tingling, heart pounding, speechless, beheld his first Christmas tree.

Dad had lifted Tim high, Mom had given him the white angel, and Tim had placed it on the treetop. The Christmas angel glowed in the moonlight.

Jennie's memory faded. Maggie and Gracie had fallen asleep. Once Tim had said he didn't read books, but he loved a good story. Jennie again heard the words of Dickens, as Amadeus read the last lines and closed the book.

Grinning, Tim said, "We got spirit friends too."

Laughing quietly, Mom said, "We certainly do, but it's our secret."

Descending the stairs, Dad carried a sleeping Maggie, her head on his shoulder.

Passing by the stone fireplace, decorated with hand-knit stockings, a gift from Aunt Madeleine, Tim and Gracie spied the musical snow globe among old black-and-white photographs and a wedding picture. Memorable books sat on the piano. On the oak table sat a plate of sugar cookies, a glass of milk, and a bag of carrots. Tim and Gracie bounced down the hall to their bedrooms. Tucked into bed, they soon floated into dreams.

After much scurrying about retrieving gifts hidden in closets and unfinished sections of the Christmas project from the workshop, Santa's helpers filled the stockings, assembled the project, and set presents under the tree.

Then, collapsing on the sofa in front of the warm fire, they sipped peppermint tea, munched on cookies, and shared their gifts. A dark blue wool coat for Jennie. "Oh, thank you." She twirled, modeling the coat. "So warm and snug. One of your shopping day secrets?"

"You look lovely," he laughed, kissing her.

For Amadeus, a white envelope filled with hundred-dollar bills and a note: *For your tractor and attachments.* "Thank you," he'd said. Then, his voice deeper, "Is this all you have?"

She kissed him and whispered, "No questions. It's Christmas."

Arms around each other, they ambled down the hall, looked in on sleeping children and kissed them. In Tim's room, his little truck, bright red and shiny, glowed in the moonlight.

In their own bed, they snuggled close together and Jennie intertwined her legs with his, sunk her fingers in his red chest hair, and laughed, "You know, the technician was not supposed to confirm our second baby blessing."

He chuckled, "She didn't need to. I spotted twins." Turning on his side and softly massaging her back, she traced his spine. Tender kisses grew longer, more intense. With one finger, a light touch, roaming over her womb, he said, "Nature's signs, my love."

✳

The glorious rising sun glistened on crusty white snow and refracted on ice-coated branches. Thin wispy strands stretched across the blue sky. The children bolted through the bedroom door, pounced on the maple bed, rolled off, tumbled to the floor, and rose to their feet in front of the French doors, proclaiming, "Mom! Dad!" "See! Come!" "Angels in the sky!" Barking, Rosie paced.

Mom and Dad sprang awake, jumped out of bed, put on the flannel robes, and followed the children onto the small porch into blinding golden rays.

Maggie pointed and said, "There, up there!"

Gracie said, "It's Mam!"

Tim said, "And Mommy! And Great-Aunt Mary!"

"And Grandma Sarah, Grandma Jennie!" said Jennie.

Holding his family close, Amadeus declared, "Merry Christmas, our angels."

One angel drew a bow across cello strings and Tim, eyes lifted to the sky, hands held prayerfully, listened intently to Mommy's music—Heaven's music. Too soon, the sun rose higher and the wispy strands evaporated. A Christmas message delivered, the angels vanished and the cello silenced.

"Where'd Mam go?" said Maggie.

"They're all gone," said Gracie.

"Don't be sad," said Mom. "Our angels watch over us. Let your hearts be happy."

"Mommy's got her music back! She plays for the angels!" Tim's heart was at peace.

"We'll see them again," said Dad. "Come inside. I'll bet Santa was here!"

Back through the French doors, the kids and Rosie ran down the hall. The plate and the glass were empty, the bag of carrots, missing! The stockings filled to the brim, Dad handed them to the kids. Dropping to their knees, they dumped them and scattered little farm animals, violin strings, ballet slippers, and more onto the floor. By the hearth sat a box of Rosie's favorite dog biscuits.

Four pairs of snowshoes and ski poles leaned against the wall, and Dad said, "We'll be hiking in the woods. You'll need to walk on them."

"How can we walk on those big things?" said Tim.

"Later, we'll practice," said Dad.

"So much fun!" said Mom, hugging her honeybees.

Amadeus ascended the stairs, two at a time, plugged in the lights, and the children scurried up behind him. Rosie and Jennie climbed more slowly. Glowing lights and the Christmas angel cast dazzling colors over the room, over a cherry reading nook with shelves of storybooks and games and a bench with a blue-and-white striped cushion.

"What's this game?" said Tim.

Dad said, "Time to strategize. Play chess with kings, queens, and knights of old."

By the tree, Maggie knelt, hugged the stuffed cow, and peered into the doll-house. Gracie checked out art supplies and an easel. And Tim spied model kits and Lego sets.

Five more presents sat under the tree. Jennie gave each child one. Tearing away paper, they unwrapped toy horses. "These look like the Morgans," said Tim.

Dad and Mom exclaimed, "At the Elliots' farm, you'll all be learning to ride horseback!"

"Annie, Mike, and Calvin, too!"

Hopping and bouncing, the kids yelled, "For real, we can ride for real?" "Yay!"

"They got cows, too!"

Maggie gave Mom her gift bag of barrettes, and Gracie said, "Dad learned how to braid your hair! He got a book at the library and practiced on ours."

Tim said, "That's why you couldn't find us sometimes. I turned the pages."

Mom said, "The perfect gift," hugging and kissing sweet cheeks.

Tim gave Dad the gift from the kids—a collage of fingerprints in bright colors, family photographs, space for baby blessings, and titled—The Blessin' Stuarts.

"We made it for you!" said Gracie.

"I kept a secret! *Shhh!*" said Maggie.

"I'll build the frame," he said, hugging his children. "We'll hang it on the wall."

Then Dad braided Mom's hair. "Beautiful!" said Tim. "Pretty!" said Maggie.

From Gracie, "Lovely!"

Amadeus kissed Jennie, said, "She is beautiful." Jennie kissed Amadeus and her sweeties. Then the family played together until Tim said, "I'm real hungry!"

In the kitchen, Mom and Dad cooked pancakes and set maple syrup and berries with whipped cream on the oak table. Upstairs, the girls still played, while Tim sat on the bench reading familiar words and puzzling out new ones on the pages of *Treasure Island.*

Under a sunny blue, cold sky, the Stuarts crossed the field from the woodpile to the stone wall nearing the tree line. The children took cautious steps on snow-shoes, fell, picked themselves up, laughed, learned to walk, and then toppled over on purpose, rolling in the snow with Rosie. Hearts healed and full of wonder, the family laughed joyously, creating a maze of huge footprints in their magical winter land called home.

Visitors donned snowshoes hidden in the pines and trekked up that snow-covered dirt road to the woodpile, crossing into the field. Amadeus saw their shadows, but Jennie did not. From behind, familiar arms wrapped lovingly around Jennie, and a familiar voice said, "Merry Christmas, Mom!"

"Oh, my goodness! How I've missed you." Teary-eyed, Jennie hugged her daughter.

The children and Rosie trudged through snow, calling out greetings to their sister, "Rebecca!" "Rebecca!" Amadeus welcomed Isaac with a hug and then enfolded everyone in family.

And sunlight danced on snow.

EPILOGUE

In the field, where a solid stone wall stood near the tree line and wildflowers grew in tall grass, high wire mesh fencing with corner posts and a gate, sunk deep into a trench, surrounded plowed and tilled land. Warm earth sheltered rows of plants, flourishing in sun and rain: leafy greens, summer's salads and autumn's root vegetables, herbs, and apple trees—Honeycrisp and Grimes Golden.

The Beast roared up the dirt road with Rosie's head out the window, ears flying.

"Dad's home!" said eight-year-old Gracie. Racing out the front door and down the steps to the field, followed by six-year-old Maggie, Gracie called out, "Did you get it, Daddy? Did you get it?"

Parked at the edge of the field, Dad hugged his daughters. "Yes, my lassies."

"Yeah, we did!" said Tim. "Cyrus was there, too, watching us real close."

"I see horses!" said Maggie.

Dad laughed, "Well, speaking of Cyrus, here he comes."

The Belgians trotted down the dirt road, past the pond, the woodpile, and halted face to face with The Beast. William and Cyrus climbed down the wagon, giving a hand to their wives, Louisa and Mary. Dashing to meet the spirits, Rosie alongside, Tim, at nine, in the lead, always in the lead, now a sprinter and a base runner, his sisters chasing him.

Meanwhile, Amadeus took his long strides, meeting Jennie on the front porch, babies in her arms. Kissing her first, he then helped her down the steps and laid their little ones in the monstrous pinewood wagon: the solid, sturdy wagon, designed and built by Dad with the children's help, stood three times higher off the ground than those mere red Radio Flyers. It sported a long steering handle, high side rails, and wide-treaded tires with shocks, hubcaps, and front and rear handbrakes.

And so, Abigail [Hebrew, *father's joy*] and Aaron [Scottish, *high mountain, exalted*], their three-month-old twins, born on a Sunday in springtime and baptized with their parents' middle names and the shared children's name of Blessing, napped on the custom-fitted mattress, designed by Mom, covered with baby sheets, blankets, and a canopy of mosquito netting. One day they would travel in comfort and style through the woods, meadows, cemeteries, homestead, and the Cyrus Deane Stream, where in the Spring crocuses and daffodils bloomed in a field of wildflowers.

Pulling the wagon across the yard to The Beast, Amadeus said, "My dear, our Cyrus is connecting with our son."

"And Mary with our daughters," said Jennie.

The spirit of Cyrus Deane, a kind-hearted man of time past, knelt before Tim and hugged him, like a grandparent holds a grandchild. Tim leaned into the hug. And Mary held giggling sisters, Gracie and Maggie, in the warm airiness of a misty embrace.

The spirits glided; the girls skipped hand-in-hand with Mary and Louisa; and Tim, with Rosie alongside, walked proudly between Cyrus and William, meeting Mom and Dad at The Beast. Gravitating toward the pinewood wagon, the spirits airily touched soft cheeks, little noses, and hands and feet, admiring a new generation, separated by centuries, of red-haired, blue-eyed adorable babies. Cooing and laughing, the twins stretched their arms and legs to everyone's delight.

"What's all this?" said Jennie. Tree seedlings—maple, oak, pine, cedar, and more—filled the truck bed.

"New growth for the woodlots and homestead. To replenish what I've cut."

"Dad, give her the special one!" said Tim.

Gracie, arms wide and palms up, said, "Yeah, Dad!"

And, bouncing up and down, Maggie said, "The Deane one!" Hands over her mouth, she giggled, "Oops! It was a secret."

"Wait! What? The Deane one?" Mom frowned.

Laughing, Dad showed Mom a pot with a miniature transplanted Deane Apple Tree, barely alive. "I found it in Cyrus's orchard hidden under dead wood. Looks like new growth." He shrugged. "I thought we could nurse it back to health. It will need tender, loving care."

Fingers to her lips and eyes watering, Jennie sighed and then softly touched the fragile trunk and frail branchlets. The tiny Deane apple had struggled to live in darkness. "Well, you brought it to the right place. There's a lot of TLC going on here." As she buried her face in his shoulder, he held her close. "My Jennie still cries at every little thing."

"I thought she'd love it?" said Gracie.

Tim, hands in pockets, rocking on his feet, and grinning, said confidently, "She does. And I knew she would!"

"She loves our gift," said Dad, and Jennie hugged the kids. "I do love it. Thank you."

"Okay, kids, you know what to do," said Dad.

Racing into the cabin, past flower gardens, hanging planters, and a lilac tree, the sisters, carefully, took the violins off the piano and, walking slowly, carried them back to the orchard.

Sprinting to the tool shed, spirits floating behind, Tim collected the tools and pails, depositing them in the empty cart. Sitting tall and proud and turning the ignition, Tim steered the garden tractor at a *putt-putt* speed to the water spigot on the east cabin wall. The spirits watched intently as Tim unwound the hose, turned on the faucet, and filled the pails. William, eyes furrowed, turned the spigot off and on again and again, fascinated by this phenomenon, while Cyrus held his hands under cold, rushing water. Buckets overflowing, Tim laughed and turned off the spigot. Only a few drips splattered.

With spirits balancing on the sides of the cart, water sloshing, and under Dad's watchful eye, Tim cruised past the workshop and the new gray Dodge Caravan, turning into the field and heading to the orchard.

Jennie opened the gate, the kids carried tools, and Amadeus lugged buckets of water, peat, compost, mulch, and the tree. Jennie pulled the wagon, and Mary and Louisa guarded the babies. Cyrus and William inspected the growing Honeycrisp and Grimes Gold, keeping a close watch on the Deane.

Digging a hole, Dad centered the little tree between healthier ones, giving it plenty of space to spread its roots and grow. With trowels, Mom and the children scooped peat and compost into the hole. Dad, sensing the pressure of spirits over his shoulders, carefully removed the Deane from the pot. He inspected the root system, showing them how and why to straighten the circular roots. Then he placed the tree in Jennie's hands, and she painstakingly set it in the hole. The kids scooped dirt, carefully covering the roots, raked with miniature rakes and spread mulch, offering sanctuary to the Deane tree. William and Cyrus watered the trees, and Dad staked the Deane. Three trees were the beginning of the Stuart Orchard.

Shouldering Alastair and the little violin called Mac, [Scottish, meaning *son*] Dad and Tim played duets from Tim's repertoire, the notes rising above the orchard, into the treetops, and floating skyward. Hugging her babies close, Mom swayed and twirled to the music and, in memory, breathed the scent of apple blossoms. Playing solo, Amadeus danced with Jennie, as Tim, Maggie, and Gracie bopped and boogied with the spirits.

In her heart Jennie knew the little Deane would take root, grow in sun and rain, and, like Amadeus, herself, and their children, would thrive, living in love and light.

The celebration lasted into twilight, the kids and Dad replaced the tools and pails, and, of course, Tim drove the tractor. The spirits climbed into their wagon. Tim and his sisters stood in the dirt road, waving, as Jacob and Mozark headed back to the homestead. Mom, cradling Abbie, and Dad, nestling Aaron, joined the children, and Dad said, "They'll be back soon."

"They'll probably water the trees," said Tim. "They know how to turn on the spigot."

Laughing, Jennie slipped her hand into Amadeus's. A natural fit. "You and I are sandwiched between generations, from children to bi-centenarian grandparents."

Amadeus laughed and squeezed her hand.

In the two cherry gliders in front of the French doors, Amadeus and Jennie rocked, cuddling their twins, he, Abigail and she, Aaron. Mugs of steamy herbal tea sat on the floor.

In the quiet of the cabin, they listened to the mellow sounds: the soft breaths of sleeping babies; three older blessings journeying into dreamland; nature's concerto of the night; Rosie's clicking nails on the wood floor.

She held the hand of her solid, yet gentle woodsman. "You have given me a life of blessings. I truly love you."

He kissed her hand, rubbed her palm softly with his thumb. "It was a long arduous journey, but worth every step home to you, my Jennie Girl. I love you, always have, and always will."

As moonlight shone through the French doors, they laid their babies, the little blessings, in their beds. Embracing, they kissed gently, then more passionately, caressing lovingly, until he said, "May I have this dance?"

"It's a starry night, my T-Bear."

Stepping through the French doors onto the porch and then the lawn, past cedar chairs and clay pots and past The Beast, they viewed the summer night sky—the Little Dipper, Cassiopeia, Orion. Her brown eyes dancing, she said, "The North Star is always there, guiding the sojourner home."

Not far away, Deane Mountain and the Deane Homestead held fast to a story of the present.

Jennie, in her soft, creamy robe and a French braid, her gold locket clasped around her neck, and Amadeus, in his green plaid flannel, his hair still cut short, embraced. Jennie lay her head on Amadeus's shoulder and he enfolded her in his arms. They waltzed to their own music, his baritone and her sweet alto. Stars twinkled above them, moonlight encircled them, and trees enwreathed them.

Amadeus and Jennie, two blessed souls, once lost, but now found, share hearts that runneth over with love, joy, peace, purpose, and new life.

ACKNOWLEDGMENTS

Sharing oral histories and memorable family moments is a gift to be passed down from generation to generation. As a child, I explored with my family the places that Jennie explored in Temple, on Voter Hill, and in Dixfield and Carthage—their cemeteries, towns, and woods, as well as the Deane Homestead—while listening to the family stories. Revisiting those places a few years ago, I shared the history with Sarah and Paul, my grown children, and Chloe, my granddaughter, the future keepers of family roots.

Five generations of the Deane family, beginning with Cyrus and Mary and ending with my father, Winslow Deane, lived on that land. It was on the homestead that I decided to write my book, to preserve their stories and the heritage of the Deane family in Temple, Maine.

My heartfelt thank-you is given to my family.

To Dale, my husband, who listened to the stories over the years and thought writing this book was an outstanding project. Sadly, though, he will not read the book, as he journeyed to Heaven during the years I was writing the book.

Winslow and Dorothy Parkhurst Deane, my parents, compiled their genealogical research of our family history. Without the internet, they wrote letters, met with people, and visited libraries, cemeteries, and other places.

My grandfather, Stephen Deane, wrote his own unpublished work, which is saved in the ancestry: *The Varnums and Their Pioneer Neighborhood* (1949).

I included a day at Grandpa Stephen and Grandma Florence Deane's in Roxbury for Amadeus and Jennie. The place and the people are a compilation of the memories belonging to my sister, Barbara, and myself. Other shared memories are of living in Carthage and Dixfield.

My grandparents, Harold and Edith Sarah Parkhurst, met and farmed on Voter Hill, where they raised my mother. This hill I climbed many times, to remember and to see the view. Like Jennie's Grandma Sarah, Edith was my beloved grandmother.

Sarah and Chloe listened to selected chapters as I read aloud from my drafts.

Through email, I connected with family historians, Susan and Annie Esther.

Susan gave me a poem by Zibiah Deane (1793–1864). Annie Esther gave me an old photograph of Grandma Jennie and her sisters as young girls.

I'm grateful for the interest given to my project by my friends, book club members, and others, and also for the time given by Gail, Tammy, and Jackie, advance readers and best critics.

Thank you to everyone I met on my trips to Temple. Betsy and Maxine, archivists of the Temple and Wilton Historical Societies, walked through the cemeteries with me. Betsy shared what she knew of the family, including the Deane apple and the Underground Railroad. She also shared Richard Donald Pierce's thesis, *The Rise and Decline of Temple, Maine* (1946). Helpful in my research were the sections about the Society of Friends and the Anti-Slavery Movement. From Maxine, her research into Stephen Deane's writings and other tidbits was of great help. Melanie shared the Knowles link in western Maine. George repaired Thankful Deane's gravestone. Jo shared her knowledge of my ancestors. Others in the area raise Deane apple trees.

Thank you, John Bunker, for permission to include your research about the Deane apple and the Underground Railroad as published in Chapter 19 of your book *Apples and the Art of Detection* (2019).

Thank you, Bill Roorbach, for the hours in conversation sharing my story and for your encouragement, writing expertise, and knowledge about the area, a valuable experience in writing.

Thank you, also, to the editors, designers and publishing staff of Maine Author's Publishing who kindly and patiently walked with me through the process.

And, finally, to the readers, I sincerely hope you enjoy my debut novel and perhaps one or more of you will be descendants of the Deane, Stolt, and Parkhurst families.